Up Close
and Personal

Jody Vitek

Published by
Satin Romance
An Imprint of Melange Books, LLC
White Bear Lake, MN 55110
www.satinromance.com

Cover Art by Caroline Andrus

DEDICATION

It is only fitting that I dedicate this book to my son, Andrew and my daughter, Ashley. This book took shape when I became a full-time mom after leaving my nine to five job sixteen years ago at the time this work was unpublished. I wrote while Andrew and Ashley took naps and eventually, while they were in school. Two books were written and pushed to the side when I wrote another book. I pulled the books out and dusted them off to see what I had to work with—nothing but the characters and premises of the stories were used for Up Close and Personal. So thank you, Andrew and Ashley, for being cooperative nappers and understanding kids.

I must mention my youngest, Alexander, for he came into our lives when my writing became more serious than just putting words on the page. He's also had to endure my writing time and has been a trooper.

ACKNOWLEDGEMENT

My thanks to the following people: Karla Edmonds, a middle school English teacher, for answering my educational questions. Mr. Nelson, who took the time to answer my architectural firm questions. My critique partners: Brenda, Joyce, Terri, and Paula, for their constructive feedback to push me to make the story stronger. My Turtle Lake Writing Retreat gals: JL, Kathy, Terri and Amy, thank you for the brainstorming sessions which bring my stories to life.

I would like to acknowledge Nan Dixon, her agent and her team at Harlequin, for granting me permission to use the main characters and their home in my story. I had no intentions of involving her story within my own. You can read more about the Fitzgerald House and its three owners in Nan Dixon's debut release, *Southern Comforts*.

Lastly, thank you to Nancy at Satin Romance and her continued belief in my writing and stories. Caroline, my cover artist, who is a saint, has worked her magic again, while dealing with my 'fix this, I don't like that' comments. Lastly, thanks to my editor, Mel, for working with me and my book to make it the best work possible.

Chapter One

Cold, damp, Minnesota air seeped into Elizabeth Farefield's bones as she stood graveside. The long, black wool coat covered the simple black dress that fell above her knees. Although the coat was unfastened, one moment she was warm and sweating, the next minute shivering from the cold. She crisscrossed her arms, wrapping them around her waist as if needing support to stand against the chill. The onset of a late fall rainstorm began. If the temperature dropped five more degrees, they'd be dealing with sleet.

The weather... the weather had ultimately led to the premature death of her husband, Gregory.

The children went with her parents to the car leaving Liz to say final goodbyes to her beloved husband. She stood beside the casket.

She dropped her chin to her chest and spoke in the silence. "Give the children and me the strength to move forward, Greg." Her love for him would last a lifetime.

Sarah, nine, knew everything about her father's death. Sarah's anger was fueled by her grandmother, Ellen, who blamed Liz for Gregory's death. This created a wall between grandmother and granddaughter. Sarah found comfort with Liz's parents, but that didn't stop her tears from flowing.

At seven, Bradley understood death but not the conflict surrounding his father's passing. Brad didn't avoid Ellen and he would often be at her side. Wanting and missing his father, he spent most of his time crying. Comfort came in the arms of whoever would hold him, much like an infant. Liz believed he'd heal faster than Sarah and be more forgiving.

Liz somberly walked to her parents' car. Her father held the front

1

passenger door open for her. Once she was seated, he closed the door, went around the front of the car, and slid behind the steering wheel. As they pulled away, the sky spattered rain on the windshield. The wipers swished the wetness away.

Brad's sweet, innocent, soft voice broke the silence. "Look, Mommy, God's crying, too."

She lost her composure. The words turned the dripping teardrop faucet on to full force. Her body shook. She leaned against the doorframe. Her head rested against the cool window. The car moved forward. Life moved forward.

They were headed to gather at the home of Gregory's parents for a light buffet and remembrance. Liz agreed to the arrangement because she didn't want to fight with Ellen about what food to serve or where to host the gathering. It was one less thing to think about or have to deal with. However, at the same time, being in the same room, let alone house, could make things difficult.

Ellen Farefield hadn't made Liz's marriage to her son an easy one. She made her dislike for Liz known from the beginning of their engagement and had been against the idea of marriage to her son. Not to mention them having children. The rest of Gregory's family accepted her, which was good and bad. Good because everyone supported their marriage with the exception of one person, which made her despise Liz that much more.

The family had run interference to keep the two women separated throughout the day. Liz had prayed to avoid any confrontation with Ellen. The extreme size of Duane and Ellen's Edina home made her home look like a dollhouse. It was easy for her to move from room to room without running into her. Ellen had remained seated in the formal living room, too grief stricken to walk around and socialize.

Liz knew her mother-in-law's actions were a ploy to place more guilt on her shoulders. Although it didn't work. Ellen entered the formal room to speak with the guests. There she sat on her throne, as Liz called the rich, mahogany colored, leather, wing-backed chair. The hatred in her squinted eyes and pursed lips would've had Liz cowering years ago. Today, she remained strong for Gregory.

Veronica, Gregory's only sibling, approached Ellen. "Mom, let's move to the family room and visit with the guests in there."

"They can come see me in here," she stated in a determined voice. "*She* can leave at any time." Ellen raised her voice and shook one thin, sharpened pencil of a wrinkled finger at Liz.

"Mother," Veronica scolded, taking hold of her mother's upper arm. She pulled her up and out of the chair. "We're going to go into the family room, now." As they left the room, Veronica turned and nodded at Liz. She'd be Ellen free for a while.

The only remaining guests were neighbors and family. The rain hadn't let up and by nightfall would turn to sleet. The drive would take longer if the rain turned to ice. She located her mother, Janice, in the kitchen cleaning. "Mom, I think we should start for home. With the sun down, the temps are going to drop and the rain will become ice."

"Okay, dear. I'll go find your father."

She gathered her children to leave. They said good night to the family and the kids dashed for the car. Hugging Duane in the large foyer, Liz wasn't lucky enough to escape without Ellen speaking some final words.

"You," her mother-in-law screeched. Ellen's husband, Duane, stopped her from grasping Liz's arm. "*You* killed him. My only son." The words echoed through the tiled entry.

Duane pulled Ellen from the room, screaming, "I *knew* you'd be the death of him."

The hurtful words did not go unheard. Fresh tears stung Liz's eyes.

Veronica embraced her. "Don't listen to her. We know that's not true. Call me... soon."

Liz nodded and dashed from the house to her parent's warm, waiting car.

She never thought it would be a possibility, but Ellen despised her more than ever. Yet, with the accidental death of her husband, it was a reality. She stared out the window for the remainder of the drive home. The home she bought and once shared with Gregory.

The headlights illuminated the front of the white colonial with its black shuttered windows as her father turned onto her driveway. She stared at the large home. The enormity of responsibility that came from one person's death weighed heavily on her shoulders. Gregory had been the caretaker of the home, inside and out. With winter knocking on the doorstep, she had snow removal to think about. Then there were the Christmas lights he had put up every year. She wasn't about to go up on a ladder to hang them. He'd also handled all things financial. The cars weren't as big a deal. She'd taken the cars to the dealership many times.

She closed her eyes, inhaled, and slowly exhaled. "Let me get the garage door open and then I'll come back for the kids."

Unbuckled from the car seat, she carried her sleeping son up the stairs to his room and tears slid down her cheeks. This was Gregory's job. She could handle the seven-year-old's body weight, but he carried Brad to bed. It was their nightly ritual, whether their son was awake or asleep. Once tucked under the covers, she regarded her son as the miniature replica of Gregory. The square jaw, blue eyes and a head full of thick, curly, dark brown hair.

"Mom?" Sarah's panicked voice sliced the silence.

Liz rushed to the hall. "Sarah, honey, I'm right here." She embraced her daughter tightly. "I was taking care of your brother. Ssh, I'm right here."

Liz's mother appeared at the bottom of the stairs. "I'm sorry, honey. She woke up in the car and ran into the house."

"It's okay." She cupped her daughter's face in her hands. "I'll be right back. I'm going to say goodbye to grandma. I'll meet you in your room."

"Can I sleep with you?" Pleading eyes stared at her.

"Please go to your room," she said gently. "I'll be right there."

Sarah wandered to her room.

Liz met her mom at the bottom of the stairs. "Thank Dad for me. I wouldn't have been able to drive. He was right. Thank you, for all of your support today. You were such a big help with the kids."

"That's what parents are for." Her mother embraced her. "You call if you need anything. I mean anything. We're not that far."

"Thank you. I'll call if something comes up."

Janice stepped from the hug. "I'll talk to you later. I love you."

"Love you too, Mom."

Her mother closed the front door, and Liz joined her daughter upstairs. Sarah's bedroom light was on, but it was lights out for Sarah.

4

Shoes off, she fell asleep dressed. Liz pulled the bedding from underneath Sarah replaced them over her, still in her clothing.

Sleet pelted the windows. Liz was glad to be safe at home. With Sarah situated for the night, Liz slogged into her room and collapsed on the bed. The tears flowed down her cheeks, and when they slowed, she staggered to the bathroom.

She popped two sleeping aids with a glass of water. Not wanting to see her reflection, she focused on the counter, unable to avoid spotting Gregory's toiletries on the ledge. A new wave of salty wetness streamed down her face. With her husband buried, the realization she was a widow at forty-one hit her. She couldn't imagine ever loving anyone the way she loved Greg. The tissue box became her sleeping partner.

* * * *

Robert Burnhamwood waited by the chain-link fence, searching the late arriving fans for his ex-wife Kathleen. *Where the hell is she?* Twenty minutes passed, causing him to miss the start of the sectional playoff football game. It wasn't every day his one and only son, a high school freshman, started as wide receiver for the school varsity football team.

"What's your excuse this time?" he scowled when Kathleen approached.

"Don't start with me, Robert." She turned from him and bent to look directly at their nine-year-old daughter. "Christine." She always used Chris's full birth name, finding Chris to be insulting for her daughter. "Be good for your father. I'll see you Sunday night when your father brings you home."

"I don't want to sit in the cold watching football," Chris whined. "Why couldn't I stay home?"

"Your mother is leaving for the weekend." He touched her shoulder. "I've brought blankets to keep us warm, Chris. I'll buy you some hot chocolate to help keep your insides toasty."

As her mother walked away, Chris darted after her and gave Kathleen a hug. She peeled her daughter from her waist and shooed her off to shuffle toward him, with her head hung.

The kids exchange made, he paid for their tickets, and they passed through the gate into the stadium. The scent of freshly popped popcorn and slow cooking hotdogs caught a breeze. His stomach growled in protest to a missed meal.

"That smells good. I'm going to get something. Would you like anything? Maybe that hot cocoa I mentioned?"

"Sure." Her response was anything but excited.

"Chris, this is a big game for your brother and the team. I know you don't want to sit out in the cold but you have to. I tell you what, let's go find a place to sit, and then I'll come back and get our food and drinks. Okay?"

"Fine." Her response was snotty.

Would he survive this? He didn't remember his other daughter, Abigail, having an attitude like this at the same age, but then he and his wife hadn't been divorced. The two of them rounded the corner of the bleachers packed with fans. He scanned the stadium seating when he heard his name and caught the waving arm. Abigail sat several rows up on the fifty-yard line.

"Chris, Abby's here and has a place for us to sit."

"Yay." Her unenthusiastic tone didn't go unnoticed.

"Come on. I know she's eleven years older than you, but she's your sister."

"Whatever." She rolled her eyes while shaking her head.

Robert shook his head in defeat as he maneuvered to the center of the bleachers where Abby sat. "How'd you know we'd be here?"

"You should know I wouldn't miss either my alma mater or my brother play. Plus, I thought Chris would like some girl company." She made eye contact with her sister. "Here, sit next to me."

"Sure." Chris plopped on the bench hunched over with her chin in her hands.

"Before I get comfortable, I'm going for food. Can I get you anything, Abby?"

"I'm good. Thanks."

"Chris, I'll get you a hot chocolate. You have the blankets so wrap up but save me one." He visited the concession stand and returned with a tray of food and beverages. "Here's your hot cocoa and some popcorn." The cold metal seat seeped past the jean material to his skin. Chris used the three blankets for herself. Rather than disrupting her contentment, he'd manage the cool temperatures. He looked at the scoreboard, "I've missed the first quarter and the score is fourteen to six. Did I miss Alex get any touchdowns?"

"No, but he's had some great catches," Abby answered excitedly.

Five minutes later, Alex ran the field, glancing back to the quarterback, who released the ball. It spun through the air. Seated on the edge of the bench Robert waited in anxious limbo. Alex caught and held the ball tight against his body while dodging for the end zone.

"Touchdown for the Wescott Wombats," the announcer hailed.

"Yes!" Robert pumped his fist into the air.

Alex ran two more balls for touchdowns and the final score of the game was forty-two to nineteen. At that moment, Robert was a proud father. The players disappeared into the high school and fans dispersed for their vehicles. Robert and Abby remained seated, but Chris stood and the complaining commenced.

"Why are we just sitting here? I'm freezing! Let's go." She tugged on his arm.

"Relax, Chris. Look at the crowd of people." His cell phone played the designated tone for Laura, his brunette lady friend. "We have to wait for your brother anyway."

She threw herself onto the bench and wrapped up in the blankets.

He answered making sure to keep the conversation short. "Hello." He turned away from his daughters to minimize what they could hear.

"Where are you? I was hoping we could get together this weekend," Laura finished on a seductive note.

"I'm at my son's football game. I told you this weekend I was busy."

"You never said anything to me," she sing-songed.

Maybe it was Kimberly, his redheaded lover, he'd told. Shit. "Well, this weekend is out but next weekend is another story. I'll call you Monday to make plans."

"Okay," came her giddy reply.

As he tucked the phone into his pocket, Chris stood and yelled, "I can't believe you're doing this to Mom." She stomped down the bleachers.

A few remaining patrons watched, but what they thought about the situation didn't matter. He cared about Chris and how to make things better between them.

Chapter Two

Four years later

Robert sat behind his glass-top metal desk, checking contracts. There was a knock followed by the door opening.

"Sir, you wanted to see me?" David Robertson, a young hard-working project manager at the firm, entered.

"Yes, David." He stood and gestured to a chair. "Please have a seat. Would you like something to drink?"

"No, thank you." He held up a to-go coffee cup.

"Okay, then." Robert sat forward on the black leather, ergonomically correct office chair. "I'll get straight to the subject. My daughter has one class remaining before college graduation. She's studying interior design and will be starting her internship today... with you."

"I don't understand, sir. I don't deal with interior design. How can I help her?" Concern, worry, confusion all muddled together on his square face.

"She needs to have an understanding of how the company operates, who she'll be working with within the firm, and about working with clients. You're one of the younger employees, in whom I have all the confidence to show her how we operate." Robert eased back in the chair.

"Thank you, sir." His face relaxed. "When will I meet her?"

"She's with Mary in HR taking care of paper work. I'll have you both come to my office when she's finished." He brought the chair to the upright position. "Can you make sure there's a space for her by your desk? I let that slip through the cracks."

9

David nodded. "I'll wait for your call." He left and as he left Robert's office another man approached the door. "Good morning, Scott."

"Hey Scott, what's up?" Robert acknowledged his good friend and partner entered the office. Robert got comfortable again on the chair.

"We need to get away from here," Scott announced with seriousness.

What was he up to now? "What are you talking about?" Robert lifted his arms, lacing his fingers together behind his head, and relaxed deeper against the seat back.

Scott plopped his tall athletic frame on a chair in front of the desk. "We need to escape the office and this cold weather."

"The weather is great." He spun the chair around and glanced out the window. There was a light coating of snow on some of the surrounding building rooftops. So far, the Minnesota December weather wasn't bad.

"It's not going to stay nice for long. You, my friend, need to take a vacation."

"And you're going to be my travel companion?" He swiveled to face his friend. "What's the fun in that? I can make plans anytime with one of my lady friends." He smiled at the thought of a warm weather getaway with one of them. Small bikini or nothing at all. Nice.

"Then you might as well get married." Scott guffawed. "My wife left me and your ex is hounding your ass to find someone to marry."

Robert's joy faded with a feeling of being weighed-down. "Ever since she became serious with this guy in New York, she's been on my case. Chris is having issues with her, too."

"Sorry to hear that, but back to discussing our vacation." He scooted to the edge of the chair and leaned forward, resting his elbows on his knees. "If things slow down enough for us, I'm thinking a New Year's Caribbean cruise."

"You've looked into this already."

Scott smirked.

"Have you booked us a romantic suite, too?" In jest, he gave his friend a seductive glance followed with a salacious wink.

"You're too much. No, I haven't booked anything. Yes, I've been looking around. Rooms are filling up on these cruises." He rose and firmly planted his hands on Robert's desk. Encroaching on his space, Scott, with icy blue eyes, stared into his. "We need to move on this if we're going to go."

Robert pushed away from Scott's looming figure. "Can I think about it? Or do I need to give you an answer right now?"

"An answer to what, Dad?" Abigail entered his office dressed in a short navy skirt with a cream blouse. She was his mini-me, but not in the looks department. Her blonde hair was a stark contrast to his now graying black. She looked like her mother, height and all.

Both men stood. "Abby, are you all done in HR?" Robert strolled around from behind the desk. Once in high school and Abby decided on a career choice, there was no stopping her. She had his drive and determination.

"I am. What does he need to decide on, Scott?" She stood next to Scott at the corner of his desk. Normally, she'd be an inch above Scott. Today with heels on, she towered over the guy.

"A vacation. You have until Monday, my friend." Scott broke eye contact to turn and speak to Abby. "It's good to see you, Abigail, and to have you here at the firm." He strode to the door. "I'll let David know to come to the office. Monday, Robert," he reminded, leaving with a wave.

Her face brightened with a broad smile. "A vacation would be good for you. Where are you going?"

Robert gave her a quick hug ignoring her question before motioning to the chair. "Have a seat. Do you want something to drink?"

"No, and you're avoiding my question." She sat on the straight-back chair.

"He wants to go on a New Year's cruise. I don't know." He shrugged. "I'd rather be with a woman ringing in the New Year," he replied with a mischievous grin, He returned behind his desk.

"Dad, isn't four years long enough to be on the market? You should find someone other than the women you're spending nights with who are half your age," she scolded.

They shared a strong father and daughter bond. Few topics were taboo between them They sought each other's advice, sometimes unsolicited.

"Abby, that's my business, not yours. Besides, just because your mother's found a new man, doesn't mean I have to find someone."

David knocked on the doorframe.

Perfect timing. No further discussion of his personal life with his daughter ensued.

"David, please come in and meet my daughter. Abby, this is David Robertson. David, this is Abigail."

"Which do you prefer, Abigail or Abby?" David shook her hand with a gracious smile.

"Whatever you'd like." Her facial expression softened, as did her voice. "I'll answer to either."

Robert didn't miss the eye contact between the two. The salacious smile on David's face implied, 'I'd like to get to know you a whole lot more than just shaking your hand'. All too familiar to Robert. He'd have a talk with his daughter later.

As much as it bothered him, he was used to young men staring at his daughter. Robert supposed she might find David attractive with his physical build, short spiky blond hair and wide, toothy grin. They were the same height, except for today. The heels had her standing above his six foot height.

"So, Abigail." Robert used her formal birth name to pull the two into focus on where they were and the reason why. "David is going to teach you everything about the business, except for the specialized fields of accounting, HR, the VP, or my responsibilities. Pay attention because he's one of our best Project Managers here at RB & Associates. You two will share a workspace. David can show you around." His eyes darted to David for a brief moment before returning to his daughter. "Abigail, can you join me for dinner tonight?"

"Sure. Where?"

"Six o'clock at the Downtowner. I'll make the reservations. If the time changes, I'll let you know. David, keep me posted as to how things are going, or if there are any issues."

* * * *

Abigail left the downtown St. Paul office at five-thirty knowing she'd run into traffic. David remained behind to work, stating he usually worked until six to avoid traffic. Three years older than her twenty-four, she wondered why her father held this young guy in high regards. David was a baby in the business, working for her father for four years, yet he was a man in every aspect.

She stood about three inches taller than David. Tomorrow she'd make sure not to wear heels. She wanted to glance into his icy-clear blue eyes at an even level. His broad smile was to die for. Yup, working with David would be easy.

She pulled onto St. Peter Street, working toward West Kellogg Boulevard. Traffic moved at a slow pace and eventually she made it to Seventh Street. Parking could've been an issue but luck was on her side today. A spot opened in the Downtowner's parking lot.

Warm air greeted her stepping into the entry. A few people waited on benches inside the restaurant. The hostess greeted her as Abby perused the bar patrons to spot her father. "I believe my father has a reservation for two. Robert Burnhamwood?"

The woman took a moment to glance at the computer screen. "Yes. He's here. This way."

Abigail walked past the large wooden wine bin wall filled with bottles and into the dining area. The hostess led her toward the fireplace, continuing to the far side of the restaurant, they strolled around to the other side of the stacked stone fireplace wall to where her father sat at a table.

"Thank you," she said to the hostess. "Dad, this was a nice invitation." He assisted her with her chair. "You've already got a drink. Have you been waiting long?"

"Not long at all." He sat and spoke sternly. "I'm going to get to the point."

"Sounds serious." She set the cloth napkin on her lap, resting her hands beneath the table.

"Not really. I don't want you to get too friendly with David."

"Where did that come from? I just met him today, Dad." She was taken aback. Sure, David was attractive, but she wasn't going to jump in the sack with him. At least not tonight.

"I saw the way you two were leering at each other. Especially the way David was eating you up."

"Excuse me?" Her eyes widened and her eyebrows shot up. Sure, she and her father had a great relationship, but jumping so quickly on her and David was… The truth.

"You're a beautiful woman and my daughter. I don't want him to think if he sleeps with you, he's going to go further in the company."

"Dad," she cautioned her father. She rested her elbows on the tabletop and clasped her hands together. "You talked him up at the office and you expressed a strong regard for his work, so why would you say something like that? We just met for the first time today."

Their waiter stepped to the table. "Excuse me. Can I get you something to drink?"

"I'd like a Cosmo, please," she ordered with a polite smile.

"Would you care for an appetizer this evening?"

"We'd like the crab cakes to start." Her father ordered and she approved of his choice.

"Very good. I'll be back with your drink."

After the waiter left the table, she returned to the subject of David. "HR didn't say anything about a no dating co-worker policy."

"Maybe I should implement something." He sipped his martini.

"Dad, come on. He's cute, but—"

"But nothing. Keep it professional. Now let's look over the menu."

Abigail perused the menu, made a decision, and closed it before speaking. "Oh Dad, the new house is great. You need to swing by and get a tour."

"Where is it again?" There was skepticism in her father voice.

"It's on Juliet between Cleveland and Fairview. It's nice having our own bedrooms. Gina and I share the same bathroom, Conrad took the large master suite, and Paul took the other room, which has a private bathroom."

"Here are your crab cakes." The waiter placed the plate in the center of the table. "Your Cosmopolitan, ma'am. And sir would you care for another drink?"

"Yes, gin martini." Her father replied.

"Are you ready to order?"

She looked at her father and received the go-ahead nod. "Yes. I'd like the Margarita pizza with a half mixed green salad with the balsamic dressing."

"Of course, and for you, Sir?" The waiter adjusted his stance to face her father.

"I'll have the black and blue burger. Medium please."

"Would you care for a salad?"

"No, thanks."

The waiter left them to dig into the crab cakes, which she swore melted in her mouth. "Oh, these are delicious."

"I knew you liked crab and these are some of the best. With the new place, you compromised, living far from school."

"I'm not that far from the U of M campus, plus I only have the one class. Remember, I planned my schedule with my internship at the firm." She sipped her martini before taking another bite of crab.

"So are you on track to graduate this spring?"

"Yes. The house is the right distance between school and work. It works out perfect for everyone. Paul is at St. Thomas."

"Shouldn't he be in law school by now and not working on getting his BA?" He finished his drink and set the remaining crab cakes on their plates.

"He's had a few bumps in the road but is determined. Cut him some slack. Gina's at St. Cate's getting her masters and working at the hospital."

The waiter delivered her salad and her father's martini.

She mixed the dressing with the assorted greens. "Conrad's teaching at St. James High School."

"I always liked that kid."

"Not happening, Dad," she warned with a stern face. Been there. Done that.

"I can always try, can't I?" Her father cocked his grey-haired head to the side, with a smirk and a raised eyebrow.

"No. He's the assistant coach for the football team."

"I thought I read something about him in the paper. It's too bad you didn't get the master suite."

"Conrad pays a higher rent than the rest of us. I'm okay with the arrangement." She ate the last bite of crab cake.

"Remind me, what are you paying for rent?"

"Nine hundred a month. It covers everything; cable, internet, electric, gas. Do I need to go on?" She moved her salad in front of her.

"I don't want to see you run into any troubles." He leaned back while sipping his drink. The relaxed look looked good on her dad.

"What kind of trouble would I run into?"

"When you're renting a house there can be all kinds of problems."

"Conrad got the lead from a co-worker, checked it out, and I trust him." She shoved salad in her mouth. "Plus, it's a new build," she added as she chewed.

"If you're happy, I'm happy."

"Dad, are you happy?" She was concerned and wanted to see her father remarried. It had nothing to do with her mother's relationship status. It had everything to do with him.

"Yes, I'm happy." He took a long sip from his glass. "Why do you ask?"

She leaned forward, resting an elbow on the table and her chin on her hand. "Are you happy with the life you have? Do you ever want to find someone you can grow old with? These young women you spend time with aren't going to stick around forever."

"I like my life." He mimicked her stance at the table. "Thank you very much."

"So you don't love your life," she commented and took another bite of salad.

The waiter approached with their main dishes. "Is there anything else I can bring you?" They both shook their heads. "I'll check back to see how it all tastes."

"You should go on the cruise with Scott."

"Are you trying to get rid of me?" He raised an eyebrow with speculation.

"No. I think it would be good to get away from the women and think about what you want for the future."

"Abby, I'm happy. I don't think a cruise is going to convince me to get remarried. I like not having to report to anyone." He bit into his burger.

"Then just go on the cruise to make me and Scott happy. When was the last time you took a vacation? Go have some fun and relax." She picked up a slice of her pizza and bit into the crispy crust.

"I'll tell you the same thing I said to Scott. I'll think about it."

Chapter Three

David stared at his computer screen after Abigail left the office. Focusing on the words in front of him was a challenge. He closed his eyes and inhaled. Images of Abigail filled the darkness. Blonde wavy hair to her shoulders. Her blue eyes had changed to a darker color as they shook hands. Her light citrus scent lingered in his cubicle.

"How was your first day with the boss's daughter?"

His eyes shot open. Scott leaned against his desk. "Good. She catches on quickly."

"I figured she would." Scott straightened. "You feeling okay? Your face is a little flushed."

"Fine. Just needed to rest my eyes for a second." His leg bounced slightly with nervousness. Scott and Robert weren't only business associates; they were friends and shared information. If Scott was aware of his attraction to Abigail, Robert would soon know.

"Okay, I'll let you get back to work." Scott straightened. "Don't stay past six."

"I won't."

Scott disappeared down the hall.

David stared at the computer. As long as he remained at work, Abigail would remain in his thoughts. He shut down his computer and organized his desk for tomorrow. She towered over him and he hoped she wouldn't wear heels again. He wanted to be at the same level, eye-to-eye.

* * * *

The following morning Robert woke with memories of last night's romp with Laura. At thirty-two and newly divorced, Laura had an understanding of what their relationship was—sex. No flowers and dinners at romantic restaurants. It was sex. No overnights at one another's place. It was a rock-my-world-and-then-go-home connection.

He clicked on the TV to catch the top stories and weather. The temperature had dropped by twenty degrees overnight and was going to drop throughout the week. The meteorologist called it a Polar Vortex. He thought about Scott's suggestion of a cruise to a warmer climate. He could go whenever and with any one of his lady friends, rather than with Scott. Scott's point was a valid one when he mentioned losing all the fun if he went with one of the women.

It wouldn't hurt to go alone. He'd have his own cabin and could meet a woman for the duration of the cruise. Things slowed in the office around the holidays. The kids would be with his ex-wife. Feeling good about his decision, he hopped out of bed and began his day.

Upon walking through the main office doors, Robert approached the receptionist. "Is Scott in?"

"Yes, Robert."

"Thank you. Have a good day." The cruise decision gave him reason to be in a good mood. He greeted those he passed with a smile and a good morning salutation on the way to his corner office.

He paused at David's workstation. "Good morning, David and Abb..." He caught himself in time with her name. "Abigail."

"Morning, Robert," David greeted him from his position at his computer.

"Good morning, Dad." Abigail stood, delivering a hug. "You're awfully happy this morning. What gives?"

"I made the decision this morning. I'm going on the cruise with Scott. I don't know the details. Will you stay at my place while I'm away?"

"Good for you, Dad," she exclaimed while embracing him again before sitting. "You need this vacation more than you know. Why do you need me to stay at your place?" she questioned with bewilderment.

"Winter is the worst time to leave a house empty. If the heat goes out, the pipes could freeze and burst." Robert glanced to David, knowing his pipes had burst two years ago and he had taken some days off.

When Abigail faced David, he nodded his head with an all-too-knowing look.

"Couldn't I just stop by and check in on the place?"

"I guess so, but I thought it would be nice for you. You'd get out of your crowded place for a while and be closer to work." Robert paused before adding an enticement. "You'd have heated underground parking."

"The house is not crowded, Dad. It would be nice, though, being a little closer to work and to have the heated parking. I'll think about it."

"Thanks. I'm on my way to see Scott. I'll talk to you later." He raised a hand in goodbye.

Reaching Scott's open door, he knocked. "Let's get this cruise planned."

"You made a decision? Yes." Scott pulled a fisted arm back like an umpire calling a strike in baseball. "Go get your computer and we'll make reservations at the same time."

An hour later, after calling his travel agent and more confident in her abilities, Robert and Scott were set to sail. They'd celebrate the New Year in the Caribbean. He'd have to let his lady friends know he wouldn't be around to celebrate with them and for them to make their own plans.

Laptop in hand, he approached the administrative assistant. "Lois, I have some dates for you to put on the calendar. Scott and I will be out of the office from Monday, December 29 through Friday, January 2. Unless something happens, we should be back on the following Monday. We'll be unreachable during that time as well."

"Yes, sir. Are you going on the Caribbean cruise?" There was a hint of enthusiasm in her voice.

"Yes. I made my mind up after hearing the future weather forecast this morning."

"You'll have a great time. Your mail is on your desk."

"Thanks, Lois." Robert strolled into his office, set the computer down, and got to work.

He had a morning office routine and the last hour and a half had thrown it out of whack. The grin on his face wouldn't go away because he actually looked forward to this vacation.

* * * *

Liz quietly sat in the family room with the Christmas tree lights illuminating the room. The children had put up the artificial tree and decorated it on the first day of their winter break from school. She helped them with the lights, but the rest they did on their own. They had grown so much in the last four years.

Sarah, now a teenager at thirteen, stood at her shoulders and had entered womanhood several months ago. Attitude came along with it, but Liz could manage it. Somehow, this young lady knew when to rein in the attitude. She also accepted and liked seeing Liz dating and moving forward. For her, Sarah was too adult at times.

Brad had troubles dealing with his father's passing, and he didn't understand her dating. At ten, she didn't expect him to understand fully relationships and moving on with life. She had trouble allowing herself to fall in love with someone because of Brad and her mother-in-law. It was hard to stand up against her son, who was growing and changing every day, replicating the man she married and lost.

A creak from the stairs pulled her from her reflections. She wiped her eyes and turned as Sarah come around the corner.

"Hey, sweetheart. You're up early." She switched the coffee cup to her other hand so Sarah could sit beside her.

"It's seven, Mom. It's not early. Can I turn the fireplace on?"

"Sure. I didn't realize what time it was." Sarah sat, leaning against her. "Are you excited about tonight?" Liz put her arm around her daughter and pulled her a little closer. It gave her a little feeling of comfort.

"Are you kidding? I can't wait. What time is everyone coming over?" She twisted quickly in anticipation.

"Whoa." Liz held her coffee cup out and away from her lap. "Don't want to spill hot coffee."

"Sorry, Mom."

"It's okay. The family will start arriving around four. We'll eat dinner at five, open gifts and then, well you know, we'll play games, eat, whatever." She sipped the coffee.

Sarah's chin dropped to her chest and her voice softened. "When do we go to Grandma and Grandpa Farefield's tomorrow?"

Her daughter knew how difficult the visits were, not only for her mother, but for everyone involved. To this day, Ellen remained bitter toward Liz for Gregory's death. Not a visit with Ellen went by without some sort of outburst from the woman. No one in the family could understand why Ellen said the things she said to Liz. They all knew, including Ellen, that the weather caused the car accident that took his life. Liz had nothing to do with the accident. It didn't help that the woman refused to seek counseling.

"We'll leave here at about noon. That gives you and your brother time to see what Santa brought you."

"Oh pa-lease, Mom. You know I know."

"But your brother doesn't." She turned and, with raised eyebrows, gave the keep-your-mouth-shut look.

"I don't what?" At the sound of Brad's voice, Liz whipped around to see him standing by the kitchen table.

"Um, that I'm making pancakes for breakfast." She rose from the couch. "How does that sound? It's been awhile since you've had homemade pancakes."

"Nah, I'll just have some cereal."

"Are you sure?" He nodded. "Okay," she replied disappointed.

The pancakes had been a cover up, but his saying no was a letdown. She glanced back to Sarah, sprawled out on the couch. "Did you want pancakes?"

"Yum. Can I help?" She sat up on her knees.

"Sure." The two walked to the kitchen.

As Brad poured milk into his bowl, Liz smiled. The secret of Santa was safe for another year.

* * * *

The turkey was in the roaster and Liz was putting the fixings in the oven to reheat when the doorbell rang.

"Grandma. Grandpa." Brad's voice exclaimed from the entry.

Liz stepped into the foyer and took her parents' coats, hanging them in the closet. "How was the drive?"

"Fine. The roads are clear for now," her father, Doug, answered.

"The weather people say we're going to get up to six inches between midnight tonight and throughout the day tomorrow."

"I'll believe it when I see it, Dad." She helped carry gift-wrapped packages into the family room.

"Well, you make sure to drive carefully out to Duane and Ellen's." Her mother, Janice, spoke trailing behind her with more gifts. "It's such a long drive for you."

"Edina isn't that long of a drive, Mom. Don't worry, I'll take it slow if we get bad weather."

"Dinner smells good, honey."

"Thanks, Dad. We should be set to eat at five. Are you going to carve the bird?" She made her way to the kitchen to check on things.

"You betcha."

Liz chuckled. After seeing *Ole and Lena's Family Christmas* play with her girlfriends, she couldn't help but laugh a little. Ole and Lena, the butt of all Minnesota jokes, made fun of the Minnesotan accent.

The doorbell rang and in waddled her pregnant sister-in-law, Allison, with their youngest, four-year-old Scott. "Doug and John are right behind me. They're getting the cookies and gifts. I think Mason and Stephanie were turning in as we got here."

"Let me take your coats and you guys join Mom and Dad in the family room." No sooner did she close the closet door in the entry, when in walked her oldest brother, Doug Jr. with his oldest son, John. Her other brother, Mason, and his pregnant wife, Stephanie, trailed behind. After delivering welcoming hugs, she added their coats to the closet.

The time to take the turkey out of the oven came and Liz's sister, Mallory, and her husband, Adam, hadn't arrived. No one had gotten a call or text from either of them. They lived in a city thirty minutes away. The family grew anxious.

"I need to take the bird out of the oven." Liz worried about their dinner.

"Your dad's calling her, dear. You go ahead and cover the turkey with foil." Her mother stood with a hand propped on the arm across her waist, with fingertips at her lips—a sign of worry.

With the turkey on the platter and tented with aluminum foil, Liz pulled the baking dishes from the oven, keeping them covered to stay hot.

"She's on her way," her father called from the living room at the front of the house.

"Well, what did she say?" her mother blurted. "Why are they late?"

"She said she was sorry and was on her way," Dad replied with a shrug.

"Well, did she sound okay?" That was a mother for you, asking questions.

"Fine, I guess. I don't know. Maybe you should've been the one calling."

"Dad," Liz interrupted, saving them from the direction it could've gone—an argument. "Why don't you carve the turkey, and we'll be all set to eat when Mallory and Adam get here."

The turkey was sliced and still no Mallory and Adam.

"Allison, what do you think?" Liz looked to her sister-in-law. "Should we let the kids dish up and get started? They could play while we eat."

"Sure. John, you can dish up your plate?"

Like Brad, her nephew took a plate and small amounts of what was offered. The kids didn't care for the turkey meal and ate what their parents required. They would fill up on the cookies and snacks later. Sarah filled her plate with everything, except the green bean dish. The kids sat around the table eating.

The doorbell startled them. They expected their stragglers to walk in unannounced.

Liz peered through the window. Headlights shined through the window. Standing at the door, she held it open.

"Mallory!" She was alone. "Where's Adam? Come in." She guided her sister into the foyer. "What's going on? You've been crying." Her voice dropped low with the question to avoid the families' attention.

At this point, the adults gathered around in the small area, waiting for Mallory to answers.

"Adam ... Adam won't be coming." Mallory broke into tears. Liz gathered her in her arms.

"What do you mean he won't be coming?" her father's voice boomed.

"Doug." Her mom silenced him with a warning tone.

"Let's go into the living room and sit." Shuffling their way to the couch, Liz sat beside her sister. "Tell us what happened."

"We got into a stupid argument ... and eventually ... he told me he was..." Mallory sobbed, cutting herself off. She left them on the edge of conversation cliff.

"What did he say?" her father exclaimed in a frustrated tone.

"Doug, please." Her mother spoke firmly. "Give her a moment. Can't you see she's upset?"

With a harrumph from their father, they patiently waited for Mallory to continue.

Her sister's head rested in her hands. "He's filing for divorce."

The room exploded with 'what's' and 'why's'. Mallory simply shook her head.

Chapter Four

Mallory broke through the sobs, "I'm sorry I ruined dinner and Christmas."

"You did no such thing." Liz embraced her on the couch. "I'm glad, we're all glad, you're safe. That's all that matters. We were worried something... It doesn't matter, you're here." She leaned into her sister's ear and whispered, "Do you think we could eat, for Dad's sake?"

Mallory nodded her head before speaking. "Let's eat, please."

"Amen," their father responded before disappearing into the kitchen.

"But Mallory—"

"But nothing, Mom." Mallory wiped her face with a tissue one of the women handed her before blowing her nose. "I'm going to be a mess for a long time." She audibly exhaled.

Liz knew the all too familiar sound. The sound of an exhale to fight back the raging storm of tears and screams of angst. She waited for the sharp inhale through the nose, followed by another exhale.

"If you want to stay here tonight, you can."

"Thanks, but I need to go back..." Mallory slumped forward clasping her shaking hands.

Liz stroked her sister's back. "You're welcome to stay here anytime. The house will be empty while I'm away."

"Thank you. Let's go eat." Mallory stood tall, counterattacking the matter at hand. "I don't want to ruin any more of our time."

Liz shared a loving squeeze before letting go. She entered the kitchen last, glad to find the children threw their dirty paper plates away before going off to play. She dished up her food and joined the adults at the dining room table.

"Liz, are you excited to leave for your cruise?" Allison said, changing the subject of conversation.

Liz mouthed 'thank you.'

"You're not going to want to come back to this cold weather."

"As excited as I am, I'm nervous to be going alone. I'll be ready to come home when it's time. I may not like the cold, but will miss the kids."

"Well, I'm looking forward to having my sweet grandkids for a week." Janice smiled gleefully before taking a bite of mashed potatoes loaded with gravy.

Mason smirked around a bite of turkey. "What does your mother-in-law think about this whole thing?" His attitude was snarky.

"She doesn't know about the trip," Liz admitted, looking to the ceiling. "God help me if she finds out."

"Why do you say that?" Stephanie rubbed her large swollen abdomen.

"Because she thinks I'm supposed to live the remainder of my life as a spinster. Stephanie, are you okay?" Liz cocked her head to the side. Due after the first of the year, Stephanie could go into labor at any time.

"Fine. Food isn't agreeing with me and the baby."

"Your plate hasn't been touched," their father pointed out gruffly.

Liz wondered why her dad was bothered this evening.

"If she's not hungry, dear, let her be. Stephanie, honey, how long has food been disagreeing with you?" Leave it to the grand pooh-bah of mothers to get to the bottom of things.

"Since this morning. Really, I'm fine. I'll take a few antacid tablets and— Oooh."

"You're not fine." Mason slid his chair back and stood behind Stephanie. "We should go to the hospital."

"Mason," their mom spoke calmly. "Let's wait to see when the next few contractions hit. What time is it?"

Allison checked her watch. "Six thirty-four."

Liz assumed the watch on Allison's wrist was to time her own contractions. "Allison, when are you due again?"

Mason sat down and they resumed eating, but all eyes watched Stephanie for the next contraction.

"A week after Stephanie. Why?"

"I forgot, that's all." Liz stuffed a piece of turkey in her mouth and chewed.

They finished their meal and cleaned the dishes without another contraction. Before going to sit with the others, Liz poured a glass of Scotch for her dad.

"Here, Dad, I thought you'd like a glass." She stood beside the lounger where he sat.

"Thanks." He tossed back a swallow.

"Another one," Stephanie stated with a mix of smile and grimace.

The adults turned to Allison. "A little over an hour apart."

"Okay, kids," Janice spoke above the kids' chatter. "Locate one of your gifts from me and grandpa, and then sit."

The room erupted with gleeful children.

"Now, one at a time, oldest to youngest, open your gift." This continued until all gifts were open.

Wrapping paper and toy packaging covered the floor. The children dispersed to the other rooms to play with their new toys and games.

"Who's ready for dessert and games?" Liz walked into the kitchen to grab some treats.

Mason stood and helped Stephanie from the couch. "If you all don't mind, we're going to head for home. It's past nine, and Stephanie would like to rest."

"Go, but you call when you go to the hospital," Janice said. "I need to know when I could expect my next little bundle of grandbaby joy."

Mason embraced their mom. "I will. I promise."

* * * *

Robert woke fully when his bedroom door clicked open. Chris entered and appeared around the corner. "Good morning. Did Santa come last night?"

"Da-ad." She swatted his leg. "I know you're Santa. Will you get up so we can open the gifts?"

"Okay. Give me a couple of minutes and I'll be out."

She left the room, and he went into his bathroom. Wrapped in a dark blue robe, he entered the dining room to find Abigail cooking.

"That smells great." He went straight to the coffee maker and brewed a cup.

"I thought we should eat some breakfast. How does French toast sound?" She flipped a slice of bread.

"Can't we open our gifts yet?" Chris whined from the living room.

They turned on the gas fireplace, which made the room warm and cozy. He didn't use the thing often.

"Yes." He strolled to the sofa and sat by his son, Alex. "Aren't you going to see what Santa got you?" Chris tore into a Christmas package.

Alex said, "Let Chris enjoy—"

"Oh, my God." Chris's voice pierced the quiet room. Kathleen and Abigail made the right gift suggestion. "No way. No fucking way."

"Hey. Watch your language." He couldn't believe the word that popped out of his daughter's mouth.

She waved the piece of paper around. "Sorry, Dad, but is this for real?" Her tone dropped with the apology but spiked again.

"Yes."

"Oh, my, God. No way." She ran around the townhouse, jumping up and down here and there. "Five Seconds of Summer. Yes."

Alex leaned into him. "You bought her tickets to a concert?"

"Two tickets. I guess it's one of her favorite bands."

"A boy band." He rolled his eyes. "The girls are crazy about these guys."

"They are not a boy band." Chris learned over the sofa and yelled in Alex's face. "They're a band because they play their own instruments." She ran over and threw her arms around Robert's neck. "Thank you, thank you, thank you."

"Breakfast is ready," Abigail called, setting a platter loaded with French toast on the counter.

"Let's eat. Chris." Robert patted her arm around his neck. "After eating, you should get ready for when your mother gets here. Abby, thanks for doing this—making us breakfast." They went to the kitchen.

Everyone dished up and gathered around the island to eat.

"It's one of the few things I know how to make. Helps too, that you have what I needed." She bit off the forkful of toast covered in syrup.

"Not bad, sis," Alex mumbled between bites. Four slices sat on his plate.

"Obviously, since you're devouring them. Slow down." Abby spoke like a natural mother.

"Chris, you like them, too?" Robert watched her as she tapped her phone screen while she ate.

"Mm, yeah. Great." She looked lost in texting land.

"Dad, I can't believe you're going on a cruise with a guy." Alex snickered tossing four more slices onto his plate.

"Nothing wrong about traveling with a co-worker. I'm not sleeping or sharing a cabin with the guy." Robert chuckled. "If Abby has it her way, I'll meet a woman, and we'll get married." He laughed at the idea.

"I just want you to get away from work, relax, and have a great time. If you were to meet someone, well so be it."

"Speaking of work. David informed me you were a big help on the Myers bid."

"That's nice to hear. I hope we're chosen." Abigail put her dirty dishes in the dishwasher. "I'm going to go shower."

"Don't take too long because I need to shower too," Chris said haughtily.

He waved Abigail off. "If she's still in the shower when you're finished, you can pack, make your bed, or even clean up the room. Alex, you can shower in my bathroom."

"Cool."

"Why can't I shower in there?" Chris whined.

"Because I don't have feminine beauty stuff in my shower. Now stop with the attitude. It's Christmas."

Abigail and Alex opened their gifts ready for the day. Their reactions weren't anything like Chris's. He was okay with that because they were older. Alex thanked him for the Jordan shoes and warm-up pants.

"Thanks for the beautiful leather portfolio case." Abigail embraced him. "I've also decided to stay here when you're away. The heated parking sold me with the forecasted freezing temps."

"I thought you'd change your mind. Let me give you a key." He went to the kitchen and retrieved a key from a drawer. "Go ahead and keep the key after I return. It would be good for someone in the family to have access."

"Sounds good. I'll put it on my key ring. I'm going to pack my overnight bag so I'm ready when Mom gets here."

"You don't have to wait for her."

"I know. I'm not sure what her plan is for the day, or where I'm involved."

Not more than fifteen minutes later, the door buzzer sounded. "I'm here for the kids." Kathleen's voice sounded through the speaker.

Robert pushed the entry button to give her access to the building. "Merry Christmas, Kathleen," he greeted on opening the door. "The kids are all set."

"I need to talk to you." It was the 'I need something' tone and no greeting in return. She wore tight fitting jeans covering her lean legs with her feet stuffed in heeled leather boots, which put her closer to eye level with him. A red loose fitting blouse with coordinating jewelry on her neck, wrists, fingers and ears, completed her ensemble.

"Okay." He walked into the dining room.

"I'm going to New York for New Year's." She hiked the large Louis Vuitton bag over her shoulder.

He swore if it were any bigger, she'd fall backwards.

"I know its last minute, but I need you to take the kids." She didn't ask, but more or less ordered him.

"Hi, Mom." Abigail's cheery voice interrupted. "Merry Christmas."

They embraced and Kathleen returned the holiday sentiment before turning to him. "Robert, please help me out." Her whining voice made him realize where Chris inherited hers.

"I would if I could, but I'll be on a cruise." He was sorry he couldn't take the kids.

"Oh." She looked taken aback. "Who are you going with?" The bag fell from her shoulder to the dining table with a thud.

"Not that it's any of your business, but I'm going with Scott." He strolled to the kitchen island and reclaimed his coffee mug. "He and Abby talked me into taking a break. This cold weather helped in the decision making, too." Taking a sip, he quickly set the mug on the counter because it had gone cold.

"What do you need help with, Mom?" Abigail leaned against the wall.

"I have plans to go to New York for New Year's. I thought your father would take your brother and sister,"—her tone turned condescending—"but he'll be out of the country."

Alex came around the corner of his room, "Hey, Mom. Merry Christmas."

"Merry Christmas, honey. We'll leave as soon as Christine is ready."

"I'm staying here when Dad's gone. Why don't they come stay here?" Abby offered as they waited for Chris.

"What are you guys talking about?" Chris went to her mother's side for a hug. She resembled her more and more, as she worked to perfect the styling of her long blonde hair.

"I'm going to New York and your father's going on a cruise, so your sister suggested she could watch you guys. She's staying here while your father's away."

"NO," she screeched, backing away from Kathleen. "Why can't I go with you?"

"It's for adults only. It's just a short trip." Kathleen stepped toward Chris, who retreated.

Abigail touched Chris's shoulder. "We'll have a great time. I promise."

"I don't want to." Chris ran to the bedroom, slamming the door closed.

"I'll go talk to her." Abigail disappeared into the girls' room.

Alex walked around him and Kathleen and plopped onto the couch. "So much for a 'Merry' Christmas."

"Alexander, please," Kathleen chided. "I'll need you to help your sisters. Abigail will be working during the day, so Christine will need you around."

"Depending on when you're leaving and how long you're gone, you did say a short time, Abby may not be working." Robert added. "The employees are off Thursday and Friday, with the option of working on Wednesday from home. Does that work with your plans?"

"Yes." His ex-wife softened a touch, probably because she could leave knowing the kids were in good hands. "I'm leaving Tuesday after the kids are home from school and I'll be home late Friday."

"Let's go," Chris demanded as she reappeared with Abigail.

"Christine, you'll only be staying here three nights. We'll go shopping before I leave and get some fun stuff for you to ring in the New Year." Kathleen put an arm around Chris only for her to shrug it off.

"What… ever. Can we go now?" Chris seized her overnight bag and stormed to the door.

"Alexander, let's go." Kathleen's curt voice revealed her upset over Chris's behavior. "Robert, I'll finalize things with Abigail. Have fun on your cruise." The last part held no enthusiasm. "Abigail, we'll see you at home."

When the door closed behind them, Abigail inquired. "I hope it was okay for me to speak up and say Alex and Chris could stay here with me?"

"Are you kidding? Thank you. You're a lifesaver. Hopefully, your sister will give you an easy time."

"Don't worry, she will. We're sisters." She snatched her little bag.

"Merry Christmas, Abby." He hugged her at the door. "I'll be leaving *early* Sunday morning for Florida. You can come over any time."

"Merry Christmas, Dad. I love you." They stepped from the embrace.

"I love you, too."

"Have a great time and relax. You don't have anything to worry about."

"I will." He closed the door, beaming. Now that he was going on the cruise, he couldn't wait to leave.

* * * *

Liz pulled in the driveway, parked next to her sister-in-law's car, and took a deep breath. "We're here. Remember to behave and mind your manners."

"We know, Mom. Don't worry." Sarah slid from the front seat and out the car door.

Brad escaped the vehicle as soon as Sarah spoke, running into the house to see his Grandma Farefield.

Inhale. Exhale. Things would be okay. It was never simple or easy with Ellen. Veronica's presence helped ease or distract the tension. She got out of the car, grabbed the bag filled with gifts from the back, and moved toward the house.

The front door opened, and Veronica appeared. "Did you have any trouble getting here?"

"No, the roads are fine." She set down the bag. "It's good to see you." They embraced each other.

"You, too."

"How is she?"

"Good. Thanksgiving time is the hardest for her and you survived." Veronica wrapped her arms around her body to fight the chilly outdoor air.

"Thanks to you. Let's get inside before she comes looking for us." Liz opened the door and entered the grand foyer. The muffled sound of voices young and old blended from one of the rooms.

"Don't worry, she won't. She's relaxing in the family room. She's having dinner prepared by a chef this year."

They talked in hushed voices.

"What?" The last time Ellen had something catered was for the gathering after Gregory's funeral.

"She said she didn't want to be in the kitchen. She wanted to be with the family." Her sister-in-law rolled her eyes.

"This has got to be costing her a fortune."

"It is, and good for the caterer." She glanced around to make sure no one could catch their conversation. "The woman took these people away from their families on a holiday. I hope they tripled their prices for their services."

Liz did, too. The two women quietly laughed. Money was never an issue for her in-laws.

"My sister-in-law, Stephanie, had a baby girl early this morning, and Allison is in labor as we speak."

"You're kidding. They weren't due at the same time, were they?"

"A week apart, but we think Allison went into 'sympathy' labor." Liz laughed.

"Wow."

"Mom," Brad's voice cried, growing louder as he neared them in the entry. Tears streamed from his eyes, as he slammed into her body with a tight embrace.

"What's going on?" She switched from friendly sister-in-law to caring mother. "What happened?" She squatted to be at his level.

"Grandma told me Santa isn't real." He huffed through teary breaths.

"What?" she exclaimed. Her teeth ground together as her jaw tensed. Heat flushed through her body, and her pulse quickened. For four years, her mother-in-law kept her undeserving spite aimed at her. Now she used it against the grandchildren.

His tears slowed. "She said you were Santa. That he doesn't exist."

Footsteps, followed by Ellen's voice. "The boy is ten-years-old."

Liz turned with a clenched tight-lipped mouth to face her.

"It's time he knew the truth, Elizabeth." She crossed her arms over her bosom with an authoritative stance.

Of course, her mother-in-law would use her full name. Liz slowly rose. Her body rigid with anger. Her voice shook, but she spoke in a low demeaning tone. "You have no right to tell *my* son what is and isn't real. You are *not* his mother." Brad hid behind her leg. She wrapped an arm around him, in a form of comfort and security.

"He's not a child anymore." With a defiant voice, Ellen stepped closer.

"He's ten, for God's sake!" Her body shook. Her heart pounded as though the nine drummers drumming beat on base drums. "He *is* a child and will be until he's a teenager, when he'll become a young man." She turned and spoke to Veronica as calm as possible considering the situation. "Will you take Brad into the formal living room?" She nudged her son toward his aunt. "Thanks."

Once they were out of sight, Liz stepped closer to Ellen. "I'm going to talk to *my* son and thanks to *you*,"—with a firm finger pointed at the woman, her voice degenerated to a guttural rasp—"I will explain this to him with deep sadness. *You've* ruined Christmas." She moved a footstep forward and stopped. "I know you want to spend time with your grandchildren, but if you say anymore to Brad about Santa while we're here, we *will* leave."

Ellen gaped as Liz turned and walked away. God, did that feel good.

In the past four years, she'd never stood up to her mother-in-law. Never raised her voice or confronted the woman. This was a step to her healing and one of the reasons she was going on the Caribbean cruise. Brad's therapist suggested she journal her thoughts and feelings during the trip.

"Thanks, Veronica. We'll join the family shortly." She sat next to Brad, wrapping an arm around him. His crying stopped, but he slumped forward, defeated. "I'm sorry about that. Grandma had no right to tell you what she did."

"You shouldn't have yelled at her." He pushed away. An angry ten-year old, who loved his grandmother, sat straighter facing her.

"I didn't yell. I raised my voice though because she did something she shouldn't have." She relaxed, resting her elbows on her knees and chin on her clasped hands, pausing a moment to find the right words. "Do you believe in Santa?" She lifted her chin and faced him.

"I ... I don't know. I've heard kids say things on the bus and ... well, now I'm not sure." His posture softened.

"Brad, Christmas is a magical time. It's a time we celebrate the gift of Jesus. He was a miracle. I won't go into detail, but I think you know enough." She smiled. "Every day we are surrounded by miracles. It's not just at Christmas time. You need to believe in these miracles because when you stop believing, you don't see them and you stop receiving the joy they bring you."

"What does this have to do with Santa being real or not?" Confusion drew his eyebrows together, crinkling his forehead.

"Your grandma told you the truth. Santa isn't real." Her voice changed from somber to a more enlightened tone. "At Christmas time there is a magic that happens all over the world where people receive gifts that make their lives happy in one way or another from strangers they never see or meet. Good things happen to them because they never stopped believing. Santa comes in many forms. Do you understand?"

"I guess so. Does this mean we won't get presents anymore on Christmas morning?"

She giggled with a lopsided grin. With his question, she knew he'd be fine. "Keep believing and you will." She tousled his hair. "Let's go join the family." A few steps out of the room, Liz quickly turned grasping his shoulders. "Oh, I almost forgot. You can't say anything to your younger cousins. You need to keep this a secret. Remember how you felt. Can you do that?"

"I think so. I'll try my hardest."

"Okay, that's all I ask, honey." She embraced him before continuing to the family room.

Her brother-in-law, William, stood as they entered. "Liz." He delivered a quick hug. "Merry Christmas."

"Merry Christmas, Will. It's good to see you."

"You, too. Should we start opening gifts?" He glanced around the spacious room. "I know the kids are excited."

"Sounds good." She sat across the room from Ellen, with the tree partially blocking their view of each other.

The unwrapping underway and everyone at ease, Veronica handed her a book-sized package. Liz opened it to find a journal with a seascape as the cover. "Thank you, it's beautiful."

"I was surprised to hear you were going on a cruise—" William was cut short by his wife, clamping his mouth with a firm hand.

Veronica shook her head at him and turned to Liz mouthing, "I'm sorry."

"You're going on a cruise?" Ellen quipped. "When?"

"I'm leaving on Sunday and will be back the following Sunday." Before it could be vocalized, she knew what was coming. The reason she didn't want Ellen to know in the first place.

"What about the kids? Where are they staying?"

Here we go. "My parents are taking care of them for the week."

She assumed a posture of superiority. "Why can't they stay here?" she demanded before continuing. "We can take care of them just as well as your parents." Her mouth pinched.

She sighed. "You can call my mother. I'm sure the two of you can work something out."

"I want to stay with Grandma Farefield." Brad jumped quickly into the conversation.

"I'll call your other grandmother tomorrow, Bradley, and we'll see what we can work out. Okay?"

Liz was taken aback with Ellen's response. She didn't make any promises. A refreshing change.

Chapter Five

Liz gleefully smiled making her way across the gangplank of the cruise ship. With the walkway covered, she couldn't see much. The air-conditioned boarding terminal masked the Miami warmth. She glanced at her wrinkled silk tank dress. What had she been thinking when she chose her outfit for the day? Wrinkled and creased from sitting while waiting for her flight and then being sedentary for the three-hour plane ride didn't help matters.

With a small carry-on, her purse, and sweater, she stepped through the ship's passageway. Greeted by a strong breeze created by the incoming passing bodies, mixed with the ships air-conditioning, reminded her of the cold temperatures and negative wind chills she'd been happy to leave behind in Minnesota. The white marble tiled floor gleamed. The ship's crew greeted and directed her to the floor for her suite. Out of the main crowd, she put on her cardigan, lifting her ponytail from the confines of the back of the sweater where it was trapped.

As she moved farther into the center atrium, the marbled floor met carpet designed with large swirls in maroon on gold. Solid gold-and-maroon fabric chairs formed small seating groups. The area opened to the upper level where chairs were situated around the edge. The grand entrance reminded her of a posh hotel lobby.

Roller bag handle in her grip, she wheeled it behind her and maneuvered toward the bank of elevators. Once she squeezed into one, the elevator slowly made its way to the tenth floor as passengers got off at the different levels with their baggage. When the doors opened to her floor, she exited and rooms lined both sides of the carpeted hallway. She hoped she wouldn't have any interior rooms across from her suite. She continued forward and the hall zig-zagged. There were no rooms in the mid-section. Luck was on her side.

She stopped in front of her door, slid the key in the lock, and opened the door. The suite amazed her. She stepped onto a dark wood floor that ended in soft sand-colored carpeting mixed with a lighter shade to create a wave pattern. Straight ahead was a floor to ceiling window and patio door, which led to her private deck. Though the room was narrow, the layout optimized the size. She had a king-sized bed and a couch. Turning to the left, she found an enclosed shower and to the right was the enclosed toilet. A bit odd to have the sink in the same area as the bed, but her room was beautiful.

She wheeled her carry-on to the couch, setting it on the cushion. The rest of her luggage would arrive once at sea, so she was thankful for the overnight bag containing bathroom items, her swimsuit, a change of undergarments, a sundress, and a short outfit. She stowed the empty bag in the closet. Contemplating whether to change or not, she opted not too because she'd be going outside in the warm muggy air as they left port.

At the sink, Liz ran a washcloth under cold water and blotted her face and neck. She could remain in her room and watch from her personal deck, but she wanted to enjoy and savor every moment of this time away. Maybe she would get a drink to ease her angst.

Her room key functioned like a credit card, so she stored her purse, which contained her passport, in the room safe. On the fifteenth level of the ship, the first outdoor level, she located the bar and ordered a fruity drink instead of her usual red wine. On deck, she shed her sweater. The pool area overflowed with passengers. Drink in hand, she meandered along the deck and took the stairs to go to the sun deck. She glanced around for an opening at the railing. Not careful enough about watching for others, she found herself up close and personal in the arms of an attractive man.

"I'm sorry. Excuse me." The beverage she held sloshed around. She regarded the man as familiar.

"No, please forgive me. I was too absorbed by the ocean." Taller than her five-eight height, the muscular arms that held her proved he was a man who took care of his body. She stared into pale green eyes and her gaze fell to his chin.

His features took on a quizzical appearance. "Are you alright?"

"I'm fine. Thank you." Her body froze in place.

"Liz?" He held her back by the arms. "Liz Farefield?"

With a mental shake of her head, she spoke. "Do I know you?" Her voice hitched.

"You resemble a woman I've met. Her name was Liz." Releasing his hold, he stepped back. "I'm sorry," he offered his hand, "Robert Burnhamwood. I believe we met at the opening of the Kids Kare Clinic. My firm, RB and Associates, designed it."

Focusing more closely on Robert, her head tipped to the side as she recognized him. It was the cleft in his chin. "Yes, you're right." She nervously drank from her plastic glass.

Another man approached and presented his hand to Liz after handing Robert what appeared to be a beer. "Hi. Scott Jordan."

He had jet-black hair with not a grey strand in sight. An olive skin tone gave him the appearance of Mediterranean descent.

"Liz Farefield," she offered while shaking his hand. "Are you two traveling together?"

"Yes. Scott's a friend and partner at the firm." Robert quickly clarified as if to indicate they weren't gay partners. "Separate suites. He's responsible for my being on this trip." He paused a moment. "Are you waiting for Greg?"

Liz avoided eye contact with either of the men, focusing on the glass she held. "No... I'm traveling alone. Greg died four years ago in a car accident." She sipped from her cup and glanced at the throng of people below on the pool deck.

"I'm sorry for your loss." Scott gently touched her forearm.

"Liz, I'm sorry to hear this." Robert embraced her for a brief moment. "You had children, but I didn't think they were old enough to leave them alone?"

"They're staying with my parents and in-laws." A level of unease mixed with intrigue made her stomach tense. "If you'll excuse me, I'd like to go back to my room and see if my luggage has arrived."

"Maybe we'll run into each other again. I'd like to buy you a drink and talk," Robert politely offered.

She nodded. "Maybe. It was nice to meet you, Scott and to see you again, Robert." She strolled inside and back to the suite.

Running into Robert flooded her with thoughts of Gregory. While working on her secondary teaching degree, she'd met Gregory on a blind date. Gregory proposed during her final year. Gregory's career prospered and he gained an excellent reputation in his field. Liz continued to substitute teach occasionally, but the children were her number one priority and Gregory's income alone, provided them with a comfortable lifestyle. Unfortunately, it also brought Ellen, his mother. The movie *Monster-in-Law* with Jennifer Lopez came to mind.

With the last sip of her drink, Liz entered her cabin to find her luggage. Disposing the plastic cup, she unpacked. Finished, she stored the bag away and relaxed by taking a long shower. With no rush to make a dining time, she took her time applying makeup and curling her hair. She picked out a knee length black skirt, cream sweater set, and a pair of heels to wear for the evening.

Dressed, she glanced in the mirror. Her workout routine of running and lifting weights kept her in shape. She figured the ensemble would fit the New York themed restaurant tonight. With time to write in her journal, she sat at the small desk.

My cabin is amazing. The view from the balcony is breathtaking. There are no obstructions. Right now, the ocean is my backdrop. I'm so happy about taking this cruise. My room is long and narrow but the layout works. I have a sitting area and TV, which I doubt I'll watch. It would be the end of the world for Brad without a TV.

Our lives have a gaping hole. Greg's presence is in every room of the house. Oddly, I've found it comforting, but at the same time, I think it may be holding all of us back from moving forward. I contemplate whether to sell the house or not. Start making new memories.

I ran into a man on the sun deck who designed and was involved in the clinic. It was difficult because of the connection to Greg. I couldn't stay and talk to him. I felt bad for excusing myself so quickly. But as I found myself taking in Robert's features, some attraction to him made me uncomfortable.

Liz wrote more detailed notes about her room before closing the journal and leaving for dinner. Near the rear of the ship, she rode the elevator to the sixth level and was transported to New York in The Manhattan Room restaurant. Dark wood, linen tablecloths, and soft paneled lighting made it warm and inviting. The diners she could see wore business casual. Her suitable attire set her mind at ease.

Candles sat on every table. A great place for couples to have a romantic dinner. She lacked the other half to make a couple. A slight heaviness in her stomach had her contemplating whether to stay or go somewhere else. Her hands ran from her waist down her sides, as she swallowed the forming lump.

"Liz." Robert stepped next to her at the hostess stand. "Would you care to join me and Scott at our table?" He gestured behind him to where Scott sat at a table for four.

"I don't want to interrupt your dinner." She glanced to the floor.

"We were just about to order when I saw you. I know you're traveling alone. You wouldn't be interrupting. Plus, I'd appreciate someone other than my business partner to talk with, if you catch my drift." He smiled as Liz nodded.

He gently touched her elbow to guide her to the table when the maître d' approached. "Thank you, she'll be dining with me, sir."

"Thank you for inviting me." Deep green eyes like a tree leaf in the middle of summer glanced at him before quickly looking away. She smelled of summer, too. Not roses like his grandmother smelled of when he was a kid, but something softer.

"Liz, I'm glad you're joining us." Scott rose when they neared.

Robert pulled her chair from the table. "What would you like to drink?"

"A red wine. Cabernet preferably." Long dark wavy hair cascaded over her shoulders.

He waved to the waiter working with the next table over. "The lady will be joining us, so if we could get another place setting and she'd like a glass of the house cabernet. Thank you."

"Yes, sir." The waiter nodded.

"So, Liz, what do you do?" Scott pounced on her.

"I'm a substitute teacher. Right now I'm doing a long-term sub job for a teacher out on maternity leave."

"Do you teach all subjects and grade levels?" Scott took a sip of his dirty martini.

"Yes, but I mostly focus on the middle school level. For the long term, I'm teaching English, which was my main study in college." She sat with her back straight. Robert didn't know if she was uncomfortable or just had good posture.

A server brought a table setting of flatware for Liz and a glass of water. He and Liz thanked the man at the same time. She flashed a demure smile. Her eyes sparkled. A brief tightness in his chest left him dazed by the immediate effect she had on him.

"How old are your children?" It was his turn to learn a little more about her. He couldn't let Scott show more interest.

"Sarah's thirteen, in eighth grade and Brad is ten, in fifth grade."

The waiter set the glass of wine on the table. He offered the evening specials and a menu for her to peruse.

"Robert, if my memory serves me correctly, you had children as well." Liz sipped the red liquid, and he found himself wishing he were the glass of wine.

He swallowed the sip he'd just taken. "Um, yeah. My oldest, Abby, is set to graduate in the spring with her Masters in Architecture." He relaxed against the chair back.

Waiters and servers, dressed in black and white, roamed about the expansive dining room as they waited on guests. Robert, Liz, and Scott checked the plates of food being delivered, to see what might interest them.

"Abby's interning for us at the firm," Scott volunteered.

"You must be very proud of her, Robert." She played with the wine glass stem between her thumb and fingers.

"Very proud. Alex is eighteen going on twenty-five. He'll be graduating this spring."

Her thin eyebrows rose.

"My youngest, Chris, is in the same grade and age as your daughter." He sipped his vodka gimlet.

Her fingers twisted a section of hair at the base of her neck. "What about your wife? I thought you were married?"

He swallowed hard. "Divorced." He coughed and cleared his throat. "She filed for divorce five years ago. The kids live with her because of school. I live in downtown St. Paul." He wanted to know her, not talk about himself. "Where are you living?"

"I'm still in Eagan. Scott, what about you? Are you married, divorced, children?"

"Divorced and single. No children. I haven't found the right woman to settle down with." Scott maintained constant eye contact with Liz.

He made Robert uncomfortable. Not out of fear, but.... Jealousy? It couldn't be. They were having a simple dinner and getting reacquainted with each other.

Their waiter approached. "Are you ready to order?"

"Yes," Robert acknowledged, thankful for the interruption. Scott couldn't ogle Liz any longer. They placed their orders.

"How long have the two of you worked together?"

He looked at Scott. "This is the nineteenth anniversary for the company and you started from the bottom, so we've worked together for..."

"Fifteen years. Three as VP," Scott finished for him.

"You're still new to the position." Liz sipped from her wine glass.

"He earned his way and does a hell of a job."

"I wasn't simply—" Her face reddened.

"I know you weren't." Robert said to ease her angst. "I was stating a fact."

"Are you signed up for any of the offshore excursions, Liz?" Scott changed the subject.

"A couple. Nothing over the top. I mainly want to relax on this trip. Self-discovery you could say."

"Care to elaborate?" Robert may have been pressing his luck with this one. He sensed unease when they set sail.

"It's been a stressful holiday, and I'm focusing on me. Or trying to. It's hard when I see kids running around on the ship. It makes me think of mine at home."

Robert sensed some sadness in her tone and decided he needed to change the subject. "My kids are staying at my place with my oldest. I asked Abby to stay there while I was away. Christmas morning, at the last minute, my ex-wife asked me to watch the kids for New Year's."

"What's she doing on such short notice?" Liz was more at ease again.

"Going to New York to see her boyfriend. I would assume she'll see her parents who live there, too."

Their meals arrived, and over dinner, they discussed the events they planned at each of their stops. Once finished, they rose to leave.

"Would you care to join us for an after dinner drink at one of the other bars?" Robert placed a hand on her lower back.

"Actually, I'm exhausted. Being up early to catch the flight, the excitement of being here, and the fresh sea air has done me in. Thank you, though for asking me to join you this evening."

"It was a pleasure having you dine with us. Maybe we can do it again tomorrow evening?" Robert didn't want her to eat alone. More importantly, as the evening progressed, his attraction for her grew and he wanted to see her again.

"I guess we'll see. I'm not sure where or when I'll be eating. Goodnight." She strolled away as he and Scott observed her retreating figure.

There was something about her that had him wanting to spend time getting better acquainted. Get closer, but not in the way he was with his three lady friends in Minnesota. Liz stirred something deep within him. She was humble and kind, genuine in her words and actions, and her eyes revealed an apprehension.

* * * *

Abigail put on a sweatshirt, left her bedroom, and padded quietly down the stairs for the kitchen. After last night's post-Christmas party, she wasn't sure who was awake, and didn't want to disturb them if they were sleeping. Entering the open concept kitchen and family room, she spotted a male body on the couch and another hanging over the loveseat. She turned the coffee maker on to warm the water, picked a coffee from the spinning pod tree, pulled a mug from the cupboard, and brewed her coffee.

Dropping a bagel in the toaster, she sipped her coffee waiting for the bagel to finish. Peanut butter smeared on the bagel, she sat at the table. Her father would be in the warm sun of Miami by now, if not on the ship. The underground parking at his place was going to be nice, as they forecasted freezing temperatures with negative wind chills. Granted, she parked in the garage at the house, but it wasn't heated.

While devouring the toasty goodness, she thought about what she'd need to pack while staying at her dad's place. Unlike her siblings, she didn't have the necessities there. She went to the kitchen and snatched a pad of paper and pen to make a packing list. As she wrote her list, Gina, her best friend, entered the room barefoot, wearing a pair of men's winter themed flannel boxers with a tee shirt.

"Good morning," she whispered and nodded to the living room. "We have a few crashers. When did you get to bed?"

"Not sure. That was some party." Gina made a cup of coffee. "Where did Paul go?"

"Who knows? You got cozy with that guy last night."

"That's putting it mildly." She sat beside her at the table where the sun warmed them through the large picture window. "I got to know him real well last night." Gina smiled dreamily, as her eyes rolled up before sighing in pleasure.

"Did he stay the night?" With a devilish grin on Gina's face, Abigail got the answer. "And you left him alone in your bed?"

"Is there something wrong with that?"

"No not really, but, well, if it were me, I'd be there when he wakes up. You know, to see what he's like when you're sober."

"You're terrible, but good point. So did you meet anyone last night?" She wiggled her eyebrows before sipping from the coffee mug.

"No, but Paul kissed me."

Gina choked on her beverage. "What?" Her eyes widened in disbelief. "And you let him?"

"Not much I could do. I was under the mistletoe. He grabbed me and his lips were on mine before I could protest." She shuddered at the remembrance.

"That bad of a kiss, huh?"

"He was trying to make more out of it than a simple kiss on the lips. A slimy, drunk's tongue searching for my tonsils is not my idea of fun."

"Ew." Gina scrunched her face in disgust. "How did you get him to stop?"

"I pushed him once and that didn't work, so I grabbed his face, dug my thumbs at the corner of his mouth, and shoved him back. He wasn't happy with my tactic."

"He didn't hit you?"

"No. Just used a few choice words." She shook her head. "I blew it all off due to his drunken state."

"I guess, but you know he likes you, so if he tries something again, tell Conrad." Gina scooted the chair back, put her cup on the counter. "I'll talk to you later."

Abigail chuckled as her friend practically ran from the room. She resumed writing her list of items to pack. Finished with a second cup of coffee and her list, she tore it from the pad and went upstairs to pack. She hit the top step and ran into her roommate, Conrad.

"What's the big hurry?" He moved her into the hall away from the stairs. She inhaled his masculine scent, as he held her in his arms. A familiar scent. The one to have ended things between them, it could be awkward at times living in the same house.

"No hurry." She backed out of his arms, putting some distance between them. Even if it was a step. "I have to go pack. I'm staying at my dad's for the week. Remember?"

"Oh, that's right. You're living the single life."

"I live the single life here, you dumbass," she razzed him back. "Unfortunately, I'll be babysitting my brother and sister for several days. My mom's going to New York to celebrate New Year's with her boyfriend."

"Well, if you want any company, I'd be glad to help." He wiggled his eyebrows playfully.

"Thanks but no thanks—"

"Oh ... oh ... yes ... oh, right ... right ... there," Gina screamed behind her closed bedroom door.

"O-kay," Abigail said, her eyebrows raised. "I'm going to pack."

"I'll talk to you later, Abs." The pet name he'd given her while they dated remained. He was the only one allowed to call her by that name.

Chapter Six

The first full day at sea, Liz woke early and headed for the ship's gym. Most of the equipment was empty, making it easy for her to get onto a treadmill. Two miles walked, she worked her upper body by lifting free weights. She spotted Scott approaching in the mirror.

"Hi," she acknowledged him before inhaling.

"Hey, how's your workout going?"

"Fine," Liz replied on an exhale.

Scott stood next to her. "Looks intense. What's your routine?"

"A little walking, running, lifting." She continued with her workout. Socializing at the gym, like some of the women back home, wasn't her idea of a workout. Why they did their hair and makeup prior to working out left her flabbergasted.

"How 'bout some company?"

"Actually," she inhaled and on her exhale continued, "I'll be done in here when I complete this set."

"Would you like to join me at the Garden Café for some breakfast?"

"Thank you, but I'm not ready for breakfast." Liz got up from the weight machine seat. Facing Scott, she smiled cordially. "Maybe I'll see you later, poolside." She left taking the five flights of stairs to the seventh deck where she ran the outdoor track for three miles.

She couldn't help but compare Scott to Gregory while running. His blue eyes, straight nose, and square chin reminded her of her deceased husband. Scott had jet-black hair versus Gregory's wavy dark brown and was about an inch taller than her. She didn't know how old Scott was, but if she had to guess, younger than herself.

Finished with her run, she stretched her muscles as she took the three flights of stairs back to her cabin. Although he was handsome, she wouldn't have any sort of romantic relationship with Scott. Theirs would be platonic.

Liz spent the rest of the morning and early afternoon exploring the passageways, browsing the on-board shops and boutiques, and getting acquainted with the amenities aboard the ship. At one of the off duty shops she purchased a bottle of red wine to keep in her cabin.

Ready for some afternoon sun, Liz went to the fifteenth level where the fun happened—the pool deck. She ordered a burger and fries from one of the deck restaurants and located a lounge chair.

A waiter stopped. "Can I get you a drink?"

"Yes, I'd love a Margarita on the rocks."

"I'll be back shortly."

"Thank you."

Liz observed the passengers while waiting for her beverage. She loved people watching. There were those who were with their spouse or a companion, those who appeared to be wealthy, and those who lived a moderate life. She hadn't seen anyone else alone. Children played with their parents in the large pool. She distanced herself from the area as much as possible, selecting a chair off to the side away from the pool, to avoid becoming emotional because she missed her kids. So far, her emotional state was stable. The frequent children's laughter put a warm smile on her face.

The hamburger was delicious along with the fries. The fries weren't soft and potatoey but crisp, which she preferred. The waiter delivered her drink when her mouth was filled with a bite of burger, so she nodded thanks.

"Do you mind if I join you?" Robert peered from behind the server.

Every nerve ending tingled at the sound of his voice. "Not at all," she replied around her full mouth.

"How was your workout this morning?" He sat on the lounger.

How? Scott must've said something. "Good." Through her straw, she sipped the libation and was in heaven. Not heavy on the alcohol. Nice and smooth.

"Scott and I were thinking of dining at the pub tonight. Go casual." He turned to sit on the edge of the chair and faced her with an endearing smile. "We'd love for you to join us." His inviting voice held a hint of enthusiasm.

"I'll think about it. What time are you planning on eating?"

She stuffed a fry in her mouth. She wasn't sure what they offered for food, but being with others would be good for her spirit. The realization of being one of the few solo travelers saddened her a bit.

"I'm not sure. I could call your suite?" His bright spring green eyes captivated her.

With a mouthful, she held up a finger. "Um, sure. I'm in 10189."

"Good. I'll let you know what time then." He adjusted his seat back into the recline position. "How's the drink?"

"Delicious. I'm full; would you care for a few French fries?" She held the basket in his direction.

"Thanks." He took the container and stuck a fry in his mouth. "Mmm, nice and crispy. I like them that way." Another fry disappeared.

A flutter in her chest caused her to smile because someone appreciated fries the same way. The kids liked theirs soft, a taste they acquired from their father. The smile faded.

"I could use a beer to wash these down." Robert rose. "I'll be right back. Will you save my chair?"

"Yes." He didn't have a defined six-pack, but he wasn't fat either. The whole package was well defined, proving once again, he maintained a healthy lifestyle. She approved of the loose fitting swim trunks he wore. Nothing tight like some of the men aboard wore.

Robert approached with a cocked smile. Casual and comfortable with his walk, he was a man of confidence. An attractive quality.

"So are you enjoying the cruise and your time away?"

"I am. I'm excited to get to Ocho Rios and the other destinations. What about you? Are you having a good time?" She took a long pull from her straw.

"Having a male travel companion isn't my idea of fun, but thank God, for having my own suite." His warm laugh made her grin. "Scott and I made an agreement to not hinder each other while on the cruise."

"So, how's that been working for you?"

"Well, he's not sitting with us, and I personally like being alone with you."

Her face warmed, and not from the heat.

"Do you like being a substitute teacher? Or would you prefer to have a full-time teaching job?" He tipped his beer bottle back taking a swig.

"I prefer substitute teaching, and I'm lucky I don't have to work full-time to support myself and the kids. One of the reasons I'm on this cruise is to figure out my, *our*, future. I've been questioning whether I should sell the house and move into something smaller."

Robert's knuckle softly grazed high on her cheek. "I'm sorry. I didn't mean to talk about something that would make you sad."

Her fingers traced where his knuckles had touched, not realizing a tear escaped. "No, I'm fine." Adjusting her chair to recline, she continued. "It's a matter of life. You just deal with it." Yet it wasn't that simple. Her decisions affected her children's lives, not just her own.

"If you want to talk it through with someone, who has an ear for listening, I'd be more than happy. When my wife, Kathleen, and I got divorced, I never thought about all the decisions that would have to be made. Then again, she made all the decisions, and I agreed to most of them without thinking. I did have to decide where I was going to live and think about how that would affect my children. In the end and looking back, I think I made the right decisions. You work through and adjust as you go along. So, what do you do when you're not teaching, that is in your spare time?"

"Take care of the kids and the house," she said with a half-hearted chuckle. "I find a little time to go out with my girlfriends, relax, or read a book." She grinned at the memory of Christmas Day. "I have two new babies I'll have fun spending time with." A laugh escaped at his surprised look. "My sister-in-laws both gave birth on Christmas Day."

"You're kidding." He genuinely laughed with her. "Were they both due at the same time?"

"A week apart. They both delivered early. The one doctor said the one could've gone into labor because she was there when the other started labor, but in the end, the baby was ready. Plain and simple. My niece was born Christmas morning and my nephew was born in the evening."

The conversation flowed on to talking about Robert's nieces and nephews, which Liz appreciated. He excused himself afterwards with a promise to call regarding dinner. After sitting with her front to the sun while chatting with Robert, she rolled to let the sun warm her backside while she rested.

* * * *

David walked into the entry area, pushed the call button for Robert's apartment, and waited.

"Hello." Abigail's voice cheerfully answered.

"I'm here. Are you ready?"

"I'll be right down." The line clicked.

Most of his day was spent behind a desk, so David passed on the two chairs in the entry. He leaned against the wall, hoping to spend the evening getting to know Abigail. A reflection caught his attention and he turned. Abigail entered dressed in snug fitting jeans with tall black boots and a sweater.

"Where's your coat? It's winter."

"I have a warm layer underneath the sweater. I'll be fine." A light masculine scent lingered as they walked outside. "Thanks for being concerned though. Where are you parked?"

"Ahead to your left. I found a spot along the street." He stepped beside her as they approached the car and opened the door.

"Thank you." She slid on the seat and he closed the door.

Quickly maneuvering around the car, he hopped onto the driver's seat and started the car. "Good, it's still warm. Since I'm driving, please don't hesitate to tell me when you're ready to leave and come home."

"No worries. I will. I've learned my lesson over the years. So where are you taking me?" There was a story behind her words. Would she be willing to tell it?

"A pub called the Pale Fox House."

"On Selby," she exclaimed.

"You know the place?" He looked at her, shocked. Then again, she did live in St. Paul and it was a well-known pub.

"I've been there a few times. Great food and atmosphere!"

"Good. I'm glad you like it. That will make it easier for us to enjoy ourselves." He hopped onto West Seventh Street heading for downtown St. Paul. "Thanks for understanding why I wanted to drive. It will be

53

easier for parking."

"Yeah, most of the time the parking lot is full and street parking in the winter can be tricky."

"Not sure if I'd rather have this frigid cold or be dumped on with snow. What about you?" He glanced in her direction.

"I've never been much of a snow bunny, so I guess I'll take the cold."

"Growing up in Seattle, I don't care for the snow that much either."

"Why did you move here, then?"

"The job was here." He smiled at her, which she returned. "Plus, Minnesota has four seasons. Three of which are awesome. Winter I would prefer for only a month or maybe two." They both laughed.

"Yeah, that'd be nice."

"Plus, it doesn't rain as much here as it does in Seattle." Turning onto Grand Avenue, he maneuvered to connect with Selby Avenue. "So, are you a born and raised Minnesotan?"

"I was born in Illinois but my parents moved here a year after because of my dad's work. I consider myself a true Minnesotan though."

"You should." He paused, not wanting to sound like a brownnoser. "Your dad's a great guy and I'm not saying that because I like you." The shake in his voice couldn't be avoided.

"Thanks, I think so, too. I'd never think you'd say that for that reason." She paused. "I like you too." She sheepishly glanced at him. "I just wish he'd find one woman. My sister still thinks after six years my parents are going to get back together. She hates him dating."

"What about your mom? Doesn't she date?"

"She's in a relationship with a guy in New York. My sister hates that just as much. My mom's relationship is more serious. My dad dates more than one woman and isn't committed to any of them."

"Wow." His head snapped in her direction. "New York? How'd she meet him?" He focused back on the road.

"She's from New York. I guess it's some guy she knew growing up. Friends of the family."

"Have you met him? Do you like him?"

"Yes, and he's nice. Let's just say he's not a Midwesterner."

"I'm not either, so does that prove bad for me?"

"No, you're fine. You're laid back versus an uptight city man, which is good." She rested her warm hand on his thigh. The warmth spread to his stomach.

"We're here." David pulled into the parking lot, driving to the back designated parking area.

"You can't park here." She pointed to the *EMPLOYEES ONLY* sign.

"It's okay. Trust me." He parked and went around to open Abigail's door, but she was already out of the car.

"If you say so. It's your car, your parking ticket."

At the entrance, he held the door for her. They stepped through the second door.

"David," his aunt Caitlin said cheerfully leaving the bar area and entering the restaurant. She glanced at him and then to Abigail.

"Hello. I'm David's Aunt Caitlin, but you can call me Cait. Welcome." Her arms spread out to include the restaurant.

Abigail did a quick take between David and Caitlin. "Nice to meet you. I'm Abigail. I work with David."

"Oh." His aunt dragged out the word, as in, 'this wasn't a date.' "Well, he's one of the best."

"Aunt Caitlin," he scolded lightly, with widened eyes, hoping she wouldn't go on about him or his work.

"My dad thinks so, too." Abigail's smile was bright and inviting.

"Oh. Your dad is his boss?" Aunt Cait was getting too much information, and he'd be questioned later.

"Yes, he's our boss." Her hand rested on his forearm. "I'm actually an intern, so you could say, David's kind of like my boss, too." She gently squeezed his arm.

When he turned, her warm expression made his heart palpitate. "Can we get a table for two, Aunt Cait?"

"You got it." She stepped to the hostess stand, glanced down, tracked the seating on the chart, and grabbed two menus. "I have a nice quiet place where the two of you can talk. This way."

She led them to a back area. A few couples sat at tables, but this was the quiet section of the restaurant.

"How's this?"

"Perfect. Thank you." Abigail sat on one of the four chairs.

Jody Vitek

David exchanged a quick hug with his aunt before sitting. "Thank you. I'll make sure to say goodbye before we leave."

"You'd better, if you know what's good for you." She delivered a gentle swat to his shoulder before leaving them alone at the table.

"Why didn't you tell me your aunt ran the restaurant?"

"It didn't come up, and she and my Uncle Dillon have always run and owned the place. I didn't think it was important. Is it?"

She unwrapped the flatware from the cloth napkin and placed it on her lap. "No, but if I'd known, I wouldn't have looked so stupid."

"You didn't look stupid. You're too beautiful." He made the endearing comment while doing the same with his napkin.

"Thank you. You can be beautiful and stupid at the same time." Her hands remained under the table.

"So, what do you normally get when you come here?"

"Beer and appetizers." She wore a lopsided grin.

"Really? We can go in the bar if you'd prefer?"

"No, no, this is fine. We won't have to talk over the bar crowd. What's your favorite thing on the menu?" She opened and peered at the menu.

"I prefer a burger, but if you want a traditional Irish meal, my aunt's Shepherd's Pie is the best."

"I'll stick with a burger and beer."

"The Mad MacGowan is good, but can be too much for some. Two Cajun spiced quarter pounders with sautéed onions, bacon, and pepper jack cheese."

The waitress stepped to the table and took their drink orders and left them to decide what they wanted to eat.

A silence fell between them as Abigail perused the menu. "So are your parents still in Seattle?"

"Yup. In the same house where I grew up. My brother's living at home right now. He's working to pay off his student loans while saving money to get a place of his own."

"How's that working out for them? I don't know if I could do that."

"Good, I guess. With everyone in the house working, it's okay. If my brother wasn't working and just living off my parents, I don't think it would be going as well as it is." He leaned forward on the table, relaxed with the conversation.

"What do your parents do?"

"My dad works for the local police department and my mom teaches English at the high school."

"Is your brother your only sibling?" She leaned back with her arms folded across her stomach.

"I have a sister a year older than me."

"And that's how old?"

The corners of his mouth slowly turned up because she didn't know his age and was being sneaky about finding out. "Twenty-eight, I'm twenty-seven, and you're twenty..."

"I'm twenty-four." She smirked. "So you have an older sister and your brother must be younger than you."

"Yup."

The waitress brought their beers and took their order. He couldn't help but grin at the nickname she gave the burger, Mad Mac. Alone again, David asked about her family.

"I'm the oldest and I have a brother who is graduating from high school this year. I told you about my sister. She's thirteen and in the eighth grade. They live with my mom in Eagle Heights, south of the river." She sat forward sipping her beer.

"I know the area. Does your mom work?"

"No." There was a tone of disgust in her voice. "I think she worked in Illinois before I was born. She's been an at-home mom ever since I can remember."

"Does that bother you?" He wondered what her opinion was about working versus non-working mothers. There was a lot of discussion of the topic on talk shows, the news, and in magazines. It was everywhere.

"Talking about it now, yeah, it does. My dad works really hard and in turn has to pay her to sit around and do nothing. I mean, what does she do all day?"

"I wouldn't know." David shrugged his shoulders.

"I'm sorry. I didn't mean to go off like that."

She sipped beer, and he used the opening to change the subject. "Your dad and Mr. Jordan went on their trip at the right time with our weather being so cold."

"They eventually have to come back to it. Plus, it's early in the winter season." A devilish grin filled her face.

* * * *

Full, with half a Mad MacGowan burger remaining on her plate, Abigail pushed the plate to the side. "I can't eat any more. The sweet potato fries were so good, I couldn't finish." She gulped beer from the glass.

David laughed, a deep hearty chuckle.

"Okay, so you were right about it being big. It will make for a great lunch tomorrow and you'll be jealous," she teased with a smirk.

"Hopefully it'll still be there. Sometimes things disappear from the refrigerator in the cafeteria."

"Oh, you wouldn't."

"Who said I would?"

She liked how he jested in return. Her face warmed. Was she blushing or was it the alcohol?

"Hmm, I'll have to come up with a burger protection plan." They both broke into laughter with her serious, joking tone. She loved to hear David laugh.

Their waitress approached. "Did you want a box for your burger?"

"Yes, please," David responded. He glanced at Abigail. "Did you want another beer?"

"No, I'm good." Being a lightweight where alcohol was a factor, she didn't want to make the wrong impression on David.

"A box and the check, please." The waitress stepped away from the table. "I forgot to ask if you wanted dessert."

"If I couldn't finish my dinner, I don't deserve dessert." Abigail gazed at his full lips and imagined the dessert she did want to sample—just not here.

"In school, I always ate my dessert first. I guess I never grew out of the habit."

"We didn't have desserts in our house, except on special occasions and holidays. Probably because my mom didn't bake, but she did know how to cook."

The waitress approached. "Caitlin covered your bill." They both opened their mouths to speak. "She said not to argue." They offered their thanks in unison.

"Your aunt really shouldn't have done that." Abigail pulled money for a tip from her wallet.

"Put that away. This was my idea and my treat." She put her money away as he pulled cash from his billfold. "Let's say goodbye to my aunt, and I'll take you home."

They approached the server's entrance to the kitchen. "I'll be right back," David uttered.

Someone from the kitchen hollered David's name. Several minutes later, he emerged with Caitlin.

"Thank you so much for dinner," Abigail said as they came through the passageway. "The food was great."

"It was my pleasure." Caitlin gave her a hug. "I hope to see you again, soon."

"Bye, Aunt Cait." David hugged her. "Thank you. I'll call you later." His large hand warmed the small of Abigail's back, along with her belly, as he guided her to the exit.

They filled the short drive back to her father's place with talk about their music preferences. He parked in front of the building.

"Here you are. I had a fun evening." He moved to get out of the car.

She grasped his forearm. "You don't need to get out. It's cold." Her hand remained on his arm, as she searched his eyes for a sign.

He shifted in the driver's seat to face her.

Her heart pulsed faster. She leaned closer to him. "Thank you for dinner. I had a fun night."

His hand cupped the side of her face as his thumb caressed her lower lip. At his delicate touch, her eyelids closed. Soft, full lips touched hers as they exchanged a brief kiss. She wanted more, but knowing her father's feelings, would take things slowly. Or at least try.

"Goodnight, Abigail." He leaned back against his seat with a sated smile.

She opened her door, slid from the car, and before closing the door, spoke. "See you in the morning."

She strolled through the apartment complex to her dad's place. In the living room, she turned the TV on to catch the ten o'clock news.

While putting her burger in the fridge, the top news story had her spinning on her heels.

"St. Paul police issued a warning this evening for females in the following surrounding college communities. St. Catherine University, St. Thomas, and Macalester College students have been asked to walk in pairs or groups at night after two females were sexually assaulted on separate occasions within two days."

Abigail leaned on the island counter for support. Her neighborhood.

"The attacker is a white male, between six and six feet five inches, with green eyes. The victims said he wore a black ski mask, making it difficult to give more of a description. The campus police for all colleges stated they would be adding additional security. The St. Paul Police Department added they would be more vigilant while driving through the neighborhoods. Back to you in the studio."

In a zone of shock, she moved to sit on the couch and shook her head in disbelief. Why? Why did men do this?

Chapter Seven

Robert walked two floors down to the sixth deck and O'Sheehan's Bar and Grill. Scott waited by the entrance.

"Any sign of Liz?"

His firm designed and handled the Kids Kare Clinic project from start to the finish in Eagle Heights. Liz had accompanied Greg on a couple occasions during the planning phase and a few more times during the construction process.

"Nope. I looked around and didn't see her inside. You told her six-thirty, here?"

"Yes, but—"

"Sorry I'm late." Liz joined them at the entrance wearing a short black skirt with a coral top.

"You're not late. I just got here myself. The sun agrees with you. You got some nice color today." Robert softly stroked her lightly tanned arm with his fingertips.

"A touch too much on my backside. Hey, Scott. Sorry about breakfast this morning."

"Not a problem. I know what it's like if you have a routine." Scott touched her other arm. "Let's go inside and get a table." She slid her arm through the crook of his arm.

The gesture prickled Robert and something deep within wanted to remove her arm from Scott's. He shook it off, remembering Kathleen's words when they divorced. "You're not capable of loving a woman. You love your job more than you love me or your children. You're never around for me. You'll never be able to give a woman what she needs or deserves—love." Kathleen had hurt him in a way he never thought a

61

woman could.

"Robert, are you okay?" Liz touched his bicep. He glanced into concerned forest green eyes.

"I'm fine. Glad you decided to join us." They entered the brightly lit pub with wooden tables and chairs in the center area and booth seating along the walls.

"I appreciate the invitation because it's better than dining alone." She wore her hair up tonight showing off her strong jaw line.

Once seated at a high-top table and their drinks ordered, they scanned the menu.

"What are you planning on doing with your day tomorrow, Liz?" Robert set down his menu.

"Go to the gym, visit the onboard stores, sit by the pool. I'll take the day as it comes."

"Maybe we'll see each other again." Scott showed her his charming smile. Working to win her over to him.

Their waiter delivered their beers. "Are you ready to order?"

They glanced at each other and Liz spoke first. "I'd like the Tuna Melt, please."

"The Fish n'Chips for me," Robert said, handing the menu to him.

"And for you, sir?" the waiter said to Scott.

"The hot dog with chili, please."

When the waiter left the table, Robert looked at Scott. "A hot dog with chili? At a pub? You should have a burger or something more pub-like."

"What's wrong with it? It's on the pub's menu, so it's pub food." Scott's eyebrows drew in as his eyes narrowed. His, 'kiss-my-ass face' evident.

"It sounded good, Scott." Liz rested her hand on his forearm. "Don't listen to him."

God, the woman loved good food, too. "I never said it wasn't good." He defended himself. "I just don't see a chili dog as pub food."

Scott leaned close to Liz's ear. "I knew there was a reason to like you." He righted himself on the high top chair. "You know how to enjoy food. I bet you don't mind watching football either?"

As he watched the two interact, a slight bitterness consumed Robert.

"I prefer to be at a football game in person. There are too many commercials on TV and you miss so much of what's happening on and around the playing field. Soccer's another story. This place is great with the games on the TVs." Liz's face brightened talking about soccer, as she glanced to the bar with the large wide-screen TV's.

"Do your children play?" Robert questioned before Scott could dominate the conversation.

"My daughter plays on a traveling team and my son is beginning his traveling soccer play. This summer was his first season. I love the fast-paced play."

"Does soccer require a lot of long distance traveling? The older my son became, the more we traveled out of state. It can be expensive." This topic gave Robert the edge and attention he wanted from Liz because Scott didn't have kids.

"Our... my philosophy is, if the child wants to participate in an activity, I'll find a way to make it happen. My daughter's team does travel and sometimes it can be hard with my son playing. Thankfully, I have family and team parents who are willing to help."

"We never had that problem. With the age gap between the kids, it was manageable. Abby didn't really stick with sports. The teen years came along and her focus changed. Alex, well, he's the one who's stuck with the sports. My money and his hard work paid off though. He's been offered full scholarships for football and made the decision to go to Florida State."

"He's leaving home and going to get some sun," Scott added. He must've felt left out of the conversation.

"I think the sun played a role in his decision. Ultimately, it was the school and what they had to offer."

The waiter delivered their meals and left to get them another round of beers.

"That looks delicious, Scott." Liz's eyes grew round looking at his chili dog.

"Would you like some?"

Robert rolled his eyes at Scott's maneuvers while cutting into his fish.

"I'd love a bite once it cools off. Did you want some of my tuna

63

melt?" She picked up a French fry and ate it.

"If after you've tried it and like it, then maybe. I'm not much of a tuna guy."

Swallowing the fry, she washed it down with a gulp of beer. "Yeah, sometimes tuna can have a fishy taste, ruining the sandwich. Speaking of fish, how's yours, Robert?"

"Too hot to eat. Looks and smells good though."

"Hey Liz," Scott said, "you want to bowl after we eat? There's a bowling alley over there." He pointed to the far side of the ship.

"Sure. Robert, are you up for a game?" Her hand rested on his. Warm and inviting.

"Why not." He moved his hand on top of hers, gently squeezing her fingers.

Her lips curved up as her eyelids fell, and she removed her hand to hold her sandwich. A beautiful smile that toyed with the notion of being coy.

Later, they took their third round of drinks into the bowling alley, rested them on a table at one of the open lanes before locating the right weight balls for themselves. Shoes changed and names entered into the electronic score board, Robert went first. The ball glided on the wood floor at a great speed.

"Yes, strike!" He spun around to face Liz and Scott, who were leaning shoulder-to-shoulder, smiling.

Liz stood to go next. "Do you do this often?"

"No. Pure luck."

Holding the ball in her hands, Liz stepped to the lane markers. She stepped a little to the side. The ball up in her hands, her arm with the ball pulled back as she approached the foul line and released the ball. Four pins fell.

"Come on, Liz," Robert cheered with Scott joining him. "Get a spare."

She returned to the lane with her ball and swung it into action. Four more pins fell.

"That's not a bad start. You've got nice form," Scott complimented as he readied for his turn.

Scott's turn was a disaster. Gutter ball on the first throw and four of the ten fell with his second throw. He sat on the red bench next to Liz.

"Care to give me some instruction?"

"I think you'll do just fine."

Robert took his turn, gaining another strike. Facing the seating, he noted the two were close again. "Liz, you're turn," he declared with more terseness than intended and cringed inwardly.

"Oh, sorry." She scooped up her ball from the ball rack.

He sat on the bench and murmured to Scott, "You're getting friendly." After giving his friend the verbal punch, he took a swig of his beer.

"Something wrong befriending a woman?" Slouching, Scott straightened and with a squinted eye, smirked. "You like her. You're jealous." He threw his head back and laughed.

The back of Robert's hand connected with Scott's stomach, while his own stomach hardened and he clenched his teeth.

Scott bent forward, snickering. "I'll back off."

"She'll let us know if she's interested in either one of us jerks." He exercised his jaw.

"Who you calling a jerk? You're the one who'd use her. Who's to say I'm not interested in more?"

Robert burst into laughter, and Liz stood in front of them. "Must be a good joke."

Not able to stop, he continued laughing. "Yeah, it was a good one." Scott's fist connected with his shoulder. He laughed more through the pain.

"Care to share the joke with me?" She sat beside him, and took a sip of her beer.

"Nope. Not appropriate," he replied as Scott got up for his turn.

"Come on." She bumped shoulders before resting her shoulder on his. "Share it with me," she spoke softly in his ear.

If she kept that up, something else would be up, and at the most inopportune time. With a gentle nudge, her body no longer connected with his.

"No," he insisted. "It's not appropriate."

"Fine, I'll ask Scott after he's bowled his frames." She picked up her glass and drank.

As soon as Scott sat next to Liz, she pounced. Her bubbly laugh caused Robert to throw a gutter ball. Waiting for the ball to return put him in close proximity to the seating.

"You're a good looking guy. From the time I've spent with you, you're funny and intelligent. Why wouldn't a woman want to marry you?"

He caught a glimpse of Scott, grinning at him. Frustrated, Robert yanked his ball from the return rack and swung it down the lane. A few pins fell, but he'd had enough. He walked back to the bench seating and picked up his beer. After several long pulls from the glass, he set it down nearly empty.

"I've had enough bowling for tonight. I'll see you two around." His muscles tightened in frustration at what was transpiring between these two. If he continued bowling, he would be forced to watch and listen to Scott make advances on Liz and her toying with him.

"What?" Scott hollered as Robert stepped from the lane.

He left the bowling lanes and exchanged the bowling shoes for his own. Pins crashed to the wood flooring as the bowling resumed. A hand snatched his from behind. A slender hand.

"What's wrong? Why are you leaving?"

Liz. He glanced into her now familiar eyes. "I don't feel like bowling anymore. You and Scott keep playing." Her hand held his. His tone softened. "There's plenty aboard to keep me busy."

"What are you going to do?" She drifted closer to him.

"I don't know." She was giving him an opening. "Maybe go up on deck and check out the stars."

"Can I join you?"

Crossing two of the three lanes, Scott interrupted their personal conversation. "Liz, it's your turn."

"Just a minute." She waved him off with her free hand. "So, do you want company? Or do you prefer to be alone."

"It'd be nice to have you join me."

"I'll be right back." Her hand slipped from his and she jogged into the alley area. She and Scott exchange words. When she turned and her back was to Scott, he bowed to Robert in defeat.

* * * *

Liz wanted to hold Robert's hand again, but remained unsure of the attraction she felt toward him. What were the odds of meeting someone she knew aboard the ship? Someone who lived in the same state, let alone area? Was Robert interested in her or a relationship? Would she know the signs?

She wasn't dead. She'd read the signs correctly.

Being away from her children, and mother-in-law, gave her a freedom to be with those she wanted and do as she pleased. Robert was attractive, nice, caring, so why not have some fun while she was away?

"What's got you so quiet?"

"Hmm? Oh, sorry. I get lost in the stars." She let her hands slide, spreading her arms wide, across the smooth wood railing. "This is amazing compared to back home." Her hips pressed against the rail as she leaned forward. What if she had too much fun while away? Would she be okay returning home? She needed to pull up her big girl panties, take a chance, and enjoy herself.

Robert's arm slid across her lower back and she jumped. "Careful." They gazed at each other. "I wouldn't want to see you fall overboard." He held her a little tighter—up close and personal.

"I wasn't going anywhere." With her hands centered in front of her, she turned into his chest, chin down. "I like where I'm at." She dared a glance into his eyes, the yellow-green was striking in the moonlight.

"Where is that, Liz?" His soft voice had a husky sound. A finger lifted her chin to look him fully in the eyes.

"Here."

Pulled into a tighter embrace, he bent and delivered a diminutive kiss. "With me?"

"Yes."

This time the kiss grew passionate. His hand glided to the back of her neck, as his fingers spliced through her hair. He stopped.

"What's wrong?" she managed to croak, anxious she had done something wrong.

"Are you sure? We may know each other, yet we don't. Yesterday, when we ran into each other for the first time in years, and at dinner, you sounded as though—"

"I've kissed other men since losing Greg. It's just been a hard adjustment, and my mother-in-law makes my dating life difficult."

"How does she make it difficult?"

Liz turned and gripped the railing, comforted by Robert's arm remaining about her waist. "To put it simply, she blames me for his death. She's never let it go and reminds me whenever she can."

How could she make any forward progress with a man when her husband's death came first in meeting and having a conversation? She hadn't brought up the topic. It was the type of question that came up in the getting-to-know-you discussion.

"You said he died in a car accident."

"He did. I had nothing to do with the accident. It was weather related. Bad road conditions."

She faced him to see his eyebrows drawn together. Hiding and not talking about the situation would be her preferred option, but not a reality. Her therapist told her the more she talked about it, the easier it would be and the quicker she'd be able to move forward with her life.

"So how can she blame you?" The confusion grew as his face scrunched and creases formed on his forehead.

"Because of the location of where we built the Kids Kare Clinic."

"What? That's absurd."

"He was too far from home. She'd say," she mimicked her mother-in-law's voice. "I don't know why he listened to you. You talked him into going out on his own. He would still be at the other clinic, closer to home, and alive if it wasn't for you." The railing was in a death grip in her hands.

Robert rested his hands over hers. Her grip lessened. He brushed his lips on her forehead. "I'm sorry." Another kiss. "She still says these hurtful words?"

"Yes." She flexed her hands. Blood rushed to her fingers.

"I don't understand though, how this affects you moving forward into a new relationship." He gently maneuvered her to lean against him instead of the railing.

"My children still have to see their paternal grandparents, which means I have to see them too. Kids talk and grandma talks. What I may say around my children can get back to her, and vice versa. Then when we see each other, she's the lesser person and well, I think you get the picture." She no longer leaned into him but continued to let his hands hold hers.

"Has she gone to counseling?"

"No. Refuses. My father-in-law is very understanding and patient. I don't know how he can live with the woman."

Robert's soft laughed, rumbled deep in his chest. She smiled at the warmth of the moment. It felt right.

"You're smiling. That's good." He gently squeezed her hands.

"What about you? How has the moving forward after a divorce been? Your kids or ex give you problems?"

"Abby thinks I need to get married again. My son doesn't say much. My youngest hates the idea of either my ex or me dating anyone. I don't share much with her for that reason." He spoke easily about his family life, and she was a bit envious.

"You mentioned your wife has a boyfriend. How do your daughters handle that?"

"As I mentioned, the older two are fine but my youngest, not very well. You should've been there when she found out her mother was leaving to be with him for the holiday. Then again, you have a thirteen-year-old. You know how they can react."

"All too well." She laughed. "Sarah's actually not that bad, but has her moments."

"You're lucky. So, yeah, that's how the relationship thing works with my children."

A silence fell between them. She leaned into him, content to listen to the slow beat of his heart. His chest rose and fell with each breath. Putting a slight separation between them, she regarded his face.

"Why does Abby want you to get married? Your ex isn't. Does she tell her mother the same thing?"

"I don't know what she tells Kathleen, and who knows why she feels I need to get married." He spoke of his ex with a bitterness, which softened with the later part.

"Have you thought about getting married again?"

"No. What about you?" He quickly turned the table on her.

"No. I haven't been in a relationship long enough to reach that point. Or, for that matter, connected with anyone on that level." The first year after Gregory's death, she never considered marrying again. The second year, her interest in the opposite sex redeveloped. In the last couple, she slowly and occasionally dated. It was in this last year she could see herself entering the bond of marriage.

"So you consider it a possibility?" His head tilted to the side.

Her pulse increased. "Don't you?" She could flip the conversation as skillfully as he could.

"Well... yeah, I guess so. If the right person comes along, I guess." Their eyes connected.

Soft lips touched hers and she parted hers to feel the burning passion they'd exchanged before. This time, her hands roamed up his back to let her fingers mingle in his hair. The embrace grew tighter with need, and this time she broke the seal of their lips.

"I think we should say good night." She spoke breathily as her heart faltered.

Chapter Eight

Abigail entered the shared workspace with a coy smile. Though their kiss last night in David's car hadn't seemed like a big deal, the sparks flew. They had to contain themselves and remain professional at the office.

"Good morning," David offered, sitting at his desk.

"It is, isn't it?" She plopped onto her chair.

"Last night I saw a report on the news and thought of you." He scooted closer to her.

"Oh?" She busied herself with the computer.

"Did you hear about the attacks in your area?"

"Yeah." Fingers tapped on the keyboard as though it was no big deal.

"Abigail." He grabbed her hands, spinning her away from the desk. "This is a serious matter, and you're blowing it off. Do you have a safety plan?"

"Whoa." She yanked her hands free. "We went out for drinks last night and all of a sudden you're acting like my father."

"I'm concerned, as your father would be if he were here."

"You aren't my father." She turned to the computer and continued typing.

"I'm sorry." The conversation hadn't gone as he imagined. He didn't want to play the boyfriend card, because they weren't there yet. He didn't plan to be father-like. "I'm just concerned for your safety."

David left to get his papers from the printer. When he returned, the sight of a small cooler caught his attention. "What's with the cooler?"

"Last night's leftovers. I didn't want anyone taking my burger."

71

He burst into laughter. "I was joking. It'd be safe in the cafeteria fridge."

"You jerk." Her hand swatted his leg before he sat. "Listen, I'm sorry for the way I reacted. I'll be fine. I'll be at my dad's place all week. When I do go back to my place, I'll be safe. The guys let us park in the garage. When I go out, I'm usually with a group." She pushed her chair so they were side-by-side.

With a glance around the office, she leaned close. "Thank you for caring." Her lips touched his for a brief moment.

He sat speechless. She'd kissed him at work.

"No one saw. If they did, who cares?" Her nonchalant air worried him.

"I care. You're the boss's daughter."

"So?"

David lowered his voice. "I'd prefer we take our time with this relationship. Warm your father up to the idea."

"Are we in a relationship?" Her thin eyebrows arched.

The buzz of co-workers conversing and phones ringing filled the silence.

"David?"

He shook his head. "I... if you don't... I just thought..."

"I'd like to pursue a relationship with you."

He slumped in his chair and then straightened again. "What do you have planned for New Year's Eve?"

"I'll be with my brother and sister at my dad's. Remember?"

"I forgot. Well, when will you be free to celebrate? With me." He smirked.

"My Mom comes home Friday. Does Saturday work?"

"Saturday it is. I'll make the plans, and let you know what time I'll pick you up. Sound good?"

"I look forward to it." She squeezed his knee.

"I guess with you babysitting, that means I won't get to see you between now and then?"

She shook her head with dramatic pouty lips. "What are you doing for New Year's Eve?"

"I'll help out at the restaurant. I've done that the past couple of years."

"That's nice of you."

"I love being with my extended family here in Minnesota and celebrating with them." He held her hands. "I'd have rather spent it with you this year, but we'll celebrate later."

"I'm looking forward to it."

* * * *

Robert hoped to see Liz enter the fitness center as he ran on a treadmill. Instead, Scott jumped on the open machine next to him.

"Nice weather, huh."

Dark skies released heavy raindrops that fell against the wide expanse of windows in front of them.

"Maybe we'll get clear skies this afternoon." Robert spoke in broken breaths.

"Care to share about last night?" Scott spoke as he walked slowly to warm up.

"Nothing to tell. We talked. That's it."

"Not your standard kind of evening."

"Well, she's not standard, so shut up."

Scott threw his hands up in front of his chest, palms out. "Okay." He backed down. "Are you adding her to your harem?"

"We talked, that's it. I don't know what will happen after the cruise."

"She's not the kind of woman who's going to want to share you with others."

"You know this how?" He scrutinized his friend.

"You can tell by the way she talks about her children and the type of woman she is. Are you willing to give up the life you have to be with her?"

Robert jumped, spreading his legs to the sides off the tread, so he spoke without huffing through breaths. "Scott, we talked, that's all. You're talking like we're in a relationship and need to make decisions. We're getting to know each other." He hopped back onto the moving conveyer belt without missing a beat.

"Well, if you hurt her—"

"I'm not going to hurt her." He didn't mean to raise his voice, but Scott's threat mixed with running, made it impossible to avoid. "Why are you being so protective of her? You don't even know her well."

"She's earned my respect. I know she's not like the others. Take care of how you treat her." Scott stopped his machine and walked away.

Irritated, Robert turned up the speed, running faster and harder. Five minutes into pounding his feet on the belt, Liz stepped onto the machine beside his. He slowed his pace.

"Tell me you don't run like that for a long time. I wouldn't be able to keep up with you." She chuckled, erasing his angst at the earlier discussion with Scott. "This weather is the pits. I guess if I had to pick between now or when we're in port, I'd rather have it be today."

"That's a good point." He huffed. The fast run pushed him and his lungs hard. "It would be nice if the rain passed by this afternoon, though."

"It sure would be nice. Later I'm going to check and see if I can connect with the kids at the Internet Café."

"You miss them." Their heads turned to glance at each other, but not for long since they were on moving treadmills.

"Kind of. It comes and goes. If I could at least get a message to them, well, it might help. What about you? Are you going to check in?"

"I'm avoiding the Internet world. It's been hard not checking email, taking calls, and all the other daily grind stuff. I'm on vacation for the first time in years. I hate to admit it, but my daughter and Scott were right about the need to get away."

"So you're enjoying yourself?"

"Yes." Robert nodded. "Will you join us for dinner again?"

"I'd love that. I'm glad we ran into each other, Robert."

"Me too," he said breathlessly.

"I'm sorry," she spoke through puffs. "Can we talk more later? Talking is difficult while running."

"Yeah, I'm almost finished here." No more than several minutes later, Robert's machine slowed for the cool down period. The machine came to a stop. "I'll call your room later if I don't see you around."

"Okay," she panted, and he left for the free weights.

Up Close and Personal

* * * *

After a light breakfast, Liz visited the Internet Café. Pleasantly surprised with the number of computers they offered, each one was contained in its own cubical type area for privacy. She logged on to her email and typed.

Mom, The ship is fabulous! The weather has been great up until this morning. Hoping it clears by this afternoon. My room is amazing. I have a balcony and hope to use it more. Surprisingly, I ran into the man who worked on designing the clinic. He's been kind, inviting me to join him and his travel partner for dinner. Tomorrow we dock for the day in Ocho Rios, Jamaica.

Hope the kids are behaving and not giving you and Dad any troubles. I'm not going to check in again until Saturday when we're at sea returning home. I'm going to send each of the kids a separate email. Thank you for watching them.

Love, Liz

She hit send and opened to write a new message.

Sarah, Having a wonderful time but miss you and your brother. The ship is so beautiful and huge! I've been bowling, spent time by the pool and looked around in the onboard shops. It's raining now and I'm hoping it clears up. Tomorrow we'll be in Ocho Rios, Jamaica. I'll take lots of pictures. Hope you and your brother are being good and helping out. If you want to write me back, you can. I'll check in again on Saturday when we're at sea on our return home. Love you, Mom

Sent, she repeated the same message addressed to Brad. When Brad's message cleared, she typed a message to Greg's sister, Veronica.

Veronica, The ship is amazing! Beautiful and huge. I'm learning my way around, which isn't too hard with the way they have things laid out. You're not going to believe this, but I've met someone on the ship. The man who handled the design of the clinic, Robert Burnhamwood. I literally bumped into him on the first day aboard the ship. He's been very kind. I've had dinner with him and his travel friend, who's a business partner. It's been nice knowing someone to eat with and talk to. It doesn't hurt that he's good looking either. Yes, there's a mutual attraction. He kissed me. OMG, Veronica, can the man kiss! Not sure if it's possible to have feelings like I'm feeling right now. I'm trying not to want to spend all my time with him. Not that that will happen, since we've booked different offshore excursions.

Today we have rain. Otherwise, the weather has been beautiful. I spent yesterday poolside and looking in the onboard shops. Tomorrow we spend the day in Ocho Rios, Jamaica. I'm okay if it rains all day today, as long as it's beautiful tomorrow. Hoping to have lots of pictures to share.

Thank you for everything. I'll be checking my email again on Saturday, when we're at sea on the return home. Liz

Her final message sent, she sorted through the messages in her inbox. Finished with email, she checked Facebook, pleased to see her two sister-in-laws had posted pictures of her newest niece and nephew. As she scrolled, two hands rested on her shoulders and she jumped, spinning around on the chair.

"Cute baby," Robert leaned in and their cheeks brushed.

Thank goodness, he didn't come by while she wrote her email to Veronica. Liz warmed at what she admitted to her sister-in-law, which was true.

"This is the niece I was telling you about." She clicked the mouse a couple times. "This is my nephew. They are too adorable. I can't wait to spend time with them."

"He has a lot of hair."

"I guess so." She hadn't given the hair much thought. Glancing at the photo, he did have a full head of dark hair.

"My kids were bald. Okay, that's not quite true. They did have some." She joined in his light laughter. "Are you hungry for lunch?"

"Not really. I ate a late breakfast." She logged out and closed the window. "Have you decided where we're having dinner tonight?" When she stood, without heels, he towered over her.

"We thought we'd give Taste a try. It's on this level, at the end, by the escalators."

They strolled, Robert leading the way, into the art gallery. "Sounds good to me. What time?"

"Would seven be too late?"

"With a late breakfast, I'll eat a light late lunch to help tide me over. It'll be perfect." Liz glanced around the area. He led her into a back corner. Her breathing accelerated with excitement. They were alone.

He gently pulled her into his chest. Intense lime-green eyes filled with seduction searched hers. "I'd like to kiss you again?"

She answered him by planting her lips on his, and her eyes closed. This man simply had to look at her and she became putty. What was going on with her hormones? None of the other men she dated made her feel this way. She wanted more from him and being alone on this trip allowed her to act upon feelings.

His hands cupped her face. "Should we continue to roam through the art gallery or was there somewhere else you were going after sending your emails?" His thumb skimmed her bottom lip.

"Let's keep looking." Their hands joined as they perused the framed artwork for sale.

* * * *

Abigail unlocked the door and entered the apartment. The TV was on, so she shouted, "Hello?" As far as she knew, she was the only one with a key to her dad's place. She took a few steps toward the kitchen. "Hello?"

"We were wondering when you were going to get here." Chris stepped around the corner of the kitchen and into the hall.

She jumped and screamed at the same time. "Jesus! You scared me."

"Everything okay?" Alex peeked around his bedroom door.

"No. How did you guys get in here?"

"I have a key." Her brother joined them in the hall area.

"I thought I was the only one with a spare key. Guess Dad forgot you had one. Did you drive here or did mom drop you off?"

"He drove, if that's what you want to call it." Chris and her teenage attitude came out attacking.

"I drive just fine. We're here, aren't we?"

"Okay, enough. I don't want to listen to you two fighting all week. What are you doing in the kitchen, Chris?" Abigail set her bag down and put her arm around her sister's shoulder. "Fixing dinner?"

"Only if you like mac-n-cheese."

"If you're fixing it, I love it."

"Seriously?"

"Sure. Why not? It's a childhood staple." She smiled at her. "But I think you'll need to make at least two boxes with big man here." They both giggled. "I'll be right back. I need to change."

In her dad's room, she put on pajamas before returning to the kitchen.

"Are you sleeping in Dad's room?" Chris said when she reappeared.

"Yeah. That way you'll have your room again. I know you don't like sharing with me."

"I don't mind. Really. It's only on the holidays we share anyways." Her tone was sad.

"What's up? Talk to your big sis." Abigail pulled a big pot from the cupboard and filled it with water.

"I hate that Mom's gone. I hate having to go between two houses." Her voice rose in anger. "Why don't they just get back together the way it used to be?"

"Chris, there's no chance of Mom and Dad getting back together. You know that. They've both moved on with their lives. You've met Mom's boyfriend. You know Dad's been dating." She set the full pot on the stovetop.

"I don't want to talk about it anymore. Am I making dinner or are you?"

"Watch your tone and keep your attitude in check. You're making it, but the pot is heavy when it's full. I'll take it off to strain the noodles when it's ready. Okay?"

"Fine."

Abigail gave her a warning look as the attitude replied.

"Sorry. Okay." Chris turned away.

"I'm going to talk to your brother." Abigail knocked on Alex's door.

"Come in," he yelled.

She opened the door to find him playing a video game. It appeared to be a war game of some sort, as blood splattered and bodies fell. "Can we talk?"

The screen was split into four. She figured he was online with his friends.

"Sure. Give me a minute." Fingers maneuvered on the controller. "What's up?"

"Since you drove here, I'm guessing you have plans for New Year's Eve with your buddies. Am I right?"

"Mom gave me orders I'm not to go out anywhere New Year's."

"And you're going to listen to her?" She leaned against the doorframe.

"Ha, ha. Ah, I died."

Abigail glanced at the TV to see a huge blood smear on the screen.

"Yeah, I'm going to listen to her." He clicked buttons and set the control on his lap. "She wants me to stay here with you and Chris."

"Well, would a couple of your buddies like to come here? Not that I have anything special planned, but it might be nice for you."

"Yeah, sure. I'll check with them."

"A couple friends. Two. No more."

"Okay. Got it." He picked up the controller. "Can I get back to my game?"

"Yes."

Alex worked the buttons and brought himself back to life in the game. She didn't understand the thrill the guys got with these games.

"Your sister's making mac-n-cheese for dinner. I'll yell when it's ready." She got a simple head acknowledgement.

* * * *

Robert waited nervously as the line rang. What's with the nerves? It wasn't like he was a teenager calling for his first date. He never reacted this way approaching any of his other dates since the divorce. So why now?

"Hello?" Liz's cheerful voice answered on the other end of the line.

He licked his lips and swallowed. "Hi, it's Robert. I was wondering if you were ready for dinner." He paced the narrow space between his bed and long counter into the seating area.

"No, but I could be in about fifteen minutes. I thought the plan was to eat at seven?" He sensed confusion in her question.

"We're still eating then. I was thinking it would be nice if you and I had a drink before dinner. Would you be interested?"

"Sure."

"I'll swing by and pick you up in fifteen." A boyish grin on his flushed face reflected from the mirror.

Chapter Nine

Robert stood outside Liz's suite. Nerves tingled in his stomach. He knocked lightly and shoved his clammy hands in his pant pockets. Heels clicked from inside and the door opened. "Hello."

She was beautiful.

There wasn't a better word to describe how she looked.

"Give me a second. I need my purse."

He held the door open. Long wavy dark hair flowed over the sheer cream fabric of the blouse covering her shoulders. The brown skirt was interesting. Different fabrics, in different shimmery colors, were sewn together in strips to make rows of horizontal stripes.

She approached the door where he stood, gazing. "I'm all set." She returned his smile. The black heels she wore brought her closer to his height. "I like not having to look up at you. I should wear heels more often. Then I can look into those amazing eyes."

Once the door closed, Robert slid an arm around her waist. "I couldn't agree more." The front of her blouse had pleats and a ruffle that ran along the button edge. She wore the neckline open and low with a necklace of jumbled pearls in a variety of sizes. His eyes roamed her chest before returning to her face.

"So where are we going to get a drink?" Her hands remained low in front, holding her clutch.

"I was thinking the Martini Bar. Unless you don't care for martinis, then we could go to one of the many other ones aboard the ship."

He wondered if he should remove his arm from her waist. She didn't seem uncomfortable.

"I love a good martini." She leaned into him for a brief second. "As a matter of fact, I'll see if they can make a Key Lime like they do at Porterhouse in Lakeville." Her hand gripped his bicep. He had his answer about the comfort level of his arm placement. "Have you ever been there?"

"No. Is it a bar? Restaurant? You sound pretty excited about the place." They waited for the elevator.

"It's a steak place. Do you know Jensen's Supper Club?"

"Yeah."

"It's very similar, but they make a Key Lime Martini that's out of this world. I haven't found another like it. Others use a cream base and it's just not the same."

The doors slid open and Robert touched the small of her back to let her enter first. The contact between them broke as they rode the elevator. "How often do you get to have one of these martinis?"

"Not often, which is okay because it makes them more enjoyable and special when I do go there for dinner."

"Well let's see if they can fix a Key Lime like… Porterhouse." He rested his hand on the small of her back as their short two level ride came to their floor. She held his free hand.

A full bar, but not to capacity, as several golden club chairs were available. The place buzzed with conversations. A good thing no one played the baby grand because there was no need for the tinkling of ivory.

"How about this spot?"

"Good for me." She sat on the edge of the large club chair.

He leaned toward her rather than raising his voice. "So, do you know how they make your Martini?"

"I know it has pineapple and lime juice, but doesn't have a cream liqueur in it."

"I'll be right back. I'll go to the bar and see what they can do."

* * * *

Liz watched his retreating figure, admiring the tight butt. The black dress slacks hid the muscular legs she'd noticed in the gym. The solid purple golf polo accentuated his attractive graying hair.

"Excuse me; can I get a drink for you?" The waitress interrupted her admiring appraisal.

"No, thank you. Someone's getting one for me."

The ceiling lights caught her attention. They looked like the metal saucers she once used for sledding as a kid. Then, her gaze shifted to the floor. The purple carpeting with its cream swirls reminded her of cursive writing. With that, her children came to mind because the school district continued teaching cursive, making it a part of the elementary curriculum.

"You appear to be in deep thought." Robert stood holding two drinks.

She struggled for a reply. "The carpet reminded me of handwriting."

"In a way, yeah, I guess so." He set their drinks on the small glass table between the chairs. "The guy at the bar did his best with the Key Lime and said if you didn't like it, he'd make you something else."

"That was nice of him, but I'm sure it'll taste just fine." She picked up her glass carefully from the table. "It's not cloudy, that's good. Shall we toast this wonderful vacation?"

Robert raised his glass. "To reconnecting on a great cruise with friends."

Was that all they would ever be to each other? Friends? In the next few days? After that, what would become of their friendship? Yet, did she want more at this moment? Staring into his eyes, the color of her drink—yes, she wanted more.

Liz sipped from the crushed graham cracker rim. Swallowing the refreshing liquid, she slowly ran her tongue across her top lip. She enjoyed flirting with Robert.

He cleared his throat. "So? How is it?"

"Not bad. I prefer a sugar rim, but this is one of the better ones I've tasted. Still not quite the same as Porterhouse." Another drink from her glass earned him another tease of her tongue.

"What are you doing in port tomorrow?"

"I'm going on the Best of Ocho Rios tour. We're going to some waterfalls, a garden, and something else. What about you?"

"Scott and I are going ziplining. I can't wait." He sipped his martini, which appeared to be pure jet fuel from his pained expression.

"Yeah, that's not for me. I guess I'm not trustworthy of those ropes and things. Knowing my luck, the line would break and I'd fall to my death." She teased with a giggle.

"Okay, thanks for putting that into my head." He laughed with her.

"I'm sure it's safe; just not my thing. It sounds as though you like to take chances."

He nodded while swallowing. "I do. Life's too short to sit around and watch it pass you by. You got to go out there with a passion for living and seize every opportunity that comes your way."

"I'll remember that. It's a great way to look at life."

"I'd like to ask you something, but you don't have to answer if you don't want to." She nodded for him to continue. "Have you dated much since Greg's death?"

Liz set her drink on the glass tabletop. She leaned against the high side of club chair and pondered the question. The few men she'd dated never asked this question. Robert was different because he knew Gregory, and her.

"I'm sorry—"

"No, it's okay. It's just… you're different from the other men I've dated."

"How so?"

"You knew us prior to meeting on this cruise. My other dates only knew I was a widow and that was that. There was no further talk really about Gregory and his death."

"So, did any of them develop into more than a date? You know, lasting longer than say a week or two?"

She corrected her posture to sit upright. "Yes, but eventually I couldn't continue seeing them."

"What happened?"

How much to reveal? She never told the other men what caused the end of their relationships. "You're a curious one." She sipped her drink.

"You can change the topic if you'd like."

For once, she'd give the man an upper hand. He might as well know what would come between them if they continued to see each other after the cruise.

"My mother-in-law is the problem." Liz took a long sip of her martini. "She blames me for Gregory's death. For that matter, she doesn't believe I should date or remarry. According to her, 'He was your one and only. You don't get another chance.' Those are her words."

"Wait. You said it was an accident. Did you have something to do with his death?"

"I had nothing to do with his death. It *was* an accident." Maybe, if she told Robert, who wasn't family or a friend, she could get past the issue and have a real relationship. "He was coming home from the clinic and the road conditions were bad. She blames me because she feels I made him leave the clinic he had been working at and opened his own clinic." The words flowing, she couldn't stop.

"I'm the one, according to her, who chose the location, not Gregory, which we both know isn't true. The roads to and from the clinic weren't safe. Her words." Liz sucked the last of the sweet lime goodness into her mouth and swallowed.

"Was he texting or talking on his phone at the time? With you?" His hand was warm on her knee, yet his question irritated her. "Could that be why your mother-in-law feels that way?"

"No. He was against texting and driving." Heat rose along her neck, and she clenched her jaw, growing more upset with his questioning.

"What about talking?"

She kept her voice low aware of the others around them. "Are you insinuating that I had something to do with his accident?" She pushed herself to her feet. "You sound as if you agree with my mother-in-law."

Robert rose. "Liz—"

"Have a nice evening with Scott." Spinning around she stepped forward to leave. His hand snagged her wrist, stopping her from any further motion.

"Please, don't leave. I'm sorry I upset you, but—"

A few people glanced in their direction.

She faced him. "But nothing." She kept her voice low. "Please let me go."

He released her hand.

She left the bar for the elevators, without another word from Robert. She never should've told him about her mother-in-law. She never should've kissed him.

* * * *

Robert finished his martini and left to join Scott for dinner. He didn't mean to upset her, but didn't want to keep pushing the subject. Nevertheless, he had pushed and failed to apply what he'd learned from his first marriage. He'd give Liz time.

Stepping off the escalator, he turned the corner and entered Taste searching for Scott. The restaurant buzzed with activity, as it was the main dining room. Searching through the throngs of diners, he spotted Scott, who had raised his hand.

"Where's Liz?" Scott asked when he approached the table.

"She decided not to dine with us tonight." He sat across from Scott, placing the cloth napkin on his thigh.

"Oh. She must've met some other people. Good for her."

"How long have you been here?" He wanted to talk about something other than Liz.

"Long enough to order a drink, which hasn't arrived yet."

"Good. You know, it's been so relaxing not dealing with work. Have you checked your email?"

The contemporary dining room hummed with discussion. Servers maneuvered around chairs and each other.

"No, that's the purpose behind this vacation—don't dwell on emails. You've been so wrapped up in work, not to mention, splitting up your free time with your lady friends. Speaking of which, how did they take the news that you wouldn't be around for the holiday?"

Robert refrained from speaking as their waiter approached.

"Your drink, sir." He set Scott's drink on the table. "Can I bring you a beverage, sir?"

"I'd like a Vodka Lime Gimlet, please." Robert waited until the man stepped away. "First of all, I haven't been on any electronic device and it's been refreshing. So don't go all anti-work on my ass. As for the ladies, Kimberly had already made plans with her friends. Rebecca ended things between us."

"Surprised by that?" Scott sipped from his glass.

"Not really. The last couple of times when we'd gone out, she was hinting at wanting more in our relationship. I guess telling her I wasn't available for the holiday was the last straw. Laura was the only one slightly disappointed, but in the end was fine spending the holiday without me."

"You and Liz seemed to hit it off. Are you two going to spend tomorrow night together, celebrating?"

"Don't know." He broke eye contact with Scott.

He tipped his head and an eye squinted. "Something happen between you two?"

The waiter set Robert's gimlet on the table. "Were you ready to order?"

The men picked up the night's menu. Robert spoke first. "I'll have the Greek salad and the braised lamb shank. Thank you."

"I would like the baked gulf shrimp and the stir fried beef broccoli. Thank you." The waiter left them and Scott reiterated his previous question much to Robert's chagrin.

"You're as bad as my ex-wife with your questions." He joked to lighten the subject.

"Answer, then I'll shut up."

"No you won't. More questions always follow. We had drinks before dinner and we talked about things."

"What things?" Scott leaned forward on the table.

"See, told you, more questions." His jesting turned solemn. "Life things. I asked a couple of questions."

"So, because of what you said, she left, not wanting to have dinner with you?" He sat away from the table.

"Yes." Robert sipped from his glass.

"You blew it with Liz." Scott relaxed in the chair. "Moving on. Tomorrow will be fun."

He leaned into the table and kept his voice calm. "I didn't blow anything."

"I told you she's different and you didn't listen." He shook his head.

"I was being myself. She'll come around." At least that's what he hoped.

"Maybe we'll meet some women on the zipline tour." Scott wiggled his eyebrows.

"Yeah." He didn't want to meet anyone else on their adventure.

Jody Vitek

He'd met the woman he wanted to spend time with on the cruise.
Liz Farefield.

Chapter Ten

The elevator moved toward the tenth floor. Liz waited for the doors to open. Solace would be found in her room. Exiting the near empty elevator, she moved briskly to her suite. She stood in front of her door with the key card in the slot. Why let Robert ruin her time on the cruise?

"This is crazy." She spoke to no one, tucking the card away in her purse. "I'm not spending the night in my cabin."

She took the elevator down four floors and then rode the escalator to the fifth, the lowest level for passengers on the ship. Taste was behind her, so she continued into the atrium and passed the art gallery where Robert kissed her for a second time.

Why did she return the kiss?

Reaching the French restaurant, she entered. "A table for one, please."

The small restaurant didn't have the French flair she expected. She hoped to see 17th century French furnishings, chandeliers, and paintings of the countryside in gold gilded frames. Instead, it was more art deco style. White table linens and fine china with a wide gold rim alluded to the fancy fare.

She perused the menu and ordered a Kir Royale to sip through dinner.

Her waiter brought the champagne cocktail and took her order for seared scallops, eggplant, tomato, pine nuts, and olive oil. But then she said, "I'm sorry. I've changed my mind. I'd like the Fruits de Mer." The lobster, shrimp, scallops, and fennel in a puff pastry, with a vermouth and chive cream sounded more filling.

"Excellent choice." The waiter nodded his head and stepped away.

89

Liz sipped the fine beverage while observing the other patrons, who were few and mostly couples. One family of four sat by the windows. The youngest, a boy about Sarah's age, dined on escargot. His sister was probably two or three years older. There would be no way she'd be able to bring her two children into a restaurant like this unless they served chicken tenders or pizza.

As she continued to observe the dining couples, it brought to mind why she was on the cruise. To figure out what she wanted to do with her life. How to move forward. Decide whether she wanted to find another man to spend her life with. To sell the house and move or stay in the home she built with Gregory.

The short time she'd spent with Robert had been enjoyable until tonight. Why did his questions make her feel as though she was the guilty party in Gregory's death? Why had she gotten so upset by a simple question? She hadn't been on the phone with Gregory at the time of the accident, or anytime for that matter when he drove. She had nothing to feel guilty about.

Deep in thought, she started when the server approached with her meal. "Merci." She used one of the few French words in her vocabulary.

"Can I bring you anything else?"

"No, thank you."

"Bon appétit, Madame."

Liz understood the universal wish to enjoy her meal and nodded. The food smelled divine. Not to mention the presentation. She cut into the puff pastry and took the first bite. Her eyes closed at the smooth, delicate flavor of the cream sauce. When she opened her eyes, a young man stared at her a couple of tables away. He sat with an older couple. After a cordial smile, she focused on the delightful delicacy on her plate.

Several times while eating, she caught the man watching her. She concluded he was traveling with his parents. Not that there was anything wrong about traveling with your parents. Everyone had their reasons as to whom they traveled with or without. Finished with her meal, she left the restaurant and stepped into the main walkway.

"Excuse me?" A man's voice repeated the words a couple of times until she stopped and turned.

It was the young man from the restaurant. Mr. Watchful. Closer, he was definitely younger than her.

"Excuse me. Hello." He stood with his hands in his pockets. "My name's Michael." He offered his right hand freed from the confines of his pocket.

"Liz." His grip was firm as they exchanged a curt shake. "I wondered if you'd join me for an after dinner cocktail."

"Michael, I…" About to turn him away, she decided see what fun he'd bring to her evening. "A drink sounds good. Where?"

He wasn't very tall, shorter than her by a couple of inches, slender, dark hair and tanned, she guessed him to be of European descent.

"Let's go up a couple decks."

Up two floors and to the right, they entered the Bliss Ultra Lounge. The décor of purple, gold, and black in velvets and leather made Liz think of Prince, the musician. The place was funky with a capital F.

"Is this okay?" Michael leaned closer to be heard over the loud music.

"For a while, sure." She thought he spoke with an accent, but she couldn't pinpoint what kind. She experienced no attraction to him. No quivers. No quickening of the heart.

"Let's find a place to sit."

They glanced around the crowd.

"Here." He grabbed her hand and led her to a velvet sofa not far from the entrance. The tables by the dance floor and around the bar were filled. "I'll get drinks from the bar. What would you like?"

"A white wine. Thanks."

This was the place to be if you were young and hip. She didn't mind the top forty music because that's what she listened to at home, although the thumping base could get to be a little too much. The bowling alley off to the side, reminded her of the night when she left the alley with Robert and their kiss. Getting off the ship tomorrow and the next couple of days would be a good distraction.

"Here you are." Michael handed her a champagne glass.

"Is this champagne?" She raised her voice.

"It's a Presecco." He sat beside her on the sofa. "A sparkling white wine from northeastern Italy, whereas, Champagne comes from France of the same region name. They are similar, yet very different. I thought this would follow your dinner drink nicely."

"Well, thank you. You seem to know a lot about wine."

Sitting sideways, he faced her, resting an arm on the back of the sofa for support. "Um, my father's family has a winery in Italy and my parents own a winery in California. I was taught at a young age all about the wine industry, and Champagne. Please try the Presecco. If you don't care for it, I'll get you something else." This explained the accent.

Liz tipped the flute to her lips. The bubbly wine sat in her mouth for a moment before she swallowed. "Very good. I think I prefer Presecco over Champagne. It's not as dry as Champagne. It's sweeter. How do they differ?"

"Keeping it simple, Prosecco comes from Italy in the Veneto region. Champagne comes from France in the Champagne region. Champagne requires that the wine's secondary fermentation take place in the same bottle it will be served from, which is how it gets its bubbles. Prosecco's secondary fermentation happens in a stainless steel tank and isn't bottled until it's complete."

She faced him by turning at the waist. "Interesting. I'm guessing there's more to the process."

"The type of grapes also play a role, but I won't get into that."

"Does your family make Presecco?" Liz sipped from the flute.

"No. If you don't mind, could we change the subject?"

She nodded.

"I noticed you dining alone." He cocked his head. "Are you traveling by yourself?"

"Yes. Escaping the Minnesota cold, and you're traveling..." She savored the sparkling wine.

"With my parents." His head bobbed with the all-knowing. "They asked if I'd like to join them, and like any kid would, I said of course. I know, kind of corny for a twenty-seven-year old to be traveling with his parents, but I wouldn't change a thing. They're the greatest."

"It's not corny at all. I think it's great that you're with them."

"You have the most amazing eyes." He leaned closer to her, his arm sliding around her shoulders.

She yelped as her back straightened. "Michael, I'm sorry but I'm much older than you." She scooted forward on the velvet seat and away from his arm.

"Liz."

Hearing her name, she jerked her head. Scott approached.

"We missed you at dinner this evening."

"Scott, hi." Calm and full of confidence, she continued. "This is Michael. Michael, Scott."

"I'm sorry I didn't mean to interrupt." Scott remained standing and slid his hands in his pants pockets, glancing between them.

Michael's eyes searched hers before turning on Scott. "Then if you don't mind, we'd like to get back to enjoying our evening together."

"Sure." Scott went to the far side of the bar.

"I'm sorry to have made you uncomfortable. I find you attractive. Does the age difference make you uncomfortable?" Michael quickly eased back to his relaxed posture on the sofa.

"A bit. I'm twice your age."

"Why are Americans so conscience of age difference between a man and woman? Age shouldn't matter if there's a mutual attraction." His eyes widened. "Oh, you don't find me attractive."

"You're a very attractive young man, Michael."

"Young being the key word then."

"Yes. I've never been with someone..." She didn't want to beat the age thing to death.

"May I kiss you?"

She opened her mouth to respond and closed it remembering what Robert said earlier. Words of enjoying life and seizing the moments that come your way. Liz leaned forward into Michael and kissed him. Michael wrapped an arm around her waist, pulling her closer as he kissed her with more passion.

The discomfort level rose enough, she placed her palm to his chest and gently pushed him away. "I'm sorry, but I can't do this. I thought..."

"I understand." He stood, picked up her hand, and kissed the top. "Have a nice evening and I hope you enjoy the remainder of your time aboard the ship."

"Michael—"

"Liz, it's okay. Good night." He left the lounge.

Her eyes darted around the room. The only person to catch her eye, watching her alone on the sofa, was Scott, who approached.

"You're not leaving, too?"

"No. Please sit."

He filled the empty spot where Michael had been. "Want to talk about it?"

"What?"

"You and the kid." His face held a playful smirk.

Her face warmed with slight embarrassment. "He asked me to join him for a drink after dinner. Heeding some of Robert's wisdom," she said in a matter of fact tone. "I kissed him. Not feeling right about it, I put an end to it and he left."

"And Robert's wisdom was what?" For the first time, she noticed Scott's cologne. A spicy aroma versus Robert's light airy scent. She preferred light and airy.

"Basically to live life without regrets."

"Speaking of Robert, why didn't you join us at dinner?"

"I didn't feel well." She sipped the bubbly.

"For someone not feeling well, you look rather good. What did Robert say to you? You two don't have matching stories."

She tugged at her skirt hem. "Would you like to get a drink?"

"I don't need a drink, and you're avoiding the question."

With a heavy sigh, she answered. "We were talking over drinks before dinner and he said some things that upset me. I didn't want to eat while angry at him and ruin your dinner." She finished her Presecco and set the flute on a small black cocktail table.

"Tomorrow night is New Year's Eve. You have to celebrate with us. I don't want you to eat alone. I'll make sure Robert behaves." He made a pouty face.

"I'm not sure. I need time and space to think. I'll let you know later."

"Can I have Robert leave a message with you, as to our plans?" He lowered his head and gazed at her with sad eyes.

With a smile at his damned cuteness, she agreed. "Yes. Let me know what your plans are."

The DJ played a techno song. The noise grew obnoxious. "I'm sorry, but this music is getting to be too much. Do you mind leaving?"

"No. Where'd you like to go?" They both stood to leave.

The night full of emotional action, she wasn't quite herself. "Actually, I think I'm going to turn in for the night."

"I'll walk with you to the elevator."

"That would be nice. Thanks." They walked in silence for a short distance, away from the loud music. "So what would be the right type of woman for you to marry?"

"Excuse me." He stopped in the hall.

She came to a halt and faced him. "I remember you saying the right woman hasn't come along yet. I'm guessing you've dated."

They strolled again, maneuvering past fellow passengers on the wide marble and carpeted center aisle.

"I have dated, but when you catch your wife in bed with another man, you have difficulty trusting again. I'm not at that stage anymore when it comes to women and being in a relationship."

"So, you just haven't found the right one." Scott made her comfortable enough to hold a conversation.

"Not yet. I'm in no hurry either."

"What about children? You said you don't have any. Don't you want children?" She glanced in his direction.

"I did. It's not important to me now. I'm close to my sister's kids and Robert's too. You never know, maybe I'll meet someone with children."

She glanced sideways when he said the last few words, and he smiled warmly. Her head snapped to the other side.

"What about you? Do you think about getting married again?"

"If the right guy were to come along, probably. You just don't know until you know. I've only been dating for a few years, and those have been hit or miss." Her shoes clicked on the marble as they passed the other bars.

"Like tonight?"

"Yeah." They laughed, approaching the bank of elevators. "Thanks for walking with me."

"I enjoyed our time together. Have fun tomorrow."

"You, too." Scott left in the direction from which they came, toward the bars.

Jody Vitek

The doors opened and she entered the elevator. As the doors closed, Liz found herself wondering what Robert was doing, and with whom? She didn't understand how the man managed to stay in her thoughts after a short time together.

* * * *

At the Martini Bar, sitting at the bar ledge, Robert took the last sip of a dirty martini. Laughter reverberated off the marble flooring out in the passageway. The musical laugh belonged to Liz. When he turned on the bar stool, his hunch proved correct. It was who she was with he didn't particularly like—Scott. Would it be any better if she were with a total stranger? Hell no, that'd be worse. They disappeared from his view as they passed the entrance.

Turning back to the mirrored bar, he ordered another dirty martini. A refill was needed. There weren't many single women on this ship. It didn't matter. There was one single woman and he was interested in her. He'd have to correct things between them if he wanted to get close to Liz again.

"You upset her big time, partner." Scott's hand landed firmly, cupping Robert's shoulder. "Drinking away the misery?" He sat on the bar stool next to Robert.

"Aren't you quick to make the moves?" He shrugged his shoulder.

Scott removed his hand. "What? No."

The bartender approached, taking Scott's drink order and halting their discussion.

"You went after Liz tonight. Don't deny it because I saw you two together not ten minutes ago walking past in the hall." He took a big sip of his drink.

"I didn't go looking for her. I found her in that lounge with a *young* guy. I walked with her to the elevator. Nothing more."

The bartender set Scott's drink on the bar.

"You're being very protective of someone that isn't yours to protect." He sipped the martini.

"What happened with the young guy?" The question held the possibility of a painful answer, but he had to know. He focused on the bar top.

96

"Liz introduced us, I went to the bar, keeping my eye on them. I didn't think she was as interested in him as he was in her. Then they kissed—"

Robert's head snapped up. "Who kissed who?" he barked with a sharp tone.

"She kissed him, but is also the one who stopped the kiss."

"How, how did she stop it?" His heartbeat quickened.

"She put her hand to his chest and pushed him back. He left and I went to talk to her. As for me, I told you I'd leave her alone. We talked, and she's going to think about joining us tomorrow night. You're to leave a message for her in regards to our dinner plans."

"Did she tell you anything?"

"If the right guy comes along, she'd marry again."

"That's it? Nothing else?"

"As I said, you upset her."

Both men sipped their cocktails.

Scott broke the silence, as well as changed the subject. "So, how do you think things are going between Abigail and David?"

"He said she was doing well and picking up on the business quickly. They submitted the Myers bid and he praised her work."

"I think David finds her attractive."

Scott tested his patience. First Liz and now talking about his oldest daughter.

"I told her to keep things professional. Although she did bring up the fact that there's nothing in our policy about dating within the company." He turned serious. "Maybe we should look at implementing something in our HR policies."

"Come on, Robert. There's no need. If the two want to explore a relationship, what's the harm in it?"

He went on the defensive. "Excuse me; we're talking about my daughter here."

"She's had boyfriends before. What difference does it make if David's one of them?"

"David's a great employee, and I'd like to keep it that way. If they date and breakup, it only complicates things in a working environment."

"Well, you can't do anything about it right now." Scott paused to sip his drink. "Why'd Kathleen have to go to New York while you were gone?"

"I don't know. She assumed I'd be around and wouldn't have a problem taking the kids. Talk about the surprised look on her face when I told her I was going on a cruise." They shared a laugh. "I'm guessing her boyfriend pushed her into the trip."

"It was nice of Abigail to be there for her siblings. She really is a good kid, Robert."

"I know. I couldn't be more proud of who she is or what she's become as an adult. You know, she wants me to settle down and get married."

He stared into his drink and thought about Liz. A kind person, he couldn't keep his mouth shut. He wanted to hold her again. Have her kiss him instead of another guy.

"She told you this?"

"Yes, but you know me, I like my lifestyle." His chest tightened.

Scott picked up his glass. "Cheers to that."

Robert held up his drink and took a deep sip. Was a monogamous relationship knocking at his heart?

Chapter Eleven

The next morning, Liz opened the drapes to the patio, slid the door open, and stepped out to her private balcony. The sun softly kissed the horizon. The rays of light would soon break through the darkness, bringing light to a new day.

Room service knocked. She directed them to set the tray on the balcony table where she enjoyed breakfast ocean-side. A cup of coffee poured, she sat with her plate of two eggs scrambled, three pieces of bacon, and two slices of toast. The ship was docking in Ocho Rios and the sky promised a beautiful day.

While eating, she thought about the night ahead. New Year's Eve. She wanted to spend it with Robert and Scott, but she was upset with Robert. Their argument disrupted her sleep last night. She finished her meal and nabbed her journal.

As I write this, we're docking in Ocho Rios, Jamaica. It's a beautiful morning. Today I'll be touring waterfalls and gardens. Tonight is New Year's Eve. Not sure what I'll be doing. Hopefully, I'll be awake to ring in the New Year. Things are going to change, starting with my personal life. I've always made sure the kids are happy and my happiness came in a distant second. Standing up to Ellen on Christmas was liberating and I need to do it more often.

The food has been amazing and I've probably been eating too much. The crew outdoes themselves to please you. I ordered room service and they brought the tray into the suite versus handing it to me at the door. The longer I'm on the ship, the less inclined I am to go home. They make the beds each morning and turn down the sheets at night. That doesn't happen at home where I'm the lone laundress and bed maker.

I've been fortunate enough to have run into Robert Burnhamwood, who is traveling with his friend and co-worker, Scott Jordan. I have been dining and socializing with them. Robert's architectural firm was responsible for the building of the clinic. It was hard at first because it brought Gregory into the conversation and my thoughts. What's hard is I'm attracted to Robert. It was an instant magnetism that I let my emotions act on. Whether that was smart or not on my behalf, I don't know. Time will tell.

Liz put the journal inside the suite. Time for another cup of coffee before having to get ready for the shore excursion. She sat enjoying the view from her balcony of white sandy beaches running into the lush green hills. Getting off the ship would do her some good. More time to ponder how to approach Robert tonight.

* * * *

Abigail rolled and squinted at the light coming through the blinds. What time was it? She picked up her cell, pushed the power button to see ten-thirty-three on the screen. Sitting a little, propped against the pillow, her eyes adjusted to the brightness.

Tomorrow would be the beginning of a fresh start. A new boyfriend and a great new job. Not only that, she would graduate in the New Year. She smiled with pride and happiness. Yup, this was going to be a great year.

She opened her Twitter account and typed.

Wishing everyone a safe and Happy New Year!

Posted, she scrolled through to read and retweet. When she finished, she started a new text message to David.

Looking forward to seeing you Saturday and celebrating our New

100

Year together. Stay safe tonight and have fun!

After pressing send, she got out of bed and strolled to the kitchen and living area to see who was awake and moving around.

"Good morning, Chris." Her sister lounged on the sofa watching TV. "What time did you get up?" She leaned against the arm of the sofa.

"Over an hour ago. Alex is still sleeping. I made myself breakfast."

Short and to the point. She was obviously bitter about having to stay at their dad's with her.

"Alex is having a couple of friends over tonight."

"Why does he get to have friends over and I don't?" Chris shrieked.

She put her finger to her lips. "Shh. If you'd let me finish. Would you like to invite a friend or two to come stay the night? Girl friends."

"Yes. Does Harry love Louis?"

"What?"

"It's a One Direction fan thing." She shook her head rolling her eyes. "Never mind. I'll text Paige and Emily first." She tapped away on her phone, grinning.

"Okay, let me know if we need to pick them up, or if I need to give their parents directions. They can be here any time after five." Abigail meandered to the kitchen for coffee and food.

Having her sister happy would make the night and week better for everyone involved. The boys would more than likely stay in Alex's room gaming and hit the kitchen for food. The girls would bop between Chris's room, the kitchen, and living room.

Her phone binged, signaling a text.

Play nicely with your siblings and we'll play on Saturday.

Aren't you bold, she replied to David.

Picking her coffee pod, she popped it in the maker and hit the brew button.

Bowling. We're going bowling. So much for surprises. Change of plans, he responded.

No, don't change what you've planned. I want to go bowling. Now I'll know how to dress.

She pulled eggs, milk, and cheese from the fridge.

Ok, bowling it is. What are you doing right now?

Making eggs. Why?

Cracking the eggs into a bowl, she tossed the shells down the disposal and washed her hands.

Curious. What kind of eggs? Scrambled, poached, omelet?

Abigail grinned. He was getting to know her outside of work.

Omelet, I think. We'll see how it goes. They could turn into scrambled.

A small amount of butter in a pan melted as it warmed on the stovetop.

Sounds delicious. Will you make me breakfast some morning?

Before she could respond to David, another message popped up.

Now I'm being bold. Too soon?

Her body warmed.

Does Sunday morning work for you?

Message sent, she quickly typed another. *Too soon?*

The butter sizzled and so did her body. She poured the egg mix into the skillet.

I think things are heating up in the kitchen. Wish I was there.
The kitchen isn't the only thing hot.

She swirled the egg around to make a bigger base for her omelet.

I'm going to go now. I'll extinguish the fire later.

Not knowing how to respond, she let the conversation end there. This relationship could prove to be exciting.

* * * *

Robert fell onto his couch, kicked off his shoes, and leaned back. What an exhausting day flying through the trees. He picked up the phone, dialed Liz's room, and got voicemail.

"Hi, Liz. Robert. Scott and I will be dining at Cagney's Steakhouse tonight. We're meeting at seven at the cigar lounge. Hope to see you at dinner and hear about your day."

The room phone back in its cradle, he set the alarm and crashed on the couch. Thirty minutes later the buzzer sounded. Refreshed from the short nap, he showered and dressed for dinner. Tonight was the first night he wore a suit and tie. He knew he didn't have to wear the suit, but tonight was a celebratory night—New Year's Eve.

On his deck, Ocho Rios slowly diminished as they left for the next port. The sun spread the last of its rays across the waters. Time to enjoy a cigar.

He entered a lounge decorated with tasteful wood walls and mirrored pillars. Black leather sofas, burgundy leather chairs, and tables created seating areas about the room. It resembled a seventies gentleman's club. The room held appeal. Four other men sat enjoying their cigars.

Lighting his cigar, he waited for Scott.

A few moments later Scott strolled in with Liz, who hobbled with a foot wrapped in a bandage. "What happened?" He stood as they approached.

"I slipped and sprained my ankle." She sat on the sofa. "Nothing major, but I won't be riding a horse in Cozumel."

Robert moved his chair closer to the sofa. "Here, rest your leg." He sat beside her, while Scott sat across from them in a chair and lit his cigar. "Do you want a drink?"

"No, I'm good for now. I'll have wine at dinner."

"So what happened?" Scott queried before Robert could.

"It's really stupid. My tour was to see three different sites, but I only saw two. While we were at the Dunn's River Falls—actually toward the end—I lost my footing. The rocks are slippery and in some spots, it was worse than others where the water was rushing. Well, I wasn't paying close enough attention because I was surrounded by all this beauty and lost my concentration."

"I'm sorry you didn't get to enjoy your outing." Robert empathized.

"Oh, I did enjoy the day. At our next stop at the Shaw Park Gardens, I got off the bus even though I couldn't walk around. The tour guide gave me ice for my ankle. The scenery was beautiful and they brought me pamphlets to read. I'm glad I didn't try to walk because it's twenty-five acres on different elevated levels.

"The tour finished driving through Fern Gully. Beautiful and stunning. Very lush with vegetation. The vendors along some stretches of the road had interesting sculptures. You could say they like to exaggerate the male anatomy." A grin formed on Liz's face before laughter escaped.

"When I got back aboard the ship, I went to medical." She patted her bandage. "They're the ones who wrapped my ankle and told me it was a minor sprain. They proceeded to tell me to stay off it as much as possible, ice, and elevate it too. The falls were so amazing! Not to mention the plants and trees. It was so worth the slip. I'd do it all over again."

"I'm glad it wasn't worse. It sounds like you were able to enjoy most of the tour." Robert held her hand and gave a gentle squeeze.

"Thanks." She returned the fingers embrace. A sign things were okay between them.

"Can you get your money back on the horse riding in Mexico?" Scott inquired.

"I'm not sure. I'll have to look into it. As of right now, I'm looking forward to relaxing on the beach tomorrow."

Robert glanced at his watch. "Why don't we head to the restaurant? It's after seven." Tamping the cigar to snuff it out, he offered Liz his arm.

"Thank you, but I'll be better off hobbling without support." She wore a stunning, simple black dress. Instead of dress shoes, she wore sandals.

"Okay. Are you ready, Scott?"

"I'll be right behind you. Go ahead." He held up his cigar, as a signal he wanted to stay longer.

The host seated Liz and Robert at a table for four. The restaurant resembled the steak places back home. Rich colors of blue and gold, with splashes of red and black accents. He sat next to Liz since Scott would be joining them shortly and he wanted to be close to her.

"Did you want to prop your leg on the other chair?"

"I think I will." She turned slightly on the chair. "I guess I shouldn't have worn a dress. It's hard to sit like this and not expose myself." He joined in her light laughter. "I'll be fine though."

"You're at the beach all day tomorrow, so you'll be able to relax. What kind of wine do you prefer?"

"With steak, red. I prefer Merlot."

Robert perused the list of available Merlots and ordered a bottle for the table. If Scott didn't want some, more for them. "Listen, I'm sorry about yesterday. I didn't mean to accuse you of anything. I was just asking."

"I'm the one who should be apologizing." She rested her hand over his. "It's a difficult subject to discuss. I took your questions too personally and shouldn't have." Her fingers squeezed his hand. There was a hint of a smile on his face.

"Good, I gave the two of you enough time to make up." Scott sat across from Liz. "Have you ordered?"

"Only a bottle of Merlot." Robert stroked her fingers with his thumb.

"I know what I'll be ordering for dinner. I checked the menu on the ships TV channel." Enthusiasm filled Scott's voice.

"Liz, why don't we see what they have to order and decide?"

The sommelier approached the table with their bottle of wine and glasses while they perused the menu. He poured a sample into a glass. Robert swirled the liquid, held the glass to his nose before sipping the fine wine. Answering the nod of his head, the steward filled the glasses.

"So you know about my wonderful, fun filled day. How was ziplining?" Liz tasted the wine.

Scott focused on him. "Go ahead."

"It wasn't ziplining like you think or at least as I was thinking, where you travel fast on a line and everything's a blur. It was a little slower so you could see the lush greenery. First we had to go through an instruction course, and then we were set up with the appropriate gear."

"Excuse me." Their waiter approached the table. "Were you ready to order?"

They placed their orders for various Angus steaks and accompaniments.

Robert continued describing their day's adventure. "We had to wear helmets, similar to a bike helmet. You have to wear gloves and a harness that you step into and pull up between your legs. Talk about an odd feeling, and I'll leave it at that. We leapt from multiple platforms, so it was stop and go. The last platform was more zipline speed. It was great."

"Yeah," Scott interjected. "While you were playing on the ground in the greenery, we were high above in the tree canopy. The chattering of the birds was pretty cool, too."

"So, what are you doing tomorrow?" Liz flinched with pain as she shifted on the chair.

"Are you okay," Robert asked quietly, solicitous about her ankle.

"I'm fine." She winked in return.

"We're going on a rum tour and tasting at three different locations," Scott responded with a joyous grin.

"I'd be under the table after one tour." Liz laughed.

"I don't think we'll get enough of a sample to get drunk," Robert earnestly responded.

"Afterward might be a different story. I may get a bottle to bring aboard the ship," Scott said with a chuckle.

Their meals arrived. They talked about going back to Minnesota and leaving the warm weather. Conversation flowed to the cruise ship, staff, food, and other passengers. Finished eating, their server asked about dessert.

"No, thank you." Liz glanced between him and Scott.

Robert and Scott declined. The porterhouse was filling along with the other side dishes.

"If you don't mind, I'm going to go off on my own for the remainder of the evening." Scott stood and pushed his chair into the table. "Happy New Year."

"Happy New Year, Scott. Have fun tomorrow."

"You, too, Liz. Take it easy and relax on the beach. Robert, see you in the morning for the tour."

As Scott strolled from the restaurant, Robert slipped his fingers around Liz's hand. "How's your ankle?"

"Sore, but not bad."

"Are you up to venturing outside? We could sit on a lounge chair." He spoke with caution though her signs lent him to believe they were okay.

"That would nice."

"Let's see if we can get some ice for your ankle." Robert flagged their server. "Would it be possible to get a small amount of ice in a sealed bag? She sprained her ankle today."

"No problem, sir. I'll be back shortly."

Removing her right leg from the chair, she shifted to face him. "Thank you, Robert."

Robert carried the bag of ice for her as they made their way to the pool deck. Liz couldn't wait to get the ice on her ankle. They found two lounge chairs in a secluded area. Liz didn't have a towel to put between the ice and her skin. Taking her shawl off, she folded and set it on her ankle.

"Would you like my jacket? I didn't think about asking for a towel." Robert sat on the edge of the neighboring chair, while she situated the ice bag.

"I'm fine, but thank you."

"Okay, just say the word and I'll give it to you." He remained sitting upright.

"You're going to make me nervous if you stay sitting on the edge."

"I can see you better this way. If I were to lean back in the chair, we'd both have to turn our heads to look at each other."

She scooted on the seat. "Then come sit here." She patted the open spot beside her with a coy smile. "I'd be more comfortable. Plus, I'd be less apt to fall asleep."

"Are you tired?" Robert sat by her thigh at an angle to face her lying on the chair.

"A little. I think the wine and filling food has more to do with it than today's activities." Her hand rested on his thigh.

"Liz, I think we should talk about us." He turned away from her. There was an awkward silence. "I find you attractive and fun to be with." Turning back, he stared into her eyes. "But I can't make any promises as to what will happen when we return home." His Adam's apple bobbed.

"Is there someone else in St. Paul?" She swallowed at the possibilities. "Please be honest."

He leaned forward, resting his elbows on his knees and his chin on interlocked hands. The action and silence spoke a thousand words. "There are two women back home."

She wasn't expecting that. He was a playboy? "They're okay with this? With you..."

"They don't know about each other." His voice remained calm and somber.

"And what? Now you're feeling guilty with me?" A bit of irritation rose, inflicting an insulting tone to her voice.

Robert unclasped his hands and turned, placing an arm to rest along her right side, propping him to hover above her. "No. You wanted the truth, and I'm telling you the truth. I'm attracted to you. I don't want to hurt you."

"So am I supposed to be a casual fling while aboard the ship?"

"It takes two, Liz. You returned the kiss. What about you? Are you using me? What did you want or expect after the cruise?"

She turned her head away from his pain-filled stare.

A knuckle softly grazed along her jaw line to her ear, tucking her hair behind. He leaned forward close to her ear. "I want to see where a relationship will go between us." He delicately kissed her ear lobe.

"Without any guarantees."

Slowly turning her head, Liz kissed his cheek. "I'm sorry. I jumped on you without thinking about my intentions. You're right, I did kiss you. I'm attracted to you, too. I guess your honesty shocked me. I want to give us a chance. If you decide, at whatever point, it won't work for you, then tell me. I'm a grown woman and can deal with whatever life throws at me."

His kiss was filled with passion. A fire ignited in her belly and the warmth spread to her outer limbs. The ice was no longer cold on her ankle. She wrapped her arms around him, pulling him against her chest.

He broke the kiss. "We need to stop. I can't…"

She searched his eyes. "My room or yours?"

"Liz—"

"Do you have protection?"

"Liz, I don't want to rush this." When he sat up, she moved with him. "I don't want to push you into something you may regret."

She slid her arms around his waist, gliding her hands down his thighs. His muscles flexed. "I'm the one pushing." Her hands skated inward and slowly inched upward. He stopped her progress to his groin.

Robert stood and pulled on his pant legs. He turned to assist her from the chair as he cleared his throat. "My room."

Chapter Twelve

Liz brushed past Robert as he held open the door to his room. Her heart pounded in anticipation. She froze in the small entry and bathroom area. Nervous, she thought his room was similar to her own.

The door clicked behind her. She swallowed.

The warmth of his body radiated against hers as his arms wrapped around her waist. "Your heart is racing." His breath on her neck sent a wave of chills down her back.

Her head fell against his shoulder as her eyes closed in the ecstasy of his nearness.

He kissed the top of her head, her neck, and another on her shoulder. "Tell me to stop and I will."

Wobbling on her good foot, he swooped her into his arms and carried her the short distance to the bed. She propped herself on her elbows, watching as he shed his suit coat and tie, draping them on the padded stool. At the sink area, he dug through a travel kit bag. When he turned, she patted the bed, and saw what he'd retrieved from the bag. He set the small package on the built-in shelving before joining her on the bed.

With one hand, he cupped her cheek, sliding his fingers into her hair holding the back of her head, while kissing her. She eased into the bed as her nerves dissipated, and Robert lessened the small space between them. The intensity of the kiss increased. She pulled his shirt at the waist and yanked it from his pants. Touching his body sent a wave of warmth and wanting over her body.

He stopped kissing her.

"What's wrong?" Liz worried she'd done something wrong.

"How do I get this dress off of you?"

She scooted from the bed to stand. He sat on the edge of the bed in front of her. As she pulled the dress up, warm, gentle hands rested on her thighs, and she inhaled as he kissed her right below the belly button. His hands glided over her hips to her lower back and he delivered a kiss beneath her breasts. Goose pimples covered her body from his slow caresses and his demanding lips on her skin. The dress lay in a heap on the floor. She stood before him in her black lace bra and panties.

Her concentration was on one thing—to breathe.

As he stood, his fingers danced up her back, resting on the bra fastening while the other hand remained low. She wrapped her arms around his waist. Her fingers tensed and relaxed repeatedly against the fabric of his shirt. She wanted this. She wanted to be intimate with Robert.

He held her snug against his body. Kissed her lips, her neck below the ear, the collar bone, and as he placed a kiss at the center of her cleavage, the bra sprang free. With the same hand, he slowly, one at a time, slid the straps off her shoulders and arms. The black lace fell to the floor.

She unbuttoned his shirt, pulled it off his shoulders, and kissed his chest. He didn't have much hair, but she liked the patch there. Pulling the shirt the remainder of the way down his arms, the cuffs on his wrists stopped any further progress.

"Hold on tightly to the shirt." He yanked an arm free from the confines of the sleeve and repeated the process for the other arm.

A bulge strained against his pants, which added a challenge when she worked the zipper down. The pants dropped to the floor with a few movements of his hips. She hooked her thumbs in the elastic waistband of his boxer briefs and gradually pulled them down. When they reached mid-thigh, the boxers joined the rest of their discarded clothing, and she wrapped a hand around his thick length and stroked. He moaned.

When she teased the slick head, he engaged his fingers at the edge of her lace boy shorts. She released her controlling grasp. He turned to the bed and yanked the covers off the bed. Using the opportunity, she removed her remaining barrier of clothing.

He turned around with a lopsided smirk. "You need to get off your ankle."

Liz lay on the bed. He opened the tiny package and put the condom on before lying beside her. His hand roamed up her thigh. Fingers intertwined through her pubic hairs and one finger slid between the wetness. She gasped with a desire she hadn't felt for years. As they kissed, hers was filled with a need for more. Her back arched with a sigh. He kissed her breast, where he tantalized the erect nipple. Her head pressed farther into the pillow as his finger pushed deeper and slowly pulled out.

He moved between her legs, his tongue slowly tasted and teased her, while fingers delved leisurely in and out. Deeper each time.

Her release came quickly, with a scream, while clutching the bed. Her body trembled as she slowed her breathing and heart rate.

Robert waited for her orgasm to subside. He kissed the inside of her thigh, moving up her stomach to her breast. He caressed her collarbone with his lips, to her neck and finished below her ear. Hovering over her, he gradually and easily glided his thickness inside. He groaned at the pleasure of her tightness. She opened her legs wider, giving him ease of deeper access. As she moaned arching her back, he gave her all of him. He paused but for a brief moment. Their bodies now one, they ebbed and flowed together. Her fingers clawed at his back, without digging, adding to the sensual sensation. In time, he shuddered, finding his own release.

He collapsed to her side, resting a hand on her stomach. Her deep emerald eyes, moistened with tears.

"What's wrong? I didn't hurt you, did I?" He lightly pecked her cheek.

She wiped her eyes and chuckled. "No, you didn't hurt me." She licked her lips and swallowed. "It's just been awhile."

"I wasn't... you've..." He wasn't sure how to ask if he was the first guy she'd slept with since her husband. She'd dated others.

"You're the first." She turned her head away from him.

He untangled their legs, pulled the bedding over them, and snuggled beside her. He didn't know what to say. Two questions buzzed in his head. Why him? Why now? She was crying, and he had to say something.

"Please don't cry."

The back of her hands swiped her face before facing him. "These are tears of pleasure. Insurmountable pleasure." She smiled then kissed him passionately.

He held her close, fitting so perfectly against him. There was a different feeling holding Liz in his arms after having... Sex? It seemed more than just sex. When he looked into her eyes, there was more than this-is-good-time-free-loving sex. It was a, I-trust-you-and-give-my-all-to-you sex. It scared him because he wanted the monogamous relationship with Liz.

She nipped his lip and encouraged his arousal to grow by sliding her firm grip up and down his shaft. He fell to his back with a sigh. A moan escaped as she sucked and teased his firm penis deeper into her mouth.

Several minutes later, she stopped, got off the bed, and hobbled to his black bag. She tore the package open before getting on the bed. With a free hand, she seized his length. She slid his engorged penis into her mouth before sliding the condom on his erection. He attempted to take his time with her, but she didn't allow him to make love to her slowly.

He listened to her labored breathing turn into a slow, relaxed, sleep induced state as Liz slept on his chest. In turn, it relaxed his own, but not his mind. Their friendship was more after tonight. He wanted to have a relationship with her beyond the cruise. Yet could he give up the other two ladies?

* * * *

Liz startled and woke to booming.

"Happy New Year." Robert kissed the top of her head. "They're shooting off fireworks. Do you want to go out on the deck?"

"Yes." She got out of the bed and pulled on her underwear and bra. "What time is it? Is it midnight?" He watched her dress and a bit of unease vibrated through her body. She knew she had a great body, so why the discomfort about him seeing her naked now and not earlier?

"Yes, it's midnight. You don't have to get dressed. I have a private deck." He slid from the mattress at her side.

"I can't stay here all night." She shook her dress as if that would remove any wrinkles. "I'll need to go back to my cabin."

He located and pulled on his briefs from where they had fallen to the floor amongst her clothing. "Why?"

"Because," she warned as though talking to one of her children. She maneuvered the dress over her shoulders and waist. "Not tonight."

Conflicted about staying or leaving, she made the decision that seemed best for her mindset. He had been a wonderful lover and made her and her body happy.

"Okay, another night then." He held his hand for her to take.

They stood for a short moment along the railing enjoying the fireworks display.

"Let's sit." He arranged it so one chair faced out to the ocean while the other faced the cabin.

She scrunched her face. "Don't you want to see the fireworks?"

He plopped on the chair and patted his lap. "Sit and put your leg up."

She did as he asked. His arms wrapped around her waist and she crisscrossed hers so she could touch him. A delicate kiss was placed on her shoulder. She turned away from the ocean and lightly kissed his lips.

When silence surrounded them, she whispered. "I need to go." They stood.

"I'll see you tomorrow." He embraced and kissed her before they strolled to the door. "I'll leave you a message about dinner."

When he opened the door, she leaned into him with a kiss before stepping into the hall. "Happy New Year, Robert."

The feeling of delight couldn't be contained. Her smile broadened on the elevator ride and remained until she entered her room. The throbbing in her ankle broke through the happy barrier. Picking up the phone, she asked room service to deliver some ice in a sealed bag. While she waited, she changed into pajamas, took off her makeup, and swallowed two ibuprofen. Fifteen minutes later room service knocked.

She lay on the bed, placed a pillow under her foot, a folded towel on her foot, and set the ice on her now unwrapped ankle. Slightly swollen, the bruising wasn't too bad. Pulling the covers over her, she opened her journal to write.

Happy New Year! Ocho Rios was beautiful! It was unfortunate that I slipped at the end of the Dunn's River Falls, receiving a slightly sprained ankle. It's enough to keep me from going horseback riding in Mexico. It also kept me from walking the Shaw Park Botanical Gardens. Fern Gully was a riding tour. The lush green foliage and chirping wildlife was spectacular!

We had dinner at Cagney's Steakhouse and my filet was out of this world. The meal was so filling, none of us ordered a dessert. Robert and I enjoyed the evening together while Scott did his own thing. We watched the fireworks from Robert's private balcony before I returned to my room.

Tonight I asserted myself with Robert and gave into my body's need. It's been too many years since I had a man love me the way Robert did tonight. He took his time and wasn't selfish about his needs. We had sex twice, and I think we both could've done it a few more. Thank goodness we didn't because my body is a tad sore. God, while writing, my nipples and lower region quivered thinking about Robert, his touch and body.

He wanted me to stay the night, but I couldn't. Not tonight. I had to step away. Because it was my first night with a man in years, I just couldn't stay. I guess a part of me worried about what others would think seeing me leave his room in the morning. I didn't worry about tonight because it was New Year's Eve.

Tonight he told me he's involved with two other women. I don't like the idea of sharing him with other women, and I told him as much. He told me this before I gave myself to him. Neither of us are making any sort of promise for after our return to Minnesota. We both agreed to see where things would take us.

Writing about his other women has made me wonder if that wasn't in the back of mind when I made the decision to come back to my room. I never thought about diseases or asking him about safety. He was the one who had protection. Do I assume he's safe when he's with others? I guess I'll need to assert myself some more and ask him about his sexual activity in the past.

In this new year, I'm going to allow myself to have a relationship with a man, and I'd be happy if that man happens to Robert.

* * * *

The Pale Fox House was hopping tonight. David helped his Aunt Caitlin and Uncle Dillon where they needed him. When tables needed moving, he moved them. If they needed clearing and cleaning, he cleared and cleaned. Dishes needed washing, he washed. He filled in for the bouncers when they went on break. No job was too small or big for him. It helped that the employees loved working at the Pale Fox House and respected his aunt and uncle.

When the clock turned to midnight, he tapped a message to Abigail.

Happy New Year! Hope you're having fun with your brother and sister.

The last part of the message made him think of his own family. He sent a group message to his parents and siblings wishing them a Happy New Year, though they wouldn't celebrate for another two hours. Then…His phone vibrated.

Alex and Chris both have friends over. Alone on New Year's Eve.

A few seconds passed and the phone vibrated again.

It's all good. I have my celebratory drink in hand. My celebration will be with you.

Looking forward to Saturday. Back to work, he replied.

Caitlin entered the kitchen. "That's a big smile. What's your girlfriend doing tonight?"

"Aunt Cait, she's not my girlfriend. At least not officially yet. She's watching her younger siblings."

"You need to be careful where you step with this girl. Being the boss's daughter and all. You don't want to lose your job over any woman."

"Speaking from experience, Aunt Cait?" He raised his eyebrows in question. A towel came from nowhere and snapped him on the hip.

"That's none of your business young man." She turned to leave the kitchen and glanced over her shoulder. "Ask your uncle." Then, she disappeared.

There was a story there, but now wasn't the time to ask.

By one o'clock, they stopped allowing people into the bar. Coffee and popcorn were free for all who wanted some. At two o'clock, the place was empty. They called cabs for anyone unable to drive or who didn't have another way of getting home. With the place cleaned and ready for another day, he headed for home.

The drive would be a little longer than leaving work for home, but tonight he wouldn't battle traffic. Tonight he worried about those who were driving impaired. Crossing the Wabasha Bridge into West St. Paul, he passed several squads with cars pulled over. Five minutes away from home a car aimed in his direction. He swerved to the right speeding quickly ahead and out of the way. At the sound of crashing, he slammed the brakes and turned around. The car ran into a light post. He dialed nine-one-one and reported the accident.

"Is anyone hurt?" the operator questioned in a calm voice.

"I don't know. I'm in my car. Just a minute." He walked near the scene. "Someone's on the ground. It looks like it's the driver." Walking around the front of the car he sharply inhaled. "Oh God, there's another person on the ground." David dropped into a squatting position as his body trembled.

"David, can you stay there until the police arrive?"

"Yes." His voice dropped low, to a near inaudible whisper. "They would've hit me if I wouldn't have swerved."

"I'm sorry. What did you say?"

He was in shock and didn't necessarily mean for her to hear him. "They were about to hit me and I swerved."

"The police and ambulance will be there shortly. David, are you in need of any medical attention?"

"No, I'm fine. Maybe in a little shock. Compared to these two, I'm great." He took some steadying breaths.

Sirens grew near.

"I can hear the sirens. I'm going to let you go."

"Thank you." David disconnected and a minute later several police cars arrived with an ambulance trailing behind.

An officer approached. "Did you witness this?"

"Yes." He tested his legs by standing and wobbled.

"Have you been drinking, sir?"

"No." He shook his head. "I was on my way home from work."

"Where's work?"

"The Pale Fox House. I was working. The only thing I've drank tonight is water and coffee." The cop was doing his job, but he didn't want to go through a sobriety test.

"You were off balance."

"I'm a bit shaken up."

"Okay. Were there any other cars involved?"

"No. They were going to hit me, and I swerved. My car's right over there." He gestured behind him.

"Okay, we'll need to ask you some questions. Please wait in your car until an officer can talk to you."

"Sure." David walked slowly back to his car and started it to warm up. In the rearview mirror, paramedics loaded one of the people on a stretcher. He turned away from the view resting his head on the steering wheel. How lucky had he gotten? Would he have survived if he hadn't moved? He doubted it.

There was a knock on his window. His head shot up and he jumped. An officer stood outside the driver's door. David opened the door and stepped out.

"I'm Officer Denton. I understand you saw what happened. Can you tell me about the incident?"

He replayed the events leading up to the crash and calling nine-one-one.

"Thank you, David. Can I see your driver's license, please? I need a record of your information."

"Sure." David pulled his wallet from his back pocket and handed the officer his license.

"I'll be right back. You can wait in your car."

He waited for the officer. Moments later Officer Denton knocked on the window. Stepping from his car, the officer returned his driver's license.

"Thank you. We'll call you if we have any further questions. Be safe."

"You, too. Good night." He waited for the officer to step away before driving in the direction for home. Tonight he'd have a shot of Scotch before attempting to sleep.

Chapter Thirteen

The ship was back at sea, sailing west toward Cozumel, Mexico. Robert dialed Liz's room. She'd been on his mind throughout the day. Last night hadn't been his typical romp with a woman. It had been different with Liz because he didn't push them into bed. Instead, he let her lead the way. Normally he was in control and the women preferred it that way.

"Hello," her groggy voice answered.

"Liz, its Robert. Did I wake you?" He sat on the sofa.

"That's okay. I've been sleeping long enough." She moaned, and he assumed she was stretching.

He hoped another man wasn't pleasing her body. He wondered what it would be like to wake up with her next to him. Where the hell did that come from? He never woke up the next day with a woman other than his ex-wife. Yet he wanted Liz to stay last night.

"I'd like to take you to dinner. Do you like Italian?"

"Sounds wonderful." She groaned. "What about Scott?"

What about him, he wanted to say. "He made plans with someone for the evening."

"Oh. What time were you thinking?"

"Does seven give you enough time to get ready?"

"What time is it?" He heard her moving around. "Oh, wow. It's five-thirty already. Yeah, seven will be fine."

"I'll come to your room then. How's your ankle?"

"It's better. I think the icing I did yesterday really helped, along with taking ibuprofen." Her voice was more alert.

"That's good. I promise to limit the time you spend on your feet tonight." He chuckled with a smile.

"No worries. I'll see you in about an hour and a half," she said with an upbeat voice.

Liz had completely missed or avoided his flirtation. Was it incidental or on purpose? Did she regret their night together? He didn't. In fact, he wanted more of her. The New Year played out nicely and he wanted it to continue while on the cruise. Oddly, he did want to pursue what he and Liz had afterwards. Liz was slowly opening a part of his psyche that Kathleen had verbally battered.

He opened a bottle of rum from the tour and poured a splash in an Old Fashioned glass. Sliding the balcony door open, he stepped into the warm air. The sun began its descent to the horizon while the moving ship delivered a gentle breeze. He sat and enjoyed his drink before getting ready for the night.

Dressed down from the night before, Robert wore casual dress slacks and a dress shirt unbuttoned at the neck. She opened her door, and he was pleased to see her dressed casually, too. She wore a red coral top with white linen cropped pants and white sandals.

"You look beautiful. The sun agreed with you today."

"Thank you. It helped that I got an umbrella to lie under when I needed shade. Give me a second." She grabbed her purse from the bed.

Other passengers were in the hall when she stepped beside him. Not wanting to embarrass her or push their developing relationship, he kissed her cheek. "We're going up to fourteen at the front of the ship."

She held his hand as they made their way to the elevators, but she seemed a little tense. Was it because of last night or because of her ankle? She walked with hardly a hobble. They rode the forward bank of elevators and strolled the short distance to the Italian restaurant.

"Wow." She glanced around the enormous room while he spoke to the hostess.

They were seated at a table for two by the wall of windows with a view looking over the ocean. The table's location was spectacular. It was as if they were seated on a patio. Where stone walls and pillars met the ceiling, eves covered in Spanish tile jutted out from the juncture. In the center of the room, a gnarled tree rose and lanterns hung from the green leafy branches. Buff and gray bricked archways with the travertine floor lent a homey feel. Old world charm came to mind. Not to mention romantic.

There weren't many people in the restaurant. Maybe forty at the max.

"So tell me about Scott's date. Did he meet someone last night or on the tour today?"

Again, she asked about Scott. Why? He didn't want to ask because it would be awkward and borderline rude in his opinion.

"Last night. Not much to tell. He said he met someone and wouldn't be joining us tonight. I wasn't about to share our evening details in exchange for the tale of his night of celebration."

"Thank you." She blushed as her eyes dropped to the menu.

He ordered a bottle of Remole Rosso and waited for the waiter to leave before continuing their conversation. "Some things are meant to be kept private." He and Scott shared a lot of things, but their sexual escapades weren't one of them. "What looks good to start with?"

"I'm going to try the spinach salad. Sounds delicious and light."

The waiter arrived with the wine. After pouring a bit for Robert to taste, he filled both glasses and took their orders.

Once the waiter left the table, Robert lifted his wine glass. "To taking chances."

"Chances." Liz lifted her glass and her tongue glided across her bottom lip.

Whether she did it on purpose or not, he didn't care. He liked it and the flooded memories of last night in his bed.

He cleared his throat. "So, how was the beach?"

"It was beautiful. The sand was heavenly, in softness and color. I even ventured into the ocean to cool off. I thought it would be good for my ankle, and it was. Although the water was warm, it was cold on my warm skin after being in the sun."

"Sounds inviting."

"You have no idea. It was so relaxing. At one point, I did take a short siesta. I was surprised how tired I was when I got back on board." Her eyes lowered to the table and looked back at him flirtatiously. "It could also be due to the lack of sleep last night." A salacious grin broadened across her face.

"You're playing the devil's advocate." He no longer thought of Scott as a possible threat.

"Whatever do you mean?" She cocked her head, wearing the naughty grin.

"Oh, I think you know." He chuckled as his body warmed with thoughts of having sex with her again. "Changing the subject, are you going to go horseback riding?"

"I am. My ankle hurts slightly, but I think it'll be okay. There's little walking involved. I'll rest once we're done riding and put my ankle up. How was your drinking tour?"

He laughed. "You don't get enough alcohol that I'd call it a drinking tour. It was very interesting though. Without going into the boring details of the brewery, it really intrigued me since I'm in building and design. We got to see the brewing process before tasting the different beers they produce. Then it was on to the Rum Cake Factory." He sipped his wine.

"Did you enjoy that tour?"

"Oh my God, the cakes were delicious. I bought a couple; they're that good. The history of how they started was interesting."

"I'm listening," she said, inviting him to continue.

"A husband and wife team built the first rum company in the early eighties, in the Cayman Islands. The Rum Cakes began in the late eighties when the wife made the first cake from a family recipe incorporating the rum. When the demand for the cakes became high, they established a bakery. The bakery produces five to six thousand cakes per day, and they hand glaze each one. It was something to see. I must admit, I purchased more than a couple of the cakes."

Her eyes grew big. "How many did you buy?"

"Six. Don't judge; some are gifts." They laughed, and sipped their wine.

The server delivered their meals.

"We finished with the tour of Seven Fathom's Rum, which was similar to the beer tour. They actually age their rum under the water, off the coast, in white oak bourbon casks. The name comes from the depth of the water where the casks are placed."

"Under the water? Really?"

"Yeah. I guess the rocking motion of the waves plays a role in the aging process. Who would've thought of such a thing? The rum was good, so you've got to give them credit."

"So, tomorrow you're doing more drinking, right?" Her eyebrows arched.

"Jose Cuervo Tequila tasting, as well as learning about the tequila making process."

"I couldn't drink the tequila straight." Liz puckered her lips and shook her head with a sour face. "Now put it in a margarita and I'm good to go."

They finished their meal talking about the cruise. With their last bites, their server approached, and they ordered dessert and coffee.

"Liz, when we get back," he proceeded with caution, "how would things work with your mother-in-law if we're to have a relationship?"

"Are you saying you want to continue seeing me after we return? Only me. No other women?"

"Yes, I'd like to see what happens. We talked about it. But I wonder about you and well, from what you've told me, I guess there's a bit of apprehension on my behalf."

The server set the coffees and cream on the table.

"There are things I need to work on personally, as far as dealing with my mother-in-law and her controlling how I handle dating." She stared into her coffee cup.

"What do you mean control? You control yourself." He was confused.

"I know, but she's very opinionated. She doesn't care who she hurts with her words. I avoid the woman as much as possible, but my children are her grandchildren. I can't keep them from her, or the rest of Gregory's family." Her hands gripped the cup.

"After the way you spoke of her the other night and now tonight, I feel a bit sorry for her." He tipped his head to the side.

"Sorry?" Her voice rose. "How can you feel sorry for *her*?" Although she lowered her voice, her face turned stern. "She refuses to seek treatment, when she obviously needs it because she blames me for something I didn't do. She's making my life miserable."

They both sat in silence until the server arrived with the desserts. Liz stabbed at the Tiramisu and shoved a bite in her mouth. Contemplating his next words, he sampled his chocolate tart before sipping his coffee.

"Liz, you control your life. If she's making you miserable, it's because you're allowing her to make your life miserable." Under the table, he rested his hand on her knee and spoke as kindly as possible. "You make your own happiness. In any of your previous dates, if you wanted to continue them, you would've. I believe you're using your mother-in-law as an excuse, when it was you who wasn't ready to commit to more."

"How dare you." She lowered her voice, scooted her chair away from the table, and rose. "You have no right to judge me and tell me what I need to do. Take a good look at yourself, Mr. Burnhamwood. Dating multiple women at once. Talk about not being able to commit to one person. Good night."

He didn't try to stop her from leaving. He believed his opinion regarding her mother-in-law was true. However, her words stung like a lone bee in search of its nectar. He was the only one who could remove the buried stinger. If he and Liz were meant to continue beyond the cruise, then both of them would need to face the issues and stop running from them.

* * * *

Why did the night start so right, only to turn south as they neared the end of their meal? Liz couldn't figure out why Robert felt the need to bring her mother-in-law into their conversation. Pushing harder than necessary, the door to her room slammed against the jam. She cringed.

Her hands in fists, she threw her arms up and grunted in frustration. "Why?"

Again, with more force than needed, she slid the patio door until it bumped hard and jerked on the stop. She plopped on the closest chair, swung up her leg to rest her foot on the railing. Inside her head, an argument played out.

Don't sit around and pout. Go to one of the shows. Do something.

Her ankle was a little sore. She wanted to go riding tomorrow and enjoy the day.

So, who was making her life miserable now? She couldn't blame her mother-in-law for this mess. She wasn't here.

She and the ensuing discussion screwed up everything.

She yanked her foot off and stood at the railing. Shaking her head, she took a deep breath before slowly releasing the air. She closed her eyes and lowered her chin to her chest, defeated. Had she responded too harshly to Robert? She thought about what he said.

"You control your life," he had said. "You're allowing her to make your life miserable. You make your own happiness. If you wanted to continue with them, you would've. You're using your mother-in-law as an excuse, when it was you who wasn't ready to commit to them."

Had her relationships failed because of her and not her mother-in-law? Did Robert have a point? Was she using Ellen as an excuse? Could she have a relationship and stand up to Ellen as she did on Christmas Day?

She went inside and picked up the phone to order ice for her ankle. If she didn't hear from Robert by tomorrow evening, then it was a sign he'd had enough of her and her outbursts. When the ice was delivered to her room, she took it and her journal to the deck.

Had a beautiful day at the beach today. My ankle is feeling better, but still sore. Icing it as I write this. Decided to go on the horseback tour, since the ankle isn't that bad. We'll be riding for the most part before relaxing at another beach resort. I paid a bit extra to have an umbrella today. Glad I did too. Being out in the strong sun with my light skin, I would've fried. I've gotten a nice tan that will make my friends jealous when I get back.

I wonder how everyone is at home. Yet, there's nothing I can do about it. I can't wait to see if the kids responded to my email messages. I've had a couple of confrontations with Robert, one tonight, about Ellen. I never realized I had a short fuse when it comes to talking about Ellen and how she affects my life.

Maybe I should take Robert's words into consideration. Maybe I get so defensive because I know he's right and don't want to admit it. Maybe it's time for me to fight for the relationship I want. Or is it too late now?

Liz reread her words. Did she even have a relationship with Robert, after tonight's incident? If she wanted a relationship with him, then yes, she could fight for it.

Ellen is in part to blame for not allowing some of my relationship to grow further. Allowing Ellen to get inside my head is my own fault. Not anymore. I will stand up to her next time. I will fight for this relationship with Robert.

Lightness filled her as she closed the journal. Life for her was about to change for the better. First though, she'd have to apologize to Robert again.

Chapter Fourteen

Friday evening, Abigail entered Doolittle's with her brother and sister trailing behind. Their mother was coming from the airport. Kathleen had texted Abigail that afternoon requesting they all meet her for dinner. Something was up with her mother. Normally, when she arrived back from a trip, she wanted to remain low key. The fact she wanted to see them together, directly after her flight, well, it was odd.

Abigail put her name on the waiting list for a table for four. By the time they were seated, her mother still hadn't arrived. As their soft drinks were delivered to the table, the hostess escorted Kathleen to join them. She wore a grin that spread wider than Abigail had ever seen before. Not quite the Joker's smile, but darn near.

"I'm surprised you wanted to have dinner out," Abigail said as her mother stepped to the table. "Usually you want to go straight to bed. Your trip to New York must've agreed with you."

She shed her wool coat and hung it on an available hook. "I had a wonderful time on my short getaway." The smile didn't fade. If anything, it grew. "Evan asked me to marry him."

"No," Chris's voice pierced through the din in the restaurant.

"Christine," her mother scolded. "Lower your voice."

Their waiter approached with hesitation. "Excuse me. What can I get you to drink, ma'am?"

"I'll have water with a lemon slice, please."

After the waiter stepped away, Kathleen continued. "I said yes, to Evan's proposal." She stuck her left hand out to flash the large diamond ring for them to see.

"How dare you," Chris blurted with petulance.

"How dare I? Christine, he makes me happy."

"No. You gave a promise to dad to live your life with him." Angry, Chris rushed the words. "You can't make a promise to another man. He lives in New York. How's that going work?" Her arms crossed over her chest as she slammed against the back of her chair.

Through gritted teeth, Kathleen spoke across the table directly to Chris. "You and I will discuss this at home. If you have nothing nice to say, then don't speak."

Alex took their mother's hand, twisting it side to side. "That's some rock, Mom. Congratulations." His voice lacked excitement, but wasn't filled with resentment either.

Abigail gazed at the brilliant round stone, set between two swirling bands of diamonds, showing the sparkling colors of the rainbow. The center diamond had to be at least two carats.

"Wow. That's an impressive ring, Mom. Congratulations." She hugged her mother. "I'm happy for you." She glanced at her younger sister. "Ah, what about Chris? She's still in school, and I'm sure Evan's not planning to move here. Are you going to wait until she graduates in four years?"

Silence reigned when the waiter approached with water. "Were you ready to order?"

"Could you give us a couple of minutes?" Mom lifted her menu. "Let's decide what we want and order before continuing our conversation."

Chris tapped with more force than necessary on her phone screen. "I already know what I want."

They ignored her, knowing best not to encourage her inner beast, and perused their menus. Several minutes later they ordered.

"We haven't made any plans yet." Kathleen's smile disappeared from her face. "Evan will not be moving here. His work is in New York City. I'll be moving there. I'll be closer to my parents, and at their age, I'm very happy to be moving back."

Abigail sensed her mother didn't want to discuss the situation with Chris present, especially in their current surroundings. "I'm sure Grandma and Grandpa Woodall are very happy with the news."

"They are." Mom's sunny disposition returned. "Evan actually asked my father for his permission and for my mother's blessing. So they knew all along what this trip was about."

"How did he propose?" With her sister upset, and her brother not into the whole relationship thing, Abigail carried on the conversation with her mother.

"Of course, he proposed on New Year's Eve." She turned and faced her, giddy as a child receiving a sweet treat. "We went to a party, where we stayed until midnight and kissed, and then he asked if we could leave. I told him that was fine. We stepped outside and there was a carriage waiting for us. It took us for a ride around Central Park and midway he pulled the box from a pocket. I had tears in my eyes before he even spoke."

"How romantic. I'm really glad you've found someone, Mom."

"Thank you, Abigail." She looked to her two other children and her smile dimmed. "So, how was New Year's for you guys?"

"It was good. Alex had a couple friends over, as did Chris."

Their food was served, and they talked while eating.

"Christine, who did you invite to join you for the holiday?"

Getting no response, Abigail answered for Chris. "Paige and Emily. They had a good time."

"You know I don't care for Paige, Christine." Kathleen regarded her younger daughter.

"She's my friend, not yours. So it doesn't matter what you think." She didn't look up, just kept tapping on her phone.

"I'm your mother, and it does matter what I think. She's a trouble maker with a bad mouth. She's not the kind of girl my daughter will spend time with. We'll discuss this later." She turned her focus back to Abigail. "What did you all do for the evening?"

That was their mother for you. Prim, proper, orderly, and it was her way or the highway. Abigail may have looked like her mother, but that was as far as the comparison went. She was definitely her father's daughter. Chris on the other hand was in the growing stages of becoming every bit of their mother. She had the orderly down, and it was her way or the highway. Prim and proper? Well, she was clean and organized but didn't have the manners or demeanor of a proper lady.

"The boys gamed most of the night, coming out for food, which we had plenty of. The girls flitted between Chris's room, the living room, and kitchen before crashing in the living room."

"What about you?"

"I watched movies in the living room while texting with a friend." Her stomach fluttered at the thought of David.

"A special friend?" her mother prompted with an arched eyebrow.

"I think so. He works for Dad."

"You're treading in some deep water there." It was vocalized matter-of-factly versus as a warning.

"I know, but there's no policy against dating someone in the office." Between her bites, Abigail added, "We've only been out once, but between the office and the one date, I like him. We're going out tomorrow night. Doing the holiday celebration thing."

"Well, you know your father as well as I do, so—"

"I know, Mom. I'm not going to hide it from him. I'm planning on telling him when he gets back." She stuffed a forkful of chicken and lettuce in her mouth.

"Have you heard from him?"

She finished chewing and swallowed. "No. He said he wasn't going to check in and was turning his phone off when he boarded the ship."

"He took this trip seriously. He never did that on our vacations. It was either the computer or phone keeping him from spending time with us."

"Mom." Abigail used the warning tone her mother used with Chris.

"Okay. I guess he's allowed to change and grow."

Abigail hoped he'd change his ways with women. Three girlfriends was ridiculous for a man his age. The fact that they were younger than him, one was too young, a few years older than her, gave her the creep factor.

* * * *

Liz boarded the ship, sore and exhausted Friday afternoon. It had been many years since she'd ridden a horse. The riding irritated her healing sprained ankle. She relaxed at the beach afterward but didn't stay more than an hour.

In her room, she ordered more ice from room service and took two ibuprophen to ease the pain. She was saddened there wasn't a message from Robert about dinner. Once the ice was delivered, she lay on the bed, propped her foot on a pillow, and took a nap while icing her ankle.

The alarm clock sounded, waking her from a sound sleep. It was five o'clock and still no call from Robert. Maybe they weren't back aboard the ship, which was scheduled to depart in an hour. She leisurely took her time getting ready for the evening. If no call came from Robert by the time she was ready, she'd try reaching him.

She pulled the black and white print, three-quarter length sleeve, wrap dress over her waist; adjusting the V-neck to cover her cleavage. Grabbing the black heels, she slid her good foot in first before testing the right. She wasn't sure if the ankle was too swollen for the shoe, or if it was stable enough to support her in the heels. It wasn't tight, so she walked to the patio door and back to the sink area. The heels were a go for the night. Now to call Robert.

"Hello?" His deep voice answered, sending a delightful shiver down her spine.

"Hi," she spoke with apprehension. "Robert, it's Liz."

Was he avoiding her after her outburst last night? She swallowed at the guilt.

"Listen, I'm sorry I upset you, again. I didn't mean—"

"Actually, some of what you said… Well, after my anger subsided, I thought about what you said, and you made some valid points. I'm not saying that my mother-in-law blaming me for Gregory's death is right though." She paced the small carpeted space between the bed and wall counter to the patio.

"No, she shouldn't blame you. It was an accident. However, if you want to move forward in your life with another man, it's your choice. Not hers." His tone was soft and caring with a dash of tough realism.

"I know." She paused for a moment of satisfaction with her own self-realization and determination to face her mother-in-law. "Can I join you and Scott for dinner?"

"I would love for you to join me for dinner. Scott's with his new found lady friend." They laughed. "Can I swing by and pick you up?"

"I'm all set. How about I come and pick you up?"

"That's sounds nice. I should be ready when you get here."

"See you shortly." She hung up the phone and primped her hair. Dressed, she left for Robert's room, down two levels.

As she stood at his door, the memory of her last visit warmed her chest, stomach, and thighs. Would they have sex again? Would he want to? She wanted to. Freedom without the responsibility or worry of her children made the sexual experience more enjoyable. Nervous, she swallowed the lump that formed and knocked.

The door opened and the deep purple golf shirt hugged his chest. "I love you in that color. With the grey in your hair and your tan, it makes you irresistible." As she entered, she ran her hand teasingly down his chest.

The door closed. "Do you have super powers to resist me?" He waggled his eyebrows.

She wrapped her arms around his waist and planted a kiss on his lips. "No. Do you have the power to resist me?"

In answer, his arms slid around her back and pulled her tight against him. The man had an erection—from a kiss? He applied more pressure to her lips as his tongue sought more from her and the kiss. She grew weak in the legs and knew if they didn't stop, they wouldn't make it to dinner. Did she care? No.

Robert eased from her lips, kissing her throat to her breastbone, and her head fell back with desire. As his lips glided into her cleavage, his hand cupped her breast and fingers teased her nipple. His erection grew.

With delicacy, he kissed her jaw. "I want you right now." His voice was husky.

Unfastening his belt, Liz undid his pants, sliding her hand down his waistband. He sighed with her touch, but it was the moan that escaped when she took hold of his engorged length and stroked, that appeased her. She continued sliding her hand up and down, while he worked to get off his pants and boxers. Next off, his shirt, putting him in all his nude glory.

She kissed his chest, stomach to his pubic area, while she moved to squat in front of him. Slowly rolling her tongue around the head of his penis, teasing and tasting, she eased his length, sucking him further into her mouth. In and out, she worked his thickness, until he backed away on an outward pull.

She squealed in anticipation as he pulled her farther into the room. "I want you out of your clothes." He yanked off her dress. Kissing her breasts, he released the hold of her lace bra. While tossing it to the floor, he sucked a nipple as his hand worked southward, removing the matching lace panties. He grabbed her butt and pulled her into him. His cock pushed at her slickness.

Her heart raced and she spoke breathily. "We need protection."

He went to the sink area, pulled the packet from the black bag, and slid the condom on his engorged manhood. Taking the benefit of her still wearing her heels, his arm slid around her back. He bent slightly to hook his arm under her right knee and pulled her leg up. She threw her head back in a moan of pleasure as his thickness penetrated her wetness. Arching her back, she pushed him deeper within. It was with his moan, he pushed himself fully in while tightly grabbing her ass. He lifted her enough to maneuver the short distance to the wall, pushing her back against it for support.

She'd never had sex while standing. Although she didn't reach orgasm, Robert's strength and stamina to hold her and bring them both the pleasure their bodies craved, was mind blowing. What was even better, was when he did bring her the release in bed and she cried out his name.

* * * *

In her sleep, Liz squeezed Robert's chest as she snuggled her nakedness closer to his own nude body. This was the first overnight he'd had in years with a woman. In part, it was being on the cruise ship and not at home. The other part was Liz and what she was doing to him. Wanting and being monogamous after five years scared the crap out of him. He wouldn't call it love yet, but he cared a great deal about her. It shocked him that in this short time span he developed the feelings of wanting to be with her, and only her.

He wanted her in his bed, all night. He was jealous when another man flirted with her. When they were together, he wanted to touch and hold her. She made his heart beat faster by simply looking at him with her forest green eyes.

Yup, he was falling quickly, and it filled him with unease as to what the future held for them.

Today would be their last day at sea before returning to the Miami port on Sunday morning. He and Liz weren't on the same flights back to Minneapolis, so they would say their goodbyes at the airport. They had yet to exchange their personal phone numbers.

Liz had to work through her own issues. The question in the end was would she be able to solve them? Would she introduce her two young children? The biggest obstacle would be her relationship with her mother-in-law. Although Liz realized she was in part at fault for the dates not going beyond dates, it was one step to moving past the issue.

He wanted to continue to see her, but could he commit to one woman? There was one sure way to find out—try.

Chapter Fifteen

Liz leaned against her cabin door for a moment and struggled with conflicting emotions. Happy. Worry. Free. Concern. Joy.

Inside, she picked up her journal and pen and sat on the deck.

Robert and I have become very close friends. We've shared a few arguments, which have caused us to spend time away from each other. I guess you could say I'm the one to blame for our separations. Things are good now since my last revelation I wrote about Ellen and myself.

I spent the night with him in his cabin. Not sure if the word is right but cheap came to mind. I think it's because I did, as they say, the walk of shame, wearing yesterday's clothes back to my own room. I'm trying to figure out why I feel the way I do after returning to my own room. Because I don't regret spending the night. I don't regret making love to him.

I'm a woman with needs. A woman who made a choice to satisfy those needs. I like the man I chose to fill the need. Yet, he's ignited the fire in my heart. I want more from him and it scares me. Will he be honest and faithful with me? There's a new learning curve being with Robert. The other men I've dated were only dates. I never moved this quickly. Blame that on traveling alone. If I would've been with a girlfriend or the children, I would never have slept with him. God, what I would've missed!

Today is our last day aboard the ship. Tomorrow I return home. What will become of Robert and me? Will he call? Should I call him? Will we find the time to go out on a date? Will I ever get the chance to make love to him again? Love? It was sex, not love making. Maybe that's part of my problem. I'm not seeing it as sex, but as making love.

Shit! Maybe I should tell Robert that we shouldn't see each other after the cruise. Maybe I did move too quickly with him. Now I'm confused. My mind is spinning with all kinds of thoughts and questions. I need to focus on here and now.

I'm off to check email and see if the kids, Mom or Veronica responded back to my messages. I promised Robert I'd meet him up top, poolside, for lunch and a relaxing afternoon.

Showered and ready for the pool, Liz sat at an open computer station and logged into her email. Everyone replied. Love filled her chest with warmth. She opened Sarah's email first.

Mom!!!! It's so cool that you could email me from the ship! They have a bowling alley on the boat too? How cool! Hope you're having a great time and I can't wait for you to come home! I can't wait to see your pictures! Brad's being his usual self—ANNOYING. I think grandma's sending him to Grandma Farefield's. I don't mind, as long as I don't have to go. I can't wait to see you Sunday! Love you, Sarah

With a smile, Liz opened Brad's message.

Hi mom. It was fun to get a message from you. Glad you're having fun. I can't wait for you to come home. I am going to grandma and grandpa Farefields for a couple of days. See you later. Brad

She was impressed he remembered to capitalize and punctuate at the end of his sentences. Writing wasn't his strongest subject at school. At least he responded. She didn't respond to the kids since she'd see them tomorrow night. Next, she opened her mother's email.

Liz, It was such a pleasant surprise to see an email from

you. I'm glad you're enjoying yourself and like the ship. I want to hear more about this man you ran into. You didn't say much about him. The kids are just fine. They have their moments. I've talked to Ellen, and Brad is spending Wednesday through Friday with them. She wasn't too happy when I explained that Sarah didn't want to stay with them. I told her Sarah made plans early on with some of her girlfriends. That seemed to satisfy the woman. I'm looking forward to seeing your pictures and hearing about your trip. Your father's picking you up at the airport while the kids and I will be making dinner for all of us at your house. We'll see you then sweetheart. Love, Mom

Liz sent a quick response to her mom, acknowledging tomorrow night and the email in general. Lastly, it was time to read Veronica's email.

Liz, What are you doing sending me an email while on your cruise? Then again, I was ecstatic to hear you met someone. Not to mention someone you already know and that lives in the area. What are the chances? Don't bother to answer. I hope you have more to tell me when you get back. Speaking of, call me, so we can set up a time to have lunch or dinner and talk in person. This isn't something to talk about over the phone or email or text. I want to see you. Plus, I need to tell you a few things. Hope the weather got better and things heated up between you and this guy, Robert. Talk to you soon, Veronica

Liz didn't reply and would call her Monday night after she was home and settled. Glancing at the time, she had time to peek in and see if new pictures were posted of her newest niece and nephew.

Sure enough, there were plenty of pictures shared on Facebook. It was the picture of Mallory holding baby Ashley that caught her attention. Mallory's eyes were moist, like she was on the verge of tears. Liz wondered how her sister was holding up with the pending divorce.

* * * *

138

Robert and Liz made plans when they were poolside to spend their last evening with dinner and a show in the theater. The show ended and they remained sitting, not in a hurry to leave. "Come sit on my lap." Robert patted his legs and winked.

"I think I'll stay safely here in my own seat. You have that naughty gleam in your eye."

He rested his elbows on the armrest between them. "Me, naughty? Never."

She leaned toward him. "Yes, you."

He seized the opportunity to kiss her and was pleased she didn't back away. They hadn't shown affection in public aboard the ship. It made him wonder if she would be demonstrative once they were at home. One is more liberated when away from their peers and normal surroundings. For him, it was never an issue. Kimberly loved taking risks in public with their sexual escapade. *What are you doing, thinking of other women?*

"What are you thinking about?" Liz cocked her head to the side and her eyes searched his.

He placed his hand at the back of her neck, and feverishly took possession of her mouth. After a moment, he put his mouth to her ear. "I would love to have you right here." He backed his head away, but his hand remained at her neck.

Large, round green eyes expressed her shock. As her eyes darted, they exposed her fear.

"Sit on my lap," he whispered in her ear. "That's all you have to do."

Her head turned. "We can't."

"Oh, but we could. Do you trust me?"

"Yes, but no, we can't."

"Trust me." He removed his hand, sat back in his seat and patted his lap.

"Hey." Scott maneuvered between the seats closer to them and out of the departing crowd in the aisle. That ruined the moment. "Robert, I'll catch up with you either once we've disembarked or at the airport. Liz, it was a pleasure meeting you. Maybe we'll see each other again."

"Scott, I'd love to share some of the pictures, if they turned out. Can

I get your contact info?"

"Sure. Since we don't have anything to write it on, Robert can give it to you or you can always reach me at the office. Have a fun night." Scott winked with a smile and joined a brunette woman waiting back a few rows.

"Since Scott interrupted, what would you like to do now?" Robert adjusted himself on the seat.

"Hijack the ship and keep it from returning?" They laughed. "But then again, I do miss my children, so living on the ship forever isn't a possibility."

"You can live on a cruise ship, you know."

"I know, but that's luxury living, and I don't live in luxury. I'd like to get to bed at a decent time since I'll be up early to get off the ship. It's going to be another long day tomorrow."

Jokingly, he said with a smile, "We could go to bed right now, if you'd like."

Her hand cupped the side of his face. "Not tonight, love." Spoken softly, his heart skipped a beat as the endearment almost held meaning.

Neither spoke. He clasped her hand to his lips and kissed the top. Slowly, he turned it palm side up and kissed her wrist. Then he kissed the crook of her elbow, her collarbone, and finished with a longer kiss to her soft lips.

When he backed his face away, she bit her lower lip and drew it into her mouth.

"Robert, I didn't mean to say love." Her words fumbled as she spoke. "I mean not that I don't have feelings for you."

The word held a lot of meaning. Although he was relieved she didn't mean it, it hurt too.

"It's okay." He didn't want her to try to explain. "I understand." And he did. "Would you like to go to your room?" If she would've admitted to loving him, he wondered if he would have reciprocated.

"I don't want to go to bed yet. Let's go for a walk." They stood and left the aisle.

"Do you want to go up to the pool deck or to the jogging track?" They slowly approached the last of the show attendees by the doorway. The passionate heat from earlier was gone. He wondered if she would've come to him if Scott hadn't interrupted. There was a hint of interest in her eyes, yet he'd also caught fear as well.

"Let's take the stairs up to the track." She took his hand in hers as he led them up the stairs.

"Your ankle must be feeling better."

"It does."

They quietly walked up and out to the track. Robert slid his arm around her waist when she stepped to the railing. "Don't want to walk anymore?"

"Robert, I'm going to be busy when we get back. With my kids, it can be difficult to find time."

"What are you saying? I thought we were going to try or are you giving up before we even have a chance to see what can happen?" His heart fell to the pit of his stomach.

"No, I'm not giving up." Her words put his heart back where it belonged. "I want you to understand if things become challenging."

"Since both Scott and I were out of the office, I'm not sure what to expect either."

"Robert, I don't know when or if I'll tell my kids about you. They only met one of the men I was seeing and it was because I thought…. Well, I regret introducing him to them because it didn't last beyond two weeks after they met him."

He pulled her into an embrace. "One step at a time." He kissed her. "The first step will be saying good bye at the airport. The second step is connecting once we're back in the real world. Now it's time to enjoy the moment we're in." He planted a firmer kiss on her lips and her arms wrapped tight around him.

She looked at him with sultry eyes. "Can we go to my room?"

"You said not tonight." He tucked stray hairs behind her ear.

"I meant that I can't stay all night. Of course I want to…"

"We can do whatever you want tonight."

"Do you have," she glanced around and whispered, "protection?"

He answered with a kiss before taking her hand and leading them inside.

* * * *

Liz opened her door and Robert walked past, sending a ripple of excitement to her thighs. The mere suggestion of having sex with her, in public, in the theater, had her aroused. She couldn't believe she gave it a thought. Thank God, Scott interrupted; otherwise, she could have made a mistake.

The door closed, and she leaned her forehead against it for a moment. When she turned around, he sat on the sofa. He patted his lap. Her heart thudded. She kicked her shoes off and under the counter at the foot of the bed. She licked her lips and swallowed in anticipation of what her last night with Robert would bring.

Sitting sideways on his lap, her hands met stubble when she caressed his face. She ran her thumb over the dimple on his square jaw. The yellow in his eyes was over powered by green as his pupils dilated. Her thumb ran across his lower lip. He snagged her thumb, sucking it into his mouth. His hands moved at her waist, but they maintained their heady eye contact.

Her breathing quickened when he spun her by the hips turning her away from him, while he drew the back of her dress to her hips. His hands skimmed across her bare thighs under her dress. He pulled the slight piece of fabric to the side and slipped his fingers between her thighs. She spread her legs and while he slightly lifted her, he slid under her and into her warmth.

He held her by the hips as he rocked ever so slightly. She cried out in pleasure and leaned forward. His hands released her hips, quickly cupping her mouth and one breast to pull her back up against him.

"I want to show you," he spoke low in between breaths, "what it would've been like… if I had my way with you… in the theater. Stay quiet and still." He thrust his hips and buried himself deeper as her body shuddered with the pleasure of his voice and body.

* * * *

It wasn't a secret they had feelings for each other, so what would tonight's date bring? With calm nerves, David rang Robert's apartment from the locked entryway.

"Hello," Abigail answered with a touch of excitement in her voice.

"I'm a little early." Maybe he was a touch excited, too, for their evening together.

"I'll buzz you in."

The buzzer sounded. He pulled the door and strode down the hallway. After knocking, he stepped inside a large entryway, which appeared to be the main hall of the apartment. "Hey Abigail, I'm here." The apartment smelled tropical with hidden notes of musk and wood.

"Make yourself comfortable." Her voice carried from the room to his right. "I need a few more minutes."

Noticing the beautiful wood floor, he took off his shoes. Walking a short distance, he met something like a trident in the road. To his left there was a bathroom and two bedrooms. If he took a sharp right to where he heard Abigail's voice, he guessed it would be another bedroom. The middle 'roadway' was where the wood floor continued to flow, and he entered the open concept dining room, which moved into the spacious, modern kitchen. The place was huge. He approached the patio door and gazed out to an open area with bare trees and shrubs. The view wasn't bad. Not that you could see the Mississippi River below, but you knew it was there below the bluff and tree line.

"Nice, huh?" Her voice startled him.

He turned from the glass and entered the living room. "Yeah. This is a nice-sized apartment." The decorations were sparse throughout the large living area, but it wasn't bare. Robert kept it clean and simple. The furnishings didn't come cheap though. Leather furniture with beautiful wood accent tables filled the room.

"My dad needed something for when my brother and sister come and stay. They each have their own rooms, and if I stay over, my sister and I share her room." She met him at the couch separating the kitchen area from the living room.

"I kind of forgot about them. It makes sense then. You look great." She wore a blue colored sweater intensifying her blue eyes. "Are you ready for a night of fun?"

She wrapped her arms around his neck with her body against him. "Yes. Starting now."

Before he could speak, her lips possessed his with a kiss. His hands on her hips slid down to cup her small firm ass, pressing her into his groin.

When they parted for air, he panted. "I think we should leave before our plans change." It was her fragrance and not a room freshener that spelled so good when he first entered the apartment.

"So you're not the flexible type when it comes to plans. Too bad." She spun out of his arms and stepped away.

He pinched her behind, making her squeal, and spun her to face him. "Oh, I can be very flexible… I just want to wait." As much as he wanted to be with her in the most personal way two humans could, he wanted to take his time with her.

"Okay, we wait. Are you ready to go then?"

"Did you want a coat tonight? Your sweater's not heavy and it's cold outside." He released her from the embrace.

"It's hanging up." She sauntered to the front door and he followed.

A suitcase sat in the entryway, piquing his curiosity. "When are you going home?"

"Tomorrow. My dad's flight gets in sometime in the evening." She opened a door and stepped into a large room with a tiled floor. It was a combination laundry, hall closet, and pantry.

"You're not hanging around to see him and hear all about the trip?"

"No, I'm ready to get back to my place. I'm sure they'll talk about it to everyone in the office on Monday. I'll hear about it then."

He helped her with the coat. She held the apartment door open, and he entered the hall.

"So, we're going bowling?" She locked the door and they headed for the building entrance.

"Yeah. You've bowled before, right?" He slid his fingers between hers.

"Of course. We learned how to bowl in elementary school."

"Well, off we go then." He swung their arms to-and-fro like school kids do when they're carefree and skipping along. This earned him a chuckle from her.

He drove to the bowling alley. "Remember when I told you to tell me when you wanted to go home, I'd take you home—when we went to dinner?"

"Yeah."

"Well, you made the comment that you'd learned your lesson over the years to speak up. I've been wondering what the story is." He glanced at her. "Care to share?"

"There really isn't much of a story. I've just been stuck in places I didn't care to stay at because I was afraid to say I wanted to leave. It wasn't until my second year of college that I found my voice and the strength to stand up for what I wanted. Sorry if you thought it was going to be a more exciting story."

"No, I'm glad it wasn't due to a bad incident." He took her hand in his.

She turned away from the window. "So how was New Year's Eve? How's your Aunt Cait and uncle?"

"It was uneventful at work. The pub was busy all night. The crowd was well behaved and didn't get out of control, which is always a bonus. I was there until after two. I've been looking forward to this night with you." Releasing the hold of her hand, he exited the highway.

"I can't believe you drove all the way out here to go bowling."

"Lakeville isn't that far." He defended his choice of bowling lanes.

"We could've gone to The Nook on Hamline and Randolph. Bowling and food all in one." She stared at the lit Brunswick Zone XL sign.

"This is a straight shot off 35." He parked the car in the busy lot.

"I know. I grew up not far from here."

Leaving the car, they met each other and walked inside the building. The noise hit them as soon as they opened the door. Kids and adults played in the arcade to the right of the entrance. The restaurant had TVs playing, music blared from somewhere farther inside, the crash of bowling pins, and the thuds of bowling balls on the alley resounded.

"Let's eat first." He gently pulled her hand in the direction of the restaurant.

* * * *

"I still can't believe you out-bowled me." David glanced at her and refocused on the road. "Are sure you're not a professional?"

Abigail laughed. "Yes, I'm sure. Elementary school wasn't the last time I went bowling. My dad likes to bowl, so we went often as kids."

At times, he seemed to get distracted, she caught him checking out her rear as she stepped to the lane for her turn. Probably gave her an advantage. With that thought, she smiled.

"At least you didn't out-shoot me in pool. That would've been an embarrassment."

"Yeah, I suck at pool, but I have fun playing. We were pretty even at air hockey though."

She liked a game of friendly competition. Her pool game was bad, but tonight it was thrown off because she was turned on by her competitor. Although his jeans weren't tight, they fit right to show off his tight ass. His muscles flexed and bulged during play through the long sleeves of his shirt.

He took the exit to Shepard Road. They were close to her dad's place.

"Did you want to come in for a while?" She hoped finally to have the chance to explore his body, minus clothing.

"Yes." He maneuvered into a parking space in front of the building.

"Let's see if we can find a movie we both like. I'll pop some popcorn, and we can snuggle on the couch." Getting out, she waited for him to come around to the sidewalk.

In front of her dad's apartment door, she unlocked and pushed the door open. She yanked him inside by the hand, kicked the door closed, pushed him against the wall, and kissed him with a burning desire. He returned the kiss, but quickly ended it.

"Abigail.... Not yet."

"It's because of my father, isn't it?" She backed away. Using more force than needed, she shrugged off her coat with a clenched jaw.

"Yes and no."

In the laundry room, she yanked a hanger from the rod. "What does that mean?" Her coat hung, she stepped partially out of the doorway. "Your coat." His jacket hung, she went into the kitchen without a word.

"I want you, you know that." He trailed behind her. "We're at your dad's place. The man doesn't know we're in a relationship. You've made it clear he's against us dating. To have our first time be at his place, in his bed, is all wrong. Plus, I want to wait, which is so not me."

"Okay, I didn't need to know that last bit of info." She tossed the popcorn into the microwave and pushed buttons with more force than needed.

"I'm sorry, I didn't mean for it to sound like that." He approached, putting his arms around her to rest on the stovetop. "It's not like I sleep around with any woman that comes my way—"

"I don't want to hear an explanation or about your conquests. I get it. You don't want to have sex here, and you want to wait. So, we'll wait until you're ready."

She may have been disappointed about not getting her way with him tonight, but he had some valid points. It could've been awkward to have sex in her dad's bed.

"Let's grab something to drink and find a movie."

Chapter Sixteen

Liz awoke to the sun rising. The patio drapes and door were open. The ship had docked in Miami. She rolled to the empty space where Robert once lay. Pulling his pillow against her, she inhaled the scent of his cologne. She wanted to remember what he smelled like. After several minutes of slowly drawing in his scent, she got up and closed the patio door and drapes for privacy.

The crew unloaded the baggage from the ship to the deportation station. She had set her large suitcase in the hall last night for the porters to take away. The next time she'd see it, would be after she'd landed back in Minneapolis. At least she hoped the bag would make it home.

As she flopped onto the couch, filled with a mix of emotions, memories of what Robert did with her on the couch stirred in more emotions. She never wanted the cruise to end, yet she couldn't wait to get home to her kids and family. To have Robert every night beside her reawakened desire, yet she was scared to death to have a man around again.

She showered, dressed, and packed the rest of her items in the carry-on bag. Checking all drawers and the closet, and certain she had everything, she glanced around the room and smiled. The time away had been wonderful, and she would always have her memories. Those final memories would remain with her for days. They made love twice more before Robert left her room. It turned out to be a late night, and he left after three in the morning. A nap on the plane was in order if she planned to have any energy for the night ahead at home.

Leaving the room, she slowly made her way through the crowds disembarking the ship and meandering through the customs checkpoint.

This saved everyone from having to deal with customs at the airport. Occasionally, she glanced around to see if she could spot Robert or Scott, but didn't have any luck.

Seated on a coach bus bound for the airport, she dug out her cell phone and turned it on for the first time in a week. It vibrated and binged, notifying her of messages. She tapped the screen and read the messages, saving Robert's for last.

Until we see each other again, thank you. xoxo

She wasn't sure how to respond. The hugs and kisses endearment was welcomed. It was the thank you that threw her for a loop. What was he thanking her for? The companionship, the sex, or both? Or was this his way of saying good-bye? Staring at the message, she thought about what to type.

I hope we can... delete. Sounded like she was giving up on them. *Call me tonight...* delete. That message would've read as desperate. *I look forward to our next date. xoxo* Perfect.

She tapped SEND, closed her messages, and rested her head against the seat as the ocean disappeared out the window. The city landscape on the way to the airport took its place. The palm trees and grass would become a thing of the past. The cold temps had reached Florida—they dipped into the low fifties. To a Minnesotan during winter, this was shorts and flip-flops weather. She had made sure to wear pants on the return flight home, but the sandals remained on her feet.

The clock seemed to stop as Liz waited for her flight. Time couldn't pass fast enough. She wanted to see her family. On the plane, she couldn't nap. Her mind filled with what she needed to do before work tomorrow, what she wanted to do when she got home, and any other little item that could squeeze into the whirlwind of thoughts. She passed the time listing items as they came to mind then arranging them in order of importance.

As the plane made the first touch on the ground, she slowly inhaled and exhaled. Landing was not her favorite thing in the world. Her hands clutched and her eyes closed as the plane bounced before stabilizing and coasted on the landing strip. The plane reduced speed.

Her eyes opened as her fingers released their death grip on each other. There was no snow on the ground. The pilot informed them earlier about the below freezing temps. Her excitement grew as they taxied to the gate, but patience would be required once they were allowed off the plane.

While waiting for her turn to deplane, she called her father. "Hi, Dad, the plane has landed."

"Sweetie, how are you?"

"I'm good. Glad to be home. Listen, I don't have time to talk because we're getting off the plane. I'll meet you outside at the baggage claim area. Remember I'm at terminal one. The big airport."

"Got it. I'm on my way."

The call ended, and she tucked her phone safely in her purse before removing her bag from the overhead. Standing in the aisle, the slow moving line of passengers made its way to the jetway. Not in a hurry, because her father was just leaving the house, she kept to the right of the walkway and strolled slowly into and through the airport. It would take some time for the luggage to be unloaded and put onto the baggage carousel.

After some time, Liz spotted her suitcase and retrieved it from the carousel's moving belt. After a double check to verify it was her bag, she managed to get through the crowd and stepped to the exit windows to watch for her father. Occasionally, she went out into the cold to see if he was waiting farther down the way. When he arrived, she moved quickly to get the suitcase in back and hopped in the car to get warm.

"Thanks, Dad." She leaned over and hugged him.

"You look great. I'm glad you took the time to go on this trip. You deserved it." He pulled from the curb, heading for home.

"I couldn't have gone if it weren't for you and Mom being able to watch the kids. Would you mind if we stopped somewhere so I could print off some pictures?"

"No, where do you want to go?"

"One of the stores closest to the house. Where's the snow?" She looked out the passenger window to see holiday decorations and brown grass and bare roadways.

"We got a dusting on New Year's Eve, but it all melted with the two warm days following. Now we're back in the deep freeze."

"It's weird not seeing snow when it's so cold. What's the forecast for the week?"

"Cold temps for the first part, but by Thursday they're saying we should be above thirty-five degrees."

"Any chance of snow?"

"There are a couple of days where there is a slight chance. How was your weather? Your mother told me you emailed and said it was raining the one day." He pulled onto the freeway and the airport was behind them.

"That was the only day we had rain and it cleared by afternoon. The sun and sand were so nice. Not to mention the beautiful ocean. As much as I wanted to come home, I wanted to stay in the Bahamas." Stay with Robert. Stay in the comfort of his arms.

"Did you meet any interesting people?"

"Did Mom tell you I ran into Robert, the man who designed the clinic?" She spoke as casually as possible.

"I think she did."

"Well, I spent some time with him and his business partner, Scott, who was traveling with him. It was embarrassing because I literally ran into him the first day aboard the ship. He recognized me, and we started talking." She gazed through the window at the brown ground.

"Does he still live here?"

"Yeah. He's living in St. Paul close to where his company is located." Her heart raced.

"Honey?"

She turned to face her dad.

"Are you going to see him again?" His eyebrows arched in that familiar concerned way. He must have guessed something happened between her and Robert, but not at what level.

Her face warmed. "We're going to try. I'm not saying anything to the kids though."

"I understand."

They fell silent until they approached the drugstore close to her place. Her father waited in the car while she went inside and printed the pictures. She didn't print all of them, but enough to show everyone the basics. There were several of her and Robert, and a couple with Scott that she printed duplicates to share. She planned to deliver Robert's copies in person.

Once in the car again, it was a matter of five minutes and her dad pulled in the driveway. Home. Family. Sadness washed over her because there was one thing missing in her life—a man at home. Although she was scared at the thought, she missed Robert. That brought on a feeling of guilt as she approached the house she once shared with Gregory. Mentally shaking her head, she put a cheerful smile on her face and opened the door.

* * * *

Sunday afternoon, Abigail walked from the garage upstairs to the main floor of her house. The ruckus of booming male voices was unexpected. She turned and entered the large open family room into the kitchen. Conrad, Paul, and five other guys focused on the football game while eating pizza from the boxes on the huge square coffee table.

"Hey," she yelled over the TV. "I'm back."

Paul turned and met her at the kitchen island. "If you want some pizza, we have plenty. How was it staying at your dad's?"

"Nice, actually. The heated garage was the best part." She opened the fridge and grabbed a beer. "How were things here? Did you guys go out or have a New Year's Eve party?"

"We all went out. Gina went with her new boyfriend while Conrad and I went to a party. How was yours?"

"Fine. You know I watched my brother and sister, so nothing spectacular. I'm okay with it though. I got to celebrate last night with my boyfriend."

"Boyfriend?" Paul choked on the word.

"You okay?" She stepped to his side in case she needed to assist him in some way.

"Swallowed wrong." He coughed to clear his throat. "When did this happen?"

"Um, it's a new relationship. You'll all meet him soon, I'm sure.

Gina working?"

"I think so. Between school, work, and her boyfriend, we haven't seen her much."

They walked together into the living room.

"Look who's back," Paul announced.

"Just stealing a slice and I'll leave you to your game." She snagged a slice loaded with everything.

"I can make room for you, right here." Conrad patted his lap, as she took a bite.

"You'll have to find someone else, bro. She's got a new guy." Paul jabbed at his best friend while she backed out of the seating area.

Conrad walked with her to the stairs. "Care to tell me about him?"

"No. You'll meet him eventually." She seized her suitcase. "When I think you're ready." She chewed on another bite.

"What's that supposed to mean?" He dropped back as she strolled upstairs.

"You tend to be a little 'in your face' when I've brought home dates."

Cheers burst out from the guys watching the game.

"I'm just looking out for you. I don't want to see you get hurt."

She swallowed. "And you didn't hurt me?"

"Ouch. I thought we'd moved past that." Hurt was visible in his eyes.

She shouldn't have brought it up. "I'm sorry. It's in the past. But you need to remember I'm a grown woman who makes her own choices. I'm not the young girl you once knew." The pizza crust remained.

"I'll always be protective of you, Abigail."

"I appreciate that. Now go watch your game. I know you're dying to find out what you missed a few seconds ago." Conrad took a few steps down while she walked toward her room. "You'll get to meet him soon. First I have to tell my dad I'm dating my co-worker."

He ran upstairs, grabbed her arm, which stopped them in front of her bedroom door. "Are you crazy?" He let go of her arm, and she finished eating. "I know your dad and he's not going to like this. Why?"

"Why what, Conrad?" She went into her room. "It's not as though I'm seeing David to upset my father. I like him, and he likes me." She tossed the bag and it settled on the bed. Unzipping it, she threw the cover open. "There's no policy against us dating."

"It's just one of those things you don't do. It creates a hostile work environment when you break up."

"When?" she screeched. "Aren't you Mr. Positive. Go back downstairs."

"I just—"

"Get out." She turned her back to him and stared into her suitcase.

When she heard his footsteps on the stairs, she closed her door. She didn't want to think about her and David breaking up. They were just starting this relationship, and she didn't want anyone to dampen her feelings.

She pulled yesterday's dirty clothes from the suitcase and tossed them in the hamper. Prior to leaving her dad's place, she did laundry, so she began putting the clean clothes away. When she opened her underwear drawer, someone had dug through them and tried to fix the mess. A bit unnerved at first, she decided maybe Gina was looking for a pair. Why would anyone want to wear someone else's underwear? She straightened the mess, and finished putting the rest away.

Unpacked, Abigail texted Gina.

Hey stranger! I'm back home. Are you going to be around tonight?

Several minutes passed.

Hey! Sorry, not tonight. I'm working and then I have class in the morning.

This might be an odd question, but did you go through my underwear drawer?

Ew!!! No, that's just gross! I mean I know they're clean but, no. Why?

Someone was in my drawer. You don't think one of the guys

would've been in there. Do you?

Why would they?

I don't know. Have you seen or heard anyone in my room?

Haven't been home much. When I have, it's to sleep. Jack, the guy from the party, has me literally swinging from the ceiling. OMG!

What?!

He has a sex swing and it is AMAZING!

Okay, now I'm not going to be able to look this guy in the face. I don't know if I'll be able to look you in the face again.

I've gotta go. Sorry I can't help with the underwear thing.

"Well, that was interesting. Not the direction I thought the conversation would go, but interesting." Abigail looked around her room and then went downstairs to join the guys watching the game.

* * * *

Liz barely got inside the front door when the kids latched onto her. The kids talked over one another.

"Wait, one at a time. It's so good to see you." She hugged Sarah and twisted to hug Brad, whom she held the longest. "I missed you guys. Let me get my bags taken care of and then I'll tell you all about it. I have some pictures to share too."

"Sarah, come help me in the kitchen." Her mother, Janice, stood in the opening of the kitchen area. "Brad, you can tell your grandpa about the game. Let's give your mom a minute." She sidestepped the kids and embraced Liz. "You look great. It's good to have you home."

"Thanks, Mom. I'll be right down. Is dinner ready?"

"Whenever you're ready."

"I'll unpack; then we can eat before I tell you about the trip."

Plopping the big suitcase on the bed, she opened it and dug between the layers of clothes to pull out the gifts for everyone. She removed the pictures of Robert and Scott from the picture envelope. On top was the picture of her and Robert at dinner in the Italian restaurant. It was the best picture of them together. She tucked them in her nightstand before joining the family.

She strolled into the kitchen area, which smelled of warm spices. "So what are we having for dinner?"

"I taught Sarah how to make chili." Her mother stepped from the counter and handed Sarah the breadbasket. "I thought the leftovers would be nice for you."

"Yum. I thought that's what I smelled when I first walked into the house. Thank you."

"Doug," Janice raised her voice. "We're eating."

"All right. I'm coming." He was slow to stand, focused on the football game.

"Go ahead, Liz."

"Thanks again, Mom." She filled a bowl and sat at the kitchen table. Waiting for her parents to join her, she spotted Sarah spooning chili in a bowl. "Sarah, are you eating chili?"

"It looked and smelled so good when I was helping grandma, I wanted to try some. I'm just taking a little." Sarah sat beside her, while Brad remained in the living room watching TV.

"Good."

Conversation focused on what happened at home while she was away. What they did with their time and who they spent it with. It was when her mother brought up her mother-in-law that sparked Brad to jump into the conversation.

"I heard Grandma say something about you going away to be wild and that you're nothing but a floozy. What does that mean, Mom?"

"It means—"

"It wasn't very nice of her to say that, Brad." She quickly silenced her daughter. Her ten-year-old son didn't need to know what floozy meant. "Did she tell you this? Or did you overhear her talking?"

He dropped his head and spoke quietly. "I overheard her talking on the phone."

"Honey, that's okay. You did nothing wrong. Floozy isn't a very nice word, but it's a way to describe a person's behavior. Particularly, a woman's. Okay?" For Ellen to speak of her this way upset her, but to have said it while Brad was around to overhear, made her angry.

"Okay."

"We're almost finished. Did you want to sit in the living room and hear about the trip, or do you want to stay in there with grandpa and watch the game?"

Her mother gave her father a displeased look. "Doug, can't you step away from the game long enough to hear about your daughter's trip?"

"No. I missed the ending of the first game because I picked her up at the airport. What's there to hear about? A beach and ocean are the same no matter where you go. She was on a ship. I lived on one for longer periods of time when I served in the Navy. Don't need to hear about it. She told me she had a good time. That's all I need to hear. She's happy. I'm happy."

"Dad, relax. That's why I said what I said. Go watch the game. Mom will tell you all about it on the car ride home."

"See," he turned to Janice. "My daughter understands." He faced Liz with a smile of thanks. "You know your mother." He took his bowl to the sink before sitting in the lounge chair to watch the rest of the game.

"Brad, you can join us or stay with grandpa." Finished eating, they cleaned up and went to the front room. Liz pulled the pictures from the envelope and told them about each of the stops. She also shared the few pictures of the ship before giving the gifts she brought back.

"I love it. Thank you," Sarah exclaimed, jumping up and hugging her. "Will you put it on?" She handed her the braided bracelet to tie securely around her wrist. "I love the shells. They're so pretty."

"I'm glad you like it. I had a difficult time thinking of something for you. Mom, before you open yours, I know it's not appropriate, but I couldn't leave without picking one up for you."

Janice unwrapped the gift and gasped when she held the statue.

"Mom," Sarah said in a scolding tone before bursting into a fit of laughter.

"Liz, what am I supposed to do with this thing? I can't very well

157

display a man with an over exaggerated penis."

"Keep it in your room then. It's art, Mom." She snickered. "You're a teacher and should know to appreciate good art when you see it." The women burst into laughter.

Chapter Seventeen

A delayed return flight home from his wonderful, relaxing cruise left Robert exhausted. He left his suitcases in the entry hall, went to the refrigerator, and opened a beer. The crying baby and loud children at the airport, and unfortunately on his flight, had tightened his shoulders and given him a headache. He plopped on the couch, turned on ESPN to catch the results of the NFL Wild Card games.

He should've been home around five in the evening; instead, it was after eight. Not feeling like talking to anyone, he sent a group text to the family.

Just to let you know I'm home. Had a great time. Exhausted. Love Dad

Abby's message popped up first.

I'll see you tomorrow. Love you.

Glad to have you home. Alex pinged.

You have to talk to Mom! She can't get married to him! I don't want to live in New York! I won't go!! Chris responded.

Whoa. This wasn't something he wanted to come home to, or deal with tonight. So much for relaxing and watching game highlights.

A response came from Abby.

Chris, I'll talk to Dad tomorrow at work.

I'm not going! I start high school next year and all of my friends are here. I'M NOT GOING.

This news didn't bode well for Chris and her struggles since his divorce from Kathleen. Not wanting to wait until tomorrow, he called Abby.

"Hey, Dad," she answered merrily. "I thought we'd talk tomorrow."

"Catch me up now, and if I have time, you can give me more details tomorrow." He took a hit from the beer bottle.

"Mom got engaged on New Year's Eve. Plain and simple."

He choked on the beer.

"Dad, are you okay?"

"Fine." He coughed to help clear his throat and return his voice to normal. "Did she say anything about moving to New York?"

"No. They haven't made any plans. Chris is over-reacting, as usual."

"Abby, cut her some slack."

"How can I cut her slack when all she wants is for you and Mom to get back together? It's not going to happen. She needs to get it through her thick skull. Ugh." Abby's frustration came through loud and clear.

"Well, she's your sister, so have patience with her and help me to help her through this. Okay?"

"Yeah," she sighed. "You know I will. That's why I sent the text."

"I appreciated that. I just got home. The flight was delayed."

"Well, since we're talking.... Did you meet anyone?"

"I met a lot of people."

"A woman, Dad."

"Oh. Yeah, there were plenty of women aboard the ship. Had a great time, if you know what I mean." Although he had a close relationship with his oldest daughter, he wasn't ready to talk about Liz.

"Okay, I'm sorry I asked. I'll let you go now."

"Good night, Abby." They disconnected and he drank his beer.

He wasn't surprised in any way with the news of Kathleen's engagement. What shocked him was that it didn't happen sooner. Still, he wondered what her plans were for the kids. With Alex graduating late in the spring, he didn't think she'd pick up and leave prior to graduation.

Chris would be the tough one to handle in the move to New York. He'd do whatever necessary to help her with the transition. Then the thought occurred to him that maybe they could send Chris to stay with Kathleen's parents for the summer. When he talked to his ex-wife, he'd mention the idea.

Finishing his beer, he turned off the TV and showered before getting into bed. He caught the local news at ten on his bedroom TV. One of the top stories caught his attention. A sexual assault occurred on New Year's Eve. Similar to two others, in and around Abby's neighborhood, it didn't make him happy.

* * * *

A new year, a new boyfriend, and a new job. Could there be a better Monday? Abigail entered the office with a happy expression.

"Robert would like to see you in his office," the receptionist stated as Abigail neared the front desk.

"Right now?" She was a little taken aback.

"Yes."

"Okay." Wondering what was so important, her face scrunched with worry. They talked last night and were touching base later today. Having returned to work after being gone for a week, she figured he'd be plenty busy.

She approached his secretary's desk when he spoke through his open office door. "Abby, come in and close the door."

This didn't bode well. No "please" followed the order. "Have I done something wrong?" She wondered if someone got to him regarding her dating David. "Dad, give me a chance to explain." Her stomach quivered.

"Explain what? Have a seat." He wasn't harsh in the tone. If anything, she heard concern.

"If something happens between David and I—"

"Nothing's going to happen between you two. I told you I didn't want to see you get involved with him outside of work." He sat on the chair next to hers in front of his desk. "I'm concerned about your safety.

Three sexual assaults have occurred in your neighborhood. What are you doing to protect yourself?"

"Dad, I'm fine." She released a sigh. One, because it wasn't about David. Two, because it was about these attacks, and three, she'd been through this with David. "I park in the garage, and when I go out it's with another person or more. You don't need to worry." She let the David topic go and would approach him later regarding their relationship.

"Make sure you stick with that plan. Do you carry mace with you? Just in case." He remained serious.

"No. I've taken a self-defense class. I'll be okay."

"Okay, but if there are any more attacks, you're moving in with me."

"I don't think so." She laughed as she spoke. "As much as I loved the heated parking garage, I'm not moving in with my father. Have you talked to Mom yet?" She attempted to change the topic.

"We're having dinner tonight. Has Chris reached out to you since your mother returned?"

"No. I worry a little about her though. You and Mom have your hands full. Good luck." The sister relationship wasn't strong because of the eleven years between them.

"Well, if she reaches out and says or does something that concerns you, will you let me, or your mother know?" An unease settled over him.

"Of course. You look great. The cruise must've been really good."

"It was. After two days, I was able to relax and not think about checking emails. I'm glad I went." His smile was bright and filled with happiness.

There was a knock at the door. "Come in."

"Have you called her?" Scott stopped talking as soon as he spotted Abigail sitting in the chair.

Her? A woman was the reason for her dad's happiness? She caught the wide-eyed, shut-up look her father gave Scott. The smile turned into a scowl.

Her dad rose. "That's all, Abigail."

"Okay." She walked to the door with a smirk. "Scott, you look good, too."

"Thanks. The weather was perfect."

Strolling past Scott, the smirk grew into a smile. Her father had met someone on the cruise. Why else would he be upset with Scott, and why else would Scott stop talking? She'd ask Scott later.

David sat with his back to her at the shared desk space. His head was down, pouring over something. She glanced around, over the tops of the work stations, quietly approached him, and slid her hands from his shoulders down his chest.

He jumped in his seat and snapped his head around. "Are you crazy?" he whispered glimpsing first right and then left.

She removed her hands from his body. "No. I'm sorry."

"Abigail, you need to remain professional in the office." His business face softened with a playful smile on his lips. "I know I'm so attractive you can't keep your hands off me, but you'll have to contain yourself until we're alone."

"And when will we get to be alone with each other?" She cocked an eyebrow while plopping on the chair next to him.

"What are you doing tonight?" He waggled his eyebrows while leaning toward her and resting his arms on his legs.

"Nothing. Why don't you come over to my place? See where I live, meet my roomies and check out my room?"

"Do you want me to follow you home after work? We'll need to eat dinner at some point."

"You could. I could make us something to eat. You like peanut butter and jelly?" She mimicked his posture. Their foreheads resting together.

"Love it," he said theatrically.

"Good, but that's not what I'm going to make. Hopefully, I'll have the ingredients I need. Otherwise, it will be pb and j for us." They shared a laugh until someone cleared their throat.

David composed himself faster than she did. "Scott, what can we do for you?"

"Can I talk to you, Abigail?"

"Sure." A giggle subsided. "What's up?"

"Let's go to my office." Scott turned and walked away.

David shrugged his shoulders and gave her the 'I don't know' look as she got up and joined Scott.

He closed the office door when she stepped inside. "You've done nothing wrong in my book." He quickly added, "That I know. Make yourself comfortable."

She sat in front of his desk. "I haven't gotten David in trouble?" For the first time she worried about her previous actions in the office.

"Not with me, but I think he might be with your father. Does he know?"

"Know what?" Close to blowing her relationship with David and earlier with her father, she played it down with Scott.

"Abigail, I'm not blind. I knew from day one something would happen between you two. Why your father partnered you with David, I'll never understand. So, are my assumptions correct?" He sat back in his desk chair.

"Yes." She sat forward on the edge of the seat. "Please don't say anything to him. I'm planning on talking to him later."

"I won't. We did talk about it on the cruise a little. I tried to soften him, if the possibility were there. With that said, you'll need to maintain a professional relationship while working. Whether it be in the office or out for a job meeting."

"I understand. David had just given me a lecture before you came by." She relaxed against the chair.

"Good to hear. Now for the reason I wanted to talk to you. I know how you feel about your dad's girlfriends and wanting to see him settle down."

"He meet someone on the cruise?" she interjected enthusiastically and sat on the edge of the chair again.

"Yes." Scott kept his voice business like. "She's younger than your father, but close to his age. They knew each other prior to meeting on the cruise. She's a widow. Your dad helped design and build her deceased husband's medical clinic."

"You've got to be kidding. What are the odds?" She shook her head in disbelief.

"I know. Well, you could say they hit it off from the beginning. She ate dinner with us and spent most of the evenings with your dad."

"So what's the problem?"

"Your dad's hesitant to call her." He leaned forward, resting his elbows on his desk.

"Why?" Her eyebrows drew in while her face scrunched in confusion about her father's lack of action. "He doesn't have an issue with calling his girl... Oh, he has feelings for her." Her face relaxed and she grinned. "That's why he won't call her. He's afraid."

"Bingo. Abigail, you should've seen how happy she made your father. I don't know if they... but he walked on air. In the beginning, he didn't like the fact that I was attracted to her and well, making it known to her I was interested."

She laughed. "Dad was jealous of you? I love it."

"We need to get him to call her. To get them out on a date again. He's going to make all kinds of excuses, just so you know."

"No worries, I'll get him to call. I'm all over this." She gleefully rubbed her hands together.

* * * *

"Welcome back." Liz started each class the same way. "Hope you all had a fun winter break. Unfortunately, it had to end for all of us." The classroom groaned. "I'm going to make today an easy day. I'd like you to write a story, in first person point of view, about how you spent your vacation." This earned her more groans. "If you'd rather, we can start discussing and reading *The Outsiders*."

The students protested against the reading and chanted for the writing.

Holding up her hands to quiet the kids, and once they fell near silence, she stepped to the white board and wrote the assignment while continuing to explain. "You'll need to pay attention to details. Give me descriptions, settings, feelings, emotions. I want to hear your excitement in what you did, see what you saw, and feel what you experienced over the break. This will be graded and is worth twenty points." She grabbed a stack of papers from her desk. "Here's the grading scale based on what I'm looking for in your paper. Any questions?"

"Yeah, what if we didn't do anything and it was the worst break ever. What do we write?"

"Chris, please raise your hand next time. I know you did something over break. If it was the worst, then write it and make me experience what you endured that was so terrible. Make me sympathize with you."

"This assignment sucks." Chris spoke the words softly, but loud enough for Liz to hear.

"Language," she cautioned with a warning tone. "You have the remainder of class to work on the assignment. It's due Wednesday." Liz sat at her desk and reviewed tomorrow's lesson while the class worked on their stories.

She glanced up to find Chris not writing; instead she was on her cell phone. Liz approached Chris's desk. "Your phone, please." She held her hand open.

"I'll put it away," she snapped in a mix of sass and pleading.

"No. You know school rules. Give me your phone."

"Fine." The young girl slammed her phone into Liz's hand.

"Thank you. See me after class."

"Fine."

There hadn't been any behavioral issues with Chris until today. Maybe her break wasn't too pleasant. She returned to her desk, setting the cell phone front and center so she remembered to return it.

The final bell rang and Chris reached for her phone. Liz put her hand over Chris's. "I'm sorry if something happened over break, but please make an effort to adjust your behavior while in school and in my class. I'll let this incident go, but if this continues, I'll call your parents."

"Good. Maybe you should talk to them. They don't listen to me."

"I hope it doesn't come to that, Chris. You've been a good student." She removed her hand and Chris swiped the phone.

She rolled her eyes. "Whatever." She walked off to presumably catch a bus.

Chapter Eighteen

"What's up?" Robert sat relaxed behind his desk. "It must be private for you to close my door."

"Don't say anything and hear me out." Abby stood and wrung her hands. "I wanted to tell you before you heard it from someone else."

"What is it? Everything all right?" He gestured to the chairs. "Why don't you sit down?"

"I'm more comfortable standing. Dad, I'm dating David." She paced in front of his desk. "I know how you feel, but it is what it is. I know the consequences of an office relationship and will handle it with maturity."

He waited for her to continue talking and when she didn't, he spoke. "I don't understand why you're defying me when I said no inter office dating. I'm guessing it's too late to nip this in the bud. Was there anything else?"

She was aware of his feelings on the matter of dating David, or anyone else in the office. It wasn't worth blowing up and repeating what he'd already said. He would deal with David at another time.

"Yes." She sat down. "You met a woman on the cruise. I know, because you're happy, or at least you were this morning. Spill."

"Scott?" His eyes narrowed.

She nodded her head with a Cheshire smile.

"I should've known he'd go to you. Yes, I did meet someone. Her name is Liz. There's not much else to say."

It was too soon to say anything about him and Liz. He didn't know what would happen between them.

"There's a lot to say. I know she lives here, so the question is, are you going to see her again?" She sat back, relaxed, compared to when she first entered.

"I don't know?" He glanced at his desktop.

"What do you mean, you don't know." His head snapped up at her angry tone.

"There's no reason for you not too." Abby stood, resting her hands on his desk. "Dad, settle down with one woman. You deserve that happiness."

He got out of his chair. "Who said I wasn't happy? Why do you think I should commit to Liz? You don't even know her. Why not one of my other lady friends? Why slow down at all?"

"Because, if you haven't settled with one of them, you're not going to. Liz is someone new in your life."

"Okay. You've made your point, Abby. I know about you and David, and now you know about Liz." He took the few steps to come around his desk. "Honestly, I don't know what will happen between us."

She grabbed his hand. "Call her, Dad." She gently squeezed his fingers. "That's the first step."

"I will if and when I'm ready. Don't push me on this, Abby. I need to deal with what's going to happen regarding your mother and her recent engagement. Hopefully, I'll learn more when I meet her in—"—he glanced at his watch—"thirty minutes. I should get ready to leave, as should you."

"Okay, but this isn't the last time I'm going to ask about Liz." She hugged him and stepped to the door.

"I'm done speaking of her with you or Scott. You may know about the women in my life, but you have no say as to who's in my life or how I spend it with them."

"Yet you do have the say about David and I?" Her voice grew louder.

"I don't have time to discuss this any further." He kept his voice firm, yet gentle. "I need to finish here and meet your mother."

She gripped the door handle. "We'll finish this discussion later. I still love you though."

"Love you." When she left, he returned to sit behind his desk. He'd deal with David and Scott later. He finished the email he was in the process of writing and sent it before leaving to meet Kathleen. Nothing bad could come of dinner and drinks with your ex-wife. She was an ex.

* * * *

Running late, he entered Pazzaluna and surveyed the busy dining area for Kathleen. Not seeing her, he approached the maitre'd stand. "I have a reservation for two. Burnhamwood."

"Give me a moment, sir." The man tapped the electronic screen a couple of times. "Yes. Your party is here. This way." He escorted him to a table situated away from the kitchen and between the doorways for the event room.

"Thank you." The host left. "Kathleen." He sat at the white clothed table. "You look beautiful, as always."

She wore black wool pants with a blue sweater he guessed to be cashmere. She always dressed in the best and latest fashions.

"You're late as usual." She sipped her Cosmopolitan martini.

"You can blame Abby. She came to my office while I was wrapping things up to leave. She's dating a guy in the office." He rested his napkin on his lap.

"You don't sound very happy."

Their waiter approached and Robert ordered a gin martini. "I'm not happy. It's not against policy, but I told her not to get involved. David's not a bad kid. It's just the whole work relation thing." He snagged an appetizer plate, poured olive oil and selected a piece of sliced bread to dip in the oil.

"Well, telling her not to get involved was mistake number one. You know she does what you tell her not to do. Her choice in school, car, her past boyfriends—"

"Okay, I got it, Kathleen," he snapped. "It is what it is, and I'll deal with it. So, you're engaged. Congratulations. What's the plan?" His voice remained indifferent.

"Wow…. Okay. Thanks."

"I'm sorry. I didn't mean to be so blunt. I'm happy for you. I really am. You've been dating for several years, so I'm not too surprised. I expected him to propose sooner. With that said, I've been wondering what your plans are for a wedding date and moving. What about the kids?" He popped the last bite of oil-dipped bread into his mouth.

"There is a lot to consider. We haven't set a date yet. Evan will wait until after Alex's graduation."

The waiter set his martini on the table and they placed their dinner order.

"What about Chris? She'll start high school in the fall. Maybe this summer she could spend a week or more with your parents. You know, help get her accustomed to being there. Maybe she'll make some friends too." He sipped the smooth martini.

"I met with my attorney today. Robert, I'm done. It's time for you to step up and be a father." Arrogance spilled from her every word.

He choked as he swallowed on what she said about him. "What are you getting at? I've been a good father."

"You haven't been there for Christine, like you've been for your other two children. As our first born, Abigail received plenty of your attention and more when she decided to follow you into the architectural business world. Then you had a son, who you embraced because he was *your son*, and you attend every one of his sporting events that you possibly can, which is a lot. As for Christine, well, you're too engrossed in your work and social life. You see her when it's your weekend and that's it."

He was jealous that she could maintain her calm, haughty demeanor because he struggled to remain composed. "In my defense, Chris doesn't participate in sports."

"There are other things besides sports, Robert. She's very active in the theater program. I guess you wouldn't know that because you don't pay attention."

They fell silent when the server set Robert's Caesar salad on the table.

He took a long sip from his martini glass. This wasn't what he expected their conversation to be like. Then again, he never knew what to expect when it came to meeting with Kathleen. Several bites of salad gave him time to cool off. What Kathleen said hurt. Was he really a bad father? Was he that unaware of what Chris was doing at school?

A nip from his glass, he swallowed, and leaned forward. "What are you thinking about Kathleen?" He ate a forkful of salad.

"My attorney is looking into transferring the custody rights to you."

The bite of salad went down hard as he swallowed. He chased it with a long drink of martini. "You just accused me of being a poor father and now you're giving up custody? Who's the bad parent now? Are you giving me full custody of Chris too?" He maintained a low voice to avoid attention.

Her eyes narrowed. "Don't you dare turn this back on me, telling me I'm the bad parent. I've been there for her since day one."

"When? When are you planning to change the custody?"

"I would wait until after Alex graduates. We will reverse our custody responsibilities, with changes due to my moving to New York. I'll have her for holiday's and school breaks. It'll all be spelled out in the new custody documents."

He swung his head side to side in disbelief.

"Robert, you said it yourself, she'll start high school in the fall. This will be the best for her." Her voice almost had a tinge of caring and gentleness to it.

His head snapped up, as well as his voice. "Do you realize that I don't live in the school district? I live here. Downtown. She'd still be looking at changing schools, missing her friends."

Their meals were brought to the table and they ate in peace for a good five minutes.

"You could always move south of the river. The south metro has nice condos, too." The tinge of snotty was back.

He gripped his fork with more force than necessary, while the other hand fisted, the thumb ran repeatedly across his fingertips. "I've only lived in my place for a couple of years and you want me to up and sell it. I'd lose money, Kathleen. I can't move."

"See, this is what I'm talking about, Robert. If this would've been Abigail or Alex, you would bend over backwards for them." She raised her voice.

Their waiter approached. "How does everything taste?"

Robert finished his bite. "Very good, thank you."

"If you would box this up to go, please. I'll be leaving," Kathleen asked politely.

"Of course." He took the plate with the margherita pizza and stepped away.

"You can't leave. We're in the middle of talking."

"It's best if I leave and give you time to think about everything we've said tonight." Kathleen pulled her wallet from her purse, yanked out a fifty-dollar bill, and laid it on the table. "That should cover my share of the bill."

"Put that away. I'll pay."

She ignored him. "Take your daughter into consideration, Robert. Summer will be here quicker than you think. I'm putting the house on the market next month."

"What if you sell it? Where are you going to move? What about Alex's graduation party?"

"I'll have to figure that out if and when it happens."

"You're something else, Kathleen." Although divorced from the woman, she continued to surprise him.

She stood and put her coat on as the waiter delivered her to go container. Picking up the bill, she handed the fifty to the waiter. "This is for my portion. Keep the remaining balance as your tip, thank you."

"Thank you. Have a good evening. Sir, can I bring you another gin martini?"

"Yes, please." Alone, he said to Kathleen, "That wasn't necessary."

"Good night, Robert. I'll be in touch... or my attorney will be."

She walked off as he tossed back the last of his drink. His phone vibrated on the tabletop. Picking it up, he tapped the message icon. Kimberly.

I know you returned yesterday, but I missed you. Care to come over for a while?

His fiery redhead wanted to play. A little stress relief is just what the doctor ordered.

What about Liz? His fingers paused in replying. He put the phone face down on the table, took a bite, and enjoyed a sip of his fresh martini. When his phone buzzed, he lifted to read the message.

I bought a new outfit.

A picture popped up. Kimberly wore a very small, revealing sailor style outfit.

I'm your cruise director and I'll be at your service all night.

His desire grew. He tapped the screen quickly in reply.

On his drive to Kimberly's, Robert's conscience battled with his libido. Sex was winning as he parked his car in her driveway. He rang the doorbell.

Her scantily clad body appeared as the door opened. He wasn't disappointed.

"Welcome back, sailor." She yanked him through the doorway and pushed him against the entryway wall. Planting her lips on his, her hands roamed from his chest to his swollen groin.

A pleasurable moan escaped from them both, as his hands glided across her bare skin. He spun her around, pushing her against the wall. He kissed her neck below her ear to her collarbone. He stopped and reared his head back.

This was all wrong. Her body wasn't the body he wanted. This woman didn't smell like the woman he wanted.

"I can't. I need to leave."

"What? Why?" she protested.

"I've met someone else."

"So. I'm willing to share." With lusty, green eyes, she grabbed his hips and jerked him toward her.

His hands pressed to the wall stopped him from making contact. "No. I can't. It's over between us. I'm sorry. I've got to go." Robert left while Kimberly pleaded.

In his car, he turned the key and hurried for home. He'd told Liz he wanted to have a relationship with her. Home for one day and he was ready to jump in bed with Kimberly. That proved him to be a piece of shit. The sexual vibes dissipated as he drove farther away from Kimberly's condo and closer to home.

Maybe a call to Liz would make him feel better. Maybe.

* * * *

Abigail left her car in the garage and strolled to meet David, who hadn't arrived yet. Several minutes later, he arrived and parked along the curb. She ran down the driveway and hugged him. Not being able to touch him all day in the personal way she wanted proved difficult, but she'd done it and would continue to control herself. As long as he satisfied her needs off the business clock.

David playfully chased her up the driveway. Paul pulled his truck in the drive and, in the blink of eye, he was out of the truck. He tackled David onto the frozen ground.

"Stop! Paul, stop. This is my boyfriend, David." Abigail yelled as she ran the short distance to where the men squirmed.

Paul released his hold and both men scrambled to their feet. He stood a good five inches taller than David. "Sorry, man. With this rapist on the loose, we're a little protective of our girls."

"It's okay. I'm glad to know someone's watching out for Abigail." David wrapped an arm around her waist.

Paul walked toward the front door.

"Are you okay? He tackled you so quickly and onto the hard yard."

"I'm fine. Is your other roommate this aggressive?"

"I'd say he's even more so. Conrad is an ex-boyfriend. Let's get out of this cold." She pushed him forward to the garage.

"Wait." Their forward momentum stopped. "You live with your ex?"

"You have nothing to worry about." With her arm around his waist, she applied a little pressure to move. "It ended on good terms and he knows about you."

"Has he ever tried to get back with you?" He moved slowly, but it was progress.

174

"Occasionally. However, it's usually in jest because he knows I'm not going back to him. You have nothing to worry about. Come on, I'm hungry." They approached the house door in the garage and she closed the garage door.

Inside, she led him up the two flights of stairs to the first floor. "So, this is where I live. We don't use much of the front part of the house. We don't have furniture in those rooms. All the action takes place in the back half or in our rooms."

"Man, this is nicer than my place."

"We got lucky. Conrad found it through a friend. Let's go upstairs." She grabbed his hand to lead the way. "Conrad has the master suite. Paul's room is next to his. Gina and I took the two front rooms with the Jack and Jill bathroom."

"Wow, nice room," he remarked as they entered her room.

"It's a standard size room."

"No, it's bigger than my guest rooms."

"Take your coat off and leave it in here. Do you mind if I change into something more comfortable?" She wandered into her closet.

"No. You all must be really good friends who trust each other, to be living under one roof."

She removed her work clothes and pulled on a pair of jeans. "We've been friends for... six years. Gina and I have been friends since middle school. We met the guys in college. You have to trust each other, otherwise it wouldn't work." She came out of the closet pulling on a tee shirt and David had his back to her. His coat rested on her chair.

Padding to where he stood at the end of her bed, she slid her arms around his waist, while placing a kiss on the back of his neck. "We all live our own lives." He faced her as she kissed the side of his neck.

"Let's go eat dinner before I have you for dessert."

"I'm not dessert, you are, and you taste delicious." He planted his lips on hers, then pushed her back, onto her bed and straddled her.

Abigail shrieked with giddiness as he grasped her wrists and placed them above her head. Her door flew open.

The next thing she knew, Conrad yanked David off her. "Abs, get out of here and call the police."

"Conrad, stop!" She grabbed at him, pulling his arms, trying to release Conrad's grip. "This is David. The boyfriend I told you about. Jesus."

Conrad and Paul were being too protective. Conrad let go of David, who fell on the edge of the bed. Abigail sat at his side.

"Sorry about that. I heard her squeal and went into defensive mode. I didn't know she had company. I guess I should've remembered what your sounds of excitement were, but it's been a while." He was making a dig at David.

"Shut up." She stood and pushed him toward the door. "Shut up and get out of my room." She slammed the bedroom door shut. "Ugh."

David embraced her. "Abigail, it's okay." His voice was as calm as his demeanor.

"No, it's not. How dare he say that in front of you?"

"He's a guy, and a jealous ex-boyfriend." Pulling back from her, he looked at her. "It's okay. I'm glad they're watching out for you."

"You're too understanding." She brought him close again. "Let's go see what I can make for us." A quick kiss and they went downstairs to the kitchen.

* * * *

David would follow her anywhere in those jeans. They hugged her slight curves in all the right places. Her living space was amazing compared to his small house, but she had to share it with others, whereas his place was all his.

"You can sit at the counter while I fix our dinner," Abigail said as they walked into the open kitchen and family room area.

Furniture filled the space compared to the front of the house. What he had seen of the front was bare of furnishings.

"Are you sure? I don't mind helping." He plopped on a stool as she opened a cupboard. "I'm good at cutting and chopping stuff."

"What're you fixing for dinner?" Paul strolled in with Conrad trailing behind.

"After the two of you assaulted my boyfriend and you..." She shoved a finger into Conrad's chest. "You said inexcusable things. I'm not fixing you guys anything."

"We said sorry." Both of the guys spoke in unison

"Well, this dinner is for me and David." She pulled items from the pantry.

"That's okay, we'll get a pizza." Conrad pulled his cell phone from his pocket.

Everyone turned their heads toward the direction of the stairs.

"Sounds like Gina's decided to come home." Paul lounged on a couch.

With the refrigerator open, Abigail pulled a bell pepper from a drawer and set it on the counter. "Gina."

"Hey." A blonde, shorter than Abigail, entered the room. "I'm glad you're here. Jack, this is Abigail." A tall, muscular guy stood next to Gina.

"Hello. Gina's told me a lot about you."

She shook his extended hand and a shade of pink appeared on her cheeks.

"Hi. I'm sorry I can't say the same, since I haven't seen her since the party. Would you two like to join us for dinner? I'm making pasta with chicken and whatever I can find to throw in with it."

"No, we're good."

"Sure, invite them but not us," Conrad hollered from the couch.

Abigail walked to where David sat on a barstool. "David, this is my roommate, Gina and her boyfriend, Jack."

"Nice to finally meet you, Gina." He shook her hand and then gripped Jack's hand. "Nice to meet you, Jack."

He glanced to Abigail, winked, and looked back at Gina and Jack. "It's nice that at least one of Abigail's roommates didn't attack me before being introduced." David raised his voice enough to be heard in the other room where Abigail's two housemates sat.

"What's that about?" Gina's face filled with curiosity.

"He's partly joking. First Paul went after him in the driveway when he got here. Then, when I was in my room, Conrad burst in and yanked David off me." Abigail pulled a pot and pan from a cupboard, filling the pot with water.

"You guys weren't, you know?" Gina's eyes darted between him and Abigail.

"No. I'd have killed Conrad if that were the case." She set the pot on the stove and lit the gas burner. "Jack, what do you do for living?"

"I'm a teacher over at St. James. I work with Conrad."

"Oh, okay, that would explain you two meeting at the party. What do you teach?"

"Physical education."

Abigail's face reddened. "Oh. Yeah, I can see that."

She's definitely blushing. Why?

"Thanks. I don't want to be one of those gym teachers that let themselves go."

"Well, if you don't mind," Gina grabbed Jack's hand. "We're going upstairs. Nice to meet you, David."

"Nice to meet both of you, too," he said as they left the kitchen.

Abigail's eyes were wide and she had a smirk on her face, leaving him to wonder what was going on. She shook her head, holding back what appeared to be laughter.

Chapter Nineteen

"Hi, Veronica!" Liz answered her cell phone as she left school. The fresh air was welcoming, compared to the stagnant school air.

"How was your first day back?"

"Fine. It's middle school. Eighth graders and their teenage years. What can you say? What's up?" She strolled through the parking lot to her car.

"Are you up for company tonight? I've been anxious to hear about your trip. I know you don't want to go out and leave the kids at home, since you just got back, so I thought I could come to your place."

"Sure. What time?" Clicking the key fob button, she opened the driver's door and set her tote bag on the passenger seat.

"I'm guessing I'd be there around seven. After dinner."

"Okay, I'll see you then." Liz tapped her phone, ending the call, and dropped it into her tote.

While driving, her thoughts drifted to the cruise and the relaxed lifestyle the islanders lived. Robert wasn't too far from those thoughts. How was he handling his first day back to the working grindstone? She could call him after Veronica left and the kids fell asleep. She'd wait and see about the time. If it was too late, she wouldn't call.

When she approached her house, Mallory's car was parked in the driveway. The kids probably enjoyed the surprise visit, but Liz, not so much. She needed the time to prepare for class lessons and make dinner. Not to mention, Veronica's visit. The Christmas divorce punch-in-the-gut had been cruel, and Mallory needed support. She pushed the button on the garage door opener and pulled inside. Entering the house, she walked through the laundry room into the kitchen where the kids sat at

179

the table doing their homework.

"Hey sis, sorry to drop-in unexpected, but—"

"No buts, you're welcome anytime." Liz wrapped an arm around Mallory and squeezed. Turning to her kids, she said, "Glad to see you guys working instead of playing. I'm going to go change and then will be back down to answer any questions on the homework." She set her tote on the built-in desk.

"I'm good," Brad answered. "Aunt Mallory helped me with the math question, and I'm almost finished."

"No questions from me, Mom. I'm just finishing my Spanish homework, then I'll go do my reading. Can I go to Cindy's house afterwards?"

"As long as you're home by five-thirty for dinner. Mallory, I'll be right back down, unless you wanted to talk while I change." Liz walked toward the foyer for the stairs.

"I can wait."

She returned to the kitchen several minutes later and Brad was already gone. "Appears we're alone." At the refrigerator, she pulled out the thawed hamburger.

"Yeah, Brad went downstairs and Sarah went upstairs to read."

"I'm making rice hot dish. Did you want to stay for dinner?" It was the cordial thing to ask.

"No. I'm good." Her sister leaned on the center island.

"Still don't care for cream of mushroom soup, huh?" At the mention of the soup, Liz pulled the canned ingredients from the cupboard.

"Ugh, no. Do your kids like that?"

"They love it. As long as I keep the onion and celery out of it. They don't mind the sliced water chestnuts either."

"Yum. I like water chestnuts."

"So...how are you doing?" She pulled a pan from the cupboard, opened the cans, and proceeded to put the contents into the pan.

"Still in shock, but doing better. I went home Christmas Eve to find all his stuff gone. Looking back, I should've seen it coming. He started packing things away in boxes months ago. When I asked him about it, because it was unusual, he said he was putting his summer clothes into the basement for storage."

"Why do you say that's unusual? A lot of people pack away clothing according to the seasons." Liz stood at the stove, browning the meat. Mallory's face scrunched. "What's wrong?"

"Oh, the smell. My stomach's churning."

"It's hamburger." As soon as she made the simple statement, she turned to the pan, stabbed at the meat to break it up and remembered. "Is it possible you could be pregnant?"

Mallory's face took on a horrifying look before breaking into tears. "I can't be."

Liz moved quickly to the ledge where her sister stood and held her hands. "Have you missed your period?"

"I'm only a few days late." She spoke between sobs. "I've been so stressed, I thought…"

"As soon as I get this in the oven, I'm going to run to the store." She grabbed the box of tissue from the counter and set it in front of Mallory. "You need to find out right now."

"What am I going to do? Adam's left." She pulled out several tissues and wiped her eyes before blowing her nose.

"Okay, let's wait and see if you're pregnant first. Then we'll worry about Adam and everything else." Liz continued cooking and finished preparing the dish. Sliding the pot into the oven, she grabbed her wallet and keys. "I'll be back shortly. I want you to turn on the TV and relax." She yanked the fridge door open, pulled out a bottle of water and set in front of her sister. "Drink this because you'll need to pee for the test."

Liz hurried to the store and completed the mission in as little as fifteen minutes. Luckily, she didn't run into anyone she knew. Wow, would the rumors be flying around. She chuckled but quickly stopped. Robert and the cruise came to mind. They may have used protection, but there were risks.

Back in her kitchen, she set the bag on the counter and took out the test. "Okay, Mallory. Take this into the bathroom. You pee on the stick, put the cap on, then set it on the counter, and come back out here."

Mallory's hand shook as she picked up the test stick and disappeared into the bathroom between the kitchen and laundry room. Several minutes later, she walked back into the living room, collapsing on the couch.

Sitting beside her sister, Liz took her hand in her own. "If you and Adam were having problems, were you still having sex?"

"The only problem I knew of was us trying to have a baby."

"How long have you two been trying to get pregnant?" This was a new development.

"A couple of years." Mallory's head hung low as she slumped forward. "That's what we were arguing about before... well, he said he couldn't take it anymore. Being around the family with the kids and the other two women pregnant."

"Mallory, are you sure there wasn't an underlying issue? If he really loved you, he wouldn't let having children break up your marriage."

"If there was some other reason, I don't know about it."

"It's time. Do you want to go look alone? With me? Or do you want me to go check it?"

"Together."

Liz stood in the doorway as Mallory slowly approached the pregnancy test on the bathroom counter.

* * * *

David stood at the foot of Abigail's bed while she closed her bedroom door after dinner. "Do you care to explain what went on in the kitchen earlier between you, Gina and Jack? You were blushing pretty good when she made introductions and more so when he talked about his job."

She snickered. "I texted Gina yesterday about my underwear drawer and she told me about Jack. More than I wanted to know." She glanced to a closed door, which he assumed led to the shared bathroom, and lowered her voice. "He has a sex swing. And when he mentioned he was a gym teacher and about staying in shape, it took everything in me not to laugh."

He joined her sitting on the bed. "I guess I can understand why you turned red."

"Was it that noticeable?" She touched her cheeks.

"I noticed, but he probably thought you were warm from working in the kitchen." He took her hands from her face and held them. "I wouldn't worry about it. Why were you texting her about your underwear drawer?

That's a bit odd."

She glanced sideways. "It wasn't anything." Her eyes peered at their hands. "I thought someone had been in my drawer."

"What? Who would be in your room?" A niggle of worry filled his gut.

"I don't know." Her blue eyes gazed into his. "Gina hadn't been in my room, and I know there's no reason for the guys to be in here. I think I overreacted. I'd been gone a week, so maybe I forgot about packing and digging through the drawer."

She pushed him backwards on the bed and she lay beside him. "Now…" A brief kiss to the lips. "I want dessert." She kissed him with a little more passion.

"Abigail, if you notice something like this now that you're back, I want to know. Maybe it's just a fluke, but promise you'll tell me."

"Boy, you know how to dampen the mood." She rolled onto her back.

He straddled her and leaned in. "Promise me, you'll tell me if anymore weird stuff is happening."

"Fine, but I think you're over reacting. You saw how protective the guys were."

"I didn't see it, I felt it." David chuckled. "Letting you park in the garage is nice of them." His hands on her hips, he slipped them under her shirt, touching her skin for the first time. Soft.

"Are we done talking?" Her stomach muscles flexed as she sat up, allowing him to remove her top. She remained in that position while removing his shirt, which kept his hands from being able to touch her.

As she lay back, her fingers slid into the waist of his pants and around to the button and zipper, where they quickly and nimbly undid both. He leaned forward and placed a kiss between her breasts, concealed behind a black bra. Slowly, he moved the kisses to her neck and shoulder. She reached for his pants, eager to remove them, but steadfast, he held his position.

"Not yet," he whispered in her ear, followed by nibbles to her earlobe before returning to her neck and breastbone.

"Then get my pants off." The demand came in breaths.

His kisses moved to her breasts where they remained covered, but not for long. He deftly removed the small piece of fabric to reveal white mounds with erect nipples, giving each a quick suckle. Abigail's breathing quickened with the touch of his tongue on her skin.

When her hands pulled at his pants, he assisted her because his growing erection was uncomfortable. As he stood to get them off the remainder of the way, he pulled a condom from his wallet. She squirmed free of her own pants and black lace thong fell to the floor. He set the packet on her nightstand as she crawled onto the bed with its covers pushed out of the way.

"I'm on the pill," she said as he slid onto the bed next to her.

"Does that mean you don't want me to use one?" This was a matter to discuss rather than avoid. Even if it meant spoiling the moment.

"No. I just wanted you to know. If you'd feel safer wearing one, then use it." A firm kiss on his lips ended any further discussion.

* * * *

Mallory didn't pick up the pregnancy test. She stood in front of the counter, turned to Liz, and solemnly spoke. "I'm pregnant."

"Do you want to call Adam? I'll sit with you."

"Um… yeah, I guess so." She snatched the test off the counter with one hand and the bag with the other, tossing the test into the bag. "He'll want proof."

They left the bathroom and stopped at the kitchen table where Mallory's purse sat. With her phone, she sat in the family room. Liz joined her, and they waited for an answer.

"Hello." Adam's voice floated through the phones speaker.

"Hi, Adam." Her eyes watered. "Can you come by the house tonight?"

"What for? I have everything I need, and there's nothing more for us to talk about." His tone wasn't one of anger, but more of despair.

Mallory released the tears and couldn't speak.

"Mallory, what's wrong?" Panic replaced his gloomy voice.

"Adam, its Liz. Everything's fine, per se. If you could, it would be best if you met her at the house."

"Tell me what's going on. It doesn't sound like everything's—"

"I'm pregnant," Mallory blurted. "We're having a baby." You

couldn't mistake the irritation at her husband for his lack of trying or wanting to meet in person to learn the news.

The room and phone line were silent.

"How… when…. I'm leaving now. I'll see you at home." His line went dead, and Mallory tapped her phone screen.

"I guess I'm going home." She stood and went to the kitchen table.

"Can you drive? Are you going to be okay?" Liz didn't want her to drive if she couldn't focus on the road.

"Yeah … on both accounts." Her sister embraced her and then stuffed the bag containing the tests in her purse. "Thank you. I'll call you later. Please don't tell anyone."

"I won't." They walked to the front door. "It's going to be okay." Liz hugged her sister one last time before she left.

* * * *

Veronica arrived shortly after seven, and Liz opened a bottle of wine, pouring two glasses. "Let's go sit in the living room. Give us some privacy."

"It's so good to see you," Veronica said, taking the glass from her. "The trip definitely agreed with you. I'm glad you went, even if my mom had a problem with the vacation."

"I came to realize that, thanks to Robert, I'm the one who's kept me from having a lasting relationship."

They sat on the couch. Each of them bending a leg and facing one another.

"So, how can you change that?" She sipped her wine.

"I need to face Ellen head on when she raises the subject about me having a man in my life. Standing up to her at Christmas felt so good."

"You shocked her. After you left, she complained how rude you were talking to her that way. Dad told her to be quiet or he was leaving the room. I was so proud of you for putting her in her place. Enough about that, I want to hear about…" Lowering her voice, she glanced to the room's entrance. "Robert."

"Do you remember him from the opening of the clinic?"

Veronica shook her head.

Liz flipped to the back of the photos. "Here's a picture of me and him."

"Oh, yeah, I remember him now. He's good lookin'. Not saying my brother wasn't handsome, but whew, he's hot."

"Yes, he's very handsome." She stared at the photo of them at the Italian restaurant. "Dressed and…undressed." The smile blossomed and she giggled.

Veronica leaned toward her, resting a hand on the knee of her bent leg. "Did you?" Although her eyebrows were raised in shock, she couldn't hide the grin as she sat back.

Liz nodded. "It was liberating and so amazing." She rolled her eyes then closed them as she exhaled and relaxed her shoulders at the memory of making love to Robert. Sharing a bed with him had been glorious.

"Um, if your reactions from just now are anything, I'd say so. The question is, what's the status of you two at this point?"

"We both want to continue seeing each other, but I don't know. With the kids and all, it's hard."

"Only if you allow it to be hard, Liz. It's obvious you like him and the… sex was great, but what about outside of the bedroom? Does he have kids and is he open to your children?"

"The whole package is great. He's divorced and shares custody of his two younger children. His daughter is graduating college this summer. His son will graduate from high school, and he has a daughter Sarah's age." She sipped from her wine glass.

"Did you talk about his divorce and his ex-wife?"

"A little. I guess it wasn't high on my list to interrogate him since we were getting to know each other."

Now she wondered why they did get divorced. What had gone wrong? Had he cheated on her? He did admit to having multiple relationships at one time, and kept it a secret from all the women.

"Liz, what are you thinking about?" Veronica searched her face for an answer.

Swallowing her wine, she contemplated what to say. "He wasn't in a committed relationship before the cruise, but had relations with multiple women." She lowered her eyes to the wine glass she held in her hand. Embarrassed? Slightly. Concerned? More so, for what would happen between them.

"Excuse me? How many other women? If you two are in a relationship, what about these other women? You're not being added to his list, are you?"

Keeping her focus on the wine, she answered her questions. "Two, that he told me about and I believe him. He said he wouldn't see them, that he was committed to our relationship. He didn't have to tell me, but he did and I trust him."

Her sister-in-law's hand rested on her knee. "I hope you're right because I'd hate to see you get invested in him and then get hurt."

Chapter Twenty

Robert's feet pounded the shit out of the treadmill belt in the apartment complex's gym. Built up sexual endorphins from his visit to Kimberly were gone. She'd gotten upset when he backed out from his visit. Images flashed across his mind between Liz and Kimberly while driving home. He made the right choice, but his libido was frustrated. Sweat covered his body.

The treadmill slowed as he entered the cool down phase. Past nine, he thought about jumping in the pool to further the relaxation period. Instead, he opted to go back to his place and shower.

As he pulled his lounge pants on, he glanced at the clock. Ten twenty-five glared at him. Too late to call Liz. Cell phone in hand, he located her contact and tapped his message.

I've been thinking of you. Would really like to see you. Can you get away Friday or Saturday? My kids will be with me the following weekend. xoxo

He plugged the charging cord into his phone. Setting it on his nightstand, he turned the TV on and got into bed. Being back home and into their regular routines, he didn't know if she would be awake or if she left her cell phone on. He'd never installed a landline phone in the apartment because of his cell phone.

The phone rang.

Liz wanted to video chat. His heart picked up a beat.

His fingers quickly ran through his damp hair. He tapped the phone. "Hey." He maintained his composure. "I didn't know if you'd be awake, so I didn't call."

Her deep green eyes were darker but smiled with the grin on her face. "I had company earlier, so I stayed up later to get some work done. You look comfortable."

"I just got into bed. Wish you were here with me."

"So do I."

Her admission and seeing her on the phone sent a signal to his groin. She wore a tank top and her hair was fastened up with random strands hanging free.

"Will this weekend work for you?" If he didn't focus on the purpose of the conversation, he'd be dealing with the same issue as earlier in the evening. He didn't feel like running off the desire.

"I'll have to see what I can do. What did you have in mind?" Her eyelids drooped while she nibbled her bottom lip. "There's one thing I'd like to do."

"Oh, you are a tease. I should get in my car and teach you that tempting over the phone is bad." So much for containing his sexual desires.

"You don't know where I live."

"Is that a challenge?" He raised his eyebrows and grinned.

She laughed softly, and he missed her more. He made the right decision not to go any further with Kimberly.

"No." Lounging in her bed, she sat upright quickly. "I know you could find my address. Stay where you are, and I'll see what I can do about this weekend."

God, was she cute. "Don't worry, you're safe for tonight. Were your kids happy to have you home?"

"Yes, very. They liked their gifts, too. What about yours?" She relaxed into her pillows.

"I've seen Abigail. Came home and found out my ex-wife became engaged over New Year's. I met her tonight for dinner. I'd rather not talk about it though."

"Okay, another time. Listen, I should get to sleep. I'll text you when I know for sure what day will work."

"Sweet dreams."

"I will now. Good night." She ended the conversation and his screen blackened.

He set the phone on the nightstand. Bringing Kathleen into the conversation eased his desires, but brought questions of his future to the forefront. If Kathleen left him with custody of Chris, his life was going to change.

He considered what Kathleen had said about his relationship with his youngest. Was he that terrible of a father? He provided for her. He spent his weekends with her. Remembered her on her birthdays. What more could he do?

* * * *

The receptionist stopped David as he entered the office. "Robert, would like to see you."

"Okay, thank you." He approached Robert's administrative assistant down the hall. "I'm here to see Robert."

"Yes, David. One moment." She left her desk, knocked at Robert's door, and cracked it open, peeking inside. "He's here." She fully opened the door. "Please go in."

Robert sat behind his desk talking on the phone, holding a finger up to gesture it would be a minute. David sat in one of the two chairs, listening as Robert ended the phone conversation.

His boss's demeanor was calm, but precise and to the point. "David, I'm going to state this simply…" He leaned back in his chair. This wasn't a social moment. "You are not to date Abigail. You two are to remain co-workers and that's it. I know there are no policies in place at this time restricting co-workers from dating, but as your boss and Abigail's father, I'm putting an end to this relationship right now."

"Excuse me, sir? Abigail said—"

Robert jerked upright in his chair and his body went rigid. His tone turned strict. "I don't care what my daughter told you. I'm telling you I don't want you to continue having relations with my daughter."

"If I said I won't end things with Abigail?" He had to know what his options were.

"I can't fire you, which I would hate to do because you are one of my best project managers, but I can make your job miserable."

"In that case, sir, I choose my relationship with your daughter. I quit." David couldn't believe he was leaving for a woman, but there was something special about Abigail.

He walked out of Robert's office and straight to his workstation. How did being pissed and yet being pleased work together? He could find work elsewhere. Robert couldn't give him a bad referral based on his relationship with Abigail. David pulled work files from his messenger bag because he was no longer responsible for them. He took the few personal items from his space, and tucked them away inside his bag.

"What are you doing?" Abigail spoke from behind him.

"I quit." There was no anger in his words. Instead, he nearly laughed while saying it.

"What?" she exclaimed, clutching his arms.

He dropped his bag. "I made a choice. I chose you."

"What are you talking about?" Her shrill voice gained the attention of those who were in the office.

"Your father called me to his office this morning. He said I was to stop seeing you."

"Oh, no." She shook her head as she spoke. Anger sparked into a fire. "No, he can't do that." She spun to leave, and he caught her by the wrist.

"Don't Abigail. It will only make things worse for us."

She yanked her hands free. "Don't you dare leave." She stormed off in Robert's direction.

A door slammed.

He glanced around as his fellow co-workers stared while he sank onto a chair. A moment of embarrassment was quickly replaced with the realization that Abigail had strong feelings for him. Enough to stand up for him against her father.

* * * *

"Who the hell do you think you are?" Abigail yelled when her father's office door slammed closed. "You have no right telling David he can't see me."

Her father came around his desk to stand in front of her. "Lower your voice." He gently clasped her hands and directed her to sit.

191

"No." She freed her hands, avoided the chair, and him, while keeping her voice loud. "There isn't a policy against us dating."

"Abigail, please sit, and we can talk like civilized people." He stepped nearer.

"If you don't go apologize to David right now, I'll leave too." Unable to contain her anger, her voice remained brash.

The door flew open and Scott stepped inside and quickly closed the door. "What is going on in here? Abigail, I heard you down the hall." His eyes flickered between her and her father.

She inhaled deeply and slowly released the breath. "I walked in and found David packing his belongings. He informed me my father told him he couldn't see me anymore, so he quit."

"Is this true, Robert?" Scott came to stand beside her.

"I didn't tell him. He made the decision to quit." Her father returned to his desk chair, as though he were running away from her and the situation.

Scott approached the desk, leaned forward, and spoke in a low voice. "What did you tell him?"

Silence filled the room.

"What do you have against David? Do you know something I don't?" Abigail bellowed.

"I don't know or have anything against him." Her father's posture stiffened. "I want to save you from being hurt."

"Hurt? You don't think your behavior hurts?"

Scott faced her and blocked her view of her father. "Abigail, give me a minute." He turned his head. "Robert, what did you say to David?"

He let out a ragged breath. "I told him to stop seeing Abigail. When he asked what if he didn't, I told him I'd make his job miserable. He quit."

Scott pressed a button on the phone. "Get Robertson in here, now." Releasing the button, he leaned within inches of her father's face. "If you want to protect the company, you will rectify this situation immediately. He could, and can, take legal action against you and the company."

He backed away from her father's desk. "Abigail, please go to your desk while your father handles this."

"Before I leave, I have one more thing to say. I will be the one to quit this job and go intern elsewhere… if… if necessary."

A knock sounded and David entered. Abigail cupped his face with her hands and kissed him passionately.

* * * *

David watched Abigail walk away as he approached Robert's desk. Scott stood off to the side. Robert rose from his chair and came around to stand in front of him.

He jutted his chin defiantly and held his head high. "David, I must apologize for my earlier words with you." The man struggled with his words. "I mishandled this situation between you and my daughter. I don't want to see you leave the firm, but if you're certain of your decision, it's not my place to tell you what to do. I'll respect your decision. You and my daughter… must remain professional when in the work place and on assignments outside of the office."

"I accept your apology and prefer to remain an employee of RB and Associates. As long as your daughter and I are dating, I will be professional at all times while in a work setting."

Scott eyed them both. "Thank you, David, I'd like to talk with Robert."

David returned to his and Abigail's workstation, relieved he wouldn't be searching for a new job. "What happened in there?" he whispered.

Abigail spun her chair to face him. "I said a few choice words to my father. Scott came in and called for you. You tell me, what happened after I left?" From her short, abrupt answers and questions, she was still angry with her father.

"Your father apologized and asked me not to leave." He sat, moving his chair close to her. "I'm not going anywhere."

"Good. Put your personal stuff back where it belongs and then let's get to work."

David removed the few pictures and trinkets from his bag. A strong woman at his side was a good thing.

* * * *

Robert changed from his work clothes into his lounge pants.

Opening the freezer with more force than needed, he shook his head in disgust. The events with David, Abigail, and Scott, didn't bode well for a good mood type of day. He pulled a pizza from the freezer, turned on the oven, and prepared to slide his dinner into the oven. He twisted the top off his beer and sipped the cold, golden liquid. Another pull from the bottle and he tossed the pizza pan in the warming oven. He didn't want to wait. Setting the timer, he strolled into the living room and turned on the TV.

Abigail defied him and defended her relationship with David. They'd never had strong arguments until her internship. She had grown into a resilient woman and was no longer daddy's little girl. Sadness filled him at the thought.

Apologizing to David had been embarrassing and uncomfortable. He had made a mistake in threatening David over his job. Scott was right about the legalities it could've brought on him and the firm. He had no valid reason for not wanting David and his daughter to be involved, other than if things soured between them, how it could affect their work.

Laura's tone played on his cell phone. He answered, knowing he would have to admit his new relationship with Liz.

"I was wondering if you were available for an evening of entertainment, Mr. Burnhamwood." She purred in his ear and brought forward his memories of their time spent in bed.

Stay strong. "I'm sorry, Laura, but I can't see you tonight." He wanted Liz.

"Bummer. I was hoping you were up to having some company after being gone for so long. You must've found someone to keep you company on the cruise."

Be honest. She's a mature woman. "I did. She lives here and we're seeing if we can make a go of a relationship." He sipped his beer.

"Well, as sad as the news is for me, I'm happy for you, Robert. Thank you for being honest and telling me. You deserve to find happiness."

"You do too, and you will."

"I'm happy for now. No relationships for me. You know that." He joined her in playful laughter. "I'll let you go. Oh, Robert."

"Yeah?"

"If things don't work out with your new lady friend, you have my number." She ended the call. She'd be okay.

Now, would he be okay until he saw Liz? He wanted to hold her. Touch her. Taste her. If she couldn't make it work for the weekend, he swore he'd combust. He knew she wouldn't take a video call at this hour because of her kids, so he texted her.

Have you figured if we can get together this weekend?

His phone pinged while he ate the last slice of the pizza.

Yes, Friday night. I'm going to let the kids stay home alone while I'm out.

This meant, for the first time ever, he would be bringing a woman to his place. Liz wasn't just any woman. He wanted to have a monogamous relationship with this woman.

What time? Do you want me to meet you at your place or the restaurant? I'm not ready to introduce you to the children. I hope you understand.

Not picking her up and wanting to have her in his bed...

You can meet me at my place and I'll drive to dinner. If you want to be here at 6, I'll make reservations for 6:45. Dress casual, like you're going out with a girlfriend. ;)

I'll see you then.

Looking forward to it. xoxo

That was the end of their conversation. She never texted back the hugs and kisses. At first, it stung, then he figured she didn't because of the kids. If they saw the message, she wanted it to be simple.

* * * *

Wednesday, while the kids did homework, Liz fixed dinner and graded the papers she assigned the students to write, which continued into the night. Grading the final class, she checked the time. It neared ten o'clock. She counted the remaining papers. Five to go and then she could go to bed. She picked the next paper from the short stack. It was Chris's. She moved it to the bottom of the pile, taking the next paper. Maybe the paper would give Liz some insight into what was happening in Chris's life.

Liz had trouble understanding Chris's sudden change in behavior. The last two days were pretty much a repeat of the day before. She gave her a final warning. Chris grabbed the cell phone and ran from the classroom again.

The four papers graded, she picked up the last one. Chris's. Written in the corner was Chris Burnhamwood.

The last name mentally smacked her across the face.

It couldn't be. Could it?

Liz read the paper. The answer to the question came in Chris's holiday paper. A child of divorced parents, having to split the holiday between them. The biggest giveaway, her father went on a cruise and her mother went to New York, leaving her to stay with her older sister and brother.

She was Robert's daughter.

Liz hadn't put the two together because as a sub of six classes, each having about thirty students, give or take a couple, she didn't learn the students' last names. She focused on learning their first names and then some of the simpler last names stuck. As she put her papers away for tomorrow, thoughts of Chris and her family pinged around her brain.

Chris didn't see her father after he returned. Her mother was engaged while away, which meant she was moving to New York for her high school years. The young girl's anger and disappointment seeped from her words.

Now what? If Robert introduced her to Chris before her subbing job finished, it could make the situation worse. Liz wondered if she'd known this information prior to her text message to Robert, what would she have done and would it have changed their conversation. Anxious to know, but wanting to talk to him about it in person, she'd wait. Wait until Friday's date.

Chapter Twenty-One

David and Abigail celebrated landing the Myers account by going out to dinner. The investment firm, based in Portland, Oregon, was opening an office in Minneapolis. With David from the west coast and her interior design ideas, she felt they both played a role in RB & Associates being chosen. They were excited to get started on the project.

Afterwards they went back to his place for some up close and personal time. When two o'clock in the morning rolled around, she left for home. Parked in the garage, she closed the door and got out of the car.

Tired, she trudged through the door to go upstairs and collapse in her bed. The back basement door opened. She let out a scream and clutched her chest as she spun around.

"Jesus, Paul. You should know better than to scare a girl like that."

"What if I wanted to?" His words slurred as he grabbed her around the waist from behind, pinning her arms to her sides.

Her heart kicked a notch faster. She twisted to break his hold with no luck. "Dammit, Paul, knock it off. You're drunk."

His breath was hot on the side of her neck. "I'll put you to bed better than that boyfriend of yours." His hands slowly slid from her waist, over her hips, and rested on her thighs. His fingers squeezing and gripping.

"I can smell your sex." He no longer contained her arms within his tight hold.

She jerked back her arms, nailing him in the gut with her elbows and ran up two steps. She paused to see him hunched with his arms wrapped around his waist.

Glowering at him, she spoke vehemently. "Don't touch me again or you'll regret it. Go to bed and think about what you just said and did."

Abigail sprinted up the stairs to the main level, which was dark except for the sliver of illumination from the kitchen nightlight. She dashed up the remaining flights to her room. With the door closed and locked, she leaned against it and caught her breath. Paul wouldn't come after her, but she was frightened just a few short moments ago.

This wasn't the first time he tried hooking up with her, but tonight he held her tighter. More possessively. The words he spoke were fouler than in the past. Did he have a hard-on? She shuttered at the possibility. If he did that again, she'd file a police report and move out.

* * * *

"I graded your papers last night." Liz announced moments after the final late bell of the day rang. Walking the rows of tables, she handed the papers to the correct student. "Some of you are very lucky to go on your warm weather trips. Some of you are very lucky to spend the time with family. Some of you are very lucky for the love shared during the holiday break."

"Yeah, well, some of us don't have any luck at all." The statement from Chris no longer came as a surprise.

To make it difficult for others to hear, Liz set Chris's paper on her table, speaking softly and quickly. "Some should reexamine their life." Liz returned her voice to normal "My winter break was a mixture of emotions. I had highs and lows, but won't bore you with the specifics. You all did a very good job. Some of you could have taken a little more time on the details, some on grammar, and others on punctuation."

She returned to her desk at the front of the class, grabbed a paper pile, and stepped to the front tables. "Please take one of these handouts and pass the rest back. This is the packet you will be using while we read and discuss *The Outsiders*."

"I say we watch the *Hunger Games: Mockingjay* instead. More action than in this piece of work."

"You're right, Chris, *The Outsiders*, is a piece of work. It's a piece of historical literature. *The Hunger Game* series, in its own right, is a literary work of fiction. Although, we will not be reading or watching any of the books in the series for class. You will though, get to watch the movie adaptation of *The Outsiders*." For Chris's benefit, Liz looked in her direction as she spoke of the movie viewing.

With her hands under the table, Chris peered down and Liz knew what she was doing. Liz continued to speak as she approached the young lady. "You will find the movie adaptation much like any adaptation of a book to film, they have differences. Wouldn't you, Ms. Burnhamwood?"

The shocked look she received didn't surprise Liz.

"Hand over the phone, Chris. Four days in a row and you still don't get it. Maybe after today you'll understand the consequences. One of your parents will have to pick up your phone from the office."

"Please, no. I promise I won't use it again. Anything but to have my mother come to school."

The pleading wouldn't work on Liz, as she had her own phone-addicted-teenage-user.

"I'm sorry." She held her hand open and waited for the phone. "Why don't you turn it off and save your battery."

Moaning was followed by the phone slapping against her hand. Liz walked to the front of the class and called the front office, explaining the situation.

Hanging up, Liz spoke to Chris. "They're calling your mother now, so she can be here as soon as possible after school. Now, back to our discussion about what is expected of you for this reading assignment."

* * * *

Robert yanked open the first entrance door, then the second to enter Chris's school. Being called out of a meeting because your ex-wife refuses to handle a situation wasn't his idea of fun. She was lucky the meeting was one he could leave. The drive south of the river hadn't calmed his frustration toward his ex or his daughter. How hard was it to stay off your phone during class?

Taking a deep calming breath, he opened the front, office door. Chris sat on a chair along a wall. Robert paused when he looked further into the office area. Liz stood talking with a man and woman, then she turned, smiled, and walked toward him.

"Robert?" Her voice sang to him in surprise. "I was expecting your ex-wife."

"You two know each other? Oh, my, God," Chris shrieked from the chair.

He and Liz both glanced at her before Liz responded. "Can I talk to you privately, please?"

"Yes." He glared at his daughter. "Don't move. I'll be back."

"Not like I can go anywhere."

"Snide comments and a rude attitude won't get you far, so knock it off." He gestured for Liz to lead the way to wherever they were going to go talk.

With the few others in the office, he kept his eyes up and stared at Liz's shoulders. Her light floral scent lingered upon the air. He wanted to wrap himself around her and inhale the familiar smell. They strolled farther into the office and turned to the right, disappearing around the corner. Privacy wasn't far off.

She stood by an open door, waiting for him to enter the small room. It was big enough for four upholstered chairs situated around a small round table. Once inside, she closed the door.

"I'm sorry about this but—"

"How…. Why?" He was befuddled.

"Please have a seat." As she sat, she gestured for him to follow. "Being a sub, I don't pay close attention to the kids' last names because I can't learn them all. While grading papers late last night I read Chris's and figured it out. That's not why you're here."

He sat on the chair beside her. "Kathleen said she was using her cell phone in class."

"Today was the fourth time I've caught her on her phone during class. I've given her warnings, which she doesn't heed. The school has a strict policy that I pushed aside the first three times, but couldn't any longer."

"I'm glad you didn't. When we bought her the phone, she was given strict rules. I'm sorry you've had to put up with this."

"Robert," she touched his knee and warmth spread up his leg. "Don't be too hard on her. As a parent, I know you have to discipline her, but go easy. From what I read in her paper, which we'll talk about at dinner, she has a lot of pent up emotions and feelings."

"Yeah," he wrapped his hand around hers. "We have a lot to talk about at dinner."

"Not sure I like the sound of that." There was a hint of worry in her joking tone. They stood and she opened the door.

"No worries. I'll see you tomorrow night at six." Her fragrance filled the room. God, how he wanted to kiss her.

They stepped around the corner. "Chris, do you have anything to say to Ms. Farefield?"

"I'm sorry."

"Anything else?"

"It won't happen again." Her words were exasperated, but spoken.

"Thank you, Chris. I hope it doesn't. You're too good of a student to be getting into trouble. Robert, here's her phone."

"Thank you, Liz."

Chris stood and shook her head. "I can't believe you know each other. That is so wrong."

Robert and his daughter were quiet leaving the building, but once in the car, he broke the silence. "I met Liz years ago and then ran into her on the cruise. Yes, we're seeing each other. No, I didn't know she was your sub. Now for this phone issue." He glanced in her direction. "It doesn't make me happy in the least that you're breaking not only mine and your mother's rules, but the school's as well. Please refrain from using it again in any of your classes. I don't want to get another phone call. Okay?"

"Got it," she responded without an attitude.

He'd take it. The remainder of the drive to Kathleen's took all of fifteen minutes, in silence. As soon as he pulled in the driveway, Chris darted from the car and into the house.

Kathleen met him at the front door. "Can you come in? I wanted to talk to Chris about what's going to happen."

"Yeah, I'm not planning on going back to the office." He followed her through the foyer and into the wide-open living and kitchen area.

"Can I get you anything to drink?" She opened the fridge.

"Water would be great."

She set a bottle on the counter and walked out of the kitchen. "Christine, please come here," Kathleen bellowed.

Heavy footfall sounded on the stairs followed with the smart-mouthed teenager response. "What?"

"Stop right now, young lady. Your father and I need to speak to you." Kathleen reappeared with Chris trailing behind. "Why don't we sit in the family room?"

"It's not a family room because we're not a family."

"Chris, we are family, regardless of marital status." He grabbed the water bottle and sat.

Kathleen wanted this, so she could start the conversation. Chris sat as far away as possible from him and her mother.

"Christine, I've made a decision, and your father is aware of it, that I'm moving to New York after Alex graduates from high school."

"No." Chris burst out of her seat yelling. "I'm not going to New York."

"Chris, sit down." Robert remained composed. "You're not going to New York."

"Thank you, Robert. Christine, my attorney is preparing paperwork for your father to take custody of you. You'll be staying in Minnesota."

"I'll still have to move, change schools, and make new friends. I'd be better off just going with you to New York. I hate you both." Chris stormed from the room and stomped all the way upstairs to her room.

"Let her go, Kathleen." He stopped his ex before she got to the foyer entrance. "She's had a lot to digest lately. When I picked her up today, her substitute teacher just happens to be... my girlfriend." As odd as it was to say, it felt right.

"What?" Her eyebrows drew together in disbelief. "You have a girlfriend. Since when?"

"I ran into her on the cruise, but I had met her years ago when I designed her deceased husband's clinic."

"Wow. I wish you the best." She went into the kitchen. Her lack of sentiment didn't surprise him.

Robert followed. "What's that supposed to mean?"

"Nothing. I really wish you the best. What's her name?"

"Liz Farefield."

"Well, from what Abigail tells me, you haven't had just one woman in your life. For you to call her your girlfriend means that you're making a commitment."

"O-kay, I need to watch how much I share with my oldest. Am I good to go?"

"Yes," she said with a chuckle.

* * * *

Liz entered the house exhausted. The exchange between Chris, Robert, and herself was both nerve racking and exciting. She worried, about how Chris would react in class, knowing her teacher and father knew each other. What if Robert told her about them as a couple? Oh, the implications could be terrible for her in the classroom. She didn't tell him about the vocal out bursts.

Calm down. No one can control the future.

The house was quiet. "Hello? Anyone here?" She walked up the stairs. "Sarah? Brad?" Reaching the top, she peered into Sarah's room and found her with headphones on, sitting at her desk. Liz entered and tapped her shoulder.

The poor thing jumped and squealed, before pulling the headphone from her ears. "You scared me!"

"Sorry. You should turn down the volume and then maybe you would've heard me yell when I got home. Is your brother in his room?"

"Not sure. I think so."

"I need to talk to you and him after dinner. I was thinking of ordering a pizza."

"Yes."

"I'm going to Brad's room." A few steps across the hall and she peered inside his room. No sign of life. More than likely, he was in the basement, gaming.

Liz went back to the kitchen and ordered the pizza. A few steps down to the basement, the sound of guns firing assaulted her ears.

"Brad," she called out. "Brad, I'm home."

He paused his game. "Hey, Mom. I finished all my homework."

"Good. Listen, I ordered pizza and after we eat, I need to talk to you and your sister. So when you come up, turn the gaming off. Okay?"

"Got it. I'll come up as soon as I finish this game." The shooting resumed as she went back upstairs.

Liz had thought about how to start the conversation while she'd waited for the pizza delivery. With the remaining pizza wrapped and put away, they sat in the family room. Her children's acceptance meant a lot, but wouldn't hinder her from seeing Robert. At least that's what she kept telling herself.

"First, I would like you two to let me talk without interruption. Let me say what I need to say, okay?" After they both nodded, she continued. "I met someone while I was on the cruise."

Both of them sat wide-eyed and slack-jawed for a minute.

"He lives here in St. Paul, and I had met him when he worked with your father on the designing and building of the clinic. His name is Robert. We talked a lot while on the cruise. We enjoyed each other's company and decided to continue to see each other after returning home."

Brad fought with wanting to speak and his head slowly shook no. A smile grew on Sarah's face.

"He has three children. One daughter is finishing college and working at his design firm, a son graduating from high school this year, and his youngest daughter is your age, Sarah. I'm telling you this because I really like him. Tomorrow night I'm going out on a date with him. I'm going to let you guys stay at home, rather than have someone babysit you. You're both old enough to be home for a night, unless you do something otherwise to prove me wrong." Her eyes darted between children.

Brad stood and shouted. "Why? Why do you have to be with someone else besides Dad? You have Sarah and I to keep you company. Aren't we enough? This guy will leave you like all the others." He darted from the room and up the stairs to his room.

With her elbows on her knees, Liz held her head in her hands. She let him express his feelings without interjecting. He needed time to digest the information before she'd go talk to him in private. She sat back and glanced at Sarah, who grinned at her.

"If you're happy, I'm happy, Mom." Leave it to Sarah to be on the opposite side of Liz's dating fence. "Do you have a picture of him?"

"I do." It was hard to match her daughter's excitement when Brad was distraught. "I'll be right back." She grabbed her purse and pulled out the small stack of photos that were of her and Robert. "Here," and handed the pictures to Sarah.

"He's cute, Mom. How old is he?"

"Four years older than me." Looking at the photos, a smile bloomed on her face. He was a handsome man.

"You two make a cute couple." Sarah gently jabbed her elbow into her side.

"Yes, I agree."

"Who's this guy? He looks a lot like Dad."

"That's Scott. Other than his hair, I thought the same thing. He was traveling with Robert. They work together."

"Was it because Scott looks so much like Dad that you didn't hook up with him instead?"

Liz jerked back and cocked her head while regarding her daughter. "Hook up?"

"I may be thirteen, Mom, but I'm not stupid. I know what happened between you and Robert on the cruise."

"Sarah!" Shocked. Horrified. Amazed. This was her daughter talking.

"Mom, really? I'm not stupid, but is that the reason why? Is it because he resembles Dad so much that you two didn't connect?"

Liz shook her head, aghast at the conversation she was having with her daughter. "Yes."

"Well, I'm glad you didn't hook up with him. Brad would be, too. When will we get to meet Robert?" Sarah flipped back to the first picture of Liz and Robert in the Italian restaurant.

"When I'm ready. I don't want to rush things."

"Then why did you tell us about your date with him?"

She took the stack of photos from her. "Because I really like Robert. There's something there between us and I want to make it work."

She bit her tongue about to speak nasty of her mother-in-law. This was something Liz wanted to change about herself—no negative talk about Ellen.

"Well, I'm all for it."

"I appreciate your support. Now," she got to her feet, "I need to talk to your brother."

Liz stood in front of Brad's closed bedroom door and rapped lightly while turning the knob to find it locked.

"Go away," came from inside the room.

"Brad, please unlock the door or I will." Her voice remained calm because she didn't want to upset him further.

Several seconds later the lock clicked. She entered, then closed the door before sitting on the bed. He crawled into a tighter ball at the head of his bed. God forbid, she come close enough to touch him. She would let him decide when to come to her welcoming arms.

"Brad, you're still young and don't understand love and life. I'm not saying I love Robert, but I do really like him. You and your sister make me very happy, but I also would like to fall in love again. When I do, that man will not be a replacement to your father. No man will ever replace him. Not for me. Not for Sarah. And not for you. You can't replace what you've lost. You can only fill the void." She spoke slowly with thought and caring words. Or at least she hoped that's how she spoke.

"Your heart can and does grow to accept and love more than one person. If it didn't, then where would we be? If my heart only loved your father, how could it accept my loving your sister? Because it grew, and my heart grew larger with more love when you came along. Our hearts will make room for others who will come into our lives. Robert may be one of them. I don't know. Only time will tell. That's all I'm asking from you, is a little time.

"As for your comment about the other men I've dated, they didn't hurt my feelings when things didn't work out between us. Usually, it was me who ended any possibility for a relationship."

Silence fell over the room as she paused.

"You know, not a day goes by that I don't think about your father. Every day when I look at you, I see him. You are a spitting image of him. You have his blue eyes with full, dark eyelashes. Your hair gets darker every fall. You're built like him too, long and lean. I love you and because of you, I will never lose my love for your father. I'm blessed to have you."

Liz remained sitting for a moment to see if Brad would say or do anything, but he didn't. She walked the short distance to the door and opened it.

Jody Vitek

"Please think about what I've said tonight. I love you."

Chapter Twenty-Two

David entered the office, set his bag in his station, and left to talk to Robert. The morning news worried him about Abigail's safety. Another sexual assault happened Wednesday night. Robert's admin was away from her desk, so he approached the open door and rapped his knuckles on the door jam.

"Can I talk to you?"

Robert lifted his gaze from the paperwork on his desk.

"Sure." After David closed the door, Robert spoke. "Sit down. Something serious?"

"It could be. Did you see the news last night or this morning?"

Robert shook his head.

"There was another assault in Abigail's neighborhood. Although it was near a different campus, the M.O. is the same as what the other victims have given. I know she parks in the garage at her place and has the two guys living there. By the way, they are protecting her because they both, on separate occasions, thought I was attacking her and came after me. I'm concerned for her safety."

"Does she know about the latest attack?"

"She wasn't here when I got in." He hesitated. Nervous and unsure of how Robert would respond. "For her safety, I was thinking of asking her to move in with me... or you."

"I agree."

David's unease subsided.

"She should move." Robert pushed a button on his phone. "Has Abigail arrived yet?"

"No, sir." The front desk receptionist answered over the speaker phone.

"Please send her to my office when she arrives. Thank you."

"Yes, sir."

"David, I'd like to apologize again for what happened the other day."

"I understand you're looking out for your daughter, but I hope you know I'm not out to hurt her. I've been strict with her about behavior between us here in the office. That we're to remain professional at all times."

"That's good to hear." A knock sounded at his office door. "Enter."

"The receptionist…" Abigail stopped once she saw David sitting in her dad's office. "I didn't mean to interrupt, but then maybe I should be."

"Please, sit down," her dad said. Once she sat beside David, he continued. "Are you aware there was another assault in your area?"

"No." She sounded so casual. "We've discussed this. I've discussed this with both of you. I'm safe."

"David and I don't believe you are. Actually, you should temporarily move in with me… or David."

"No. You two need to stop." She bent and stared straight at David. "*You*. What right do you have to come to my father and discuss my well-being? Please keep your thoughts to yourself. Please leave, so I can talk to my father."

He glanced at Robert.

"Go ahead. I'll talk to her." Robert nodded to the door.

David closed the door behind him. She wasn't happy with him, but he didn't care. He worried about her. He wanted to protect her.

"I can't believe you." Abigail rested her hands on her father's desk and leaned in. "One minute you're telling the guy to leave me alone and the next you're saying I should move in with him." She pushed away and stood straight. "I'm not moving out of my house. I told you, I'm safe. In two weeks, I start my final class. I'll be careful when on campus."

"I'm not saying to move permanently out of the house. I just want you to move out until this guy is caught."

"Dad, do you realize there are assaults happening all the time on and off campus? It's not just college students at risk, but everyone, and every day." She softened her stance. "I will always be at risk, no matter where

I am, Dad. I love you and that you care about me enough to want me to move, but do you understand what I'm saying?"

"I do. Please promise me you'll carry your mace at all times."

"I do and will continue to do so." She plopped on to a chair. "What's going on? Have you called Liz yet?" The ball had better be in motion or she'd continue to push.

"Yes, I've talked to and seen Liz." He put his hand up to stop her from interrupting. "Your sister has been using her phone in school, during class, and yesterday had it taken away. They called your mother to come to the school to pick her up. Your mother called me at work, refusing to deal with the situation, so I went to the school. You're not going to believe this, but the teacher who took it away, was Liz. You can't imagine the surprise for me and the horror for your sister. Chris was mortified and even more so when I told her in the car that Liz and I were dating."

Abigail shook her head. This didn't bode well for Liz or Chris.

"As for Liz and me, we're going out tonight. The first time since the cruise."

She waited for him to continue, but he didn't. "I'm glad to hear you're dating. As for the situation with Chris, it could get worse before it gets better."

"She'll be fine, eventually. As for you, stay safe and know you can stay at my place anytime. Now, I have work to do and so do you."

* * * *

While Liz changed her clothes for tonight's date with Robert, she wondered if she should bring up Chris's recent classroom behavior. Today the girl had been abnormally quiet and remained off her phone. She'd see what direction their conversation would go and then decide. Back in the cold Minnesota weather, and not in the tropical heat of her cruise, she opted for jeans and a sweater. Robert had said casual. In her bathroom, she freshened her makeup by adding darker eye shadow, a touch more blush, and a new shade of lipstick.

A knock on her bedroom door was followed by Sarah's voice. "Can I come in?"

"Yeah. What's up, honey?"

"You're wearing that on a date?"

"Something wrong with this? Robert said to dress casual. Like I was going out with my girlfriends." She slipped a foot into her tall leather boot.

"Well then, I guess you look good." Her daughter sat on the bed.

"I'm glad you approve. Not that I needed it." She pulled up the zipper, and slid the other boot on her foot. "I'm not sure what time I'll be home tonight, so don't wait up. Call me only if it's an emergency. Blood, broken bone, that sort of emergency." Boots on, next came jewelry.

"I got it, Mom. I won't bother you." She rolled onto her stomach. "Do you want me to make sure Brad gets to bed at a decent time?"

"Being a Friday night, I'm not worried about what time he goes to sleep." She turned from her jewelry box with two different earrings. "Which ones?"

"I like the dangling ones."

She put the one earring away and retrieved the mate to the dangling one. "I want you to leave your brother alone. Only if he's getting into trouble, then you can bother him. I'm guessing he'll either be in the basement or up in his room."

"Okay. Got it."

"What do you want for dinner?" She slid a chunky ring on her middle finger that had a yellow-greenish stone in the center. The stone's color played nicely with the chartreuse color of her sweater.

"Chicken?" Her daughter got off the bed, as Liz was finished getting ready for her date.

"Let's go see if that works for Brad." Leaving her room, they went to the kitchen where she'd last seen him at the table doing homework. Although it was the weekend, the rule in the house was to complete your homework on Friday.

No longer at the table, she went downstairs where he sat gaming. "Are you up for chicken strips for dinner? I can make waffle fries too." The fries were his favorite.

"Whatever." He spoke with a bit of attitude.

"I'll get dinner in the oven." She returned to the kitchen, fixed their dinner, and cleaned up the dishes before leaving for Robert's.

On the way to his place, her nerves kicked in with fingers tapping on the steering wheel. Her stomach fluttered. She didn't understand why she was nervous. For once, she felt good about going on a date that her children knew about. Although small, she was making progress with having a man in her life regardless of what others told her.

She exited off 35E onto Shepard Road and followed Robert's directions for the rest of the way to his place. His apartment building sat along the Mississippi river on the edge of an older housing development, but downtown was only a few minutes away. Parking was a bit of a challenge, but she managed to locate a spot. She entered the building and buzzed his apartment.

"Hello."

"Hi, Robert. I'm here."

"Come on up."

The door buzzed, along with her insides. She'd seen him yesterday at school, but it seemed like a lifetime since she last saw him. He stood in the doorway when she approached and her legs weakened. He wore jeans, loafers, and a navy three-quarter zip pullover sweater with a tee shirt underneath. Different from his cruise attire. More relaxed. Damned if she didn't like it.

He took her hand, leading her into the apartment. "You look great." He pulled her in for a kiss. Her legs buckled, and he held onto her. "You okay?"

"Uh, yeah. Wow." The effect of his kiss left her dazed since too much time had passed from the last time they'd seen each other. She wanted him. "What a kiss."

"That wasn't a kiss. This is." Taking possession of her lips and mouth, his tongue sought hers, as he pulled her into a tighter embrace.

Her inner thighs quivered, and she didn't want to leave. She wanted him in bed. He was hard and wanted the same thing as her. A pleasurable moan from her and he took his kiss to her neck.

"I don't want dinner." He maneuvered his hands inside her coat and under her sweater. His breath fell warm on her ear.

The simple contact ignited a passionate fire within her. "Nor do I," Liz said breathily working her hands underneath his top layers.

* * * *

Lying under his covers, sexually spent, Robert held Liz close to his body. He knew before she arrived that he wouldn't be able to control himself and was glad she'd wanted the same thing. Although he'd turn fifty this year, his body didn't fail him in the bedroom. Here he was with a woman in his bed. The bed he swore he'd never share.

"What are you thinking about?" Her quizzical voice broke the silence, as she glided a hand on his chest, running her fingers through his chest hair.

"About how hungry for food I've become. The question is, do you want to stay here or go out? I know a great Chinese place that delivers... if you like Chinese."

She propped up on an elbow and spread her hand flat on his chest. "You never planned on taking me out tonight." She teased.

He suddenly felt guilty. "I had every intention of taking you out to dinner." He sat up, making her fall on to her back. "Let's shower and dress, then I'll take you out to eat."

"No. Robert, I'm having fun. Let's stay here."

He leaned toward her, placing his hands on each side of her body, to hover above her. "So you're not hungry?"

"No, I need food to re-energize. I'm glad I ate a few of the kids waffle fries before coming here."

"Yeah, you came alright." He grinned at his own dirty joke.

"Robert," she chastised with a smile. "Chinese sounds good."

He leaned in for a quick kiss. Food before another round of pleasure in bed. "I'll be right back." He slipped out from under the covers and went into the bathroom to put on a pair of lounging pants. "Here's a robe, or if you'd prefer, I can find lounge wear for you."

"The robe will be fine." His robe fit her body well, as she cinched the belt around her waist.

No other women had shared his bed let alone worn his robe. The idea of Liz being a part of his private world set his heart on fire for the possibility of a future for them.

"How does it look?" Liz turned around. Her small frame remained hidden in the bulkiness of robe.

"A bit big, but otherwise, I like it on you." Robert took her hand and led her to the kitchen. He rummaged through a drawer where he kept his takeout menus.

Locating the Chinese flyer, he opened to the menu. "So what do you like?"

"Cheese Wontons." She stood beside him, resting a hip against the marble countertop.

"How about something with a little substance? Protein to replenish your energy."

"Sweet and sour chicken?"

"And cheese wontons." Robert winked as a pleasing smile blossomed on her face.

With their food ordered, he led Liz to the couch. "I have to ask, after yesterday's visit, how was Chris today?"

"Unusually quiet. I hope you went kind of easy on her."

"I discussed the situation with her. I think what took her by surprise was the fact that you and I are seeing each other." He put his arm around her.

"I can understand why she kept to herself."

"There's something else you should be aware of, Liz." As she faced him, uncertainty fell over her face. "I'm going to be gaining full custody of Chris in the near future. I told Chris this yesterday as well. There's a lot going on with my ex-wife. The man she's engaged to lives in New York City. She's moving there after Alex graduates from high school. Chris will be starting high school in the fall and well, she was angry about moving."

Liz sat up and out of his arms. "Are you moving so she can remain with her friends and in the same district? Because you are definitely out of our school district."

"No, I'm not moving. She'll have to make a change in schools and make new friends."

"Robert," she held his hand. "Don't take this the wrong way, but I think you should give great consideration to either moving into the area, so she can go to the same high school as her friends or finding a way to transport her daily to our district. This is an important time in her life and with all of these changes going on between you and your ex, it's going to be tougher for her if you remove her from friends and the normalcy."

He inhaled and audibly exhaled. "As of right now, I'm staying here but will consider your words of advice."

The door buzzed and he let the delivery guy into the building. With the money and food exchanged, Robert pulled two plates from the kitchen cupboard. "What would you like to drink?"

Liz joined him at the island. "Water, please, and tap is fine." They dished the food onto their plates. "How's Abby doing? She's interning at your firm, right?" She broke the wooden chopsticks apart.

"She's doing great with the firm, but I worry about her. She lives in the area where the assaults are happening and I'm concerned about her safety. We can eat at my dining room table that never gets eaten at."

"Never?" She set her plate on the placemat.

He sat down, as did Liz. "Never. The kids eat anywhere but at the table."

"You don't eat together as a family?" She maneuvered the sticks with precision between her long, slender fingers.

"Everyone has their own food likes. If we do eat together, it's at the ledge of the island. You must eat with your children." He mixed his rice and sweet and sour chicken before taking a bite.

"Yes, even when they eat something different from me. As they're getting older though, I'm finding it harder to cook and eat together. I think we're headed down the path you're on, but back to the assaults. Does she feel safe where she's living?"

Robert finished chewing and swallowed. "Yes. She feels safe because she parks in the attached garage and has two male roommates. She's also dating a guy she works with at the firm."

"You allow that?" She choked with surprise. "Don't most companies have policies in place regarding dating within the workplace."

"No. Bigger firms usually have some sort of statement about not being able to date someone you report to. I never thought about inter-office dating being an issue until now. It all happened when I was on the cruise."

He enjoyed watching her eat with chopsticks. The way her tongue darted out and her lips closed around the sticks, he'd never found eating Chinese to be arousing—until now.

"You don't sound happy about this guy dating Abby."

He cleared his throat. "His name is David. He's actually a great employee and kid. I just don't want to see Abby get her heart broken."

"Who says she will? Sometimes, you have to take a chance at love. Even if it means getting hurt."

He set his fork down. "I'm not going to hurt you, Liz."

"I can handle it, and so can your daughter."

"You and Abby would get along great. You two are on same wave length." They ate in peace for a few minutes. "Have you talked to your kids about our relationship?"

"I did. Sarah handled it well, but Brad not so much. Kind of getting the cold shoulder. He'll come around."

Chapter Twenty-Three

Sunlight broke through the shades as Liz woke and stretched her body in her own bed. Last night, she didn't want to leave Robert or his bed, where it was warm, and go into the cold January night air. Staying the night wasn't an option. The children were expecting her to be there during the night and in the morning.

She sat on the edge of the bed, gave her body another long stretch of the arms before going downstairs. Voices drifted from the kitchen. At first, it was difficult to decide if it was the TV or the kids. Entering the kitchen, she stopped dead in her tracks and stared at her son's head.

"Bradley, what happened?" She approached like a tortoise, taking what seemed like forever to reach where he sat at the kitchen table, eating his bowl of cereal. Her hands touched his poorly shaved head. "Who did this to your hair?" Too stunned, she didn't raise her voice.

"I did. Now I don't look like Dad." He jerked away and moved to the next chair. Then he pulled his bowl in front of him.

"Why?"

"Because I don't want to look like Dad." He was angrier than she originally suspected.

The words hurt. Surely, he didn't mean them.

She stared at his patchy head of hair. "What did you cut it with?" There an amazing calmness came over her while talking to Brad.

"I found Dad's shaver in your bathroom." He shoved in another spoonful of cereal.

"Hmm." She thought she'd gotten rid of all of Gregory's belongings. "Where did you cut it?"

"In your bathroom."

"What…. Did you clean it up?"

"No, I did." Sarah came around the corner. "I found him in the process of doing the damage and figured it was too late to stop him, so I let him finish. I didn't call or text you because, what good would it have done?"

Liz turned on the coffee machine, picked a coffee flavor, and waited for the water to heat. "True, on all accounts. Thank you for cleaning it up. You did a great job, because I didn't see any signs of it when I came home."

"So you're not mad at him?" Sarah popped waffles into the toaster.

"Will you put two waffles in for me? Thanks. Not much I can do about it. The damage is done. Plus, it's only hair. It'll grow back."

"Wow. I remember when I cut my bangs once and you went ballistic on me."

"It was also for good reason. School pictures were the following week. Would you like me to show you?" she replied with a cock-eyed grin. "This is his whole head and he's a boy."

"Good point."

"Brad, when we're finished having breakfast, you and I will go fix your hair."

The cutting of his hair didn't bother her. However, she was apprehensive with his behavior behind the reasoning of shaving his head.

"Fine." At least she got a response from him.

"So how was your date last night?" A slow smile built on Sarah's face.

Brad humphed at his sister's question followed by a glare.

"I had a great night. It was good to see Robert again, but that's all I'm going to discuss with my daughter." She grabbed plates for her and Sarah's waffles.

"Oh come on. What did you do? Where did you go to eat?"

"Sarah, I'm not talking about my date." A need for a knife and the peanut butter kept her from making eye contact with her daughter.

"Get the hint, Sarah. They had sex."

"Bradley!" He had gone through sex education, but this was too much.

"It's true though." He put his breakfast dishes in the dishwasher.

"Just ask Grandma Farefield."

The waffles popped up and Sarah pulled hers from the toaster.

"Okay, enough. I'm not talking about my personal life with you two. As for your grandmother, she assumes too much and speaks too freely to you kids. Now let me eat my breakfast."

With the haircutting incident and problems with Chris at school, Liz questioned if maybe she and Robert should step back from their relationship. Was their relationship worth the trouble it's caused with their children?

* * * *

After a couple of drinks with Scott Monday night, Robert entered his apartment, when his phone vibrated. He had gotten a message from Kimberly, and he'd texted it was over between them. Unfortunately, she didn't get the hint, even after telling her in person and via text. She texted him again, pleading for him to at least join him for a drink or two. He politely told her he was out with a work partner and wouldn't be able to make it. Closing the door, he checked his cell to see another text from her. This time with a picture attached. He deleted the message without a response. Maybe she'd get a clue.

Liz had been on his mind all day. Friday night was enjoyable, yet he found himself at odds with his single status. There was a growing need inside of him of wanting a strong relationship with Liz. Wanting to be with her more than for a short period of time. Wanting to wake up with her in his bed on a regular basis.

Yet they had steps to take. Slow steps when it came to their children. More so with Chris than with Abby and Alex. He picked up the phone and called Liz.

"Hi, Robert. Miss me already?" There was a playful tease to her voice.

"Yes, which is why I'm calling. I've been thinking and was wondering what you've got planned this weekend. Saturday in particular." He hung up his coat.

"Um, nothing as of right now."

In his bedroom, he stripped off his business attire and pulled on lounge pants. "I have my kids this weekend. I thought it would be a good time for everyone to meet."

"Robert, I don't know." Her words were spoken with heavy hesitation. "Chris is having a hard enough time, and I found Brad Saturday morning at the table with a shaved head."

"He shaved his head?" His fingers ran through his hair as if on autopilot. He couldn't image a young boy shaving off his own head of hair. "Why?"

"He's mad at me. If he's acting like this, I worry about what else he might try, and for that matter, what Chris might do if we rush things."

"If we wait though, the situation may not change for the better either. That's one of the reasons I think it would be good to make the introductions. It would be us, showing them, that we care enough about each other that we want to have this relationship, and they're going to have to accept us being partners."

Silence.

"Liz?"

"I just don't know."

"I'm worried. You sound like you're caving. I don't want you to give up on us." If he wasn't ready to throw in the towel, he wasn't about to let her toss hers in on them.

"Are you certain about this? About us? You haven't called any of the other—"

"No, I haven't called any of them. I told them it was over and I wouldn't be spending time with them. Liz, I really enjoy my time with you. I want you to meet my older two children and at the same time meet your two children." For a brief moment, he paused. "I care about you."

"Okay. Let's see how it goes." She lacked enthusiasm.

He kept his excitement hidden and spoke calmly. "It's going to be fine. Would you prefer to be at your place Saturday?"

"I think that would be best for my kids. Did you want to come for dinner?"

"No, that would be asking too much from our kids. I was thinking maybe after dinner."

"That works. Should we say seven then?" Her mood picked up, as she sounded delighted about making the plans.

"We'll see you Saturday at seven. Until then, can I text or video call you after the kids go to bed?" He didn't think he'd make it all week without talking or seeing her. She had grown on him that much.

* * * *

Friday afternoon, Robert left the office early. He was meeting with his attorney, Kathleen, and her attorney. The new custody papers were ready. He entered the St. Paul office and was directed to a sleek, contemporary designed conference room. Located in the corner, the room overlooked the Mississippi River. The formality of shaking hands upon his entrance completed, the proceedings commenced.

The agreement left nothing for Robert to object to or argue about. He had given Kathleen his okay to the changes in person. To him, as a man, you don't back down on your word. The first weekend that school was out for the year, he would take over parental responsibilities. He wasn't sure what the date would be until today, but for some reason, he hadn't expected it to be as soon as June.

He would schedule some time off to move Chris into his place. Maybe spend some time showing her around the area to make her feel more comfortable. They would also need to work on getting her registered for high school. Liz thought he should move so Chris could remain in the same school district with her friends. He wouldn't start this new relationship with his daughter by giving into her every whim. If he decided to move, it would be on his terms.

They shook hands after things were finalized. "Can we talk?" Kathleen asked.

"Sure. Here or back at my place? The kids will be arriving soon."

"Here. Give me a minute to see if we can sit in here or if they need the room." Kathleen left the room with her attorney.

A couple minutes later, she returned. "We're fine to stay in here." She sat on the square leather seat.

"What's going on?"

"I got another call from school yesterday. Christine has been disruptive in class and her counselor said this has been going on for some time. It's now at the point where it needs to be dealt with. Not only that, she's continued to use her phone in school. I've taken it away from her. Interesting enough, she's been relatively quiet in your girlfriend's classroom, but her grades have slipped dramatically in English."

He stood by the windows and looked out to the snow-covered frozen waterway. "Liz never said anything to me."

"I wouldn't expect her to. Teachers don't call parents about the children's grades. As parents, we should be checking the grades on-line. Plus, she's not failing yet. I would think maybe if she were failing then maybe we'd get a call. She's not troublesome any longer in Liz's classroom."

"She's just not doing the homework or not applying herself." He faced his ex-wife and leaned against the window frame.

"I think it's a combination of both. I've had a long talk with her. No phone until she brings her grades back up. I'm also going to take her to see a family therapist. The school counselor mentioned it, and I informed her that it was already on the calendar."

"That's good."

"I wouldn't be surprised if we're asked to do a group session. Will you make yourself available if needed?" Kathleen approached the window where he stood.

"Of course. I'll do what I can."

"Robert, Christine's going to need you to be there for her during this transition. You're not going to be able to run off whenever and with whomever you want. She's going to be dependent on you for everything."

With her last words, his composure broke and his voice rose. "She's not a baby any more, Kathleen. Stop treating her like one." He stepped away from the window. "As for me, I'm an adult and know how to take care of my own children."

"Do you? You haven't been there to take care of them for the past fifteen years." She crossed her arms over her chest, taking a defensive stance.

"I *was* there. Maybe I haven't been there for Chris as much as I should've been. Since the divorce, I've been there when I was supposed to be. Things are about to change. As of Sunday, June fourteenth, Chris will be in my custody." He paused. "If I wasn't there, as you say, why would you then be so quick to give me custody of Chris?"

"You're too much. You want to flip this situation on me and make me the bad person? I don't think so."

"What mother would up and leave her teenage daughter during a time when she's going to need her the most?" He didn't care if the words stung. He spoke the truth.

"How dare you?"

"It's a two-way street Kathleen, and you've trudged all over my side. I'm going to be there for Chris. It may be difficult at first for both of us, but we're going to work through all those tough times. I wish you the best in New York."

He left the law office and waited for the elevator. There were many things he'd need to prepare for before gaining custody of his daughter. Maybe this weekend would be the start to making changes—in his and her life.

* * * *

Liz and the kids finished eating dinner Saturday night and she let them go off to do their own thing while she cleaned. Her nerves on edge, keeping busy with clean up occupied her hands and mind.

Earlier in the week when she'd fixed Brad's self-shave job on his hair, she used the opportunity to talk to him about Robert. She had reiterated that Robert, and other men that might come into their lives, would never replace his father. Ever. If he wanted to accept Robert into his life, he might find a new friend. A new confidant. A new mentor. As the week went on, Brad would ask her simple questions about Robert. He grew more accepting of meeting Robert.

The doorbell rang.

Her heart leapt.

Sarah and Brad came into the entry area.

Regaining her composure, she ran shaking hands down her jean-clad legs before opening the door. "Hello. Welcome. Come in out of the cold."

A beautiful tall blonde entered with a genuine smile on her face. A young man with black hair, who towered above his older sister, came through the door and nodded in greeting. Chris strolled through next with Robert trailing behind.

As he moved in for a kiss, she turned to offer her cheek. "Let's hang your coats up in the closet before we make introductions and sit down."

Robert assisted her with their jackets. "You have a very beautiful home."

"Thank you. Did you have any trouble finding it?"

"No problem at all." With the last coat taken hung, he turned to their two families. "So, you must be Sarah and you're Brad. The man of the house. I'm Robert and these are my three children." He gestured to his kids. "This is Abigail, my oldest; Alex, who will be graduating high school; and my youngest, Chris. You and Sarah are the same age."

Liz didn't miss Chris's eye roll at her father's attempt to make a connection. "Why don't we go into the family room?" Liz gestured to the opening that led to the great room. "Can I get anyone something to drink?"

With no one in need of a beverage, she sat on the sofa beside her children, away from Robert. Chris had perched next to him, Alex beside her and Abigail sat on the lounger. Awkward, was the word that came to mind.

"My Mom says you're a nice guy and that I should like you." Leave it to Brad to speak freely. Everyone chuckled, but Chris.

"I'd like to think I'm a nice guy and easy to get along with. You'll be the one to decide whether you like me or not. Your mom tells me that you started playing traveling soccer this year. Did you enjoy playing?"

Brad glanced between Liz and Robert, as though he was surprised she had told Robert about him and that he remembered. "It was fun. We're doing indoor training now."

"That's pretty cool."

"So, you must like my mom a lot because you wanted us to meet." Sarah offered her insights on the conversation.

"I do like your mom. She's important to me which is why I thought it would be a good idea for everyone to meet each other."

"I'm going to barf. Seriously, Dad?" Chris shook her head.

Robert's head dipped low to face his daughter.

"What?" Chris threw her arms into a crisscross across her chest before throwing herself back against the couch "Don't give me that look."

Liz knew exactly the expression Robert had given her. 'Keep your mouth shut if you don't have anything nice to say' stare.

"Brad, do you prefer Brad or Bradley?" Robert leaned forward, resting his forearms on his thighs.

"Brad. My Grandma Farefield is the only one who calls me by my full name. I don't like that."

Robert chuckled. "My ex-wife calls the kids by their full names too. I don't though. It's too formal." Brad snickered and fought the smile.

"Hey Brad, my dad says you play video games. What do you play?" Alex turned the subject around.

"I play Call of Duty, Destiny, and Battlefield."

"No way. Your mom lets you play those? How cool."

"Mom, can we go play," Brad asked with pleading eyes.

"Sure, if you're okay with that, Robert?"

"Yeah, why not." It would be good for Brad to lighten up a little. Maybe Alex would talk about Robert in a positive way.

"Come on." Brad jumped from the sofa full of excitement and waved his arm to Alex. "It's all setup in the basement."

"Chris, do you want to go to my room?" Sarah followed her brother's lead to make their guests feel welcome.

"Sure." The two girls left the room to go upstairs.

"Liz," Robert spoke when the footfall was on the upper level. "I'm sorry about Chris."

"Don't worry." Robert came to sit beside her. High pitched squeals penetrated the upper floor. The girls found something in common.

"You two make a cute couple. I'm glad Dad met you on the cruise, Liz." Abigail admitted with a warm expression.

"I'm glad I ran into him." She glanced into his caring gaze before grinning at Abigail. "Did he tell you that I literally ran into him with a drink in hand? I'm glad he caught me before I spilled my drink on him."

"I believe he did mention something to me. Some things are meant to be and you two meeting on that ship was meant to be."

"Some things are meant to take time too, Abby," Robert spoke to his daughter.

"How is it, working for your father?"

"I don't see him that often during the day, so it's fine. I think if I were working side-by-side with him, we'd have issues."

"No, we wouldn't," Robert interjected. "We get along great."

"Dad, we get along great as father/daughter, but we're too alike to have a close working relationship."

"Does that mean you're not going to work for the firm after graduation?" His question was filled with concern and possible regret.

Robert loved hearing his daughter engage in conversation with his… girlfriend. The term was new for him. He had women, not girlfriends. Yet Liz was his girlfriend because there were no other women in his life now. Only one. He did want to take time where Liz was concerned, like he told Abby. He would wait a lifetime for her.

"Let's not talk about work. Liz, my dad said you're a substitute teacher and are teaching at Chris's school."

"I am. I sub for middle school English. Chris's teacher is out on maternity leave, so I'm filling in long-term."

"Ladies, would you mind if I went downstairs and checked in with the boys?" He wanted to see if he could bond a little more with Brad. Make things a little more comfortable between them.

They shook their heads, and he took the stairs to the basement where familiar noises assaulted his ears. The gunfire was loud, as was the talking between the boys and the game characters. He stood for several minutes behind them, watching the large sixty-inch screen and listening to them interact with each other.

"Looks like you two are having fun." Robert broke his silence and approached the worn sectional.

"This is an awesome set up, Dad."

"Liz, has the right house for it. I don't. As for your mother, well, you could've done something like this but not anymore."

"Kill him," Alex yelled out.

"What are you two playing?"

"Call of Duty." Brad's fingers ferociously maneuvered on the controller.

"D-A-D! Chris is gone." Abby's voice shattered the peacefulness.

Chapter Twenty-Four

Taking the stairs two at a time, Robert hit the top step and found Abby, Liz, and Sarah standing by the kitchen table. "What do you mean Chris is gone?" He was befuddled as to what Abby meant.

"She left to use the bathroom, but never came back to my room." Sarah spoke shyly, hugging Liz around the waist as if she'd done something wrong.

"How long ago? Just give me your best guess." He squatted to be at an even level with her. "Don't worry. She'll be okay. How much time, honey?"

The boys came up the stairs.

"Twenty… thirty minutes now?"

"Okay." Robert straightened. "Did she take her coat?"

Liz walked to the hall closet. "No. Robert, it's cold outside."

"It's warmer than normal. She had a sweatshirt on." He glanced at Abby. "She doesn't have her phone. Your mother took it away."

"How can you remain so calm?" Liz exclaimed, unnerved.

Robert looked back at Liz. "Kathleen lives about ten minutes away from here. Chris has friends close by too. More than likely she planned this out when I told her we were coming here."

"How would she know she'd be close enough to leave? She didn't know where I lived." Liz wrapped an arm around Sarah. Her eyebrows drew in expressing her worry for his daughter.

He took the few steps and embraced her. "I'm not sure, but kids are tech savvy these days. She'll be okay." An arm remained around Liz's waist, as he faced his children. "Abby, Alex, do either of you have her friend's numbers? If I can, I'd like to avoid calling your mother." They both shook their heads. "Did she use either of your cell phones to make a call or text a friend?"

"I haven't been around for her to use mine," Abby said standing next to Alex.

"Alex, what about your phone?"

"I got to your place late last night. Remember?"

He shook his head in defeat. "I'll need to call Kathleen. Liz, I'm sorry this happened. Do you mind if we stay here until we've found her?"

"Of course, you can. Brad, you can go back to gaming and Sarah, go ahead and go up to your room."

"Sarah," Robert gently said. "Thank you for coming downstairs and saying something."

"You're welcome." She hugged him tightly and just as quickly let go. "I hope she's okay."

"Sarah?" The possibility dawned on him.

"Yeah?"

"Did she use your cell phone?"

Sarah's gaze darted. Her chest and shoulders rose as her eyes widened. "Yes." The word burst from the young girl before she dashed from the room.

"I never would've thought about that." Liz collapsed on a kitchen chair.

"It just hit me."

Sarah's footfall thudded on the stairs.

"Here." She slid through the hall's entrance into the kitchen. "She texted someone named Paige."

"Thank you, Sarah." Slight relief washed over him because this saved him from calling Kathleen. "Alex, why don't you go ahead and join Brad? I'm not sure how long we'll be."

With a nod, his son disappeared into the basement.

"Abby, I want you to call Paige. If I call, more than likely, Chris won't talk to me." He rattled off the number to Abby who tapped numbers on her cell phone.

"Let's sit in the living room," Liz suggested.

They followed her and waited as the phone rang. No response. They called two more times, unsuccessfully.

"Dad, I'm going to text Paige. She may not be answering because she doesn't recognize the number."

He nodded. Liz gently took his hand in hers, stroking his fingers. Whether it was meant to soothe him or her he didn't know, but he liked the gesture all the same. Minutes passed and they sat in silence, as though they were having a contest to see who could be quiet the longest.

"She's there." Abby's voice sliced the silence. "Paige says she got there about twenty minutes ago. She made good time. Do you want me to go get her?"

"That would be easier for her than if I go. I'll deal with her later."

Abigail sent another message. Five minutes passed without a response and then her phone rang. "Hello." She put the call on speaker.

"I'm not going home with him. Can I stay with you?" Chris said with defiance.

"No, my place isn't up for grabs. It's your weekend to be with Dad." Her father shook his head after she'd answered Chris. David was meeting her later at her place. What he didn't know, didn't hurt him.

"I don't want to be with him or Mom right now. I'll stay with Paige then." Abigail could hear Chris was fighting back the tears.

Her dad lost his resolve as he slumped forward with his head in his hands. Liz wrapped an arm around his shoulders, and Abigail knew there was a bond. Her father may not have said as much to her, but tonight was showing otherwise. She liked Liz and hoped this thing between Liz and her father would survive.

"You can't stay there. You and Dad are going to need to talk. And probably with Mom tomorrow."

"No. What's there to talk about? Mom's leaving me with Dad when she moves to New York."

Her father sat up, rigid.

Abigail's eyes widened. "What are you talking about?"

"Mom told me yesterday. After Alex graduates, she's leaving and I'm moving in with Dad."

Abigail mouthed the word 'what' to her dad and his eyes closed as his head nodded in confirmation.

"I don't want to change schools, Abby. I don't want to move." The dam broke. Chris was bawling.

"Chris, calm down. I'm going to pick you up." She'd deliver her safely to her parents.

No response.

"Hi, it's Paige."

"Paige, I'll need directions to your house. If you don't give them to me, I'll call our mom."

"No. Don't call Mom," Chris pleaded through sobs.

From what their mother had said at dinner when she arrived home from her New Year's Eve trip, knowing their mother didn't care for Paige, playing the 'call mom' card made sense. "Chris, I knew nothing about Mom and Dad's plans. My number will be in Paige's phone, so I want you to text me back with her address. I'll use a map to find my way there."

"Fine."

The phone call dropped, Abigail hung up on her end. "Before I pick her up, would you care to tell me what she was talking about?"

"Your mother and I met with the attorneys on Friday. We signed the new custody agreement papers."

"You're assuming custody of Chris?" This shocked her because of her mother's need to control everything in her life. "When?"

"Yes. After your brother graduates."

"Dad, you can't move her now. She's starting high school."

"Abigail," her dad cut her off. "We're not going to discuss this here and now. We can talk later."

She shook her head and looked at her phone. The address popped up on her screen. "I'm going to go get Chris and I'll see you back at your place." Abigail stood. "Liz, it was a pleasure to meet you. I hope to see you around more. I'm sorry my sister pulled this tonight."

Liz got off the couch. "I'm just glad she's safe." Opening the hall closet, she pulled her coat off the hanger.

"I'll see myself out. Dad, text me when you're on your way home."

"I shouldn't be too far behind." He held Liz's hand. They looked good together.

"You and your ex-wife move quickly." Liz walked away from him. "She gets engaged and the next thing you know you're getting custody of your daughter."

She spun around to face Robert. "I can see why Chris is upset. She's been with your wife for thirteen years and all of a sudden, she's leaving her, only to see her on certain agreed upon times. Did you two think this change would be as smooth as silk?"

"My ex-wife moves quickly. Especially when it's something she wants." He clasped her hand. "I don't know what you want me to say. I agree with you. Chris has every right to be upset, but what you don't know is that she's been mad at her mother and me since the day we announced we were getting a divorce." With a gentle tug of her hand, he persuaded her to sit in the living room. "Since I got back from the cruise, I realized I needed to get my relationship with Chris on the right path."

"I've said it before and I'll say it again. You should highly consider moving out this way—"

"You don't understand. We, I, can't keep giving Chris everything she asks for. She uses and manipulates to get what she wants."

"No, *you* don't understand." She removed her hand from his. "I can see I'm not going to get anywhere with you." She got off the couch. "I'm glad you found Chris and hope you two can figure this out."

"Liz," he pleaded as he followed her into the kitchen. "Honey." She turned at his choice of word usage. "Don't walk away mad at me."

"I'm not mad and you're stubborn, darling."

Whether she was being facetious or not, he didn't care. He smiled at her word choice. "Okay, you win for now. I am stubborn at times. We should probably be leaving." At the door to the basement, he hollered, "Alex, time to go."

"Just a minute."

"You heard him, we have a little time. Can I get a hug and a kiss?" She stepped into his waiting open arms.

* * * *

Robert walked through the door to his apartment behind Alex. Abby sat in the living room, alone, but got up and met him in the foyer.

"She's in her room. I talked to her a little. She knows what she did was wrong, but she saw it as an opportunity. Oh, I like Liz. Don't let her go, Dad." Abby hugged him and left.

He found Alex digging in a kitchen cupboard. "Hope you had a good time. I wanted you to meet Liz."

"It's cool she lets Brad play those games. He's not a bad player." He yanked out a bag of chips. "Oh, Liz seems nice, too. Not bad looking either."

He found his son's comment about Liz amusing. "Thanks. I'm going to talk to your sister." He walked the short distance to her room and lightly rapped on the door. "Chris, I'd like to talk to you." No response. "I'm coming in." Turning the doorknob, he cracked open the door.

She was lying across the width of her bed with headphones on. He closed the door gently behind him and sat on the bed by her feet. Startled, she flipped on her side and glared venomously at him.

"Take out your earbuds." He purposely didn't raise his voice. "We need to talk."

She popped a bud from her ear.

"Both of them, please."

With a heavy sigh, she flopped back onto her stomach, resting on her elbows. While removing the other earbud, she straightened her arms with another dramatic sigh and let her face bounce near the edge of the bed.

"I know you've wanted your mother and me to get back together since the day we told you kids we were getting a divorce. You've done everything possible to get us back together."

Chris snorted.

"I've also let your mother be the one to handle it all. I have to admit, she's the one to point out I've been absent from your life without being absent." He earned another groan from his daughter. "At first when she mentioned this, I pushed it aside. Told myself I was a good father."

She delivered a hearty, "Ha."

With a slight cringe to her reaction, he continued. "I told myself I did what I was supposed to as a father. I remembered the birthdays and holidays, and took you on my weekends. However," he rested a hand on her calf, "I wasn't there for you, Chris. My attention and focus was on Abby and Alex. A great deal on Alex. And for that, I'm sorry." Robert paused.

He thought he heard her sniffle, but didn't say or do anything. She needed time to hear what he had to say, soak it all in, and then decide how she was going to proceed. He didn't expect her behavior to turn around in one night. It would take a little time.

"When I returned from the cruise and your mother told me her engagement news and plans, I was taken aback. I realized she was right and that's why I made the decision to sign the custody papers. I needed to stand up and be a father to you. To be there for you."

He garnered a sniffled laugh. Again it hurt. He meant what he said about being more attentive to Chris. To take a more active interest in her life.

"We're going to make the transition work. We can go look at the school nearby."

"I don't want to change schools!" She snapped to a kneeling position on the center of the queen bed. Tear-filled eyes glowered in his direction. "I'm not moving away from my friends." She flung her body back to lie across the bed and kicked her feet enough to bounce her legs on the mattress.

"I'm sorry, but that's one decision that's not up to you."

A sudden shift and she was propped on her side. "I haven't been able to make one decision about any of this. Not one. It's my life and you and Mom are making all the decisions." The bed shook as she fell back onto her stomach and resumed kicking.

"This isn't about you getting to make the decision because you are the child. Your mother and I are your parents. We have to make the ugly decisions, and that's exactly what they are, ugly."

"I'm thirteen. I'm not a child. Isn't that what you've told Mom?" In her typical teenager, snotty voice, she threw his own words back at him.

"You're not an adult either." He kept his calm. "That's why your mother and I make the decision when it comes to you. Now, let's talk about tonight.

"Your sister says you're sorry, but I don't know if you really are. If so, I'd like you to write an apology to Liz. If you write an apology and leave it on your bed before you go with your mother, I'll make sure Liz receives the note. That's all I have to say." He walked toward the door. "I love you, Chris," he added before leaving her room.

With his back to the door, he inhaled deeply and, while exhaling, relaxed his body. That was the best he could say to Chris to make her understand their situation. He prayed it would be a smooth transition. Two important women in his life had given him the same advice. Was there some value to their words? Should he consider the notion of moving?

* * * *

Abigail left her father's place as it neared ten o'clock, and sent a text to David saying she'd be home in about twenty minutes and to come inside. They'd planned to be together, but her father's request to meet Liz overruled the earlier plans with David. It was all good though. She smiled at the thought of her dad with Liz. Liz was a beautiful, friendly, and caring woman. She and Liz got along great when her dad went downstairs, until her sister ruined the evening.

It angered her that Chris would do such a stupid thing—like run away—when her father was introducing Liz, someone special to him. Hopefully, the few spoken words they shared in the car would help matters and their dad would be able to talk to her. Maybe explain the situation, of which Abigail really knew little.

Approaching the house, she glanced around to see if anything or anyone was out of the ordinary. The guys were having a party, and with all the cars, getting to the garage would be iffy. As she neared the driveway, there was a pathway. A tight fit, she managed to get the car through and into the garage. Gina's car was gone, which helped make parking her car much easier.

She went inside and music reverberated the basement ceiling. As she walked up the stairs, the bass of the song thumped louder, and everyone practically yelled to be heard. She made eye contact with Paul on the other side of the family room, jerking her head in a man's way of acknowledgment. Turning to go upstairs, she spotted Conrad who waved before moving in her direction.

He leaned close to her and spoke in her ear. "Did you get in the garage okay?"

"I did. Thanks. Listen, David's on his way and should be here shortly. I told him to come right in and up to my room."

"You're not joining the party?"

"Not tonight. I've had enough fun for one night." She rolled her eyes. "Remind me to tell you about it."

"Okay. Don't be too loud up there." He nudged her shoulder.

She laughed in return. "I don't think you'd hear us if we were howling like wolves."

Conrad walked away making sounds of a wolf's cry.

Upstairs, in her room, she closed the door, which drowned the ruckus below. She used the toilet and then peeked out the high bathroom window to see if she could see David or his car. The door to her room opened as she walked out of the bathroom.

She ran to greet David but stopped as she faced Paul. "What are you doing?" House rule—knock on closed doors first.

He closed the door. "You are the only one I can think about when I'm with them."

She stepped back, turned, and ran for the bathroom.

Not quick enough.

His arms wrapped around just below her chest and trapped her arms, forcing her to expel a lungful of air. He stood five inches taller than she did.

She worked to catch her breath as her lungs rapidly expanded and contracted.

Warm air fell on her ear as he lowered his head. "None of them were you."

He was drunk, but she didn't smell beer or other alcohol.

"Help," the barely audible word escaped from her on a breath.

"No one's going to hear you." He kissed her ear. "Tonight it all comes to an end. Tonight I'll have you." He ran his hands up her arms. "I can't wait for you to spread your legs for me."

Her stomach lurched as the reality struck her.

Paul is the rapist.

"Help!" She flung her hands up and quickly, with her elbows bent, threw her arms back at her sides.

Free from his hold, she darted for the bedroom door. Her head and body slammed against the closed door. Pain shot through her neck, shoulders, and head. His body, and erection, pressed against her backside.

Dinner worked up her esophagus.

He yanked her hands behind her back. "Time to go to the bed."

Her ears whooshed and thumped with the blood rushing through her veins to reach her walloping heart.

Chapter Twenty-Five

As David stepped from his car, thumping music vibrated the air. He followed Abigail's instructions and entered the house without knocking, as if anyone would've heard anyway. The party was in full swing. A hand clasped his shoulder as he walked to the staircase to go to her room.

"Hey, you'd better take care of my girl."

David turned to Conrad. "Your girl?"

"Abs is special to me, and I pity any guy who hurts her." Conrad squeezed his shoulder.

He slapped Conrad's upper arm. "I hear you."

A thud sounded on the ceiling.

He glanced up and back to Conrad before darting up the stairs. The door to her bedroom was closed, and he grabbed the knob. Locked.

"Abigail?" he yelled. He backed up and ran into the door with his shoulder. It didn't bust open and he repeated his actions. With more force and a better connection, the door swung wide. David lost his balance for a moment.

The bathroom door rattled, but his focus was on Paul and Abigail on the bed.

"Get away from her!" Blood coursed through his veins. His heart pounded to keep up.

Paul held her hands above her head. "No." He worked with a tie to bind her hands. "The other girls never satisfied me. She's mine."

In a blind rage, David used his head to hit Paul on his backside, right at armpit level. They landed on the floor, and he swung at Paul as the beast ended on top of him. Conrad came up from behind and yanked Paul off him, holding him in a tight bear hug.

"Let go of me." Paul squirmed. "You've had her. He's had her. It's my turn to have her."

"Shut up, you piece of shit," Conrad yelled, shoving him to the floor. He crammed his knee in Paul's back. "David, get me something to tie him up with." Conrad wasn't as tall as Paul, but built with more muscle, giving him the edge on the asshole.

He hustled to Abigail who sat with her knees pulled against her on the bed. She was dressed, and he thanked God for that much. He grabbed the binding Paul had used on her and handed it Conrad.

"Do you have any other scarves," he asked her.

She sat stunned on the bed for a moment before going into her closet. She tossed several scarves beside Conrad as he sat atop Paul.

"I loved you," Paul yelled, "but you never gave me a chance."

"I said, shut up," Conrad growled, applying pressure with his knee to Paul's back.

Abigail stood close against David as he pulled the cell phone from his pocket.

"Nine-one-one. What is your emergency?" a male voice answered.

"My girlfriend was just attacked." Keeping a normal tone of voice wasn't possible as the words rushed from his mouth.

"Is she okay?"

"The guy was going to rape her, but we stopped him. We tied him up." Slowly his breathing and heart rate slowed down.

"Okay. What's your location?"

David gave the address and the dispatcher informed him the police were on their way.

He shoved his phone into his pocket, "Get him out of here," he snarled. "Away from Abigail."

Conrad kicked Paul's feet and yanked him by his hands. "Get up." They walked into the hall area.

David gathered her closer against him. "You're okay, right?"

"I'm fine. My head hurts a little from hitting the door, but I'll be fine." Her head rested on his shoulder. "You got here at the right time. Thank you." Her arms squeezed him tightly around the waist.

"I'm just glad Conrad followed me upstairs. If he hadn't pulled Paul off, things could've turned out differently. I want you to pack a bag.

You're coming home with me after the police give the okay."

"Only for tonight." She went to the closet and reappeared with a bag. Items were tossed inside and she set it by the door.

Sirens wailed and grew louder as they approached the house. The music stopped, car doors closed, and the sounds of partygoers leaving echoed up the stairs.

"Do you want to stay in here or go downstairs?" he asked holding her again.

"Let's stay here."

Moments later footsteps sounded on the stairs. "Let me see your hands. Is there anyone else up here?" The police. They directed the orders to Conrad and Paul in the hall.

"The girl he attacked and her boyfriend are in the bedroom." Conrad's voice wavered. "This guy's the attacker."

"One at a time," an officer ordered, "come out with your hands up."

Abigail walked out of the room first followed by David.

"Are you the one who was attacked?" A tall officer addressed Abigail.

She nodded.

"Okay. Let's go downstairs." He escorted them to the kitchen area.

A few of the partygoers remained at the front of the house talking with other officers.

"Stay here." The tall officer searched the seat cushions and scanned the tabletops in the family room. "Okay, come in here. I want each of you to sit on separate pieces of furniture. No talking."

The policeman sauntered over to talk with several other officers, while keeping their eyes on the three of them. A shorter officer, with a bit of weight on him, entered the area where they sat.

"We need statements from the three of you. We'll talk to each of you separately."

Two other officers carried chairs from the kitchen table to the front rooms for additional seating.

A petite female officer entered the mix of policemen. She approached Abigail. "I'm Officer Maxfield. Please come with me."

Abigail stood. The officer gestured for her to go ahead. David wanted to be there for her. Hold her hand. Comfort her. However,

Abigail seemed unfazed by the incident. Like the attack was nothing. The whole situation angered him. So why wasn't she angry? Was she in shock?

Two male officers approached David and Conrad. "Which one of you was first to respond to the attack?"

"I was," David offered.

"Come with me, please." The other officer stayed behind with Conrad.

The officers were professional yet courteous to them. David really hadn't known what to expect when they responded, but a part of him expected to be pushed to the ground when they first got to the house. He'd watched too many cop shows to assume this of them.

The tall officer led him to the front part of the house, in a large room opposite of where the female officer had taken Abigail. Although the three large rooms were open to each other, he couldn't hear Abigail talking. He guessed these rooms to be a formal dining and living room with the third being a possible office space.

"Please sit down." The tall guy gestured to a chair. "I'm Officer Ramirez. I'll be taking your statement." He pulled a notebook and pen from his front shirt pocket, as they both sat. "Please start by telling me your name, contact information and how you're related to the victim."

David gave him the information and the officer scribbled away on the pad.

"Now tell me about the events that led to our being called to the house," he prompted.

He told him everything that took place and what Paul had said about Abigail and the other girls. The officer's face remained unreadable during the entire statement process. David finished by giving his own opinion about Paul.

"I think Paul is the guy who's been attacking women in the area."

No reaction from Officer Ramirez, but David caught some mumbling as he continued to write on the notepad. "Is there anything else you can think of?"

David didn't answer, interrupted by the paramedics entering the house. They continued on to the room where Abigail was being questioned.

"Sir, is there anything else you need to tell me?"

"No, that's it." Panicked, he asked, "What's going on? Why are the medics in there with my girlfriend?"

"I'm not sure. I'll go check."

"Thank you." David's feet bounced, jiggling his legs.

The officer returned. "She's okay. They're checking her over to make sure she doesn't need to go to the hospital. We'll be in touch if we need to talk to you again."

"When can my girlfriend and I leave?" David remained on the chair.

"When Officer Maxfield is finished taking her statement. You can wait for her here."

"She packed a bag while we waited for you guys to get here. Can I go up and get it?"

"I'm sorry, no. We're going to need to check her room."

"Okay, thanks."

An officer escorted Paul, in cuffs, past them through the front door. Several minutes later, two guys in suits arrived. Officer Ramirez joined them as they strolled to the back of the house. David wondered why it took so long for Abigail to give her statement. She started before him. Fifteen minutes passed, and then she came into the room where he waited.

"Thank you, Officer Maxfield." Abigail shook the woman's hand. "David, can you leave?"

He stood and joined her in the entry. "Yeah, but we can't take the bag you packed."

"I don't care about the bag. I'm tired and want to go to bed." There was an air of attitude when she spoke, which David didn't mind. He took it as her way of releasing anger.

"Keep an eye on her," Officer Maxfield cautioned. "The medics don't think she's at risk for a concussion, but said to stay aware."

"I will. Thank you." David shook Officer Maxfield's hand. He and Abigail strolled outside to David's car.

* * * *

The drive to David's was quiet. Abigail didn't want to talk about what happened and was glad David didn't ask. When they arrived at his place, it was well past midnight. Tired, they crawled into his bed, and Abigail snuggled into him and fell asleep. She woke to an empty bed and smelled bacon. With a stretch of her arms, she swung her legs over the edge of the bed and took in the surroundings.

David's room was painted a dark tan. His bedding was a brown and aqua floral pattern. Black picture frames adorned the walls and furniture. There were two pictures on the low oak dresser. Picking up one of the photos, David stood between a young woman and young man. Probably his brother and sister. Replacing the photograph, she looked at the other photo of an older couple, which she assumed were his parents. She glanced between the two frames and saw the resemblances. His sister was a spitting image of their mother, his brother was a replica of his father, and David was a mix of them both.

Her stomach growled.

Barefoot, she padded from the room and down the hall toward the enticing smell. Light poured through the large window at the front of the house. She squinted against the brightness and followed the smell of bacon to the kitchen.

"Good afternoon, sunshine." David greeted her with a smile, followed by a kiss. "There's coffee in the pot. Cups are in the cupboard right above it."

"Have you been up long?" She grabbed a mug and filled it.

"About an hour. Hope you're hungry. I've made us some bacon, eggs, and we'll have toast soon. How's your head?"

With fingertips, she gingerly touched her head, moved them to the right side, and flinched. "A little tender there."

"Let me take a look." He looked at her face and then lifted her hair in sections. "You've got some bruising, so you'll probably be tender for a few days."

"Yeah, that's what the EMT said. After breakfast, can we go back to my place?" She sipped the coffee while leaning against the counter. The small cozy kitchen opened to the main living space.

David moved the scrambled eggs around in the pan. "Sure. Then you can pack some of your things to stay here. Unless you wanted me to take you to your dad's."

"Um, I'm not staying anywhere but my home." It irked her that he assumed she would be staying at his house.

"Are you going to tell your dad about this?"

"What?" Her voice cracked. "Why are you asking?" Her face scrunched.

"He has a right to know. You're his daughter." He pressed the toaster button down.

"One," she held her pointer finger in front of him—"it's none of your business if, or what, I tell my father. Two," she flicked her hand, making a peace sign with her fingers—"it would be in your best interest to not saying anything. I will handle this my way."

"You've made your point. The eggs are ready." He dished a plate of eggs for each of them and handed her one. "You can pick your own bacon and the toast should pop up—"

The toast was done.

She selected a few pieces of bacon and took two of the four slices of toast. "I'm sorry for how I just spoke to you. I shouldn't have been so mean." She sat at the table. "I'm fine, David. He didn't hurt me. You got there in time. If you hadn't, well, I don't want to think about what could've been. It didn't happen, and I'm fine. A little bruised, but fine."

"You need to talk to someone about it."

"I did. To Officer Maxfield. She knows everything. Do you want to know what happened up until you arrived?" She didn't give him time to answer and filled him in with the details. "Then you came in and you know the rest. He didn't even kiss me on the lips." She shoved a forkful of fluffy egg in her mouth.

"I'm sorry I wasn't there for you." He worked on eating his own breakfast.

"Don't you get it? You were, when it counted. David, I'm fine. He's been arrested and will be going to prison."

"You don't know that. They have to find evidence first and then he'd go to trial. The girls he attacked, they'll need to come forward."

"They have, when they reported the incidences to the police. My question, how many others are there that may not have reported it?" She took another bite.

"God, I hope there aren't any more than those reported."

"Me, too." She smeared jelly on her toast. "So, because I want to change the subject, I start my final class Monday. I'll be working around my class hours."

"Your dad told me on Friday. What are your plans after graduation? Are you staying with your dad's firm?" He took the last bite of egg from his plate.

"I'm not sure. A part of me says to step away from my father and move on. Yet another part says to stay for the experience."

"You've got the automatic in, so I'd stay. Your skills will be a benefit for the firm."

"I know, but I worry about my father's personal relationship with me if I do stay. I don't want to lose the close bond we have."

"Where would you go? Have you looked for a job elsewhere?" David picked up his plate and put it in the dishwasher.

"Not yet. I think I need to talk to my dad. A father/daughter versus an employer/employee talk." She chewed a bite of egg and swallowed. "It might be better to work elsewhere to make it easier on all of us."

"What do you mean easier? That would make it harder. We probably wouldn't see each other as often. I like being able to see you every morning."

"It's been fine for now at the office, but if I become an actual hired employee versus an intern, well, things would change. You and I wouldn't work together, except maybe on occasion." She picked up her plate and handed it to him.

"Nothing would change between us. If anything, we'd grow closer."

"Do you mind if we leave for my place? I'd like to shower and change out of these clothes." She didn't want to talk about their future. Right now, she needed to focus on her future. Hers, and hers alone.

* * * *

"You don't need to come in. Conrad's here. I'll be fine," Abigail told David as he pulled onto the driveway and parked beside Conrad's truck.

"You're sending me home? Just like that." His eyebrows shot up and his eyes expressed hurt.

"I need to shower and talk to Conrad." She looked at the house. "I need to tell Gina about what happened, too." She turned to face him.

"Okay." He glanced out the windshield. "I guess I'll see you tomorrow at work." He tilted his head away from her as he dipped his chin.

She bit her bottom lip. "I'll call you later. Can I have a kiss?" He turned and delivered a quick peck to her lips. "Why are you mad?"

"I'm not mad. It's just that our night together wasn't much, and I'd hoped we'd get to spend a little time together today. Instead, you're spending it with your ex-boyfriend."

"I've told you there's nothing between Conrad and I. You need to get past him if we're going to have a relationship."

"I don't want to keep you any longer from your shower. Or your roommates." He put the car in reverse. He may have said he wasn't mad, but his actions were showing he was upset.

"I'll talk to you later." Out of the car, she watched him back out and drive away. She turned around and wandered to the front door.

Inside, she shouted, "Conrad?" No answer.

As she approached the stairs, a buzzing noise from a machine drifted down. Going up to her room, she found him working on her bedroom door.

"Hey." She tapped his shoulder.

Conrad turned off the sanding device and removed big headphones. "Hey. I didn't expect you home so soon. Hoped to have this repaired before you got back. You okay? We didn't talk before you left with David."

"I'm fine. You?"

"Bruised knuckles." He held up his right hand. "Otherwise good. Some detectives came and searched his room and left with—"

"Hey, can we talk about this after I shower?" She didn't want to talk about Paul or the attack. It happened. She was okay. It was in the past.

"Yeah. Do you mind if I keep working on the door?"

"No, please do." She carefully stepped by him and his tools to enter her room. "Have you heard from Gina?"

"Nope. Does she know about…"

"I haven't talked to her. I haven't seen anything on the news. You?"

"No."

"You keep working, and when I'm out of the shower we can talk."

With a curt smile, she left him to finish installing a new door.

The bag she'd packed last night now sat on her bed instead of by the door. The items were tousled inside the bag. While getting clean clothes for after her shower, she put the items away. Locking the bathroom door, she turned on the water, stripped and then stood under the warm spray. She tipped back her head to wet her hair, while relaxing the slight tension that had remained since her conversation with David.

When the water spray hit her bruised head, she was reminded of being shoved into the door. What had triggered Paul's awful behavior? Despite his obvious attraction to her, she never got the feeling he was obsessed. Not to the degree of raping other women. A shiver went down her spine, and she turned the knob making the water hotter.

She worked the shampoo through her hair and thought about all the nights she heard someone coming in late. There was the night he scared her as she came through the garage door into the house. Then she thought about her underwear drawer. She rinsed her hair. Could he have been the one who dug... Oh God, no. She shuddered.

David's question as to whether she was going to tell her father popped into her thoughts. He'd been worried about her safety, so it'd be best for her to tell him what happened. Should she call and tell him over the phone or tell him in person? She'd wait to see how the rest of her day played out.

She finished showering, got dressed, opened the bathroom door to her room, and screamed.

A man's voice spoke as arms wrapped around her.

She fought back, swinging her arms and punching with her hands. "No."

"Abby. Abby."

They dropped to the floor. She sat between the man's legs. The male voice was comforting yet firm. It was Conrad.

Gently, he rocked them side-to-side. "Abs. Calm down. It's okay. I'm here," he repeated.

As her body relaxed into his, he released the firm hold around her while he stroked her damp hair, the tears poured free.

"Want to talk about it?"

She shook her head while sniffling.

"Okay. Let's sit here until you're ready."

She wasn't sure how long they sat there, but when she stopped crying, she rasped, "I'm sorry. I opened the door and it all flooded back. As though I was slapped back into the moment. Did I hurt you?" She looked up at him.

He chuckled. "No." His head dipped close to her ear. "You weren't swinging hard enough." His arms briefly tightened around her.

"Conrad." She spoke his name in a scolding tone. He never stopped trying to win her back. She got up off the floor. "I'm with David."

"I wasn't—"

"You were. Are you finished with my door?"

"Yup. Do you want to go downstairs and talk?"

"Yes. First, let me grab my phone." Locating her purse, she snatched her cell from the front pocket. "Okay, I'm ready."

Downstairs, she flicked the switch turning on the fireplace before sitting on a chair close by the warmth. "What happened after we left?"

Conrad plopped on the couch. "So, detectives showed up with a search warrant for Paul's room. They left with bags and boxes."

"Do you know what they took?"

Was any of it admissible as evidence to prove him guilty as the rapist? A chill came over her body. She wrapped her arms around herself.

"Nope. I couldn't go upstairs until they were finished. Which was at about two or three this morning."

"Have you gotten any sleep?" If she would've stayed the night in her own bed, she didn't think she would've slept as well as she had at David's. If at all.

"A couple of hours. How's David handling this?"

"He wants me to move in with him. I told him I wouldn't do that, which he didn't like, but he has no choice in the matter. My dad even tried getting me to move out. I haven't talked to him yet about what happened." The tension returned to her shoulders and neck.

"He's not going to be happy."

"I know, but I'm not moving out. I'm not going to let him or any other rapist scare me into running home. Are you going to find someone to move in to fill his vacancy?"

"Yes. I talked with Paul's—"

"Don't say his name anymore, please."

"I talked with his dad and they'll be over to clean out his belongings this week. His parents can't believe he attacked you, and more so, the possibility that he's linked to the other assaults."

Abigail could only shake her head in disbelief at his parents. He was guilty of raping those women. In her gut, she knew it, though how to prove it? With his father being a lawyer, she knew they'd fight for his freedom.

Chapter Twenty-Six

Abigail knocked on her father's office door with her stomach in knots. This would be tough news to tell her dad.

"Come in," he called.

She swung the door open. "Hi, Dad." She stepped inside and closed the door. "Can we talk? Is this a good time?"

He came around his desk to sit on the chair beside hers. "I always have time for you. I need your advice. Valentine's Day is coming up and I want a woman's perspective. I'd like to take her to Vegas."

"Why Vegas? Are you planning on marrying her out there?" She laughed at the thought of her dad getting married so soon after meeting a woman. He'd had his girlfriends for years and never once thought of settling down.

"No." His eyes widened. "I was thinking it would be warm, with plenty to do and see. Do you think that's what she would think?"

"I don't know about Liz, but it's the first thing that came to my mind. Why not go somewhere south? Las Vegas isn't romantic. Isn't that what you want?"

"Yeah, but I want it to be fun too."

"Call your travel agent and ask her where you can go that would be warm, romantic, and fun. Think about the Carolinas, Georgia, or Louisiana." She could see he was mulling the possibilities over in his head. "You really like Liz, don't you?"

He was quiet for several moments. "Honestly, I can see myself having a future with her and her children."

She jumped from her chair and embraced her father. "I'm so happy for you!"

"Thanks, but there's a lot we both need to work through. I have your sister to deal with, and Liz has things on her end. It'll be a slow moving relationship."

"It's not that slow if you two are introducing each other to your children. I don't have to ask if you two have slept together because that happens before introducing the kids. If she means that much, don't take her to Vegas, Dad.

"Listen, I need to tell you before you hear it on the news. Eventually."

As she told him about the attack, his jaw tightened and his hands fisted. Not until she moved to the point of David and Conrad bursting into the room, did his hands open and his fingers flexed.

"That's the final straw. I want you out of the house, now."

He stood and pushed on his phone. "Please get David Robertson for me. Now."

"There's no threat anymore, Dad."

At a knock on the door, her father responded. "Come in."

David cringed as he entered. "You wanted to see me?"

"My daughter just informed me about the incident you two were involved in at her house. I want to thank you for being there for her."

"You're welcome, sir, but Conrad was the one who took care of Paul. I want you to know I've asked her to stay with me, but she insists on staying at the house."

"Abby, why aren't you moving out of the house? Why would you stay there?" Robert sat behind his desk.

"I'm an adult and make my own decisions. The daughter you can feel free to make decisions for, is Chris."

She couldn't control her frustration and had raised her voice to her father. Bringing Chris up was close to stepping over the line.

David remained by the door, not moving closer to her or her father.

"You are still my daughter, Abigail. I will always be a part of your life."

"Not if you're going to continue to hover like a spy drone."

"Abigail." David approached speaking in a low voice. "Move temporarily until we know Paul is not going to get out of jail. He could make bond."

"I'm done discussing this. I'm not moving. My decision is final."

"Thank you again, David. You can leave." Her father looked at her while speaking to David.

She followed in David's wake.

"Abigail, we're not finished." Her dad's calm returned.

She spun around. "What more could there be to talk about?"

The snotty tone couldn't be helped. She didn't like the way her father and David pushed.

"Please close the door."

She did as asked, as an employee, but chose to stand in defiance as his daughter.

"I'm worried about you and your safety. Paul may be in police custody, but can be released on bail. I don't want him coming after you in retaliation."

"He's not going to be released. He's the rapist. I'm safe, Dad."

"You told me that before and that you could defend yourself. With what you just told me, you can't protect yourself." He came around the desk.

"I'm done repeating the same conversation with you and David. I'm not moving out of my house." She crossed her arms over her chest. No one controlled her life but her.

"Why do you minimize the severity of this matter?" He grabbed her by the shoulders. "You were attacked in your home by someone you know."

"First of all, he didn't do anything to me sexually." She shifted her shoulders and her father removed his hands.

"He attacked you, honey," he said firmly with a stern face.

"The only physical attack was when he slammed my head into the door. I'm fine. I had my breakdown yesterday with Conrad. He took care of me. It's all good."

"You need to talk to someone about this."

"Dad, I'm done talking about this with you, David, or anyone other than the law. Understand?"

"Will you promise to keep me posted?" He embraced her with a gentle squeeze.

"I will."

"One more thing. Please think about moving—"

"Dad," she said in a warning tone.

"Think about moving out or having David stay with you. That's all. I can worry about you."

"That's all you can do. I'll talk to you later."

* * * *

Wednesday night Liz lounged in bed reading *The Outsiders*. The last time she'd read it was as a teenager. Her cell phone rang precisely at ten-thirty. Robert. They had a standing call date on Wednesday nights.

"Hello," she answered while looking at her phone, waiting for Robert to pop up on her screen.

"Hey, beautiful." When he smiled, so did his eyes. "Hope you had a good day at work."

"I did. Is Chris okay? I was informed she would be out of school for the week and possibly next week as well." His daughter didn't create any further issue for her, but her assignments were lacking which lowered her grade.

His eyelids lowered. "Kathleen's pulled her out of school. She's taking her to a therapist for counseling."

"Sorry isn't quite the right word because I'm glad she'll be getting help, but, Robert, I am sorry." It didn't feel right to ask if school kicked her out, or if, as parents made the decision.

"It's okay." He shook his head. "This should be a good thing. I know we just came back from a cruise, but Valentine's is coming up and I'd like to take you away, somewhere warm. I know you'll be done subbing by then, so it would be a matter of finding someone to watch your kids."

"Robert, I can't afford another trip."

"I want to take you on a trip, Liz."

She couldn't fathom the idea of why he'd want to take her away. "I need to think about it. Can I ask why we can't do something here?"

"We could, but I'd like to go away with you. I have the kids that holiday weekend, so I was thinking we would go the following weekend. The twentieth through the twenty-second or third. I did some searching on-line and Savannah, Georgia looks romantic and warm."

"Okay. I'll think about it and let you know when I decide one way or the other." She yawned. "Excuse me."

"Before I let you go, I haven't told you about Abby. I told you about the rapist in her area, well, one of her housemates attacked her on Saturday night."

"What?" She sat up. Her hand rested at the base of her throat.

"She told me late Monday afternoon. She believes he's the guy that's been raping women in the area. They don't know anything for certain though. The cops haven't told her anything and there's been nothing on the news."

"Nothing?"

"His attack on Abby isn't news worthy, but if he is the rapist and they get the evidence to link him to the other assaults, then it will be a major news story. She said they searched his room. I'm guessing they're waiting on DNA results to tie him to the other cases." He appeared relaxed.

"Is she okay?"

"Yeah. Too well, if you ask me. She won't move out of the house. David's asked her to move in to his place. I told her to move out of her place. She's not going anywhere. She says there's no threat." Concern showed on his face. He'd held his worry in check.

"I'd have to agree with Abby. If she feels safe, then she should stay at her house."

"Well, she'll like to hear you're on her side." A smile ticked to one side of his mouth. "I wish you were by my side right now. We wouldn't be talking, that's for sure."

Her face warmed. If the lighting were better, she was sure he'd see her blushing.

* * * *

"Robert!"

Robert turned, David jogged to catch up to him as he left the office. He stopped and waited. "Is something wrong?"

"No." They walked to the elevator together. "I wanted you to know that I'll be staying at Abigail's all weekend. I figured she wouldn't tell you, but I know you'd appreciate knowing. I'll talk to her a little more this weekend about moving out."

"Thank you. Don't push too hard. She's been stubborn since the day she was conceived." The men laughed.

"I'll heed your warning."

The elevator doors opened, and his cell phone rang. "Go ahead. Oh, thanks, too." He stepped away to answer. Kathleen.

"Hello, Robert. Christine's therapist asked me to contact you. She wants to have a session with Christine and you, so I scheduled an appointment for Monday at four. If you can't make that appointment, call the office right away. I'll send you an email with all the details."

"I'll make it work. Will you be able to get Chris there? I can bring her home."

"Wow, no argument?"

He clenched his jaw to avoid starting one.

"I'll have her there on time. You are changing. I'll see you Monday."

She ended the call, and he took the elevator to the parking ramp level.

* * * *

Liz had put off a visit to her in-laws as long as possible since her return from the cruise. Veronica would be there, which would help ease the tension between Liz and her mother-in-law. Brad was excited to see his grandparents. Sarah, didn't mind as long as her grandmother behaved.

Brad rang the doorbell and rushed in, shedding his boots, coat, and gloves.

"Grandma. Grandpa. We're here." He yelled before running off to search for them.

Veronica greeted them in the foyer, delivering a big hug. "You look fabulous." She lowered her voice. "Things must be going well with Robert."

"Sorry I haven't called. I'm so busy with my sub job." Liz removed her coat and hung their coats, as Sarah took off toward the back of the house. "His daughter is in my class."

Veronica's eyes widened. "You're kidding?"

"No."

"Ladies," Ellen surprised them as she came around the corner. "Please, don't be rude. Come join us in the family room." The woman turned, peered over her shoulder to make sure they followed behind, and then marched through the house.

Liz rolled her eyes at Veronica who did the same while shaking her head. "My sister, Mallory, is expecting."

"What?" she exclaimed.

Ellen's head snapped back with narrowed eyes directed at them.

Veronica whispered, as though they'd been scolded by the nun while walking the halls of a convent. "I thought they were getting a divorce?"

"They're going through couple's therapy. I came home the night you stopped by, and she was there. I fixed dinner and things weren't right with her. I ran to the store to get a test. She took it, and there you have it."

They entered the family room. Duane got up from his chair to embrace her. "You look great. That trip must have been a good one."

"It was, Duane. I brought pictures to share, and I have gifts." She opened her bag and pulled out two small boxes. "These are for Frank and Joe."

The two teens opened the simple shark tooth necklaces.

After their thank-yous, she took a larger box and handed it to William. "This is for you and Veronica."

Veronica sat by her husband as he tore open the gift. When he lifted the well-endowed naked Jamaican statue, Ellen gasped loudly.

"This is going in my office," William exclaimed. "I love it. Sorry, darling, but this can't sit around the house for you to ogle on a daily basis."

"William, please," Ellen said, exasperated. "That is terribly disgusting, Elizabeth. Why on Earth would you purchase such a thing? Put it away, William. Right now."

"It's art, Mother," Veronica defended the statue, taking it from her husband.

"A laughable art." Liz chuckled.

"It's so exaggerated, one has to laugh. Are you that prudish, Mom?" Veronica stroked the enlarged penis.

"Veronica," Ellen scolded. "Don't speak to me that way. William, please take that thing from your wife and put it away."

The dutiful son-in-law took the art from his wife and smiled as he placed it back in the box.

"This is for you and Duane." Liz handed the medium-sized box to Ellen.

Ellen opened the package and removed a small handmade vase. "This is beautiful, Elizabeth. Thank you." She spoke with affection, which took Liz by surprise.

"I had a hard time thinking of what to get and found this in one of the shops in George Town. Sorry, Duane, I know the vase isn't up your alley."

"Oh, that's okay. I'll go visit William at his office." This earned her father-in-law a stern glare from his wife.

"You will do no such thing." Ellen reprimanded her husband. "So, Elizabeth, tell us about your cruise."

Liz pulled the pictures from her purse and told them about her trip. She'd decided to tell them about running into Robert and Scott, and left out the more intimate pictures of her and Robert to avoid questions. When she talked about Fern Gully in Ocho Rios, where the carvings were made, Ellen excused herself to check on dinner.

Returning to the room, Ellen announced, "Dinner will be served in ten minutes. What are you telling us about now, Elizabeth?"

"Our stop in George Town. The Grand Cayman's were beautiful." She continued talking about her offshore excursion and the cruise until the time came for them to go to the dining room.

Once seated at the table and grace said, Ellen started the dinner conversation. "So it seems you spent a lot of time with these two men." She tilted her head. "Did you spend *all* of your time with them, or did you meet others aboard the ship?"

"During the evenings, I spent time with Robert and Scott. We didn't do any tours together, so I met plenty of others during the excursions."

"How *much* time in the evenings did you spend with the *two* men?" Her mother-in-law cocked an eyebrow.

"Mother," Veronica said, when Liz was about to speak. "Why don't you just ask what it is you're dancing around?"

"It's okay, Veronica. Ellen, I spent a lot of time mostly with Robert. We're seeing each other now and the children have met him and his children. As a matter of fact, I'm going to be joining him on a trip to Savannah, Georgia."

"I knew you were a hussy. You went on that cruise and flaunted your body in front of those men." Ellen stood, rigid with accusation. "You probably slept with the men. You whore. I can't eat with you, let alone be in the same room." Her face was crimson.

"You don't talk about my mom that way," Brad shouted.

Chapter Twenty-Seven

"Bradley," Ellen's tone was shocked and parental.

"No." Brad's voice echoed off the walls. "You've said some mean things to her, and you don't even know Robert." His face flushed.

Liz thought Ellen's eyes were going to bulge out of the sockets. Ellen closed her gaping mouth.

"He's the nicest guy, and his kids are cool, too. Mom's happy. She has a picture of Robert and her on the refrigerator. You should see her smile." Moisture built in his eyes. "They love each other." He shoved away from the table. "Dad... Dad would want her to find someone else to be happy with." He choked out the last words before running from the room, crying.

Her son's words blew Liz away. He saw more than she thought possible. Love each other? She questioned that one herself. Her pulse rushed. Not chasing after Brad, Liz remained sitting.

"Is it true you love this man?" Ellen stood behind her dining room chair. She gripped it as though she had it in a chokehold.

"Mother," Veronica raised her voice. "You're a tyrant. Leave Liz alone. If she's content with Robert, which I know she is, that's all that matters. If she loves him, which I don't even know the answer to, so be it. Gregory is gone. We've all grieved, healed, and moved on with our lives—except for you. I love you, Mom, but you need to let go."

"Yes, Gregory is gone. He's gone because of that woman." Ellen pointed in Liz's direction and spitefully shook the thin digit. "It's *her* fault my son was taken from me," Ellen shouted. "She doesn't deserve happiness. She took *my* happiness away five years ago." She dropped onto the chair. "The only pleasure that remains of my son, are my two beautiful grandchildren."

Liz pushed her chair back. "Sarah, please go find your brother. We're leaving."

Once her daughter left the room, she stood beside her mother-in-law at the end of the table. "I have lived the past four years allowing you to steal my joy. Not anymore. I loved Gregory with all of my being. I grieved for a long time, but with help, I saw I could be happy again. You've seen your grandchildren for the last time." She stalked to the foyer with her head held high.

"No, don't do this, Elizabeth," Ellen cried out, "Don't take my Bradley."

Either she stayed in the dining room by choice, or was held back by her husband. Liz didn't care which it was, as long as she didn't see her again. The children pulled on their winter gear. Brad's eyes were red and swollen.

Veronica came around the corner with her purse. "Your pictures are inside. I'm so sorry about Mom."

"Don't apologize for her. Thank you for what you said. I'll call you this week." They hugged, and Liz left with her children.

In the car on the way home, she spoke to her son. "Brad, thank you for defending me, but you will write an apology to your grandmother."

"Why? She doesn't say nice things." He had stopped crying.

"Because you're ten and you shouldn't speak to an adult in such a manner. I was there and could defend myself. Okay?" She didn't scold or raise her voice. She made a simple explanation.

"Yeah, okay." In the rearview mirror, she saw him glance out the rear passenger window. "Are you going away with Robert? Like you told Grandma?"

"I haven't given Robert an answer yet."

"When would you be going and for how long," Sarah questioned from beside her on the front seat.

"He wants to go for a long weekend in February. I'd have to see if my parents would be willing to watch you guys again." She glanced sideways and in the mirror to see if there were any body reactions. "Would you guys be okay with me leaving again? I just got back from my cruise and to leave again—"

"Yes," Brad said from the back. "He makes you happy. You love him."

"Brad, I don't love him. Love is a strong word. Yes, he does make me very happy." She was a little surprised and pleased by her son's turnaround about Robert.

"Call Grandma and Grandpa when we get home." Sarah said with a grin.

"I'm glad you two are accepting Robert and his children."

Brad burst into a conversation about Alex and their gaming experience together. In fact, he talked the entire way home about Alex.

* * * *

Robert parked the car in the lot and entered the non-descript, brick, business building with narrow, vertical windows spaced evenly apart. Taking one flight of stairs, he located the office and pushed the glass door open. Chris sat off to the right on a grey utilitarian couch. His ex-wife met him close to the doorway.

"She knows you'll be bringing her home. I'll see you there in a little over an hour." Kathleen strolled out of the office.

Before sitting beside his daughter who wore her usual earbuds, he nodded and mouthed a hello. She returned the nod and shifted her focus to her phone. He picked up a sports magazine and flipped through the pages. Five minutes later, a short, thick woman, identified herself as the therapist and invited them into her office. Chris unplugged when they sat on the chairs in the therapist's room.

The chairs in the office were as simple as the reception area furniture.

The therapist sat and leaned comfortably back in the office chair. "Robert, I'm glad you would come in today. Chris, how are you?"

"Fine." Chris slouched in her chair.

"Would you like to expand on that a little more? You've been out of school for a week now. Do you miss school? Your friends?"

"Miss school? No. Are you crazy? Friends? A little. My life's complete with my bed, laptop, and phone."

Robert refrained from speaking, letting the therapist lead the direction of their discussion.

The office was business like with the framed certificates hanging on the wall and bookcases filled with studious books. Whether real or not, there were two potted plants sitting on the floor.

"Let's talk about your parents and the new custody arrangement. You've expressed how angry you are, for not being included in the decision process. If you've discussed this situation with your father, can you tell me about the discussion?"

"The only time I see or speak to my dad is when it's his weekend." She scowled sideways at him.

"Do you ever call or text him when you need or want to just talk?"

"No," she huffed. "He's too busy for me. And when I do tell them how I feel, I'm told I'm the child and they're the parents." She hastily threw her arms across her chest.

"Robert, would you care to say something?"

He held eye contact with the therapist while speaking. "If it's during working hours, it can be tricky, but she should be in school at the time. As for during evenings and weekends, more than likely I have time to talk to her." He faced his daughter. "You are the child."

She declared with a snort of dismissive laughter. "I've tried in the past, but you're always too busy with things or your girlfriends. I gave up."

"I'm sorry. I want to change that and be more available."

She spun in her chair, glaring at him. "Then don't make me move and leave all of my friends."

"Chris, your father is the adult who will be supporting you and making the decisions where you're concerned until you become an adult, which is recognized by the state as the age of eighteen. You need to comprehend that he has an established career and home. He would be giving up a lot for you at a great expense."

"Can I say something?" He received a nod of approval from the therapist. "Chris, I want to know if you truly understand and are accepting that your mother and I are never getting back together."

"Yes." Her chin fell to her chest.

He sighed with relief. One low hurdle jumped.

"Robert, you introduced Chris and her siblings to a woman, Liz. Can you tell me about her?"

"I first met her years ago when I worked on designing her then husband's clinic. He's since passed away, which I found out when I ran into her on my cruise this past New Year's. We got reacquainted and developed a personal friendship. By the end of the cruise, we decided to continue seeing each other." He shifted on his chair. This meeting was going smoother than he anticipated.

"When I returned from my trip, I learned of Kathleen's engagement. Chris is having trouble accepting her engagement. Chris is in Liz's classroom and first learned about her and me when I had to go to school. Liz is a substitute teacher."

"Chris, it was noted that you created problems in all of your classes. Your behavior did improve in English, but your grades fell in all, especially English class. Care to explain the differences?"

"Silence.

"I like Liz." She spoke, the words barely audible.

When moments passed, the therapist continued. "If you like her, then why are your grades failing when you've been an A student until now? Why create trouble in all your classes, but hers?

"Let me tell you my thoughts on the matter, and you tell me if I'm close or way off." She leaned forward, her focus on Chris. "You haven't been happy about your parents' divorce since the beginning and thought if you were a good student and daughter, they'd get back together, but it never happened." Her voice was calm and soothing as she spoke.

With her chin tipped to her chest, Chris sat quietly biting her bottom lip.

"They dated other people, and you didn't like it, but maintained your schooling while acting out on your parents. Now with your mother's engagement, it pushed you over the edge. You saw the reality that your parents were really and truly never going to get back together and it hurt. You thought, if you created enough trouble that maybe your parents would think twice about the separate directions they're going in their lives. Am I close?"

"Yeah," she whispered.

Chris's simple reply slapped him in the face. Kathleen was right about missing so much of Chris's life. If he had been present and more aware, maybe things would've been different. He needed to change and make things right with her. This was a beginning.

The therapist leaned back. "Chris, you and I will continue to talk at our next appointment. Right now, I'd like to talk to your father. Would you please wait for us in the reception area?"

The woman didn't have to ask his daughter twice. She bolted from her chair and out the door.

"Robert, let's talk about your relationship with Chris first. She has expressed a great deal about you not being around for her or her school events."

"It's true, and I intend to change that."

"How?"

The question rubbed him the wrong way. "Well for starters, I'm going to be her only guardian when her mother moves away. I'll need to pay attention to her schooling and whatever else it is she decides to participate in."

"My question of how seemed to bother you. I'm only trying to help Chris and the family come to an understanding and heal."

"I'm sorry. It's just that having full custody of Chris will be new for me. It'll take time to figure out how things will work for us. I haven't thought much in great detail. I'm working on the small stuff right now." He paused. "I realize I need to pay closer attention to Chris and listen to her when she wants to talk to me."

"Would you like to tell me about, Liz?"

"She's the first woman I've had a monogamous relationship with since my marriage. Kathleen wasn't a very kind person when she announced the divorce. She said some cruel things, and I accepted them." Robert explained how he met Liz and about the two families meeting.

"Okay, back to Chris. I do have some concerns about the change in custody and her moving into a new home, school, basically a new life. As the parent, you make the decisions, as I told her earlier. If I can make a recommendation, it would be for you to strongly consider keeping her in her current area of living."

This was the third woman to advise him to keep Chris in her current area. Maybe he should heed their advice.

She glanced at her watch. "We're nearing the end of today's session.

I want to thank you for coming. It shows Chris and me that you are on your journey of change in your relationship with your daughter."

They walked to the door.

"Thank you." If he moved south, he'd also be closer to Liz. Maybe it would show her his willingness to make their relationship work.

They joined Chris in the small reception area.

"Chris, I'll see you Friday. Robert, we'll talk again." The therapist shook his hand before leaving the area for her office.

He and Chris left the building. "How about we go to dinner? I'm sure your mom wouldn't mind."

"Sure."

"Where'd you like to go?"

"I don't care."

The lack of daylight in the cold north, they stepped outside into the darkness of winter. Once in the car, he texted his ex-wife letting her know their plans. They remained quiet on the short drive to Applebee's. He used the time to contemplate the idea bouncing around in his head.

Seated in a booth, they ordered as soon as their waitress came to the table. Chris avoided eye contact.

"So," he said, when the waitress left. "I thought that was a good talk. She said some things that others have told me, which is why I wanted to talk to you over dinner."

She continued to look down. He assumed she was on her phone.

"Will you please put your phone on the table? What I want to talk about is important and concerns you." He waited and she did as asked. "I will consider buying a home in this area—"

"Really?" she blurted with excitement.

"Yes, if you're willing to work with me." He held up a finger to keep her from interrupting. "When you go back to school, you need to turn things around. Behavior and grades. We need to work together and communicate more about what's happening in school and life. Is this something you're willing to work on with me?"

The waitress delivered their beverages and when she left, Chris erupted. "Yes. Oh, thank you, Dad."

"Okay. I guess we need to talk about a house. I don't want a big house. You have to remember I haven't had to take care of a yard in years."

"Can we find one with a pool?" Her enthusiasm was high.

"That would require more yard work and maintenance. How would you feel about living in a nice apartment? They have everything, like my place."

"No," she whined.

"What about a townhouse? Some of the nice ones sometimes have clubhouses that have the pool and stuff."

"I'd rather have a house."

"I'll get in touch with a realtor. I'm not making any promises. When I find something, I think we both would like and agree on, we'll go take a look. How does that sound?"

"Okay, good. Thank you."

A high hurdle jumped, he had plenty more ahead yet to leap.

Chapter Twenty-Eight

The doorbell rang and Liz glanced at the clock. Seven ten. Who would be ringing their doorbell at this hour? The kids weren't expecting any friends. As she neared the door, Robert peered through the side window, startling her.

She opened the door and stepped aside for him to enter. "What are you doing here?"

"I didn't mean to scare you. I saw you jump. I was in the area and thought I'd stop by. I hope that's okay?"

"You were in the area, huh?" She quirked an eyebrow. "Of course, it's okay. Here, give me your coat." She hung it in the closet.

"No, really, I was in the area. I met with Chris's therapist, took Chris to dinner and then home." He wrapped his arms around her waist from behind as she closed the closet doors. "I've missed you."

Slowly, she turned in his arms. "I've missed you."

On tiptoe, she kissed him. He pulled her tighter against him and deepened the kiss. When the moan escaped her, she pulled away.

"Mmm, kids. Let's go sit in the family room. Can I get you anything to drink?"

"You." In the family room, he reached and pulled her onto his lap. "No, I'm fine."

"You're in a good mood. What happened today?"

"The session with Chris's therapist was good." He leaned over her, forcing her to rest back on the couch cushion, and kissed her. "I'm moving into the area."

"Really?" She relaxed lying on the couch.

"Yeah. I talked to Chris at dinner and we've struck a deal. She improves her behavior and gets her grades back up to where they belong, and I become more involved with her activities and life."

"Robert, I'm so happy for you. Have you found a house?"

"No." His head shook. "I need to get a realtor and start the search. Unless you want to do the Brady Bunch thing?" His eyebrows wiggled, followed by a chuckle.

Good thing he chuckled because for a minute she thought he was serious.

"I'm joking, Liz." His pulled his vibrating phone from his pocket, glanced at it before returning it into the pocket. "Have you thought about our trip?"

She smiled. "Yes, I'd love to go to Savannah with you."

Her head was crushed against the cushion with his kiss. Her body hummed with desire.

"I'm so glad. I think my agent found the perfect bed and breakfast called the Fitzgerald House. It's run by three sisters whose mother opened the B and B."

"It sounds lovely."

His phone vibrated against her hip. "You're lovely." Pulling out the cell, he glanced at it before setting it on the floor. A quick kiss followed.

"I'll call my travel agent tomorrow."

"Do you need to answer that?" Someone was anxious to reach him.

"No, it's not important. I'll take care of it later. How was Saturday at your in-laws?"

"Interesting to say the least."

Robert's phone vibrated again. He picked it up, and she strained to see the screen. It was a text message. She couldn't see much else. He dropped it to the floor.

"Care to tell me more?" His nose nuzzled against her neck.

"My mother-in-law said things and my son yelled at her before my sister-in-law, her daughter, lashed into her. Brad stood up for you, Robert. You made an impression on him when you were here. He also thinks we love each other." She chuckled at the last part.

"Would it be so bad if we did love each other?" His eyes searched her face, while he remained serious and focused.

She swallowed the lump that had formed in her throat.

His phone vibrated, again, but he left it on the floor. "Liz?"

She rolled to the edge of the couch, grabbed his phone, tired of the interruption, and swiped the screen.

She stopped breathing.

Clutching the phone, while staring at the screen, everything blurred.

"Liz, it's not what—"

"Get out." She shoved his phone into his chest, pushing him up and off her. For the sake of the kids, she kept her voice low. Heat flushed through her body as her pulse sped.

"Liz, I'm not seeing anyone but you."

"It looks like you're seeing a whole lot of Kimberly." The image on his phone was disgusting. "What is she, all of the age of twenty?" The redheaded woman was scantily clad in a bra and panties of sorts, posing in a position that revealed more than Liz wanted to see.

Jumping off the couch, she marched to the entry closet. As she whipped the door open, he grabbed her hand.

"I love you, Liz."

She yanked his jacket from the hanger, then freed her other hand. Jamming the coat at him, she stormed to the front door, and yanked it open. "Get out. I don't want to see you again."

"Liz, I love you." He stood in front of her by the door. "That's my past. You're my future. Don't do this. Let's talk. Please?" He was actually begging.

"Out," she growled loudly. Her chest heaved with every breath as she fought the onset of tears.

He stepped outside. She slammed the door. Along with it, she slammed the door to her heart.

How could she be so stupid to believe him when he said he wouldn't see the other women? She closed her eyes, with her back to the door and slid to the floor. How could she be so careless and give her body to him? Why did she think it was safe to introduce her children to him?

She wiped her eyes, stood and took a deep cleansing breath before walking away from Robert, and the door. There would be no crying over him. At least that's what she repeated in her head.

* * * *

Like a tranquilized animal, Robert entered his apartment. He turned on the TV and collapsed on the couch. The one woman he cared about, the one woman he proclaimed to love, kicked him into the gutter. Taken away because he was foolish with a young woman.

The messages continued to come. Kimberly attached a photo more risqué than the previous one Liz had seen. Kimberly had gone from being classy to trashy. She held a dildo between her legs stating if he didn't come take care of business, she would. He furiously typed a message.

I'm done with you. This is inappropriate. If you don't stop harassing me, I will go to the authorities. Do not text or call me again.

He deleted the message and her contact info, while blocking her on his phone. Why hadn't he done that sooner? Because he didn't want to believe he'd fallen in love with Liz. With one woman.

He closed his eyes and rested his head on the back of the couch. What was he going do to get Liz back? He wouldn't let her go so easily. There was something special between them. They were meant to be together. Why else were they on the same cruise? What were the odds of them bumping into each other with hundreds of people aboard the ship? It was destiny. Just like Abby said, they were meant to be.

"An arrest has been made today in the sexual assault cases in the St. Paul community surrounding the college campuses," the news anchor reported.

Robert's head and eyes shot open. He focused on the TV news.

"The St. Paul Police released a statement today regarding the assaults in St. Paul. Paul Logan, a twenty-four-year old male, has been arrested on a separate incident, which led police to the other attacks. Mr. Logan is at the Ramsey County Jail awaiting arraignment."

Happy and relieved to know Abigail and the women in the area were now safe, he had one less thing to worry about. The house hunt and travel plans would be put on a back burner until he fixed the situation with Liz. He sent her a text. Whether she would read and respond was a different story.

I would like to talk to you and explain the situation. It's not what you're accusing me of. I have kept my promise to you. I haven't seen any women other than you. I can't control who sends me text messages. Please, can we talk? I love you.

He went to the fridge and grabbed a beer. After a long drink, he snagged his laptop and went back to the couch. He searched flowers to express his apologies for how sorry he was. Overwhelmed, he decided to send a single red rose. Satisfied, he closed his computer, polished off his beer, turned off the TV, and retired for the night. His text message to Liz went unanswered.

When he arrived early to the office, he called his realtor after deciding not to wait. If he put the house hunt off, he'd more than likely never follow through, which would create conflict between him and Chris. He told his realtor the details of what kind of house he was looking for and where. Forward progress. He had to keep moving forward.

He stopped by David's workstation later in the morning. "Hey, I saw they arrested Paul for the other assaults. That's a relief." He rested his butt against the desk.

"Yeah, but his bail hasn't been set and that worries me. Hopefully they won't give it to him."

"Do you think he'd be stupid enough to come after Abby again?" He had never thought about the possibility.

"I do. You didn't look into his eyes or hear the way he talked about her. He's obsessed with her."

"Are you worried? Should I be worried about her safety?" Robert rose from his resting position.

"If he gets out on bail, yes, I'll be very concerned."

"Well, if you hear anything, let me know. If he does get out, stay with her at all times." He stepped away and turned back. "David, I know I wasn't happy about you two from the beginning, but I'm glad she has you." David nodded an acknowledgment and Robert returned to his office.

* * * *

David lay naked on his bed. Abigail shifted her long, lean, body against his. "Abigail, we need to talk." She rubbed a leg along his with a hmm. "New Year's Eve I was involved in an accident."

"What?" She propped up on an elbow and her eyebrows were drawn inward.

"I was on my way home from the pub when a car came heading for me. I swerved, and they crashed into a post. The driver and passenger were ejected."

"I saw that on the news," she exclaimed. "Why didn't you tell me sooner?"

"Shock. Not finding the right time. Hiding from the horror of it all."

She relaxed against his chest, but kept her head raised. "Why tell me now then?"

"Because I need to talk about it at some point with you. I couldn't wait until we'd been married for ten years to bring it up."

"Married?" She sat up on her knees. Bare breasted and all.

"I'm not proposing. It was an example. We need to talk about the bad, crazy, shit that's happened to us in the last couple of weeks." He sat up and reached for her, but she got off the bed.

"So you thought that if you told me about your New Year's Eve incident, I'd talk about Paul attacking me? Do you have any idea how asinine that is? Do you know what it's like to have your body disrespected without being physically violated?"

She was talking and he wouldn't interrupt because it was a step in the right direction for her to expunge the internal turmoil within.

"First, he's polite in asking me out on a date. Next, he gets touchy before kissing me at a party. Then he's stealing underwear from my room, doing who knows what. When he grabbed and wrapped his arms around me from behind one night, I should've known. I should've stopped him then. I should've filed a police report."

"What did he do to you, Abby?" He spoke softly.

She was breaking down. Tears flowed down her cheeks. He stood in front of her.

"He kissed my neck. Ran his hands on my thighs and squeezed. Said revolting things. The bastard had raped a girl earlier that night."

It happened on their first night together. He was upset, but wouldn't go there. It wouldn't do any good.

"I'm to blame for him attacking me. It's my fault because I didn't report him sooner. It's my fault." Before she could crumple to the floor, he wrapped his arms around her waist and got them to the edge of the bed.

"You are not at fault. You did nothing wrong. He did."

She cried in his arms until she fell asleep. Why didn't she tell him about the first time Paul assaulted her? He told her to tell him, and she didn't. Robert's one word to describe her was stubborn. That she was. She didn't tell because she was too proud. Too confident. Maybe, too afraid. Whatever the reason, he didn't want to push her about it tonight.

* * * *

Last night Liz read Robert's text but deleted without responding. The photo that woman sent proved to her there was still something very sexual going on. Not to mention what she said in the text. Now to receive a single red rose at work sent a buzz around school. She didn't want the flower, but out of privacy and respect for Robert, she took the card and left the rose in the front office.

Alone at her desk she read it.

I'm sorry. I love you, Robert

She threw the note away.

Pulling her cell phone from her purse, she then sent a text to Veronica.

Need to talk. Can you meet me for drinks?

While eating her lunch, she kept her phone out and on. Five minutes before her next class, she went to put her phone away when it vibrated.

Tell me what time and where and I'll be there. Hope you're okay.

Six o'clock at the Factory. I'm in need of a good piece of cheesecake.

See you then.

She put her phone away and locked the drawer.

Veronica was waiting on the cushioned bench when Liz entered the restaurant. "Hi." A brief hug followed. "Are we waiting for a table?"

"It's not too busy so I decided to wait."

They approached the hostess stand and were seated.

"So, what's going on?"

"Let's order first. Was William okay with you coming tonight?"

"I don't give him much of a choice where my favorite sister-in-law is concerned. Honestly, he's fine with it. He never says much about my girl time out."

"That's nice." Liz stopped talking when their waiter approached. With drinks and food ordered, she started the purpose for their meeting.

"I ended it with Robert."

She closed her eyes while cupping her hands over her face. Saying it aloud, telling someone, brought the emotions forward, yet she didn't want to cry. She'd cried too much last night in bed before falling asleep.

"What? Why?"

She clasped her hands on her lap. "Monday night he made a surprise visit. I told him I'd go to Georgia with him and while we sat on the couch, his phone kept going off. He'd check it, but never responded. I'd finally had it when it went off another time so I picked it up and looked to see what was going on. It was a young woman, and she'd sent a picture. Jesus, Veronica, she looked all of about twenty years old. She was texting him wanting him to come to her place."

"You said he wasn't responding to the text, right?" Liz nodded her head. "Was he trying to leave your house?"

"No. So what? It doesn't make a difference. He's cheating on me."

"What did you say to him after you saw his phone?" Veronica's voice was calm, unlike Liz's.

"What do you think?" Her voice pitched, but then she dropped it low to avoid attention. "I told him to get out of my house. That it was over between us. That I didn't want to see him again."

"I'm guessing he tried explaining, but you wouldn't hear him out."

"Oh, he tried all right. He said he hadn't been with anyone but me since the cruise. The kicker... He told me he loved me. How can someone claim to love you when they're with someone else, too?"

"He said he loves you?"

"Crazy isn't it?"

"No. Liz, is there anything to what Brad said at dinner this weekend? Do you love Robert?"

"Perfect timing," Liz said when the waiter delivered their drinks to the table.

"Your meal should be out shortly, ladies." The waiter left them alone which meant she would have to answer Veronica's question.

She sipped from her wine glass to stall the conversation.

"Do you love him?"

"No. Brad is a young boy who doesn't understand what love is between a man and a woman." Her heart raced.

"Maybe I should be a little more specific. Did you love him before Monday night?" Veronica's head cocked to the side.

"A person can't fall in love after being with someone for several weeks."

"Okay, I'm going to back up. Why would he ask you to go away with him if he's with someone else?"

"That's normal for him."

"What's normal?" Veronica's face scrunched.

"He told me on the cruise that he was seeing two other women. At the same time. When I, we, decided to continue seeing each other afterwards, he told me he'd stop seeing the other women and be with only me. Obviously, he didn't stand by his words, as the messages show. He'll take me on a trip and sleep with her at the same time. Just like he did before the cruise."

"Why did you agree to go with him on the trip?"

The servers arrived with their dinners and left after making sure they had all they needed.

"Liz, I know you wanted to talk to me to help you through this. So talk honestly with me. Why did you say yes to the trip and do you love him?"

Liz moved her fork around in her salad. "I said yes because I do love him."

* * * *

Wednesday, Liz received two red roses. Each with individual notes.

Card one read: *I love to hear you giggle and see you smile from your eyes. I love you.*

Card two read: *What are the odds with over four thousand passengers that we should meet? Destiny. I'm sorry. I love you, Robert*

She brought the roses and note home, setting them upstairs on her bedroom dresser. The roses and note confirmed why she was doing tonight, as she and Veronica discussed. She knew it was the right thing to do. Face him. She freshened up and went down to the kitchen where the kids sat at the table doing homework.

"Okay, guys, I'm leaving. Thanks for understanding."

Brad looked up from his paper. "I'm just glad you're making up with him, Mom."

"Me, too," Sarah said.

"I'm not sure when I'll be home, but it won't be too late because it's a school night."

"Don't worry. I'll make sure Brad gets to bed on time. Love you, Mom."

Liz kissed the top of their heads before leaving.

* * * *

Liz parked along the curb in front of the building. Abigail opened the front door as she approached with a bag of groceries. "Thanks for helping me out."

"I'm glad you called." Abigail opened the second, secured door. "I enlisted Scott's help to keep Dad there until at least five-thirty." She turned with a grin.

"That gives me a half hour. How are you doing? I know your dad was worried about you."

"Good. They've charged him for the other attacks. His parents are moving his stuff out of the house and Conrad told me his parents aren't paying to bail him out." She opened the apartment door. "Well, here you go."

"Thank you, so much." She set the bag on the floor and gave her a hug.

"Thank you. You've changed him and made him so happy. I'm going to go and let you get cooking. Don't forget to lock the door behind me."

Liz did just that, picked up the bag of groceries and went to the kitchen. Digging through drawers and cupboards, she located what she needed. One pan had water coming to a boil while another heated the olive oil. She added chopped garlic and pine nuts into the oil, opened the can of sliced black olives and drained them. Once the garlic and nuts browned, she tossed in sun-dried tomatoes and the pre-cooked diced chicken. She set the oven to warm for the bread. With the water boiling, she tossed in the rotini noodles and set the timer on the stove. She added a couple tablespoons of butter to the garlic and nut pan. Once it melted, she added the black olives and Italian seasoning. While setting the table, the door lock clicked.

Her heart pounded.

He was here.

Her stomach fluttered.

She quickly tossed the bread in the oven. Stepping into the foyer, she fluffed her hair, as he opened the door.

"Wha... How..." His mouth hung open briefly as his head shook. Dropping his briefcase, he ran the short distance to her, wrapped his arms around her waist, and lifted her in an embrace before setting her feet back on the floor. "I don't care. You're here and that's all that matters. Liz, I'm sor—"

Her hand rested over his mouth, which he kissed. "Let me talk, but after you take your coat off and hang it up."

He stripped the jacket off and tossed it over the back of a dining room chair.

"Go hang it up. I'm not going anywhere, and I need to take care of our dinner." She left him to stir the mix and while she strained the noodles, he swooshed her hair to the side and kissed the back of her neck. Her legs weakened. She mixed everything together, tossed in some parmesan cheese, and scooped some into their bowls.

The oven timer beeped.

He trailed kisses toward her collarbone.

The beeping dissipated.

She leaned into the counter for support. Rapid breathing and light headed from a growing desire, she turned her neck away from him.

The beeping of the timer continued.

"The rolls!" Her hands flew up in a flutter.

He stepped back letting her tend to the oven.

The rolls were tossed into a basket and set on the table. "Let's get our bowls." As they walked to the table, his hand touched the small of her back. A shiver of pleasure coursed through her body.

"I forgot something to drink."

"I've got it." He got a bottle of red wine and two glasses. "To our future." He held up his glass and after a moment, she lifted hers.

"To our future." She sipped and prayed she wouldn't screw up. "Robert, I'm the one who should apologize. I didn't give you the chance to explain or defend yourself. I have only one question. Am I the only one you've been with since the cruise?"

"Yes. As soon as we got back, I told the women it was over. I texted the woman from the other night back and told her if she didn't stop, I'd file a police report."

Liz swallowed a sip of wine and coughed.

"I want to be with you, Liz. I'm ready for a relationship where I can give my everything. I want to make you laugh. I want to be there when you cry. I want to be your one and only to bring you pleasure in and out of bed. I need you in my life."

"You make me laugh. You make me cry. You're there when I cry. You bring me pleasure, especially in bed. I need you in my life. Robert, I love you and I want to go to Georgia if you're still willing to take me."

He slid from his chair, took her hands in his, and pulled her into his arms. "I'll take you anywhere you want to go."

The delicate kiss undid her. "Take me to your bed."

Robert dipped her back. "First say yes."

"To what?"

"Will you marry me?" His tone of voice revealed he was serious.

"I…"

He brought them upright, and cupped her face with his hand. "We don't need to get married right away. I don't even have a ring. We can be engaged as long as it takes, even if it's for the rest of our lives, I just want us to be together."

He bent on one knee. "Elizabeth Farefield, will you marry me?"

* * * *

Abigail put the last box in the back of her car. Her parents were helping with the remaining lease payments for her room rent at the house. Conrad waited as David closed the back of the small moving trailer.

She approached the guys. "I'm going to miss this place. I hope you can find new roomies soon. Not just for my sake, but for yours. You'll go crazy all alone in this big house."

"Nah. I can run around naked and not worry about offending anyone."

"Have fun with that." They embraced and she whispered, "Thanks, for everything, Conrad."

He whispered, "I may have been your first, but he'll be your last." He kissed her cheek and stepped back. "Take care of her, David." They shook hands. "Don't be strangers. Come visit, anytime."

"I think we'll call first. I don't want to see you naked. Plus, you can't get rid of me too easily. Are you ready?" she said to David.

"Yup. Conrad, thanks. We'll see you around." David walked her to the car and gave her a kiss. "I'll see you at home."

"Should I park in the driveway?" She slid behind the steering wheel and started the car.

"Yes. Make sure to pull all the way up, so I fit with the trailer."

"Will do. See you there." She pulled away from the curb and headed for David's place. It was their place now. They would drive to work together, once she was a full-time employee at RB and Associates. She talked to her father, before his and Liz's trip to Georgia, about what she wanted after graduation. There were formalities she'd have to go through to become a full-time member of the firm's team, but she had the job. Life was good.

Jody Vitek

Epilogue

The June morning sun lit the sky. A day of new beginnings. Robert and Chris followed the moving van to their new house. Trailing behind them were Liz with her children, Abigail and David, Alex, and Liz's parents at the back of the caravan. He paid a small fee to end the lease on his St. Paul apartment. Liz's house sold in a month for above asking price.

He and Liz were able to find a home that fit everyone's wants and needs. What he liked best was the layout of the bedrooms upstairs. The master suite was on one end with an office and bathroom to separate them from the other bedrooms. Chris got the pool she wanted, with Sarah and Brad happy to agree they should have one.

The moving truck pulled along the curb in front of the house. He led the rest of them to park on the driveway. Everyone got out of their vehicles and congregated off to the side of the driveway.

"Okay, everyone," Robert threw up his arms to quiet the group. "Here's how we're going to do this. Number one rule is to stay out of the moving crew's way. Let them do their job. We work around them. No unpacking until everything is unloaded and the moving company is gone. Any questions?" All heads nodded. "Good, then let's move into our new home." The group cheered before dispersing to unload the cars and trucks.

The highlight of the trip he and Liz had taken to Savannah was when she told him she wanted to get married. He was shocked when she made it clear she wanted to get married while in Georgia. They had extended their stay by two days. The sisters at the Fitzgerald House helped them with the legalities of making the wedding happen. One of the sisters,

Dolley, took pictures of the small private event. Another sister, Bess, put together a beautiful floral arrangement for Liz to carry down the short aisle in the Fitzgerald's amazing garden. Abigail, yes, the same as his daughter's, was a professional chef who cooked amazing meals for the guests. The small, beautiful cake she made for them and their special day made everything perfect.

At ten in the morning, the Minnesota humidity was on the rise, along with the temperature. They forecasted a record-breaking high of ninety-six degrees. By noon, Robert dripped with sweat and wiped his brow.

"Who thought it was a good idea to move in this kind of heat?" he asked his wife in passing.

"You did, dear." Liz reached for a box from the back of the truck.

Robert snagged her into an embrace. "Have I told you how much I love you?"

Liz smiled. "Yes, you told me this morning, but I'll never grow tired of hearing you tell me."

"Well in that case, I love you, Mrs. Burnhamwood." He dipped her low while planting a kiss on her.

"There will be enough time for that later on. Get to work you two."

"Yes, Mother," Liz said with a laugh, as he lifted her upright. "I love you, Mr. Burnhamwood."

About the Author

Jody is a multi-published author with Satin Romance, an imprint of Melange Books, LLC. She has been a member of Romance Writers of America (RWA) and Midwest Fiction Writers (MFW) since 2001 and is a Provisional PAN member of RWA.

Born and raised in Minnesota, Jody remains close to home living with her husband of twenty-five plus years, three children and a cat named Holly. Growing up, she enjoyed reading V.C. Andrews' the Dollanganger series, starting with *Flowers in the Attic,* S.E. Hinton, and Stephen King to name a few. Today her tastes run across the board in fiction and non-fiction, in all genres.

She has traveled throughout the United States, to the Bahamas and Cancun, Mexico. Between watching her youngest son playing soccer, maintaining one of the many scrapbook albums, gardening and being the COO of the Vitek household, she writes contemporary romances.

Author Contacts

Website: www.jodyvitek.com
Email: info@jodyvitek.com
Facebook: https://www.facebook.com/pages/Jody-Vitek-Author/142820225824162
Twitter: @JodyVitek